THE
AIDE

· ·

WARD CARROLL

A SIGNET BOOK

SIGNET
Published by New American Library, a division of
Penguin Group (USA) Inc., 375 Hudson Street,
New York, New York 10014, USA
Penguin Group (Canada), 10 Alcorn Avenue, Toronto,
Ontario M4V 3B2, Canada (a division of Pearson Penguin Canada Inc.)
Penguin Books Ltd., 80 Strand, London WC2R 0RL, England
Penguin Ireland, 25 St. Stephen's Green, Dublin 2,
Ireland (a division of Penguin Books Ltd.)
Penguin Group (Australia), 250 Camberwell Road, Camberwell, Victoria 3124,
Australia (a division of Pearson Australia Group Pty. Ltd.)
Penguin Books India Pvt. Ltd., 11 Community Centre, Panchsheel Park,
New Delhi - 110 017, India
Penguin Group (NZ), cnr Airborne and Rosedale Roads, Albany,
Auckland 1310, New Zealand (a division of Pearson New Zealand Ltd.)
Penguin Books (South Africa) (Pty.) Ltd., 24 Sturdee Avenue,
Rosebank, Johannesburg 2196, South Africa

Penguin Books Ltd., Registered Offices:
80 Strand, London WC2R 0RL, England

First published by Signet, an imprint of New American Library,
a division of Penguin Group (USA) Inc.

First Printing, July 2005
10 9 8 7 6 5 4 3 2 1

Ⓟ REGISTERED TRADEMARK—MARCA REGISTRADA

Printed in the United States of America

PUBLISHER'S NOTE
This is a work of fiction. Names, characters, places, and incidents either are
the product of the author's imagination or are used fictitiously, and any resem-
blance to actual persons, living or dead, business establishments, events, or
locales is entirely coincidental.

For the staffers

ACKNOWLEDGMENTS

I'd like to thank the following people for helping to fill in the blanks or just taking the time to share ideas as this story came together: Vice Admiral Tony Less, USN (Ret.); Don Swanze; Tina Mayberry; astronaut and Navy SEAL Captain Bill Shepherd, USN (Ret.); and Ken Baile.

Thanks to Captain Kevin Wensing, USN, for his decades of friendship and for sharing his in-depth knowledge of the Pentagon.

Thanks to my MiLES FRoM CLEVeR bandmates, Steve Wallo and Kent Nichols, and to all of the club owners and fans in southern Maryland who support us.

Thanks to Steve Coonts for his ongoing support and the fellowship of Deer Camp.

Thanks to Carson and Briggs, the two best brothers a guy could ever have.

Thanks to my editor, Dan Slater, for his guidance, encouragement, and "brand development."

Thanks to my agent, Ethan Ellenberg, for going way beyond his job description and giving me the occasional pep talk or push and knowing when one or the other was appropriate.

Thanks to Bertha Thompson for the kick save.

As always, thanks to Giles Roblyer for spending countless hours challenging me to complete the thought.

Thanks to my sons, Hunton and Reid, for keeping me honest and young. You guys never fail to make me proud.

I'm eternally grateful to my wife, Carrie, for letting me be myself—the greatest gift a husband could receive. I cherish your friendship and thank you for sharing your life with me. I love you.

ONE

At times like these, Murdo Edeema missed the old days. Back then, he would stand in the jungle clearings, dilapidated warehouses, dusty armories—wherever the deal required—and crack open the wooden boxes and bathe in the smiles of the warlords, insurgents, separatists, rebels, or whoever the clients were. He'd traded in many forms of goods during that period of his life—specially machined maritime fittings, bolts of proprietary Kevlar, flare-rejecting shoulder-fired surface-to-air missiles—but the draw of the business had little to do with the goods themselves. Edeema had no agenda, political or otherwise; the job just seemed exciting, and it beat working at his father's Scheveningen fish market. The payoff had been a young life punctuated by suitcases full of cash, high-speed runs in unmarked trucks, and late-night border crossings without passports.

But shepherding high-value items to their proper destinations was an entry-level position, and when a man lost a step on his former agile self he needed to consider other ways of serving the organization, not to mention over the years the collection of weapons manufacturers, money launderers, and smugglers grew into the Paris-based Le Monde Internationale—a company with a lot of offshore accounts, several legitimate fronts around the world, and a loose, unorthodox notion of career progression. After smoothing his profile with a company-funded master's degree from the Sorbonne, Edeema was one of two men sent to Washington, D.C., to stand up the Huntington Group, Le Monde's operations and manpower wing posing as a garden-variety defense consultant firm, one with considerable expertise in the international arena.

Edeema got busy making contacts, forging relationships, and generally establishing himself inside the Beltway. He was urbane, elegant, and worldly—the perfect guest at an embassy reception or Department of Defense open house. His methodology was simple: achieve access. Access was the key to success in Washington. Access led to information, and information—used correctly—led to success; in his case, more success than he ever could have imagined during that first harrowing night bouncing around the cargo hold of a rusty DC-3 bound for Jakarta.

But whatever his successes to date, Edeema was still having trouble with access at the moment. His level of frustration was heightened by his ignorance of who was on the other end of the speakerphone. He paced in front of the large picture window and looked beyond the Potomac River, across the Washington Monument and Jefferson Memorial to the Capitol dome, and attempted to calm himself with thoughts of earlier days.

"What did you say your name was again, sir?" the grating alto with a phlegmy vibrato asked, making Edeema think that she was a smoker and probably fond of the grape, as well. In spite of never laying eyes on her, he was sure he knew everything about her—where she liked to shop, where she did lunch, what sort of car she drove. But why had she answered this number?

"Isn't this the congressman's personal line?" he asked in return.

"It was," she replied. "But we had to change the number because of a security review the office just went through."

"Can you give me the new number?"

"The *new* number?"

"To the congressman's personal line. I called you on what you're telling me is now the old personal line. Obviously I knew the old number, so I'd suggest it's safe to give me the new number." He heard traces of his Dutch origins coming out in his voice—*olt* number . . . *gif* me the new number. That could happen when he was upset.

Edeema took a deep breath. One of his mentor's lessons was never to show your roots, and in this job that meant coming off as Yankee Doodle Dandy. National pride was such a flawed concept anyway, too often out of synch with profit.

Dead air indicated his logic regarding the new number to the personal line was lost on the woman. Edeema felt his temples starting to pound. He had spent months grooming key players of the outer office of Congressman Pete Charles of California, current chairman of the House Committee on Immigration Policy, only to have the most important among them—the personal secretary—change overnight, and, worse still for a man who dealt in information, without warning. He had plied the last one with enough niceties and wampum to guarantee direct access to the lawmaker for what he thought was the rest of his working life, but suddenly he was just another misfortunate at the palace gates, begging for an audience.

Edeema took stock of his reflection in the full-length mirror against the near wall. Tanned, fit, and trim, with just enough gray in his full head of brown hair to radiate wisdom as well as style, he was satisfied that his appearance belied his fiftysomething age. He didn't look like a misfortunate. And last he checked, misfortunates didn't live in $1.2 million homes in northern Virginia.

After a time she asked, "Could I have your name, sir?"

"Murdo Edeema," he said.

"Can you spell your last name, please?"

Now he was spelling? "E . . . D . . . E . . . E . . . M . . . A."

"*Ehd*-a-mah?"

"It's pronounced Ah-*dee*-ma."

"Hold, please."

Edeema strained to hear what her now-muffled voice was saying, but he couldn't make out any of it. A few seconds later she was back with, "And what company are you with?"

He could feel himself teetering between civility and rage, so he snatched a therapeutic stress ball from between two jet fighter models perched on the window ledge and repeatedly squeezed it in his fist as he gave his answer: "I'm a vice president at the Huntington Group. The congressman knows me quite well. If you'd simply—"

Edeema spat a string of profanities under his breath as the woman's voice muffled again. He wanted to slam the phone back onto the cradle, but he couldn't afford to have his first impression with the new help end on a sour note. Administrative types around the Hill tended to remember that sort of thing; it gave them something to talk about during their smoke breaks behind the congressional office building.

"I'm sorry," the secretary purred with a by-the-numbers pleasantness as she returned to the line. "Congressman Charles just left for testimony on the Floor. I can either leave him a message or direct you to Mr. Cullen."

Edeema didn't stop with staffers—not even chiefs of staffers. "No, I'll try to get in touch with the congressman later."

But he still didn't hang up. It was time for the rebuilding to begin. He dreaded starting over out of nowhere with this particular office, but he'd also been inside the Beltway arena long enough to know when to suck it up and press on. "I apologize, but I missed your name," he said with an appropriate amount of cheer.

"Gloria," she replied.

"Where did you come from, Gloria?" Edeema hadn't met a secretary yet who didn't love talking about herself, most likely a by-product of spending inordinate amounts of time focused on the boss's problems.

"Sacramento. I worked in the congressman's home office."

"Sacramento? Wow, that's a long way from Washington."

"Tell me about it. But it's not all bad. We like it here—except for the traffic, of course. Washington's got better arts."

"Oh, you're a patron of the arts? Do you like classical music?"

"I love it."

"Really? Who's your favorite composer, if you don't mind my asking? I've always found you can tell a lot about a person by their favorite composer."

"Oh, that's easy: Aaron Copland."

Of course. Musical bathos. Manna for American dimwits posing as sophisticates. "Good choice," Edeema pandered. "Isn't the National Symphony Orchestra doing a salute to Copland soon?"

"Yeah, but it's sold out," the receptionist said with the same tone of voice she probably used when telling members of her call tree that a bunco partner had been caught shoplifting.

"You're not subscribed for the season?" he asked.

"No, my husband and I got into town too late for that."

"Gloria, this is quite a fortunate coincidence for both of us. I have two tickets that I can't use. I'd hate to see them go to waste, especially knowing that true aficionados like your husband and you were missing out. I would be honored if you would take them off my hands."

She gasped with excitement, then caught herself and said, "I don't know if I should. . . ."

"Please, Gloria, as a favor to me. I'll have them couriered over to you immediately."

"You're a very nice man. How can I thank you?"

"What's my name, Gloria?"

"Murdo Edeema," she said firmly.

"That's all I ask."

As Edeema cut the connection, he saw Ned Reynolds, the Huntington Group's Vice President for Operations, hurry past the doorway. Together, Ned and he ran the company. "What's the rush, Ned?" he called into the hallway.

Reynolds came back, poking his head around the edge of the door, and between breaths said, "I need to review something in the SCAR." His normally pale face was crimson at the cheeks; sweat matted wisps of hair against a tall forehead.

"Serious?"

"From what my source in the Pentagon tells me, it could be."

"Mind if I join you?"

Reynolds simply shrugged in response.

The two men started down the hallway toward the company's Special Classified Access Room, the place where they helped their industry clients pitch future systems to military procurement officials. They strode past the receptionist station—a traditionally appointed island on the near end of the main lobby—where Allison sat working the phones through a headset while simultaneously typing on two keyboards like a church organist. Allison was Edeema's conception of everything an administrative type *should* be: efficient, quiet, gorgeous, and clean. In short, she was the anti-Gloria.

"I'm going to the SCAR, Al," Reynolds said as he passed. "Hold my calls."

"I'll be in there, too," Edeema added.

Allison pushed the mute button and said, "Murdo, Mr. Chavez called from Jacksonville. The stevedores' union is angry that they were taken off the job loading equipment bound for Iraq, and they're suing the Army for wrongful termination. He wanted to talk to you as soon as possible." As she spoke, Edeema couldn't help but notice how her skirt rode up, revealing her tanned thighs mashed against the padding of her chair. And that tasteful hint of cleavage, as sexy as it was understated. He reminded himself, as he often had to in her presence, that he was a happily married man. Okay, he was middle-aged; that didn't mean he was dead.

"I'll call him back after this," Edeema said. "And get the lawyers on standby to conference in, please."

The lighting was more subdued at the end of the hall-way, where they came to a stainless steel door. Edeema placed his palm against an adjacent screen located on the wall, waist-high, and a second later the door opened. Inside, Reynolds moved swiftly across the room and worked the knobs and switches along a rack of electronic equipment. Soon classical music poured at low volume through the speakers mounted in each corner of the ceiling—real classical music: Rachmaninoff. But the music wasn't for pleasure. It was a precaution against any electronic bugs that may have been planted since the last bimonthly sweep for them.

As Edeema slid into one of the high-backed leather chairs around the long oak conference table and watched Reynolds bring other gear to life, he was reminded of the "Le Monde Paradox." The organization's executives knew everything about those with whom they dealt out-side the company but little to nothing about their co-workers. Edeema and Reynolds had arrived in Washing-ton at the same time over a decade ago, but Edeema knew little about the other VP's life outside of the office. He didn't know where Reynolds lived around D.C., what his hobbies were, or even if he was married or not. Reynolds was very average-looking, from his build— neither athlete nor couch potato—to the conservative way he styled his thin brown hair to his off-the-rack two-button charcoal suits. Edeema had seen evidence of a dry wit and a temper, but most times Reynolds suppressed both of them well. He wasn't much of a conversationalist and tended to say only what needed to be said. These attributes would have killed his chances for upward mobility at a Fortune 500 corporation, but they were the keys to his success with the Huntington Group. Being invisible was a handy trait when trading in access—a different sort of access from that Edeema prided himself on.

What Edeema did know was that the tension between them had grown over the last year, and he wondered if it was the beginnings of a power play, one that would see Ned as the undisputed head of the Huntington Group. Perhaps it had been inevitable—operations always seemed to trump personnel—but Edeema wasn't going to roll over without giving his best shot in return. He hadn't worked his way to vice president by being someone's nephew. Edeema had no idea what Reynolds had done to earn his place in the organization—he wasn't even sure that his name had been Ned Reynolds before his arrival stateside—but he was sure of his own accomplishments. And if Reynolds thought getting the right people into the organization and maintaining contacts was so easy, why didn't he try it for a while?

"So, what do you have, Ned?" Edeema asked as Reynolds powered up the seventy-two-inch plasma screen that dominated one end of the SCAR.

"This brief was just given to the Joint Chiefs of Staff," Reynolds said as he produced a thumb drive from a suit coat pocket then sat down and pushed a button on the edge of the conference table. Part of the table slid away and a computer workstation rose into place. He stuck an index finger into an electronic fingerprint reader mounted on the side of the monitor, and the system powered up. The lights dimmed and both the monitor and the plasma screen displayed in bold type: THIS BRIEF IS CLASSIFIED TOP SECRET. Although neither man held an active top-secret clearance, they didn't balk at the warning. Huntington execs treated matters of clearance the same way Edeema treated outer office personnel: bumps in the road to success, things to put in the rearview mirror with as little hassle as possible.

Reynolds advanced to the next slide and said, "Events have moved the timeline to the left for one of our projects."

"I can see that," Edeema said with a nod as he took in the information on the screen. "Isn't that project already pushing schedule?"

"Yes."

Reynolds clicked to the next slide, one accompanied at the top by an even more serious warning: THIS PORTION OF THE BRIEF IS CLASSIFIED TOP SECRET/SPECIAL COMPARTMENTED ACCESS ONLY.

Edeema considered the slide and asked, "What are those lines?"

"Special operations mission routes," Reynolds replied.

"The blue one looks like it comes awfully close to the site."

Reynolds walked over to the screen and performed a quick measurement using his thumb and forefinger as calipers, then announced: "We should be fine."

"Our fingerprints are all over it at this point."

"I know that, Murdo, thank you."

"Does Paris know about any of this?"

"Please, let me worry about that. This is an operations matter, obviously."

"It could quickly become something that all of us are forced to deal with." Edeema snorted himself a sardonic laugh and sat down at the conference table. "I knew this was a risky venture."

"I don't remember you saying anything when we were briefed on this effort a few months back," Reynolds returned as he quickly marched through the balance of the Joint Chief's slide show. "You just keep scouting and working your contacts, and let me handle our situation in the desert."

"Working my contacts, huh?" Edeema laughed again, louder this time. "If we're discovered, we won't have a single friend. Even those on retainer will scurry for cover."

"Then let's hope we don't get discovered."

TWO

With a forty-foot runner named *Temptress* and the guts it took to break a law he considered ridiculous, Ashton Roberts started his fortune by orchestrating a simple supply chain, moving spirits from New Jersey's underground distilleries to Manhattan's speakeasies across the Hudson River. The family never used the term "bootlegging" to describe his efforts, and before they could worry themselves too much about it, Prohibition was repealed. Roberts emerged from the shadows and grew his previously covert operation into the nation's largest liquor distributorship, drawing heavily on the contacts he had made during what he referred to as the "silent times." Any grumbles that lingered among the gentry on the topic of how the man had come into his money were stilled in the years that followed by the exponential rate at which the company expanded. By the time Ashton Roberts Jr. seized the reins from his father, Roberts International was a conglomerate boasting the world's largest shipping fleet among its myriad assets. And although Ashton Roberts III had refurbished his grandfather's legendary boat to entertain high-powered guests, he had never cared for the sea. He used his flair for numbers to branch out of straight maritime commerce and into high finance, adding several zeros to the family's net worth in the process.

Ashton Roberts IV had taken a still more radical turn. Without offering any explanation and ignoring his father's offer to spend a summer or more in Europe purging the impulse, he had bypassed Princeton for Annapolis. Four years later, just as the family had reluctantly accepted the notion that one among them would be a military man, young Ashton had done further damage to the natural order by choosing the Navy SEALs as his service selection. He wasn't going to be conning submarines; he was going to be attaching himself to their hulls as they passed under him. He wasn't going to be piloting airplanes; he was going to be jumping out of them. And then he'd done himself one better by joining Delta Force, although that fact remained unknown to his parents.

Now, bathed in the red light of a C-130 Talon's cargo bay, Lieutenant Ash Roberts slouched in one of the nylon sling seats along the side of the modified transport and considered his distorted and dim reflection in the chrome bumper of the weathered Chevrolet Suburban strapped to the airplane's deck. Ash was no stranger to the routine, if that's what it could be called—no two missions were ever alike. He had cut his fighting teeth in the mountains of Kosovo, and there he'd killed his first man. After months of hearing about it in training, instructors going on ad nauseum about how the trainees wouldn't know shit about the business until they watched an enemy die at the end of their rifles, he'd actually been glad to get it behind him—sort of the same way he'd felt about freeing himself from the burden of virginity.

He'd killed a dozen more men since then, and although each final grimace or contortion when the bullet hit was etched in his memory, he didn't dwell on those events. He'd survived, and in his line of work, survival was its own statement. The successful completion of a

Delta Force mission didn't lead to an awards ceremony or a parade; it simply led to the luxury of another mission.

Task Force Bravo wasn't alone; four other Special Mission Units had been charged with capturing high-level Iraqi officials—"snatch and grabs," in special operator speak—as part of Operation Medusa. "Nothing like making important men disappear in the night to break the will of an enemy," a colonel on the headquarters staff of the theater's special forces had said during the video teleconference that kicked off the final mission briefing. But of the five SMUs, only Bravo was dropping out of an airplane to enter the country, and only Bravo was headed into downtown Baghdad.

Almost subconsciously Ash reached into a pocket and removed a deck of playing cards, each adorned with the face of a different Iraqi official—evidence that the Department of Defense had a sense of humor. He flipped through the deck until he came upon the Eight of Spades: Deputy Minister of Information Tarmal E Hassid. Ash studied the face scowling up from the card, a face the members of Task Force Bravo had memorized from every angle.

"Does he know we're coming?" Senior Chief Billy White asked from the seat next to him, the volume of his southern drawl raised enough to be heard over the din from the Talon's four turboprops. The senior chief was Task Force Bravo's highest-ranking enlisted man who had also emerged as the team's spiritual leader. Ash had felt comfortable with him from the moment they were introduced a few months before. He had that light in his eyes that all the good ones had, the one that told the lieutenant that his right-hand man would thrive when things got interesting.

"I don't know how he would," Ash replied. "But, like most gangsters, these guys have survival instincts."

"Is he worth the effort?"

Ash's expression caused the senior chief to pause momentarily before continuing: "I'm just saying, maybe we should be going after somebody higher up."

Ash shook his head and said, "One card at a time, Billy. Hassid's the right guy for our part of Medusa. His movements are predictable. Plus, by the time we're done, the locals will know a change is in the works." He began to speak in Arabic: "*Assalamu alaikum*, people of Iraq. Your nightmare will soon be over."

"*Wa barakatuhu*," the senior chief replied. "You're going to be a regular *hajji* radio celebrity."

"*Shukran, akh.*"

"You're welcome." Senior Chief White pointed toward the card in Ash's hand. "I'll tell you one thing: He's an ugly cuss, even by Mississippi standards."

Ash brought the card closer to his face. "No argument there, although I've never been to Mississippi."

"You don't know what you're missing."

The senior chief focused on the card for a time before zoning out altogether. Ash scanned the rest of Task Force Bravo, the four other men along the opposite side of the cargo bay. It was the smallest force Ash had ever joined, much less led. Delta Force SMUs were always carefully constructed, but this one seemed more so. That Task Force Bravo consisted of a balanced mix of three SEALs, two Green Berets, and a Marine Recon was of less importance than the fact that the six of them were all just over average height with slim to medium builds, statures that hid the havoc they could wreak with their bare hands. All had dark complexions that were made even darker by the thick mustaches they'd grown to better blend with crowds of Iraqi males. Several of them had allowed a week's worth of stubble to grow along their jawlines.

They were specialists in the region: fluent in Arabic, with master's level understanding of Iraqi culture and traditions. Navy Petty Officer Second Class Brent Stephens and Army Staff Sergeant Renaldo Hidalgo were electricians and demolitions experts. Army Sergeant Mac

Phillips was a medic. Navy Senior Chief Petty Officer Billy White and Marine Corps Sergeant Jason Tangredi were the go-to guys in matters of kidnapping and assassination. And Lieutenant Ashton Roberts IV was there to run the show and make the hard calls.

Task Force Bravo had trained six weeks for this mission without any contact with the outside world, first in the woods of North Carolina and then in the desert of Kuwait. "Isolation," they called it, and it had reminded Ash of why he had no life. Maybe a life would come later. Maybe not. In any case, he hadn't had much time to worry about it since he'd left the Academy.

Ash went through the mission sequence for the umpteenth time, and then again, before his mind wandered onto the road not taken. What about the family business? What was his problem with power and affluence? And was his younger brother Winston, now a Roberts International vice president, happier for having never questioned their father's plan?

Ash tried to picture Winston, the Roberts son with fewer varsity letters but better grades, seated between Sergeants Phillips and Tangredi across the cargo bay, but the image wouldn't form. Not even in his wildest daydreams would his brother fit into this world, even less so than he would on the parade fields or sports turf of the Naval Academy. Ash wondered if Winston ever had the same thought in reverse, mentally wedging his Navy SEAL sibling in the boardroom between two button-down executives.

In time the roar of air and engines announced that the Talon's aft ramp was dropping. Ash stared into the dark sky 30,000 feet above Iraq.

THREE

"One minute, Lieutenant," the loadmaster shouted into the right ear hole of Ash's helmet, wiggling an index finger in front of his face.

Ash focused on the Air Force tech sergeant bathed in red light and gave the man a thumbs-up. The lieutenant stood up, strapped his oxygen mask across his face, and lowered his goggles, which cued the other members of Task Force Bravo to do the same. As they stepped behind the pallet that held the automobile, each of them made sure he had good flow into his mask while he adjusted the straps of his parachute and checked that the rest of his gear—weapons, food, and water—was secure.

The status light went green, and with the pull of a single lanyard, the loadmaster commanded the pallet to thunder down the rollers. Before the SUV cleared the ramp, Ash was in full sprint behind it, and then hurtling headlong into the night, followed in rapid succession by the rest of Task Force Bravo. Even if the Iraqi radar operators had managed to track the C-130, they wouldn't have seen any blips from the things tumbling out of it.

The initial acceleration as Ash fell through the darkness took his breath away, as it always did during night jumps, and only when he reached terminal velocity—about 120 miles per hour—did he grab his wits enough to glance at the altimeter strapped to his wrist. The lights of the capital blazed to the east, and he studied the pattern they made—the distinctive bend in the Tigris River, the brighter lights around the palaces and cultural centers. He had never been there, but knew it well.

Ash shifted his attention to the void below. Task Force Bravo's landing site was down there somewhere, roughly twenty-five miles west of the city. He hoped it was deserted, as the intelligence reports had suggested it would be, but the reports also carried the disclaimer that it was hard to predict the movement of the locals. It wouldn't have been the first time in Ash's experience that the intel had been off or that he had been forced to detain innocents.

But Serbian peasants were one thing; Iraqi city dwellers would be another. This wasn't some sort of low-intensity conflict the members of Bravo were falling into. It was a war, or at least it would be by the time they got to work. He was keenly reminded of this by the folded barrel of the modified Kalashnikov pressing against his back.

Ash brought his wrist in front of his face again while using his other arm to maintain a good free-fall attitude, trying to keep his head from dropping. He wanted to fall without sailing downrange and to stay over the landing zone. Passing fifteen hundred feet. The chutes of his fellow jumpers should have started opening above him. A few more seconds and it would be his turn. He counted the remaining time off in his head and then found the D ring of his rip cord and yanked it away from his torso.

The parachute filled with a snap, digging the harness hard into his collarbones and crotch—a good kind of pain, the kind that meant his chute had opened. He unlatched his oxygen mask and checked the readout on the global positioning system strapped to his other wrist for the range and bearing to the landing site: He was directly over it.

Ash rummaged through a pouch at the front of his harness, found the pair of night-vision goggles he'd placed there, and clicked them to his helmet. Then he ran his hands up the risers and wrapped his fingers around the steering toggles. He gave the left one a steady tug, starting a controlled spiral designed to keep him close to his intended destination, and scoured the ground for a sign of the Suburban. The chute over the pallets had been set to open at one thousand feet, below all of the jumpers, and if it had failed the mission was a bust. Mission planners never liked single-point failures going into an operation, but sometimes they were unavoidable. They had toyed with the idea of dropping two vehicles, but had scrapped it once the loadmaster on the planning team said that more than one car would overly complicate the drop. So the number crunchers redid the risk assessment and deemed the operation a go with a single vehicle. "Dropping palleted loads is a science now," one of them had said, which made Ash cringe the same way he had cringed when one of his lacrosse teammates back at the Academy had crowed, "There's no way these guys can beat us."

But he'd long ago given in to the idea that sometimes it was his job to just salute and go. If the SUV was destroyed, Ash would round up the team and hump it to the abandoned airstrip just over ten miles to the west to lie low while waiting for the transport they had just jumped out of to pick them up. He peered under his goggles at his watch. Time was already tight, and they weren't even on the ground yet.

There was little slop built into the time line, by design. Bravo's success was predicated on them being on the ground as briefly as possible. And "Shock and Awe," as the Pentagon had labeled the opening salvo, would kick off as planned regardless of what happened to this newly isolated band of special operators. At the appointed time, the bombers would strike their targets nearby. That was no problem . . . as long as the Suburban wasn't smashed to bits.

Ash steadied himself toward the east, into the lights of Baghdad. He wanted a good horizon to judge his final flare. He glanced between his boots to find the ground, but getting little from what he saw, looked to the horizon again.

Right when he was sure he was going to hit, Ash pulled hard on both toggles and waited for his feet to kiss the sand. When they didn't, he pumped the toggles several times, trying to step himself down while his legs paddled to find terra firma. Once both feet were on the ground, he twisted around and collapsed his chute. He balled the silk in his arms and then checked the GPS again.

After discarding his chute and harness (he planned to be long gone by the time anyone found it), Ash unfolded his AK-47 with the tubular titanium stock. Once the rifle was loaded and at his hip, he slinked eastward. With each step he became more the predator, senses heightened, powers of perception well beyond what men who'd never been isolated in an enemy's land were capable of. He felt the grains of sand and bits of rock beneath his boots. He noted the subtle shifts in the breeze against his face, and from it he pulled down scents. He listened for the trampling of spiders and the distant batting of mosquito wings. His night-vision goggles gave him the eyes of a wolf.

Some of the others drifted to earth around him along the way. They traveled until they had nothing but zeros on their GPS readouts and then waited for the rest of Bravo to arrive. Beams of light visible only to those wearing NVGs fanned across the flatness—pleas for friendly contact, answered in kind. No words were spoken between those crouched in the sand. Eyes searched the vastness, looking for troubling movement or unexplained glints of light.

After several minutes that felt like hours, Senior Chief Billy White leaned over and whispered into Ash's ear: "We're all here."

Another step in the operation was complete. Ash needed to focus on each step, to stay in the present. Mission mind-set was about process, not outcome. To look beyond the next step was to allow doubt to creep in, and doubt was the enemy. Doubt clouded judgment and slowed reaction time. Doubt could kill.

Ash came out of a kneel and started to move while checking the range and bearing to the Suburban with the homing device. The readout flickered. Never mind the risk assessments and the parariggers' estimates: This wasn't theory anymore. His gut churned with the possibility that they were closing in on a smashed hulk instead of a working automobile. He picked up the pace.

Although the night was clear, the absence of starlight kept the NVGs from showing the details that punctuated the desert around them. Just as he had convinced himself that his homing device was leading the team on a wild-goose chase, Ash noted a lump in the distance. It had to be the Suburban. Closer, Ash could see that something wasn't right. He then heard caterwauling in Arabic. Ash hunkered down, and the others matched him.

The senior chief silently sidled up to the lieutenant and whispered into his ear: "Single nomad would be my guess."

"Okay . . . what's his problem?"

"Dunno. I'll take two and circle around the other side. Give us a couple of minutes to get over there."

"Check."

Ash waited two minutes and then moved toward the nomad. The Iraqi didn't see the men surrounding him, and his tirade continued. As the team closed, Ash figured out what he was wailing about, as well as what had caused the palletized SUV to flip onto its right side: a camel.

The senior chief grabbed the Iraqi from behind and,

with Sergeant Tangredi's help, the nomad was bound and gagged. He continued to struggle, however, distraught over the fate of what was most likely his sole asset in a harsh world.

"What do you want to do with him, L.T.?" Senior Chief White asked in a low voice, using the common field abbreviation for Ash's rank.

"How are we fixed for sedative?" Ash asked back.

"One vial," White returned. "Enough for the mission."

"Doc, get up here," Ash called over his left shoulder in a loud whisper. One of those watching the darkness around them came over. Even with night-vision goggles across his eyes, Sergeant Mac "Doc" Phillips was instantly recognizable. His sharp jawline and aquiline nose pushed the limits of passing as an Iraqi, but that element of his profile was eclipsed by his talents as a combat medic. Like Ash, Doc had fled the predictability of his legacy. Phillips had left the Johns Hopkins University pre-med program his freshman year and joined the Army. But he'd softened the blow to his family, in his own mind, anyway, by first qualifying as a medic and *then* joining the Special Forces.

"How much morphine do we have?" Ash asked.

"What are you thinking, L.T.?" Senior Chief White asked before the medic could get an answer out.

"We can't leave this guy out here tied up," Ash said. "If somebody finds him our cover will be blown. With a little shot of morphine, he'll come across as a simple infidel who got into the firewater on a lonely night. I'm not talking about making him an addict; just give him enough to make him woozy. Nobody's going to believe a nomad out of his mind babbling about men in the night."

"What about his crushed camel?"

"A tragic hit-and-run."

"And the pallet?"

"It fell off the truck that hit the camel," Ash shot back. "Look, we don't have much time here."

Phillips had already pulled a needle out of his kit, prepped it, and without any further discussion plunged it into the Iraqi's biceps. Soon the man's movements went from aggressive to sluggish. A minute later, he didn't move at all.

FOUR

"All right, let's get the Suburban ready to go," Ash said. After dragging the dead camel out of the way and propping the nomad against its back, the team rolled and righted the SUV. Ash ran his hand over the right side. The damage seemed only cosmetic, but would the thing start?

Knives sliced through duct tape and quick-release fittings were flipped open, loosening the straps that had mated the SUV to the pallet and the parachute rigging. Tires were repressurized, shock absorbers charged.

"Is this junker going to make it?" Petty Officer Stephens asked as he stepped back and considered the Suburban from a few feet away, sounding every bit the team youngster that he was. Steve-O, as they called him, was barely twenty, but Ash had seen during their training that being the junior man agewise didn't make the petty officer any less capable of mentally hacking the program.

"It's only beat up on the outside, or at least it was before it hit a camel," Ash said before looking to Tangredi. "See if it'll start up."

"Bring the magic, Tang," the senior chief coaxed. "Just like your repo man days back in Detroit."

Jason Tangredi slipped behind the wheel and took a

deep breath. He drew his mouth tight across his face and held his crossed fingers aloft before twisting the ignition. The Suburban's engine stuttered and then roared to life. Tangredi pumped his fist and drove the vehicle clear of the pallet. At the same time, the rest of the team began to transform their appearances.

They stripped off their black coveralls, revealing a variety of local clothing styles. Some, including Ash, wore *farrujs,* half shirts–half robes, while others sported white dress shirts with an open collar and plain black slacks. Sandals and loafers replaced boots. The removed coveralls and other equipment, including the NVGs, were shoved into several equipment bags, which were, in turn, covered with a tarp in the Suburban's cargo area.

Phillips slid into the specially modified forward center seat, and Ash jumped in next to him. He checked his watch. The nomad had put them a few minutes behind, but if traffic was as light as the intelligence officer who had briefed them said it would be, they could make it up along the drive to the city.

The senior chief pulled out a ruggedized laptop computer and fired it up. Soon the screen displayed a map with a blue line that scribed their route into the city. He selected a larger scale to check the position of the C-130 they'd just jumped out of and saw it was now orbiting over northern Kuwait. The team also had a miniature SATCOM set, but because the Iraqis could triangulate radio transmissions, the senior chief would only use it if they were in deep shit.

After a brief and bumpy ride southbound across the countryside, the SUV came to a four-lane divided highway, Highway 9, one of the main arteries into Baghdad. In the columns of light that repeatedly washed over the Suburban as it passed under the long row of streetlights that lined the road, Ash studied each of those in the vehicle with him. If he were an Iraqi, would he have bought the notion that this was a carload of laborers making their way back to the capital? Their disguises seemed to be working so far. They passed some cars and yielded to others without any reaction from the local drivers or their passengers. All the same, the team's weapons remained at the ready; there was no telling when their acting careers might abruptly end.

Several miles later they drove past an exit for Saddam International Airport. The exit was marked—like all of the traffic signs—in both Arabic and English, and although Ash didn't think about it for too long, seeing the Iraqi dictator's name in writing gave him pause. They had a long way to go through the enemy's backyard.

Focus on the next step. Ash called into the backseat: "Billy, how's the computer look?"

"Tight. How's your GPS?" the senior chief said.

Ash peered at the dimly lit global positioning system screen perched on his right thigh and replied, "Looking good so far, but keep us honest."

"Roger. Stay on Matar Saddam al Dowli for another two miles, Tang," the senior chief said across the medic to the driver. "It'll bend around to the north and turn into the Qadalya Expressway. After that we want the third exit."

"Copy," Tangredi replied. As was the case for the other members of the team, he didn't really need the input; they had all long since memorized the way to the Ministry of Media, even driven the route a dozen times each using a simulator at Fort Bragg. But in spite of that, Tangredi knew it didn't hurt to have the senior chief back him up. The last thing they needed to do now was to get lost.

Ash looked at his watch again. The deputy minister should have just left his residence in the affluent Karada section of the city, near Baghdad University, driving north on Arbataash Tamuz Street, across the bridge over the Tigris, and into the center of the capital. In just over an hour, Hassid would begin his weekly radio broadcast over the Baath Party's airwaves. The show was simply titled *Masa alkhair, Sa'b—Good Evening, People*—and was billed by the station as an entertainment program, but after listening to several months' worth of one-hour segments, Ash hadn't heard much that he would have labeled as entertaining. *Good Evening, People* was nothing more than propaganda, a chance for Deputy Minister Hassid to rant about infidels and the Jews, and to remind Iraqis everywhere about the supreme power of their leader. And as civilians knew they might be quizzed by the police on the streets about the last show and that a wrong answer meant jail time, Hassid had a large audience.

Matar Saddam al Dowli turned into the Qadalya Expressway. The Suburban reached the third exit and turned left onto Arbataash Tamuz Street. Now they were following the same route Deputy Hassid should have traveled just minutes before; now they were less seekers and more hunters. Palm trees lined both sides of the street. Ash scanned ahead of them for Hassid's car, a black Mercedes beefed up to repel anything short of a tactical nuclear device, but saw nothing but battered Datsun pickups and Fiat compacts. To the right he could see the spires of the Iraqi leader's palace complex that stood on the banks where the Tigris made a ninety-degree turn through downtown. Although he hadn't seen the target list, he was certain the complex would be in flames before morning. A half mile later, they came to their first stoplight.

"Maybe I'm just paranoid," Tangredi mumbled, "but I think those people are staring at us."

"I always found a little paranoia comes in handy at times like this," Hidalgo quipped in a raspy whisper.

"Stay cool, fellas," Ash replied without moving his lips, eyes averted but seeing all. "No worries here."

A slow roll got slower as traffic intensified along the southeastern end of the military air station at Tarablus. Ash checked his watch and cursed under his breath. They'd planned on some congestion, but not this much. What the hell were these people doing out on the streets? Didn't they know a war was coming?

"Oh, fuck," Tangredi said, stretching his neck to see over the cars strung out in front of them.

"What is it?" Ash asked, attempting to match Tangredi's view ahead.

"We've got a checkpoint or something up here," Tangredi said.

"Well, that explains the traffic jam. Did I miss the part in our intel briefings about checkpoints, Billy?"

"Negative," Senior Chief White returned dourly.

"Put the laptop away."

"Done."

"What do you want to do, L.T.?" Tangredi asked.

The lieutenant quickly considered their options. The adjacent sidewalk was wide enough to drive on, but scattering pedestrians would certainly draw the attention of those working the roadblock. He looked over his shoulder. There was no way to turn around, plus they didn't have time to try another route to the Ministry of Media.

"Are they stopping every car, Tang?" Ash asked.

"I can't tell," Tangredi replied.

Ash slipped his hand down and found his rifle. "All right, boys," he said. "Hide your gear. Keep weapons out of sight but handy."

The two cars in front of them were waved through without stopping, and for a moment it looked as if the Suburban would get the same treatment. But as the dusty SUV neared them, the helmeted Iraqi regulars stopped waving. Tangredi slowed but didn't stop as he rolled his window down and called in Arabic to the closest soldier: "*Insha'allah,* you will please not delay us. We are late for a meeting with a government *rasmi.*"

The soldier banged on the Suburban's hood and barked, *"Qif!"* several times.

"Kaif halak, sayyid?" Tangredi returned as he continued his slow but steady roll, doing his best to play the ignorant laborer simply trying to go about his business. "How are you, sir? You are busy men with more impor-

tant cars to search. We should get out of your way. *Shukran.*"

The soldier barked an order, and two others flanking him lowered their rifles at Tangredi's head. The sergeant came to a complete stop.

"Where are you coming from?" the soldier asked as he ran a flashlight across the occupants of the Suburban.

"We are construction workers," Tangredi replied in fluent Arabic. "We were working at a site west of the city." The other soldiers reslung their rifles across their shoulders and began working their ways around the outside of the vehicle.

"Is this your car?" the soldier asked.

"No. It belongs to my employer."

"What is his name?"

"Mr. Burdukali Ailul," Tangredi said without hesitation. He'd memorized these replies months ago.

The soldier pursed his lips while his cold dark eyes fixed on Tangredi then Phillips then Ash then back on the driver again. It was impossible to tell from the Iraqi's reaction whether he was buying the program at all. "Show me your identification," he said.

The sergeant reached into one of his pockets and produced a tattered card that the Iraqi soldier studied for a time. Suddenly there was a tapping on the Suburban's rear window. "Ask them what is in the back," another soldier said.

"What is in the back?" the soldier at the door asked.

"Construction equipment, of course," Tangredi said. "Tools for digging and such."

The soldier called to the others behind the SUV: *"Iftah sunduqa s-sayyara!"*

Ash heard them fumbling with the latch, and then one of them shouted back, "It's locked."

"Unlock the door," the soldier ordered.

"I'll have to get out to do that," Tangredi explained. "As you can see, this is a very old car."

"Then get out!" the soldier barked, patience wearing thin with this truckload of buffoons.

In a split second, Ash checked the traffic beyond the checkpoint and then said, "Clear ahead, Tang" under his breath. He didn't have to say it twice. Tangredi shoved his door hard into the Iraqi, knocking him to the ground. The rest of Task Force Bravo threw themselves below window level as the accelerator slapped against the floorboard. The tires squealed; Tangredi crouched low, keeping sight of the road by peering between the steering wheel and the top of the dashboard.

Shots rang out, and the bullets hit the SUV's rear window, holes forming with a series of pops before the glass exploded altogether. Tangredi didn't let up on the gas pedal. As bullets continued to tink against the sides of the Suburban, he swerved around the cars in front of them like a teen playing a video game. A few seconds later, the shooting stopped.

"Where to?" Tangredi asked as the others sat back up around him.

"Right at the next intersection—Qahira Street," Ash said.

"That's not what I meant."

"We might want to think about scrubbing this one, sir," Senior Chief White added across Ash's left shoulder. "The last thing we want to give the Iraqis at the outset of this war is six POWs."

"Then we'd better not get caught," Ash said before repeating his directions to Tangredi, firmer this time: "Take a right on Qahira. And you can slow down now."

"We're made," White said.

"We're fine, Billy," Ash returned.

Any lingering air of dissention vanished once they made the next turn. To a man, Bravo was comprised of professionals, and they all knew what Ash knew: dissention induced doubt. Plus, they were only a few blocks from the objective now.

"Grab the first parking place you see, Tang," Ash instructed.

"Don't we want to get closer to the building?" the sergeant asked.

"No. If they're looking for us, we don't want to lead them right to the ministry's doorstep. And depending on how things look once we've got our man, we may or may not be using this car to get out of town. You still remember how to hot-wire, right?" Tangredi nodded, and with that Ash began folding the stock of his rifle. He looked over his shoulder and said, "Kit up, boys."

They were in a market district now, low-roofed hovels at the feet of the ministries and other government buildings that loomed over them. The street was awash in yellow light. A crowd filled the sidewalks in front of shops that were just closing. For now, none of them paid the Suburban any mind, even with its rear window shot away.

"There's a parking spot," Senior Chief White said, thrusting his arm across Tangredi's right shoulder. "Across the street there."

Tangredi threw the Suburban into reverse, and with a single fluid motion worked the big car between two smaller ones and against the curb.

"Okay, nothing but Arabic now," Ash said before pushing the passenger door open.

One by one the team slid out of the Suburban and onto the streets of downtown Baghdad. The still air teemed with rich scents. Stephens, Hidalgo, and Phillips feigned interest in the produce that lined the front of the adjacent grocery and kept tabs on the Iraqi policemen patrolling the other side of the street. Ash opened the Suburban's rear door, and Tangredi and the senior chief joined him in brushing the broken glass out of the way before rummaging through the equipment bags. In short order, they transferred the required gear—NVGs, short-range radio headsets, a camera, stun guns, and a medical kit including the sedative—into a couple of satchels.

The team started the block and a half to the Ministry of Information, uncoordinated to the casual observer but each very much aware of the others' movements. The lieutenant led the way with relaxed yet purposeful strides, employing one of the lessons he'd learned in his earliest days as a plebe at the Naval Academy: You could get away with most anything as long as you looked like you knew what you were doing. No sudden glances over the shoulder. No widening of the eyes when catching a local's stare on a busy street. His expression also hid how strange the night breeze felt as it crept under his *farruj*.

The blare of a siren sent a jolt through Ash's body, but he saw it was only an ambulance speeding down the street. Around the next corner they would be able to see the Ministry of Information on the southern side of the roundabout. He checked his watch.

"Inta," a gruff voice called from Ash's left. "You, *qif!"*

A policeman approached from the other side of the street. Although Ash didn't look over, he knew the official was talking to him. "You," the man shouted again, louder. "Stop!"

Go away, Ash thought. *Just go away.*

A hand wrapped around Ash's biceps, and he turned and saw that a fat man holding a broom had grabbed him. "That policeman is speaking to you," the man said.

In spite of an increased pulse rate, Ash casually raised his eyebrows and faced the street. The fat man released his grip and went back to sweeping the sidewalk.

"Na'am, sayyid?" Ash asked as the policeman reached him. *"Matha tureed?"*

"I want to see your identification and what's in your bag," the policeman said.

The lieutenant shrugged and said, "Certainly, sir, but why don't we move out of the way of all of these people?" As he spoke, he took stock of the man: frail-looking, rail thin. Ash was sure he could crush his windpipe with one hand. There was the matter of the pistol, however. . . .

The policeman didn't voice any objection to Ash's suggestion and followed him a few steps around the corner into an alley along the side of the fat man's store. The light was poor there, and as Ash went through the motions of slipping the satchel off his shoulder to show the policeman its contents, he missed how the Iraqi's face contorted for the half second it took Tangredi's blade to slit his throat. No noise. No screams of agony. Only the silent spilling of blood.

The two Americans quietly dragged the dead body several more feet down the alley—away from the busy street—and dumped it behind a pile of discarded boxes. Ash felt no remorse. A policeman in Iraq was not a servant of the people; he was a dictator's henchman.

Back on the sidewalk, a subtle nod from the lieutenant told the others to keep moving for the objective. Around the corner and diagonally across the intersection, and they were at the main entrance to the Ministry of Information. Two guards stood at the base of the steps.

Ash hailed them, extending his hand as he approached: "*Masa alkhair,* gentlemen." He swept an arm across the others. "We are here about the electrical problem."

The guards exchanged quizzical looks. "We know nothing of an electrical problem," one of them said.

Ash continued to speak as the rest of Bravo ringed the uniformed Iraqis. "Well, I'm very sure you have one. Is there someone else we should talk to?"

The guard never got his reply out, nor did his partner have time to react before knives plunged deep into their chests, acts unnoticed by the passersby beyond the ring of Americans. They didn't fall but were held up with their mouths covered by the men who had stabbed them. The group moved up the stairs and through the ornate metal doors as if the two dead men were escorting them.

Inside, after discarding the bodies in one corner of the alcove, Ash reached into one of the satchels and passed out radio headsets before donning his own. Then they split into two groups: The senior chief, Stephens, and Hidalgo set out for the building's main electrical junction box while the remaining three pulled night-vision goggles from the other satchel and then started down the passageway that led to the studio where they hoped to find Deputy Minister Hassid perched in front of a microphone, nearly halfway done with the evening's segment of *Good Evening, People.*

The three who comprised the takedown team slinked through the office door adjacent to the studio and crouched behind some furniture. They could see Hassid through the glass now, bathed in fluorescent light, ranting, head jerking as he spoke, arms flailing with each angry word.

"How are you doing, Billy?" Ash whispered into the small microphone against his lips.

"We're at the box," the senior chief replied.

"We're ready for lights out anytime."

"Copy. Give us a second here."

Waiting for darkness, Ash reviewed the next step: Once Stephens and Hidalgo took out the lights, the others would don their goggles and rush the studio. They'd take down the deputy minister with a stun gun. What they did with the engineer working the control room was up to the engineer. If he remained disoriented in the dark and out of the way, he would be left alone. If he tried to be a hero, he'd join the policeman and the guards in the afterlife.

The clicking of footsteps echoed in the passageway outside the studio door, and before Ash could duck down a bit more, another person walked into the room. From under the desk he could see her, face peeking from a hole in her *abaya,* the black cloth that wrapped her from head to toe. Who was she? There were only supposed to be two people in the studio during Hassid's broadcast. And how long was she going to be there? He crouched lower and watched her feet step across the floor toward the engineer's booth.

"Hold the lights," Ash murmured into his headset the moment the door to the booth clicked shut behind her. "We've got a woman in here."

"A woman?" the senior chief said. "Who is she?"

"I don't know. Some administrative type, I guess."

"So what are we waiting for? It's not our fault if she's in the wrong place at the wrong time."

"Hold on. She's—"

Ash cut himself off as the building shook with the thunder of a distant explosion. "What the hell was that?" someone asked over the headset frequency.

Before anyone could guess, another explosion rumbled through, and then a handful more in rapid succession. The concussions rattled the studio glass so violently Ash thought it would shatter. He glanced at his watch amid a growing cloud of plaster settling around him: It was too early for the air strikes. Or was it? Had the planners at CENTCOM called an audible?

Ash shifted his focus back to their target, and he watched as Deputy Minister Hassid, without fanfare, signaled the engineer with an index finger across the neck, put on a black beret, and then walked out of the studio through a back exit. He was soon followed by the engineer and the woman.

Ash waited for the door to shut then spoke plainly into the headset: "Skip killing the lights, Billy. I say again: Skip the lights. Hassid is headed out of the building with another man and a woman. We're in trail."

"Roger," Senior Chief White returned. "We're closest to the north exit. You want us to watch that one?"

"Okay," Ash said as he led his part of Bravo through the studio in the direction just taken by the Iraqis, keeping the NVGs at hand. With each successive rumble, Ash expected that the lights would go out by themselves—if the building didn't start coming down around them first. Through a door, past a maze of narrow corridors, and down a long hallway and they were into a part of the building they'd never planned on occupying. Checking around each corner before he rounded it, the lieutenant tried to recall the lesser-studied part of the floor plan as he worked to keep contact with Hassid. With each turn he saw less and less of the trail Iraqi, the woman—an ankle, a flash of a heel, and then nothing.

"We've lost contact," Ash said into his headset. "Where are you, Billy?"

"We're stashed by the north exit," the senior chief murmured.

"Any sign of them?"

"Negative. Any chance they went for the basement?"

"I doubt it," Ash said. Intel showed that in the years since the start of the first Desert War, the locals had learned that when American bombs were falling, the last place they wanted to be was in a government building—even the basement of a government building—unless it was made of steel-reinforced concrete—which this building wasn't. The three Iraqis were most likely headed for the street and as deep into the adjacent neighborhood as they could get. Bravo had to reestablish contact before Hassid made the street. Once he blended into the bomb-fueled chaos, it would be tough to find him again. "Watch that door for now, Billy. We'll go for the east exit."

"Roger. What about your radio speech?"

"I'm skipping it. We don't want to announce we're here until we have Hassid."

"Too bad. That would've been a nice touch."

"Let's get this guy."

The door to the east exit was closing as it came into view, although Ash didn't see who had just passed through it. These were crucial seconds; at the moment the stealth approach was on the back burner. "We're going out, Billy; meet us on the street," Ash said just before he ripped his headset off and rushed through the exit.

The four Americans passed outdoors in time to catch the latest explosion blossoming over the rooflines to the south. The growing clouds were highlighted in bright flashes of white and orange and punctuated by thin plumes from secondaries that arced wildly across the night like Satan's own skywriting.

If there had been guards posted at that exit, they were nowhere to be seen now. Ash snapped his head in the other direction, trying hard not to look frantic while scanning the hurried masses for the deputy minister. He doubted that he'd be able to pick out an individual among this crowd, the men in their light-colored *farrujs* and the women wrapped in black *abayas* made more uniform by the yellow streetlights. Then he spotted a black beret, the only one of its kind on the street.

"There he is," Ash said to those behind him, speaking Arabic once again.

"Na'am," Tangredi replied. "I see him."

FIVE

Ash wasn't going to lose Hassid again, and he and those with him quickly made their way to the other side of the street, closing fast while still careful not to let their prey know they were there. And then the lieutenant saw something straight out of a team leader's dream: Beyond Hassid, White and Hidalgo approached, walking the opposite direction with their hands in their pockets, stun guns at the ready.

Ash almost smiled. Although this wasn't how they'd planned to spring the trap, in some ways it was better: They wouldn't have to thread through the building. They were already on the chaotic street, and the bombs would be the perfect diversion—if they didn't obliterate them all first. All they had to do now was surround the deputy minister, zap him, inject him, carry him to the Suburban, and get the hell out of Baghdad. Before the engineer and woman realized their boss was missing, Task Force Bravo would simply disappear in the night.

Another string of bombs erupted behind Ash—the palace complex was taking quite a pounding—and with that, Hassid took a sharp right turn and led the other two through the wrought-iron gate of a private residence. The Iraqis made their move so abruptly that Ash nearly ran headlong into White and Hidalgo coming the other way. The team stood on the sidewalk and watched through the bars of the gate as the front door closed behind the Iraqis.

"Whose place is this?" Senior Chief White asked under his breath.

"I don't know," Ash replied, moving against the wall and sighting through the gate.

"Did he see us? Is that why he bolted?"

"Like I said: These guys have survival instincts."

"So, do we go hard or easy here?"

Ash drew his weapon from under his *farruj* and said, "We're done with easy." He looked past the senior chief and gave the rest of the team a simple order: *"Tabi'a."*

Without any further discussion, Ash slipped through the gate and stepped to the front door. As the rest of Bravo tucked themselves to either side of him, he used his fingers to test the condition of the painted wood around the handle. Material assessment complete, Ash took a step back and nodded toward Petty Officer Stephens, the team's master of forcible entry. Stephens put his martial arts skills to good use: He took a couple of quick steps and with a powerful kick of his right leg, smashed the heel of his sandal against the door just below the lock. There was a loud crack and a slight budge, but the door didn't completely give way. Tangredi threw his shoulder into it, and the six of them stormed into the home in a single mass, repeating the fluidity they'd used pouring from the C-130.

Inside, they trained their rifle barrels in all directions, efficiently splitting their attention about the room. The occupants had been caught off guard. The woman from the ministry threw her hands above her head while next to her a startled teenaged girl bounced in place and made strange whooping noises. In the opposite corner, Hassid scrambled over the engineer and another man in an attempt to make it to the back of the house.

"Qif!" Ash shouted, very much wanting to avoid another chase. But the three of them kept moving. It was time for more dramatic measures; concerns about drawing unwanted attention were old news now with the city blowing up all around them. Ash aimed his rifle at a portrait of Saddam Hussein that dominated the far wall and pulled the trigger.

A burst of bullets cooked off, and the women shrieked. Glints of light flashed wildly as the glass shattered. The frame jumped off the wall and crashed against a small wooden table that, in turn, split in two and clattered against the cement floor. The engineer and the other man dropped to their knees. Hassid kept going, disappearing into the dark hallway.

"Where are you from and what do you want?" the woman asked through her tears.

"Be quiet, woman!" the man shouted across the room to her. "Do not be a fool. They are Americans."

"Secure them. Steve-O and Go-man will grab the car and wait in front of the house," Ash ordered as he rushed to catch their primary target. "Billy, Tang, goggle up. Billy, come with me." He pointed toward another doorway along the opposite end of the wall shared by the opening through which Hassid had just passed. "Tang, see if you can get to the back of the house by circling around the other way." The sergeant nodded and disappeared.

Ash put the NVGs around his head but didn't slide them over his eyes until he eased around the corner and into the darkness. He hugged one side of the hallway while the senior chief took the other some distance behind.

"Kana'aqil, Wizar Hassid," Ash called toward the back of the dwelling, a request for reason. "You are outnumbered." He got no response from the Iraqi, so he added in Arabic, "It is going to get very dangerous in the city in the next hours. We want to take you to a safe place. We will not hurt you."

Hassid hadn't been wearing a holster, but that obviously didn't guarantee he was unarmed. "We will not hurt—" Before Ash could finish his sentence, two bright flashes came from the end of the narrow passageway, causing his NVGs to gain down to the point that he was blinded. The twin reports were deafening, and Ash dove to the floor and lifted his rifle while waiting several lifetimes for his goggles to start working again and the stings to let him know where the bullets had hit him.

But he felt nothing, and before he could bring his AK-47 to bear, someone kicked it out of his hands. Ash barely saw the man—much bigger than Hassid—before he was on him. Ash was lifted off his feet in a bear hug around his chest. The man's arms were the size of Ash's legs, and they bore down on the upper part of his rib cage, painfully knocking the wind out of him. Ash couldn't breathe. He couldn't make a sound.

In the half second it took Ash to realize that the senior chief was somehow unaware of his situation, it also struck him that he was quickly losing consciousness. He had to make a move now or he'd be crushed to death under the noses of his teammates. He put his chin to his chest and then threw his head back as hard as he could.

Ash knew he'd made good contact the same way a golfer knows he's hit a good shot from the feel at impact. The cartilage of the man's nose gave way against the back of his head, followed immediately by the splattering of warm blood against his neck. Remarkably, the NVGs remained in place.

The man screamed and released his grip, and before his hands reached his face, Ash wheeled around and kneed him in the groin and then, as he bent over, smashed him in his broken nose with a sharp uppercut. The Iraqi didn't fall fast enough to avoid Ash's karate kick to the side of his right knee, so by the time he hit the floor he had a broken leg to scream about as well. Ash quieted him with a roundhouse to the cheek.

The senior chief came up from behind with the stray rifle in hand. "Is this yours?" he quietly asked.

"Hell, yeah, it's mine," Ash seethed in a loud whisper. "Where the fuck were you?"

"What do you mean?" the senior chief said as he spotted the human lump at Ash's feet. "Who's that?"

"I don't know, a bodyguard or something. I have a feeling this is his house."

"That must be why Hassid chose this place."

Their brief exchange was interrupted by the dull thud of flesh against flesh, followed by a man's groan and several flashes of a stun gun.

"Hassid is secured," Tangredi reported from the far end of the corridor. "I side-doored him."

Ash helped Tangredi lug the subdued deputy minister and the unconscious bodyguard to the front room. The other Iraqis sat on the floor with their backs against a wall, hands and feet bound with zip ties and mouths covered with pieces of duct tape.

Doc Phillips kept one eye on their captives and the other out the window to the street. "No SUV yet," he reported as the lieutenant and the senior chief laid Hassid at the feet of the others. In the light they studied his face, relaxed now, mouth slack and brow not intensely knit as it was in the photograph on the playing card.

"That's him, all right," Senior Chief White said. "I told you he was an ugly sonofabitch."

The deputy minister let out a long moan, head lolling from side to side. "Want me to stun him again?" Tangredi asked.

"No," Ash replied. "Get the camera and take his picture. Doc, you ready with the sedative?"

As Tangredi took dozens of photos of Hassid with a digital camera, Phillips let the curtain over the front window fall back into place and dug into one of the satchels on the floor. All of the Iraqis' eyes widened when the medic moved toward them with the syringe in hand. He

crouched down and, after waiting for Ash to finish rolling up Hassid's sleeve, stuck the needle into the upper
part of his biceps and pushed the plunger home. Hassid's
lids fluttered, and then he went out cold.

"That should buy us six hours or so," Phillips said as
he returned to the window and parted the curtain again.

"You want me to take their pictures?" Tangredi
asked, pointing toward the other Iraqis along the wall
and across the floor.

"Go ahead," Ash replied before turning toward the
medic. "Doc, you got our car out there?"

"No," Phillips returned, which caused Ash's mind to
race with the decision matrix surrounding what the remaining four of them would do if the Suburban failed
to show up. He'd barely passed the step of stealing a
car on the street when Phillips turned from the window
and said, "They're here, L.T."

Tangredi and Phillips bent down and threw Hassid's
arms around their shoulders. On the third try, they suc-
cessfully synchronized their efforts and propped the deputy minister upright and then shuffled him out of the
house. Ash and Senior Chief White followed after grabbing the satchels off the floor. Before he shut the front
door behind him, Ash looked back to the bound Iraqis,
and in their eyes he saw something between fear and
hatred.

By the time Ash reached the Suburban, Hassid had
already been slid over the backseat and into the cargo
area and covered with a blanket. Hidalgo had assumed
driving duties, and he hit the gas even before Ash had
the passenger door shut.

More quarters of the capital were sprouting explosions, and the sky was blazing with an eerie orange. But
in spite of the ever-growing risk to the team's well-being,
the bombing intensity had caused people and cars to
desert the streets. The roll out of town looked like it
was going to be a lot smoother than the one into it
had been.

A calm settled over the Suburban. The tough phase of Bravo's part of Medusa was over. Now they just had to keep their heads down and make it to the rendezvous for their flight out. But Ash still felt like something was missing, and he figured out what it was as the SUV made the first left turn around the Ministry of Information.

"Stop the car, Go-man," he said.

"What the hell are you talking about, L.T.?" Hidalgo returned. His Latino accent grew thicker when he was stressed or confused, and, as he looked at the lieutenant as if he had sprouted antennae from his head, he sounded every bit the kid less than seven years removed from L.A.'s roughest barrios.

"Stop, I said. Right here." He looked into the backseat. "Billy, come with me."

"Where are you going?"

"To talk to the people."

Senior Chief White wrestled with the answer for a beat before folding the laptop shut and growing a grin. "The radio broadcast?"

"Why not? The general's going to want to know why we skipped it if we didn't have to. This is the psyops part of the mission."

"How long is this going to take?" Hidalgo asked.

"Five minutes, max."

The lieutenant and the senior chief exited the Suburban with rifles in hand. A second later, Tangredi said, "I'm going with them," and jumped out of the backseat. He caught the other two before they made it to the far side of the street. The three of them passed unnoticed through the east entrance of the Ministry of Information, the same door Ash and Tangredi had come out of no more than a half hour earlier.

Ash knew if he was going to pull off this part of the deal, he needed to do it quickly and without making contact with any more Iraqis, especially civilians. Past the entryway, he struggled to retrace the twisted path to the studio, but if he hesitated at all, Tangredi was there to point the way. Although some of the offices showed evidence that they had been recently occupied—desk lamps were lit, computer monitors glowed, a cigarette burned in an ashtray—the three met no one.

They wended from the wide corridor to the smaller hallways and alcoves, moving so fast that Ash almost missed the door marked STUDIO in plain English. Inside, he noted that the rack of electronic equipment in the engineer's room was still alive in small dots of green, red, and white. He put a finger to his lips and slipped into the glass enclosure that Deputy Minister Hassid had abruptly vacated.

Ash tapped the microphone perched on the long wooden table and saw the needles on the VU meters flicker in response. He took his place in the announcer's chair, cleared his throat away from the mike, and addressed a nation in Arabic:

"*Assalamu alaikum.* People of Iraq, your nightmares are almost over. Do not fear the explosions you hear. Those bombs are not intended for you. They are aimed at the headquarters and palaces of the tyrant that has held your nation hostage for too long. He and his henchmen are thieves who have stolen your very lives. They will be soon be punished for their crimes against you and your families.

"The only goal of the liberators is to return your freedom to you. They will bring no harm to innocents. It is in the interest of peace and harmony for you to support the liberators and encourage your neighbor to do the same. With your help the conflict will end quickly. *Allah alim. Ma'assalama.*" Ash smiled toward the pair of Americans pressed against the glass as he flicked the power switch next to the VU meters and watched the needles die to the left of the gauge. "And now a word from our sponsor."

They hurried out of the building unimpeded until they turned the final corner into the main corridor and came face to face with a feeble elderly man whose saucer eyes and agape mouth suggested he was more shocked than the intruders about the chance meeting.

"I know who you are," the old man barely managed to say in stuttering Arabic, sweeping an index finger across them. "You are the illegal broadcasters."

"Broadcasters?" Ash said, with his eyebrows earnestly arched. "*La*, we are not. We are cleaners."

"*La!*" the old man shot back, "*I* am the cleaner." He looked past them as if he was about to scream toward the east exit, but before he could get anything out Tangredi quieted him with a single rabbit punch to the jaw. The Iraqi crumpled across the tile floor.

"Good work, Tang," Ash cracked.

"What's the price for your silence?" Tangredi asked as he bent over the old man to make sure the fall hadn't killed him.

"Silence?" the senior chief chuckled in return. "Sure, your secret's safe with me. I guarantee nobody else will hear about you beating up geriatrics."

Hidalgo was obviously eager to get moving again. He started a slow roll the moment he spotted his three teammates hurrying out of the building and around the corner. Ash recaptured the shotgun position while the other two piled in the backseat, and the Suburban was past the speed limit before the doors were shut.

On the way out of the center of the capital, explosions reverberated through the SUV's broken rear window and lit the night all around them, at times so frequently that Ash was sure that every bomber in theater was directly overhead. They traveled several blocks north and west of where the roadblock had been, just in case the strikes hadn't convinced the Iraqi soldiers to focus their efforts elsewhere, and eventually rejoined Matar Saddam al-Dowli close to the international airport.

Once westbound on the four-lane, Hidalgo picked up the pace to one hundred kilometers per hour. Ash brought his GPS back to life and checked his watch. At this rate they'd make the abandoned strip with plenty of time to spare. But just as the passengers were about to sit back and relax a bit, Hidalgo hit the brakes, hard enough to throw one of the satchels from the cargo area across the supine Hassid and into the backseat.

"What the fuck, Go-man?" the senior chief exclaimed. "You break these NVGs and supply will have your ass."

"I've got some fires on the road up here," Hidalgo said. "Tanks or personnel carriers or something."

A handful of burning hulks dotted the way ahead, splitting the highway with flames that shot high into the night. The smell of burning rubber and death wafted through the Suburban. Hidalgo rolled slowly forward but then skidded to a complete stop.

"We're not going to be able to get around these things," he said. "The road's completely blown to hell."

"Double back then," Ash said, looking over his shoulder. "Look at the laptop, Billy. Let's figure out another way west."

Hidalgo threw the shifter between reverse and drive as he performed an aggressive three-point turn, shooting rocks and metal across the road in all directions. When he steadied the wheel, the lights of Baghdad were before them once again, and whatever euphoria the team had allowed to settle over them disappeared with the sight. Ash felt like a dumb-ass newbie for decompressing at all. The mission wouldn't be over until they were back aboard the C-130 headed for Kuwait. No, the mission wouldn't be over until the mission report was in the general's hands.

"Next left ought to work, L.T.," Senior Chief White said. "We can follow that north for a few miles and then pick up this other highway and start working it west. I'm not sure what the road's called, but it should be obvious when we get to it."

Ash ran the beam of his penlight across the map on his lap, tracing the route the senior chief had described. With his thumb and forefinger he roughly figured the mileage to the rendezvous point and then checked his watch again.

"I figure that way will put us at least a half hour behind," Ash said. "At best we'll get there right when the C-130 lands. So much for gravy."

"And that C-130 crew didn't seem terribly interested in waiting around for us," the senior chief added.

"Can you see where they are?"

"I'm not showing their symbol on the screen right now, but their signal has been coming and going all night."

"We're going to have to haul ass, Go-man," Ash said to the driver.

"*Sí,* I can do that as long as the road's in okay shape," Hidalgo replied.

"Billy, Archangel is probably freaking trying to figure out why our track is off. Let's give them a quick blast on the SATCOM that we might be a bit late. I think it's safe to break radio silence out here."

"I'll give it a shot," the senior chief said. He rooted through a satchel and found the phone. After a minute of holding the long antenna out of the window, he reported: "I can't get a signal."

"All right, try again later," Ash said. "Doc, what's up with the deputy minister?"

The medic leaned across the back of the seat and slipped an arm under the tarp. "Pulse is good," Phillips said. "He's fine."

"Is that his cologne I'm smelling, or what?" Tangredi asked.

"It's nasty, ain't it?" Phillips said, passing his pulse-checking fingers quickly under his nose for a tentative whiff.

"I don't think that's cologne . . . ," White quipped.

"All right, be polite, you animals," Ash said. "He's our guest."

Hidalgo followed the senior chief's recommended

route, heading north for a time and then west. The lights of Baghdad were behind them again, hopefully this time for good. Ash watched the bombs go off in the passenger's side rearview mirror and wondered what the jets' ordnance tally would be before the sun rose again.

Once they'd cleared the outskirts of the city and no more lights were visible in front of them, Hidalgo and Ash donned NVGs, and Hidalgo killed the dashboard lighting. He then flipped the headlight switch a click past the ON position, which turned the lamps pale green, a shade practically invisible to the naked eye. With the goggles on, the modified headlights aided those looking forward just like regular headlights, but unlike cars using regular headlights, the Suburban hurtled down the road unseen by any who might have heard it pass in the distance.

Task Force Bravo had switched to their "stealth mode," as the senior chief put it, a mode that would get them stopped by the authorities in populated areas but would buy them time across the vast stretches of unpatrolled road away from the cities. The night was black, no lights at all now, but the highway was straight and clear of any other cars or obstacles of any kind. Even the flashes of the bombs hitting the capital were gone, a memory below the rear horizon save the occasional five-thousand-pound bunker buster that momentarily set the entire hemisphere aglow. Hidalgo urged the accelerator closer to the floor as he grew more confident in the view through the NVGs. Soon the Suburban's speed was back into the triple digits.

Ash peered under his goggles at the GPS and noted the range to the rendezvous: twenty-three miles. At this speed, they'd make it before the C-130 got there, which, among other things, would allow them to outline the runway with glow sticks as the pilots had requested. Ash had been stranded enough times to appreciate that it was best to keep pilots happy: Unhappy pilots didn't always bother to pick teams up before heading back to their bases.

"I've got a signal," the senior chief reported. He put the SATCOM phone to the side of his head and attempted to contact the C-130: "Archangel, this is Dirt Farmer; how do you read?" Nothing but static in return. "Archangel, this is Dirt Farmer; how do you read?"

A faint voice barely made its way through the earpiece: "Dirt Farmer, this is Archangel. Go ahead."

"Archangel, Dirt Farmer is inbound to rendezvous but behind our timeline due to a divert to the north. Estimate twenty minutes out."

"Archangel copies."

"Tell them we have the Eight of Spades," Ash prodded once he heard White stop talking.

"Dirt Farmer is in company with the—*aahhh!*" The senior chief ripped the phone away from his head. "Damn it!" he exclaimed. "That thing just shocked the shit out of me."

"Is that smoke coming out of it?" Sergeant Tangredi asked in the backseat's limited light.

Ash turned around and raised the goggles away from his eyes. He flashed his penlight toward the end of the senior chief's arm. "It *is* smoking," he said. "Turn it off before it explodes or something. And roll your window down some more. I'm sure we shouldn't be breathing those fumes."

"I wonder what—"

Senior Chief White cut himself off as Hidalgo hit the brakes again. Ash twisted back around and braced himself against the dashboard with one hand while flipping the NVGs back down with the other. He was shocked to see they were suddenly driving across the sand, with nothing but desert stretching to the horizon before them.

SIX

"What happened to the highway?" Ash asked.

"It's gone," Hidalgo replied as he finished bringing the Suburban to a full stop. The skid caused a cloud of sand to grow around them, temporarily stealing their view beyond the hood.

"What do you mean it's gone? Did we miss a turn or something?"

"Negative, L.T. The road just ended."

A cloud of sand caused by the skid billowed outside as acrid smoke from the SATCOM phone filled the interior of the SUV in spite of the open window. The back of Ash's throat burned, and he joined several others who had started to cough. He lowered his own window, which allowed the dust inside, and his coughing fit intensified. He fought to get himself under control, to keep a clear head. He pulled a canteen out of the glove box and took a drink.

Once he could breathe again, Ash considered their options. The desert was flat, for the most part, and the Suburban had good off-road capability. Did they need a paved road to get where they were going? What would keep them from driving straight to the abandoned airstrip from where they were? Ash removed his goggles and focused on the GPS in his lap. To his growing frustration, instead of the normal high-resolution map labeled with letters and digits, Ash's screen showed nothing but a jumble of wavy lines. "Billy, how's your computer look?" he asked.

"Hold on for a sec," the senior chief returned in a raspy voice, having just weathered his own respiratory crisis. He shifted his focus from the broken phone to his digital map display. "It's not working. And it's not just that I don't have a satellite signal; I can't read anything on the screen at all."

"What the hell is going on?" Ash asked as he put the goggles to his eyes. He stuck his head out of his window and scanned the night sky for evidence. "Did we get fried by an airborne jammer or something?"

"I didn't hear anything fly over," the senior chief said.

Ash pulled his head inside and said, "Whatever. It's old-fashioned time now. Break out your compass, Billy. We're going to do a little dead-reckoning."

"What was the last good range and bearing you had?"

"I had fifteen miles at two-four-zero degrees about three minutes ago," Ash said.

"All right, we'll subtract four miles then. And the highway was running due west, so why don't we steer just south of two-four-zero?"

"Sounds fair." Ash turned toward the driver. "You ready, Go-man?"

"Give me a steer," Hidalgo said.

"Bring it left thirty degrees, and tell me when you reach a comfortable speed."

Hidalgo nodded and urged the Suburban forward again, slowly at first.

"Is that it?" Ash asked after about thirty seconds of poking across the sand.

"I need a little comfort time here," Hidalgo said.

"We're trying to DR this bitch," Senior Chief White shot back, nerves obviously fraying at the edges as the long night threatened to get longer. "We need a steady speed now, and we don't have time to pussyfoot around."

Hidalgo didn't reply but eased the accelerator down. A minute later he sighted under his goggles as he quickly flipped the dashboard lights on and reported, "That's it: Forty kilometers an hour is the best I can do without fucking killing us, amigos."

Ash worked the problem through his head: *Ten miles is about thirteen kilometers, and at this speed we'll cover thirteen kilometers in about twenty minutes.* "Okay, I've got it," Ash said after a long exhale. "You know, when I selected SEALs, I was told there would be no math."

"That's why we bring you college boys along," Senior Chief White said.

They'd only gone a short distance when Ash spotted a glow on the horizon in front of them. "Now what?" he asked.

"You want me to go around?" Hidalgo asked.

"No, not yet, anyway. We don't want to vector all over the desert. Keep going. But be careful." Ash looked over his left shoulder. "Everybody goggle up and have your weapons at the ready."

Closer, the glow transformed into a large ring of stadium-sized fluorescent lights mounted atop tall poles. Beneath them were knots of activity; large vehicles rolled into view from the west and cranes dangled large cylinders. Nearer still, the lighting was bright enough that they had to remove their NVGs to make out the detail. They could see different types of trucks now, flat beds and containers. They heard the roar of engines and grinding of gears.

"What is this?" Hidalgo asked. "Why are they building in the middle of nowhere after dark?"

"I don't know, but I think we need to take some pictures of it," Ash said. "Tang, you got the camera?"

"Yeah." Tangredi pulled the camera out of the satchel at his feet and aimed it across the front seat.

"You want me to get closer?" Hidalgo asked.

"If you can," Ash replied. "But we want to avoid contact here. As interesting as it is, this isn't our mission."

The stadium lights suddenly went dark. A second later, a pair of headlights aggressively swung toward them.

"All right, show's over," Ash said. "Did you have enough time to get any pictures, Tang?"

"I think so," Tangredi replied as he dropped the camera from his face. "The lighting wasn't the best."

"Let's get out of here, Go-man. Goggles back on, boys."

"How did they see us?" Hidalgo asked.

"Maybe they have NVGs, too," Ash replied.

"Which way should I go?" Hidalgo asked.

"Swing around to the south," Ash said. He looked back to the approaching vehicle, a white pickup. "And hurry up about it."

As they sped off, Ash saw a handful of flashes from the pickup, and then they all heard the cracks of gunfire. "Duck!" Ash cried, but the rest were way ahead of him, including the driver.

Hidalgo raised his head back above the dashboard just in time to see they were about to plow into a chain-link fence. He jerked the wheel to the left and stomped on the brakes, but it was too late. The Suburban hit the fence, but it gave way easily, as if it had been hastily erected. The rear of the SUV threatened to overtake the front until Hidalgo released the brakes and threw the wheel the other way. The Suburban straightened out, and they raced along just inside the fence line with the pickup still closing on them.

"We need to get back on the other side of the fence," Ash said.

"You want me to smash through it again?" Hidalgo asked.

"Do you see any openings?"

"No."

"Then I guess you'll have to smash through it again."

Without any further prompting, Hidalgo eased the wheel to the right to build some distance from the fence, and then he turned hard into it. The fence gave way as easily as it had the first time, and they sped into the night, more southbound than westbound now.

"Need to bring it right some," Ash said.

"That'll bring us pretty close to that factory or whatever it is," Hidalgo said.

"This guy's closing fast," Senior Chief White reported as he focused through the broken rear window.

Ash cut his eyes toward the passenger side rearview mirror and above the headlights he saw more flashes. "Keep your heads down!" he ordered. "We don't need a lucky shot to smoke one of us now." He tapped a finger against the front windshield. "Go-man, take it back to the fence line and follow it around until we get to the west side of this shit. Then we'll pick up our original heading to the landing site."

"Copy."

"And can you go any faster?"

Hidalgo nodded and steered the Suburban to the right. In short order they were hugging the fence from the outside as it wrapped around the complex. They were only about a mile away from the structures now, and although the lights remained out, through the goggles Ash could make out some of the shapes: the latticework of the cranes, several low-roofed buildings, and two tall chimneys. The noise of engines had been replaced by silence. If only they had thought to bring a night-vision lens for the camera. But those things were heavy, and besides, that hadn't been their mission. Hopefully Tangredi's pictures would be enough for the photo interpreters to do something with.

The pickup continued to close the Suburban and instead of the occasional flash of a single shot or two, it was now erupting in flickers of automatic gunfire. The three in the Suburban's backseat trained their rifles across the motionless Iraqi in the cargo area and let fly with a fusillade of their own. The pickup swerved but didn't falter, still decreasing the distance between the two vehicles by the second. The tick of lead against the steel of the tailgate told the team that their pursuers were within their weapons range, and Ash wondered if the same was true for the modified Kalashnikovs they were using. Probably not. Those had been designed for relatively close-in work.

"I hope those self-sealing tires on this bitch work," the senior chief said between squeezes on his trigger.

"How much longer do you want to follow the fence, L.T.?" Hidalgo asked.

Ash did a quick mental plot and replied, "Give us another quarter mile then peel off to the left. I'll give you a steer once we're headed into the desert again."

"Maybe they'll drop us once we're away from here," the senior chief offered.

"Maybe," Ash said. "How's your ammo?"

"I'm running low."

Tangredi and Stephens simultaneously added, "Me, too."

"Here, take my spare cartridges," Ash said. He held his hand out to the medic seated next to him. "Give them yours, too, Doc, and grab Go-man's from his rifle."

The last of the team's bullets were passed into the backseat, and the three continued to lay down a wall of fire in an effort to ward off those chasing them. They could see sparks as their bullets hit the hood and grill of the pickup without slowing it down at all.

"That's got to be a damn hard car or something," Tangredi declared. "Our shots are bouncing right off them."

"Just keep shooting," Ash said. "They've got to honor that."

A few seconds later, Hidalgo turned the wheel to the left and pointed the Suburban back into the nothingness of central Iraq. Ash sighted through his compass and said, "Bring it ten more degrees to the right . . . there, steady up."

"They're still on our ass," the senior chief said between bursts. "And I'm down to the last clip."

"Same here," Tangredi said.

"My RPG might work here," Stephens offered matter-of-factly.

"You've got an RPG?" the senior chief said.

"Yeah, I always bring one or two rounds for emergencies."

"Well, this is an *emergency,* son. Get busy."

The young petty officer dug into a satchel and produced something that looked like a miniature torpedo. He clicked it into place on a rail along the bottom of the rifle barrel then took aim. Before he squeezed the trigger, he glanced toward the senior chief and asked, "Do you think this'll work against a hard car?"

"Just shoot the fucking thing!" the senior chief snapped.

Stephens took aim again and pulled the trigger. The rocket roared through the broken window and streaked toward the pickup, marked by a bright plume along the several hundred feet it traveled before it hit. The resultant explosion consumed the pickup and its occupants in an expanding ball of flame. The earsplitting blast radiated out, and the Suburban lurched forward as the shockwave slammed into it.

They distanced themselves from the burning wreckage, and after a few minutes of silence between the team, Senior Chief White offered dryly, "Make a note: RPGs work just fine against hard cars."

Ash checked his watch: Just over ten minutes had passed since the last time he'd attempted to fix their position. What had the trip around the factory—if that was what the complex could be called—done to their track across the countryside? They had to be behind where the straight-line track would have put them, but by how much? And where had the southerly jaunt put them coursewise?

"How fast are you going now, Go-man?" Ash asked.

"I'm back at forty," Hidalgo replied.

"Hold that. What do you think, Billy?"

"I like this heading," the senior chief replied. "What about the timing?"

"Based on the size of the arc we made, I'd add about five minutes to our timing."

"That gives us another fifteen minutes, right?"

"Right. All the same, you guys sing out if you see something that looks like it used to be a runway."

"Used to be a runway?" the senior chief said. "Hopefully it still works."

"We'll know soon enough." Ash looked back into the rear view mirror to see how high the flames were climbing above the pickup's hulk and saw nothing. He twisted over his left shoulder and checked the view through the broken window. Still nothing.

"What happened to the fire?" Ash asked.

The three in the backseat turned around and joined the lieutenant looking to the east.

"Maybe it went out," Stephens offered.

"Not that quickly," Tangredi said. "We've gone far enough. It's probably below the horizon."

Ash noticed the screen in Senior Chief White's lap flicker to life, and he asked, "Is your computer okay now, Billy?"

The senior chief tapped several buttons and announced, "I think it is. How's your gear?"

Ash looked at his own lap and saw his GPS was working again, too. He also saw his dead-reckoning estimate had been very close. "Heading's good, Go-man," the lieutenant said, pride poorly muted. "Three minutes to go."

"You were a minute off," the senior chief said.

"What's a minute between friends?" Ash replied.

"More than half a kilometer."

"A mere stone's throw. And you didn't seem to have any trouble with my numbers."

"I was just being a good subordinate."

Ash pulled off his NVGs and shot the senior chief a look. "Bring the real headlights on, Go-man," he said as he turned forward again. "Let's find this runway."

"It runs north-south, right, L.T.?" Hidalgo asked.

"Yep."

Hidalgo slammed on the brakes. "We're here."

Ash put the NVGs back to his eyes and surveyed the area. Sure enough, they were in the middle of a strip of smooth ground that looked a lot like a runway. He checked his watch: It was a minute after the planned land time for the C-130. He reached for the satchel at his feet and said, "Quick. Let's run along the edge of it and lay down the glow sticks."

They weren't sure exactly where they'd arrived along the length of the runway, so they drove north. Ash cracked the glow sticks to life and then chucked them out the side of the Suburban like a newspaper boy on his morning rounds. Several hundred yards later they reached the northern end of the strip, so they turned around and drove the other way, holding the glow sticks until they got beyond where they'd started.

"Isn't it past the rendezvous time?" Senior Chief White asked.

Ash looked at his watch and replied, "Yeah, by two minutes."

"Those bastards better get here."

"I'm sure they're . . . hold it. I think I hear them."

In the backseat Stephens and Tangredi rolled their windows down and stuck their heads into the night. "You're right, L.T.," Tangredi said. "Those are definitely turboprops I hear."

"Let's get the rest of these glow sticks down before they get here," Ash said.

Hidalgo sped up and Ash delivered the sticks at a

frantic pace. He was down to the last few when out of the corner of his eye he caught a glimmer of spinning propellers entering the headlights' circle of light. The C-130 was already on the ground and was headed right for them.

"I just got their signal back on the computer," the senior chief announced. "That's the C-130."

"No shit," Ash shot back. He almost screamed an order at Hidalgo but saw that the transport was going to pass a reasonable distance abeam. The C-130 came to a quick halt, locked wheels and props with their pitch at full thrust reverse kicking up dust along the way. The roar of its four engines accompanied the huge silhouette of the plane. The transport spun around, and once the dust from the prop wash cleared, the team saw the aft ramp was already down. The red lighting from inside the cargo bay beckoned like the lodge's hearth after a long day on the mountain.

"Time's a-wasting," Ash said.

Hidalgo drove across the sand and up the ramp, and the crew chief and loadmaster nearly had the Suburban completely strapped down before the last member of Task Force Bravo had slid his road-weary frame out of it. Sergeant Phillips pulled a stretcher from where it hung on one of the bulkheads, and Tangredi joined him in getting Deputy Minister Hassid lashed to the deck. Once the Iraqi was secure, the medic covered him with a blanket and rechecked his vital signs.

Ash buckled himself into one of the sling seats, and after what seemed to be a very short takeoff roll, they were airborne. He peered out of the small round window behind him, looking for the fire from the burning pickup or the ring of stadium lights, but could find neither. He focused farther to the east and saw that Baghdad was still taking a pounding.

"I see we got our man, Lieutenant," the loadmaster said, startling Ash a little as he stepped over unannounced. "And it looks like everybody made it back in one piece. I guess it was just another routine mission, huh?"

Running a hand across his matted hair, he smiled politely and said, "You got it, Tech Sergeant: just another routine mission."

SEVEN

Murdo Edeema was jolted awake by the melodic ring of his cell phone. He snatched the device from the floor next to the bed and flipped it open, hoping that his sleeping wife, supine on the other side of the California king-size mattress, or the borzoi at his feet hadn't been disturbed. "Hold on," he murmured into the phone before slipping out of the bedroom and padding downstairs to his study. He switched on the light and closed the door behind him.

"Hello?" he finally said in a normal tone of voice.

"Reynolds?"

"No, it's Edeema."

"*Merde!* I have the wrong number here. Well, no matter. *C'est Paris, ici.*" The man's French threw Edeema off in his still-waking state, but once the fog cleared he realized it was Bertrand Vélanges, the Huntington Group's overseer at Le Monde's headquarters. "We have a problem," the Frenchman said. "I need you to call Reynolds and get him to call back from the SCAR *immédiatement.*"

"Tonight? Can't this wait until the morning?"

"*Non!*" Vélanges hung up.

Edeema hit the END button, then immediately started punching in another series of digits. He put the phone to his ear and listened to it ring. Where the hell was Ned?

"Hello?" a man said after the sixth ring.

"We need to meet," Edeema said.

"Excuse me?"

Edeema paused. He didn't recognize the voice. "Is this Ned Reynolds?"

"Hold on."

There was a short exchange at the other end of the line, and then another man's voice said, "Hello?"

"Ned?" Edeema asked.

"Yes?"

"Sorry to disturb you," Edeema said, fighting off the images entering his mind regarding what might be going on at Reynolds' house or wherever he was. "Apparently we have a problem. I just received a call from Paris. You need to call Vélanges."

"They called you?"

"I think he meant to call you first, but he misdialed or something. In any case, he wanted you to call back right away."

"I'm on my way."

"I'll meet you there."

"It's late, Murdo. I can handle this."

"I really think I need to be involved in this, too. I might need to start crafting a strategy from my angle."

"Whatever." Reynolds hung up.

EIGHT

Ash was dead to the world until the door to his hooch—nothing more than a large tent with a plywood floor—opened and daylight rushed in. He winced as he raised his head from his inflatable pillow and tried to figure out who owned the approaching silhouette.

"You going to sleep all day, L.T.?" Senior Chief White asked.

Ash reached across his cot to the crate he'd fashioned into a nightstand and fumbled for his watch. "What time is it?"

"Just after nine."

"I didn't get to bed until after three."

"Okay, so you've had a lot more than your duty four hours." The senior chief mopped his face with a towel draped around his neck. "Hell, I've already PT'd this morning."

Another silhouette filled the doorway and called tentatively into the darkness: "L.T.? L.T., are you in there?"

"Jeez, the whole world is here," the lieutenant said. "What is it, Tang?"

"You got a call on the bat phone," Sergeant Tangredi

said. The "bat phone" was slang for the encrypted, or "covered," circuit used for classified discussions. "It's a general or something."

"A general?"

Ash scrambled out of his sleeping bag and threw on a set of desert cammies, some boots, and a pair of stylish sunglasses favored by professional golfers and beach volleyball players. As the senior chief went to shower and change into his working uniform, Ash and Tangredi headed the opposite way through Officers' Country, pausing briefly at the prefab latrine trailer so Ash could empty his bladder, or, as he put it, get his head right.

Ash had thought the base in northern Kuwait a busy place the day before, but it had been nothing compared to the current level of activity, and he wondered how he'd been able to sleep with so much going on around him. A war had definitely started. Humvees loaded with fifty cals choked the air with dust as they sped along the company street. Choppers raged overhead in all directions. Soldiers and Marines moved in a jog if not a full-out sprint instead of moping about with their normal hangdog shuffle.

Across the asphalt from the tent city that the regular Army had relegated to the special operators, Marines and other cats and dogs based at Camp Doha were the more permanent structures, and among them was a former Kuwaiti Army truck warehouse that now served as the tactical operations center for the Special Operations Command. The two members of the newly deactivated Task Force Bravo waited for a break in the convoy of giant-tired trucks hauling shipping containers northbound in support of the forces already deep into Iraqi territory, and then sprinted across the street and to the TOC's steel door. Ash punched a combination of keys on the adjacent cipher lock and the latch popped open with a loud click. Once inside, Ash let his sunglasses dangle and searched the space. Beyond the rows of soldiers feverishly tapping on plastic-sheathed laptops and watch officers yelling into handsets stood Petty Officer Stephens, waving a telephone receiver over his head. Ash threaded his way through the maze of chairs and long tables and eventually reached his fellow SEAL.

"Who is it?" Ash asked quietly as he approached.

"General Dupree?" Stephens replied. The general was SOCOM's deputy commander and the officer in charge of all special operations in the Iraqi theater.

Ash relieved the sailor of the receiver, took a deep breath, and put it to the side of his head: "Lieutenant Roberts, sir . . ."

"Ash, this is Dupree in Qatar," the general said in a graveled voice, using only his surname as many flag officers did—power and access in a simple package, like a well-branded Fortune 500 corporation. But the general was no politico or rear-guard poseur; he was a living special ops folk hero. Since his earliest days as a Green Beret in Vietnam, when he had freed himself and several comrades from a Vietcong prison camp deep in the jungle, killing twenty-one VC with their own weapons in the process, he'd done nothing but build on his reputation as a no-nonsense, kick-ass war fighter. He was a guy who'd ascended in spite of the system, by most accounts, and the special ops community shared the collective dream that he might one day be the first of them assigned as the Chairman of the Joint Chiefs of Staff.

"Good morning, General," Ash replied, trying to keep his voice from catching. He'd never been comfortable around admirals or generals; in fact, Ash was probably more at ease in the presence of an enemy than an American flag officer. They made him nervous, even the most pleasant among them—a feeling he could only attribute to his first experience with one of them. During his plebe year at the Academy, the superintendent, a three-star admiral, had come out of nowhere to dump on him in front of his friends for wearing his cover the wrong way.

"I know you're busy up there, so I won't waste your time." As he listened to his voice come through the encrypted line, Ash pictured the general—tall and broad-shouldered, with a cue ball head and a rugged face that had for years silently convinced men to charge death. "I just finished reading your mission report, and I wanted to send my personal congratulations for a job well done. Of the five missions that went out last night, only three managed to get the gomers they were after, and only Bravo came back without any casualties. That's good stuff, Ash, and a real tribute to your leadership."

"Well . . . uh, thank you, General, but it wasn't just—"

"I know," the general interrupted, "you've got a great team. Well, they're *all* great teams. We don't field anything but. But that didn't get the job done for the others last night. I also wanted to relay word from the intelligence chief down here, who said that your radio broadcast had a real impact. That was a true stroke of genius. Did you come up with that?"

"Ah, no, sir. I'm not sure who . . ."

Ash allowed his words to trail off as the general, voice muffled now, conversed with someone on his end of the line. "I've got to take another call," he said back into the receiver. "Again, congratulations on a great mission. Keep it up."

"Thank you, sir—" The line went dead. Ash dropped the handset into its cradle.

"What did he say?" Tangredi asked across his shoulder.

"He just wanted to say congratulations," Ash said.

"That's it?" Stephens said. "Did he read our mission report?"

"I think so. He said that intel had passed to him that our radio broadcast had big impact."

"So Tang didn't deck that old guy for nothing, huh?" Stephens quipped.

"You'd better watch it, squid, or I'll deck you," Tangredi returned. "Did he say anything about the desert complex?"

"No," Ash said. "It was a pretty short conversation."

"I'm dying to find out what that place was," Tangredi said.

"The photos were pretty blurry," Stephens said. "They might not be able to make anything out of them."

"The light was bad, and the car was banging around."

"Whatever, Tang. I'm just saying they were blurry."

"I think a couple of them were decent enough to do something with," Ash said. "And now that you mention it, I guess I am sort of surprised the general didn't mention anything about it."

Senior Chief White, now in his desert cammies with his wet hair slicked straight back, materialized between the other two. "What's up?" he asked.

"Who put our misrep on the wire?" Ash asked back.

"That tall redheaded intel officer. Captain . . . Seymour, I guess it is."

"Do you see him around here?"

The senior chief twisted his head back and forth a few times and then said, "Yeah, he's standing over by the fax machines."

Ash did a quick assessment as to who might be senior. The Army officer looked pretty young, plus he was an Army officer. "Tang, ask him to come over here for a second, please."

Tangredi hustled across the space and soon returned with the lanky captain in tow. The Army officer stood with his arms folded in front of him, wearing an expression that told that he wasn't terribly interested in spending much time with these three. "What do you need, Lieutenant?"

Ash cut his eyes to the man's last name embroidered over one of his breast pockets, just to be sure, and said, "Captain Seymour, I was just on the phone with General Dupree. He was fresh from reading our mission report and wanted to pass along his congratulations."

The captain raised a red eyebrow and shrugged. "Okay . . . *and?*"

Ash narrowed his eyes slightly, a subtle signal for the

Army officer to keep his attitude in check. "And I just wanted to make sure the misrep was transmitted without any glitches."

"Glitches?"

"Problems . . ."

Captain Seymour's head shuddered slightly. "Look, I don't have time for games, Lieutenant. If you're trying to say something, just say it." So much for keeping the man's attitude in check.

"You transmitted our mission report earlier this morning, right?" Ash asked.

"Yeah."

"In its entirety?"

"What, you think I have time to edit those things?"

"So, as far as you know it went through exactly as we wrote it?"

"Affirmative."

"What about the photos?" Tangredi asked.

"Which ones?" the captain asked back.

"The ones we reviewed last night," Ash said. "The photos of Hassid are pretty straightforward, but the shots of this industrial complex we came across are definitely going to need some computer enhancement and analysis. And those are the ones we're curious about."

"All of the photo interpreters are down in Qatar. All we do here is attach your photo files to classified email and then send the disc to CENTCOM headquarters in the daily snail mail run. We're not allowed to even look at the files at this end."

"How long will it take to get something back from Qatar?"

Captain Seymour shrugged again, a move he seemed to have perfected. "There's no telling. Plus, your geographic coordinates were sort of a swag, right? That could delay the process some."

"Our GPS and laptop malfunctioned," Ash said.

"Along with our SATCOM," the senior chief added.

"And little green men came out of the sky," the captain said, putting the backs of his wrists against his temples and wiggling his fingers in a B movie ghoul imitation. "No, I'll bet what you saw was the Disney folks getting a head start on *Hajji* World."

Ash rose out of his chair and stood toe to toe with the Army intelligence officer—albeit while giving away an inch or two in height—and intoned drily, "You're a funny guy, but this isn't a joke. That complex could be important; hell, it could be the key to the whole damn war."

Captain Seymour blinked a few times and took a step away. Flashing his palms, he said, "Fellas, it's not for me to decide anything. All I'm telling you is whatever information they manage to get from your stuff is only going to be one piece of a very big pie down there. Plus, intel isn't just about access; it's about the need to know. I mean, think about it: You guys captured Hassid, touched him with your very hands, but do you know where he is now?"

"No," Ash replied. "Where is he?"

"I don't *need* to know." He splayed a hand across his chest as he continued: "But I'm on your side. I'll try to find out what they come up with. I talk to them all the time. If I hear anything, I'll let you know."

"Yeah," Ash said as he turned away. "We don't really *need* to know. We're just the guys actually fighting the war."

Captain Seymour's eyes widened, and he said, "Hold it, I do have something for you." He raced across the space to his work area and returned waving a sheet of paper. "I have the analysis of the bullet holes in your SUV." He lowered his eyes and began to read aloud: "Ballistics analysis of the damage to the rear of the Suburban used by Task Force Bravo during Operation Medusa showed conclusive evidence of two different types of ordnance: a standard fifty-caliber automatic weapon round of Russian origin and a nonstandard APLP round." He looked up from the page and said, "I'm not sure what APLP is."

"Armor piercing, limited penetration," Ash replied.

"That's bad shit," Tangredi said. "Those are those five-point-five-six-millimeter blended metal mothers that shatter instead of penetrating. The wounds they create are untreatable. You get hit in the ass with one of those, it'll blow the lower half of your body off."

"Why don't we have those?" Stephens asked.

"Because like the report says, they're nonstandard," Ash said. "They haven't passed our military approval process. If you got caught using one, you could be court-martialed."

"Figures."

"Looks like the Iraqis are playing hardball this time," the senior chief said.

"It also looks like they were serious about guarding that complex," Ash added before focusing back on the Army captain. "Does headquarters have that ballistics report?"

Captain Seymour studied the list of addressees at the top of the page and said, "Yeah, they're on here."

"Well, here's hoping they can put the pieces together," Ash said as he hoisted a plastic bottle of water from a nearby table.

"Have faith in the system," the captain said. He grew a devilish smile as he flipped to a second sheet of paper and held it in front of Ash's face. "In the meantime, it's a happy coincidence you called me over right after this came across the wires. You guys might want to start planning your *next* mission."

Ash took the tasking from the captain and slid a chair up to an adjacent table. Before he started to read the operational overview, he fished through a pocket for the briefing card from the previous night's mission. Normally he would have chucked the card into a "burn bag," a specially marked paper sack that was thrown into an incinerator once it was filled, but this time he elected not to. He scanned the card, assessing the range of hand-written data scrawled over it—waypoints, frequencies, the serial number of the ruggedized laptop, etc.—and then folded it in half and slipped it back into his pocket. He'd never kept a briefing card before, but something told him he might need the information later.

NINE

The night watchman was asleep at his desk when Murdo Edeema stepped out of the elevator from the underground parking garage and walked across the lobby of Crystal City Gateway Number Seven, the high-rise where the Huntington Group's offices were located. *Fucking typical,* he thought. He thought about letting the old codger slide; Edeema had enough to worry about, and Reynolds was probably already in place upstairs. But the fact that part of the firm's rent paid the watchman's salary combined with the requirement for a security company to actually provide security drove him in the direction of the desk.

"Psst," he hissed, hoping to avoid giving the man a heart attack. "Wake up."

The watchman bolted upright, slinging a stream of drool across his chin as he did. "I wasn't asleep," he slurred mechanically, wiping his face with the sleeve of his uniform jacket. "I was just resting my eyes."

Edeema flashed his building access badge and said, "I could've walked right by without your noticing."

"Oh, no, sir. I heard you the whole time."

"Sure. The tenants of this building need you to stay awake."

Edeema started for the bank of elevators that fed to the upper stories, and the watchman called to him: "I apologize, sir. What say we keep this between us?"

Edeema turned around and said, "Just stay awake."

When the elevator doors opened on the fourteenth floor, Edeema saw Ned Reynolds headed for the SCAR in full stride, and he suddenly felt a bit guilty for showing up in jeans and a sweatshirt with Reynolds dressed in his suit and groomed as if it was the start of just another working day.

"I got us a couple of coffees on the way over here," Edeema said, holding up a pair of Styrofoam cups. "Black, right?"

"Sure," Reynolds returned with muted appreciation.

"The guard in the lobby needs this more than I do," Edeema said before peeling the plastic top off the cup and blowing across the surface of the coffee. "He was dead to the world when I walked across the lobby. I'm going to give the security company a call once the day starts."

"Did you catch his name?"

"Had 'Henderson' on his nametag." Edeema took a cautious sip of the coffee and then said, "I'm sorry if I disturbed you when I called."

Reynolds offered no explanation or excuses but simply shrugged and said, "No problem."

Edeema raised the cup to his lips again while considering how to address a delicate matter. "I was surprised you didn't answer your phone."

Reynolds didn't waver. He looked Edeema in the eye and calmly said, "That was my mistake. It won't happen again."

"I was . . . surprised, you know?" Edeema tried to read Reynolds's expression but got nothing.

"I need to call Paris," Reynolds said in return.

"Yes, of course."

Reynolds took a step and then stopped. "Again, Murdo, you don't really need to be here for this."

"Please, Ned," Edeema said in return, trying to maintain an air of authority in his voice. "Let me decide where I need to be. If this turns out to be a waste of my time then I'll be the first to say so, trust me."

Inside the SCAR, the classical music was cued up again—Bach this time—and the top secret brief was beaming over the plasma screen in short order.

"Can you hear me, Bertrand?" Reynolds asked into the black obelisk at the center of the conference table.

"I can," Vélanges replied. "Let me, as you say, cut to the chase. We had an incident in the desert a few hours ago. Two Russians on the security detail were killed by a rocket propelled grenade that was fired from a vehicle that passed very close to the facility."

Edeema and Reynolds exchanged furrowed-brow glances, and Reynolds asked, "What kind of vehicle?"

"A civilian vehicle," Vélanges returned. "What you call an SUV. The plant manager thought it might have been a group of insurgents. He has had some trouble with them in the past."

"They weren't insurgents," Reynolds said. "They were Americans, a special forces team."

"*Oui?* Are you sure about this?"

"Sure enough."

"Then you also know what we need here."

"I'll poke around across the street in a few hours."

"*Alors, plus vite.* We need to control damage here. This isn't just about us. Lucrative deals always draw a lot of firms that otherwise might not undertake such risks. We have a lot of companies working this one: French, Russian, Polish . . ."

"The impact would be huge," Reynolds opined.

"*Oui.* So you get me information; we activate *Les Affreux.*"

"Already?" Edeema returned. "Perhaps we should employ others measures first."

"What other *measures* are you talking about?"

"I don't know . . . something less drastic than turning those thugs loose."

"They are not thugs," Vélanges said. "You sound like one of those American hypocrites on the television."

"Don't worry yourself over *Les Affreux,* Murdo," Reynolds said. "That's operations."

"We are wasting time here," Vélanges said. "Let us keep this off the BBC or the front page of *Le Figaro, n'est pas?*"

"I think we need to take this to the higher-ups before anyone does anything," Edeema said. "I'm not entirely comfortable with the course of action you recommend."

"I am the president's chief advisor!" the Frenchman ranted. "I speak for the so-called higher-ups. Ned, you have your tasking."

"This is what happens when we get too cute," Edeema mumbled, twisting his fists against his eye sockets.

"It was smart business," Reynolds said.

"No, it wasn't."

"Well, that's an easy position to take now, isn't it?"

"And *Les Affreux* won't be damage control—they'll just make our situation worse," Edeema said. "We've got to accept the consequences. We should just weather the hit and move on."

"You cannot be that naive, Murdo," Vélanges said. "We would not just take a hit, as you say. We would be crushed. The American government alone would see to that."

"Maybe or maybe not."

"Paris will not accept *maybe*. And this is the wrong time for our efforts to be discovered, even though these damn sanctions are nothing more than the will of America thrust on the world."

"Let's keep our heads here," Reynolds said, reaching

across the table and patting the back of Edeema's wrist with a cold, dry hand. "Murdo, you're not new to this. I'm sure you've been around the business when things got, let's say, interesting."

"I did what I had to do to stay alive," Edeema said, drawing his arm back. "I never murdered anyone."

A heavy silence followed, and then Vélanges said, "I will thank you never to use that word again. Whatever happens, it is business. Do you understand, Murdo?"

"Sure," Edeema begrudgingly returned. "Whatever you say, Bertrand. Just tell me this: Is there an officer on the American special operations team?"

"Probably," Reynolds said. "These task forces are usually led by a junior one, a Navy lieutenant or an Army captain. What about it?"

"Then at least let me have the officer."

"The officer? Why?"

"Look around the organization, Ned. I've had some success with that type. Our business is not all operations, you know."

"What would you do with this one, Murdo?" Vélanges asked.

"Isolate him," Edeema replied. "Even groom him, perhaps. As I said, his sort of pedigree has worked to all of our benefit before."

"Sounds risky," Reynolds said.

"It is *not* risky," Edeema shot back. "This is what *I* do. You think the right people simply march through our front door?"

"Arrête, s'il vous plait," Vélanges said. "Murdo, do some research. If you like the profile, get him somewhere where we can keep a close eye on him. I must go now. Like all of us, I have a lot of work to do. We will speak again soon, I am sure." There was a click through the speaker as the Frenchman cut the connection.

Edeema crushed the cup in his fist as he looked to the bank of lights in the ceiling. Again, his thoughts went to the early days when, for all of his wanton zest, he'd been ignorant of the full ramifications of any given action. With a heave of his chest, he muttered, "This is already too messy."

"Not to worry," Ned Reynolds said. "We know how to do messy if we have to."

TEN

Lieutenant Saul Schoenstein awoke with the same thought that he had greeted each new working day with for the last six months: *I hate my job.* He crawled out of his bed with the mattress that made his back hurt, shuffled his bare feet across the cold tile floor to the bathroom sink, and unwrapped the bar of complimentary soap the maid had placed there the day before. As he balled the wrapping in his fist and chucked it into the plastic wastebasket at his feet, he wondered what had happened to the bar he'd just opened yesterday. *Typical government waste,* he thought. In some dark room somewhere, a corporate rep had presented a contract stipulating that the bachelor officers' quarters had to provide a new bar of soap to its guests each day, regardless of the condition of the old bar, and the government agent had willingly signed it. The very idea of it bugged Saul to his marrow. In fact, he'd tracked down the housekeeper during the first week of his stay in the BOQ and asked if she couldn't just leave the old bar until it was used up. Without making eye contact, she'd impassively shaken her head and mumbled that she just did what she was told by her supervisor. That was where he'd left it. He was too busy with this job he hated to do anything about it right now. In time, he swore, he'd make a difference, and not simply in matters of wasted soap. It was this promise of a brighter, productive future that kept him going.

He stood with the shower's stream beating against the back of his neck and thought about how he'd come to accept this duty. After a successful first sea tour aboard an Arleigh Burke class destroyer, he'd never expected to wind up in Millington, Tennessee, for shore duty. But Millington was home to the Navy Military Personnel Command, and that was where fast-track lieutenants went to be detailers, the folks who arranged orders for other officers. His mentors had told him that the detailer job was a tough, thankless duty, but an important check in the block, as well as a great way to meet everyone in the surface warfare community. What they hadn't mentioned was that he wasn't going to be a detailer for the surface warfare community, and once he arrived he discovered he was the new redheaded stepchild among the detailers, charged with giving orders to SEAL officers, the guys who made even fighter pilots look humble.

The former Miss Ruth Rollins, now known as Mrs. Saul Schoenstein, had told him there was no way in hell that she was living in Tennessee, never mind Millington, and she'd grabbed young Master Jon Schoenstein and moved in with her parents, who lived in an affluent suburb west of Philadelphia. So, Saul was forced into geographic bachelorhood, and as there were no decent rentals available this side of Memphis and he didn't feel like caring for a house anyway, he'd taken up residence in the BOQ and endured a too-soft mattress and the gluttony of a daily fresh bar of soap.

Along with not having a wife in the area, he didn't have a car, so, after stretching his back and throwing his khakis on, he pedaled his secondhand beach cruiser across the base to his office, or rather, to his cubicle. By the time he'd chained his bike to the stand and rushed through the double doors and down the corridor to the common area, the morning briefing was already in progress.

"Now that the war's started, we have to be ready to ramp it up a notch," his immediate boss, the chubby-cheeked Commander Donahue, said. "Here's a good example." He held a piece of paper aloft. "Is Saul here?" Saul raised his hand nonchalantly, as if he'd been in place for the duration of the meeting. "This is a hot one. This is to replace that admiral's aide who got cancer a month back or so. I think the admiral's finally sick and tired of not having an aide." The commander handed the sheet over.

Saul scanned the sheet and saw it was an email exchange between organizations in the Pentagon, including the Joint Staff—commands he normally didn't deal with. "This *is* a hot one," he said in amazement.

"Right," the commander returned sardonically. "And I guaranteed the boss we'd have orders cut on this guy before noon today, so don't screw it up, please." He dismissed the group with, "Okay, everybody. Go out and pedal some flesh."

On the way to his cubicle, Saul again scanned the sheet of paper. The Joint Staff, the Secretary of Defense's office, SOCOM? A powerful bunch, indeed. But he sensed he didn't have time to marvel over the trail across which this request had traveled. After grabbing a cup of coffee from the community pot, he sat down in front of his monitor, currently displaying the phrase PLEASE KILL ME in thick block letters that were spinning around a black background, and checked his watch. With the time difference between Millington and Kuwait, what were the chances "this guy" was at his desk? Ten after eight in the morning here, dinnertime there. Never mind the time difference. With a war going on, what were the chances a Navy SEAL wasn't out killing bad guys? And what if this guy refused to accept the orders? What if he, like so many others, called his equally cocky sea daddy and had him make big trouble with the higher-ups about how the timing of the proposed job was bad and how it would kill his career, blah, blah, blah.

Orders cut before noon, huh? "Did I mention how much I hated this job?" Saul mumbled to himself as he brought his computer screen to life and reached for the phone.

After two days spent buried in the sand, real food was welcome, even if it was prepared by the lowest-bidding contractor who provided meals for most of the units at Camp Doha. The activity around the dinner table showed that the men fresh from the war were hungry. Flanked by his teammates, Ash sawed into his over-cooked steak and washed the pieces down with a brown-ish liquid that tasted like a mixture of iced tea and cherry Kool-Aid. But the desert had given them fresh perspective; none of them was about to criticize the meal.

The mission had been straightforward, as far as Delta Force missions went. The former Task Force Bravo had been joined by a handful of others to form Task Force Golf. Ash had figured Operation Scout to be along more traditional lines than the previous op as soon as he'd met the first two new members of the team, neither of whom spoke Arabic or looked the slightest bit Iraqi. After another C-130 ride and another night jump, they'd concealed themselves in the desert twenty miles ahead of the rapidly moving front line and used IR binoculars and NVGs to count Iraqi men and equipment, and then relayed their findings to the approaching U. S. Army division.

With the notable exception of a couple of Apache helicopters stumbling across an Iraqi elite Republican Guard unit and absorbing a few rounds before limping back home, Operation Scout had been uneventful, even boring. Ash and his men had simply waited for the Army to roll past them as they motored toward Baghdad, and then climbed into a southbound convoy of Humvees for the hundred-mile drive back to Kuwait.

Ash had occupied his mind during the return trip with scenes from Operation Medusa. What was that complex for, and how long would it take intel to figure it out? And even if they did figure it out, would he ever hear anything about it? It seemed unbelievable that he might not have a "need to know" in the view of those tasked with figuring out that sort of thing, but at the same time, considering the number of self-important bastards who had gravitated to support roles like intelligence, it made perfect sense.

"Poker game after chow, L.T.," Tangredi passed from across the table when Ash pushed his chair back to leave. "You in?"

"I'll think about it," Ash said noncommittally as he got to his feet and brushed the crumbs from the front of his cammies. "First I want to swing by the office and see if anything's come up. In any case, if I don't make it, I don't want you guys pulling another all-nighter. You're studs and all, but even you need to pace yourselves. We're only three days into this bitch."

"We'll be good boys, Mom," Senior Chief White quipped.

Ash smiled and ran his eyes across the group, briefly considering each man. With a casual salute, he walked out of the mess hall and onto the company street. Calm winds and the brilliant burst of orange in the western sky at sunset instantly put him in a contemplative mood, and it struck him that the senior chief and the others were as good a bunch of war fighters as one could ever serve with. Ash rode the sanguine wave of emotion; maybe it was the weather or the fatigue or the full belly, but for now it just felt good to feel good. He was tired and lonely, but most of all, he was lucky, dammit. Brother Winston could have Manhattan. He'd take the rest of the world, or at least the parts of it where there was ordnance to be expended.

Several hundred yards across the base, Ash dialed the

cipher lock and pushed his way through the steel door to the tactical operations center. He was pleased to see that a few of the workstations lining the long tables were not being used. He plopped himself into a folding chair and punched the nearest laptop to life.

As he typed his password into the appropriate field, one of the phones among a bank behind him rang. He looked around to see if anyone was reacting. No one was. Murphy's law. Stop by for a quick email scan and wind up with the phone watch.

Ash scanned the bank for a couple of rings before he figured out which of the phones to answer: "TOC, Lieutenant Roberts speaking . . ."

"Ashton Roberts?" the voice on the other end asked.

"That's affirmative . . ."

"*Lieutenant* Ashton Roberts, the Navy SEAL?"

"Yes?"

"Man, this never happens to me. I'm surprised I reached you right off the bat. I usually wind up playing phone tag with guys over there."

"Who is this?"

"I'm sorry. I should've identified myself. This is Lieutenant Saul Schoenstein. I'm your detailer."

Detailer? Why the hell would his detailer be calling? "What can I do for you?"

"I know you're in a joint job right now, but those guys handed this steaming turd—I'm sorry . . . *this good deal*—to the Navy to take care of." After a few beats of silence on the other end of the line, a delay that felt like an eternity to Ash, Lieutenant Schoenstein said, "Right up front I'll admit this is a bit of an unorthodox situation, even by SEAL standards. I'm not here to bullshit you, Ashton. That's not my job. If you and I don't have trust, then we don't have anything. Do you agree with me there?"

"Uh . . . I'm not—"

"Does the name Brooks Garrett mean anything to you, Ashton?"

"No," Ash replied.

"*Vice Admiral* Brooks Garrett?"

"Nope."

The detailer hummed in confusion and then softly said, "Then why would you be a by-name call?"

"Excuse me? What are you talking about?"

"A by-name call. Admiral Garrett has asked for you by name."

"To do what?"

"To be his flag lieutenant."

"His what?"

"His *aide*."

Ash felt a bolt of adrenaline shoot through his veins, wracking his system more severely than anything he had gone through in recent days under fire. "There's got to be some mistake," Ash said. "Trust me; you've got the wrong man. I'm not the aide type."

"Of course, there will be an interview process, Ashton," the detailer explained, "but in this case I think it will be a mere formality."

Ash's head was spinning faster with each of the detailer's words. "I'm completely lost here," he said mechanically. "When does this so-called job start?"

"As soon as possible."

"Who am I relieving?"

"Nobody. The guy rolled a couple of weeks ago—medical reasons, I think."

"Where is it?"

"The Pentagon. Admiral Garrett is an assistant principal to the Joint Chiefs of Staff." Ash heard the rustling of paper on the other end of the line. "Let's see here: J-three-alpha-six, deputy assistant chief of staff for international liaison."

"I don't—"

"You're single, right, Ashton? It looks like this billet is going to have you on the road a lot."

"I don't get this," Ash said, desperately trying to slow the pace of the discussion. "I wasn't supposed to roll from this tour for a year or so. I shouldn't be up for orders now."

"I'll say you don't get it. You're a *by-name call,* and a three star's by-name call at that. As your detailer, I must advise you that this is a very career-enhancing job."

Ash released an involuntary burst of sarcastic laughter and shot back, "More career-enhancing than fighting a war?"

"Uh . . . it can be, I guess. Unless you piss somebody off." Ash wasn't sure whether to interpret the comment as sage counsel or a threat. "Look, I've got a lot of calls to make today. Keep an eye on your email in-box. I'll follow this conversation by zapping you your official orders."

"Do I have a choice here? What if I say no?"

"I would advise against saying no to a three-star, Ashton. That's *not* career-enhancing."

Ash ran a palm across his forehead in exasperated disbelief, and said, "I can't believe you're pulling me out of the war for this."

"Think of it as simply changing fronts," Lieutenant Schoenstein said.

ELEVEN

Traffic wasn't bad, and for that Ash was thankful. Washington, D.C., was notorious for its congestion, and not just during rush hour. He checked the time: 12:45. He was playing it closer than he'd wanted to, but that was due to factors out of his control. The itinerary had been tight to begin with, and the shuttle bus taking forever to pick him up in front of the airport and the clerk at the counter twice sending him to the wrong numbered space to grab his bright red econo-clone rental car hadn't helped.

He had only been stateside for a few hours when he steered off New York Avenue and onto I-395 South. The contrast of the scene with the last time he'd been in a civilian vehicle—Operation Medusa—mixed with his jet lag and compounded the surrealism of it all. He vacillated between a keen, battle-honed sense of the present and a hazy detachment from his surroundings—a defense mechanism that protected him from his confusion and, perhaps, anger. He stroked his face under his nose, marveling at how smooth his upper lip felt without a mustache on it.

A few miles later, he reached the 14th Street Bridge, and halfway across the Potomac River, the Pentagon came into view. He'd passed the building a number of times during his Annapolis years without giving it much thought, but now he saw the brownish-gray wall that faced him as a battlement, a structure out of synch with the other, more graceful architecture that dotted the landscape around the capital. He fought off a sense of foreboding, reminding himself that he'd just come out of a war zone. This was just a stupid interview, a no-risk no-brainer. Besides, he didn't even want the job. But, all the same, his heartbeat pounded in his chest.

The long plane rides between Kuwait City and Frankfurt and Baltimore-Washington International Airport had given him plenty of time to think, but his main questions remained unanswered. Why would Vice Admiral Garrett—whoever he was—have asked for him by name? Why would General Dupree and the others in charge of special operations in Iraq allow an officer with his credentials to be transferred out of the theater just as a major war was cooking off?

And what the hell did an aide do? He wasn't sure he wanted the answer to that one. He saw himself—the once proud warrior—holding car doors open and chasing down dry cleaning. He cursed the speed at which the system had sent him back to the States. Why didn't things happen as quickly when the teams needed new gear or even a basic resupply?

Ash cursed himself for his compliance. He should have bitched; he should have called every high-ranking officer he'd ever worked for. But there hadn't been time.

But it wasn't really about time; he simply didn't do business that way. He wondered if somehow that made him morally superior to those who did, or if he was just a chump.

His cell phone rang. He managed to fish it out of the duffel bag on the passenger's seat without driving off the side of the bridge and answered it with his signature greeting, a personalized twist on standard radio procedure: "Ash is up. . . ."

"Hello, homo." There was no mistaking that voice, the same one that had at once buoyed and plagued him during his SEAL training days in Coronado. "Wild" Willie Weldon was Hollywood's conception of a SEAL: physically imposing, coifed with a California surfer's blond locks, permanently tanned, and as full tilt in his approach to life as his nickname suggested he would be.

"Hello, Wild," Ash said.

"I guess the fact your phone is working means you're on the ground and in the Greater Washington metropolitan area."

"I'm just crossing the Potomac."

"You got the directions I emailed you?"

"Yes."

"Take the Route One exit south after the bridge. Once you cross Army-Navy Boulevard, my apartment building is the first complex on your right: Pentagon Towers. Parking is under the building. Tell them you're my guest. Apartment fourteen-one-twelve."

"I've got it already. You sure you don't mind me crashing at your place for a day or two? I'm sure I could get a hotel room."

"Stop with the Mr. Polite Guy routine. You're not good at it. What time is your interview?"

"Two thirty," Ash replied.

"You're okay, then. Take the Metro from the Pentagon Mall one stop to the Pentagon."

"I've got the directions, Wild."

"Which uniform are you going to wear?"

"I'm already wearing service dress blues. I changed at the airport."

"Is that what they told you to be in?"

"They didn't say."

"You may be overdressed, but that's better than the

other way around, I guess. What room are you going to?"

"E Ring somewhere. I've got it written down."

"You've never been inside the ol' Puzzle Palace, have you?"

"No."

"I guarantee you'll get lost."

"I had an Army major on the airplane explain the room number system to me," Ash offered. "Plus, I think someone from the admiral's staff is meeting me at the main entrance."

"Of course," Wild chided. "You're one of them now."

"I appreciate your support."

"Oh, trust me, I support you getting this job. If you don't, they'll send you back to the war, and I'll still be the only SEAL out of the action."

"That's support, huh?"

"Make good eye contact and don't talk too much. Answer the questions and then shut up."

"Priceless advice, Mr. Trump."

"Stop by my office once you're done. Maybe I can even skip out a little early."

"Where's your office?"

"Room 4C312."

"How do I get there from where I'm going to be?"

"You're a SEAL; you figure it out."

TWELVE

Other people in uniform—a few of them in service dress blues—surrounded Ash for the short ride to the Pentagon Metro stop. He figured from those around him that what he had heard about Crystal City being nothing more than an extension of the Pentagon was true. After surfing the flow of humanity out of the Metro car—the end of the lunch rush—Ash rode the escalator from beneath ground level, unsure of how close to the Pentagon he would be once he broke the surface. Back in the daylight, he was pleased to see the building looming over him and the entrance he'd been instructed to go through only a few hundred feet away. At the approach to the massive doors, doors fit for a fortress, he queued up in the line marked NO BADGES.

"Open all bags, show two forms of photo ID," a guard dressed in dark blue utilities with a submachine gun slung over his shoulder chanted repeatedly from behind a folding table. Ash offered his military ID and driver's license, and after studying both for a time, the guard waved him on. Ash passed more armed guards before passing through the entrance. He'd no sooner had time to remove his uniform cap than he found himself in another line, this one caused by visitors waiting to pass through a metal detector. Although he emptied his pockets and removed his watch, Ash set off the detector. As the guard took him aside and ran a wand around his body, he heard a female voice calling his name.

"Lieutenant Roberts," she said. "Excuse me, are you Lieutenant Roberts?"

An attractive woman moved toward him, waving an arm in the air. He noted her bright blue eyes and bouncy blonde hair just past the collar. His eyes drifted lower, just long enough to avoid the obvious, and he noted that her hair wasn't her only bouncy attribute. Even with the unflattering lines of the female khaki uniform, he could see she was very well built. It reminded him, as it had in the presence of every remotely good-looking woman since he had walked on the airplane in Kuwait City, that he hadn't had sex in an awfully long time.

"Yes, I'm Lieutenant Roberts," he replied as the guard gestured that he could move away. A second later she was close enough that he noted her aiguillette—the three gold braids flecked with bits of blue that circled her left arm at the shoulder—the device that marked her as a member of the admiral's staff. Now he could make out her collar devices, and he felt guilty for his sexual thoughts. Actually, it was more disappointment than guilt. The future between them he'd conjured up in the time it took for her to transform from a knockout to a chief would, alas, not be coming to pass. Fraternization was a rap he'd never mess around with.

"I'm Chief Monroe," she said as she extended her hand. "I'm here to escort you to Vice Admiral Garrett's office."

The security guard standing behind the desk seemed to know Chief Monroe, or in any case was pleased to see her, and in short order Ash was awarded a temporary badge. The chief led the way up an escalator where another security maze awaited them, this one ending with a turnstile that didn't budge until one of the laminated security badges was inserted into it. Ash couldn't seem to crack the code with his badge, so the chief had to turn around and use hers to get him through.

"I understand you were just in Iraq," she said as they rounded the first corner and came upon a line of retail stores that seemed out of place.

"Yeah, I was," Ash replied, head swiveling around like a country bumpkin on his first day in the big city. "I'm actually still in the middle of my return-to-civilization culture shock. Can anyone shop here?"

"Anyone with access to the Pentagon. This is known as the concourse. You'll hear people refer to it a lot. Do you think we're in for much of a fight over there?"

Ash shrugged and said, "I don't think they're going to just hand us the keys to Baghdad." He didn't feel like talking about the war. He needed information about what he was walking into. "Do you work for Vice Admiral Garrett?"

"I'm his flag writer."

"What, do you write his speeches and stuff like that?"

"No, sir, I mostly answer the phone. I'm Mrs. Wood's assistant."

They turned the corner past the stores and started up a shallow ramp several hundred yards long. "Who's Mrs. Wood?"

"She's the executive secretary. But don't call her 'Mrs. Wood.' She hates that, for some reason. She goes by 'Miss Dubs.' "

"Miss Dubs?"

"Yes, sir. 'Dubs' as in W for Wood. You don't get in to see the admiral without going through Miss Dubs. That's Rule Number One around the outer office."

At the top of the ramp they turned another corner, and, once through a side door, they walked along a plain hallway that came as close as anything in showing the building's age. Many of the terrazzo floor tiles were missing, and most of those that weren't were badly cracked. The cream-colored paint on the walls was peeling, and the ceiling tiles along the edges of the hallway were water-stained.

"I'm taking you the short way," Chief Monroe explained. "Obviously, we don't bring VIPs through here. We keep hearing stories about how they're going to renovate this, but I've been here for six months and it hasn't happened."

"Times are tight everywhere, I guess," Ash said.

Around the next turn Ash was happy he hadn't been made to find his way to the admiral's office alone. "How long did it take for you to be able to get around this place?" he asked.

She chuckled and said, "I still get lost all the time."

The surroundings turned progressively more presentable as they continued down another long passageway where the walls went from plaster to burnished mahogany, punctuated by bigger-than-life oil paintings of former secretaries of Defense. He locked eyes with several of them as he passed, and each sent the same subliminal message: *What the hell are you doing here?* His disorientation increased by the gilded frame.

The chief made a left then a right and suddenly stopped next to one of the doorways and gestured for Ash to enter. The atmosphere across the threshold sharply contrasted with that of the hallways—floor and desk lamps instead of fluorescent lights overhead and thick carpeting to absorb the echo of footsteps and conversation.

"This is the reception area," Chief Monroe explained. "Please have a seat, and I'll tell Miss Dubs you're here."

The chief disappeared through another doorway. Ash decided against sitting down, a combination of nerves and the fear he'd be caught off guard by someone bursting into the room. He paced along the wall and feigned interest in the American naval history prints that hung there. He smelled hazelnut coffee. Phones rang incessantly in the adjacent offices.

"Lieutenant Roberts?" The voice startled him. He

looked over and saw a diminutive woman with short, black hair striding toward him with her arm extended. She was dressed in a dark business suit with a knee-length skirt—exactly how he imagined a middle-aged female civilian working in an admiral's office would be dressed. "I'm Miss Dubs. Welcome to Washington."

Ash thought she might have been a beauty as a younger woman. The lines of her nose and jaw were sharp, a bit too much so, perhaps, and gave her a delicate edge. Her weapon against time was makeup—and lots of it. As she drew closer, he noted her artificially white pallor, which made her red lipstick look that much brighter. Her cheekbones, high or not, were accentuated with matching rouge. Her eyebrows were drawn in dark pencil. Her fragrance was a bit overpowering and wafted in sharp contrast to what Chief Monroe wore. And her hair wasn't just black; it was jet-black, a color too dark to be natural.

"Can I get you some coffee or something?" she asked as she took his hand in a grip that belied her small frame.

"No, ma'am, I think I'm fine for now."

She fanned the air near his chin, mocking slaps to his face, and said, "You stop with that *ma'am* stuff right now, mister. You sure I can't get you some coffee? You've got to be exhausted."

He wondered if this was part of the interview used to judge how much of a whiner he was. "I feel fine, actually."

She returned a closed-mouth smile and nodded. "Okay. The admiral is on the phone with the Secretary, and once he hangs up we'll get you in to see him."

"I thought you were the secretary."

She smiled and said, "Around here when we say 'the Secretary,' we mean the secretary of Defense."

"Oh . . ."

"It shouldn't be too much longer. Why don't you have a seat?"

This time Ash thought it might be rude if he didn't follow the recommendation, so he sat down in the middle of the nearest brown leather couch. Miss Dubs waited until he was situated and then spun on her heel, gone as fast as she'd arrived. In spite of her somewhat clownish appearance, her disarming aura was calming; his heart rate had slowed a bit with her presence.

Ash leaned forward and leafed through a few magazines lying on the coffee table before settling on the morning's edition of the *Washington Post*. The main headline read SANDSTORMS SLOW AMERICAN TROOP ADVANCE, and a large color picture of an Army soldier wearing goggles that had been made opaque by blowing dust dominated the front page. Ash focused on the photo. He knew the soldier's pain, the irritation of sand clogging every pore, exposed and otherwise, and the constant grit between the molars.

The article stated that the storm had not only slowed the Americans' advance on Baghdad but that it had injected a dose of reality in the minds of military and civilian leaders who had become convinced after the first two days that the war was going to be an easy go. There was a quote from an Army meteorologist who said there was no telling how long the storm would last. "Maybe days, maybe weeks," he said. An Iraqi cleric claimed it was the will of Allah. Air support was grounded. Supply chains were strained. Ash wondered where Billy White and the boys were.

A pair of brown shoes suddenly came to Ash's attention, parked just beyond the end of the coffee table. He looked up from the paper and saw an officer standing over him in khakis, wearing a leather flight jacket. He caught a glimpse of a silver eagle peeking out from behind the jacket's fur collar and popped to his feet.

"You must be the SEAL," the captain said with a smile that revealed a gap between his two front teeth. He was a head shorter but had a wider build, like a wrestler or rugby player. What little hair he had was combed straight back and matched the color of the freckles dotting his ruddy face, especially around his nose and forehead. "I'm Bill Bradford," he said as they shook. "I'm Admiral Garrett's executive assistant."

"Ash Roberts, sir."

Captain Bradford pointed at the newspaper. "Looks like things didn't go as smoothly yesterday as they had the day before."

"No, sir," Ash agreed. "I was just reading about that."

"I flew Hornets in the first Gulf War. In fact, Admiral Garrett was my air wing commander. People tend to forget that wasn't any cakewalk, either."

"Yes, sir," Ash said. "I think they do."

"I understand you saw a little action on the first night, huh?"

Ash wore a poker face as he wrestled with matters of classification. Operation Medusa had been a highly classified mission. What details did the captain have at his disposal, if any? And even if he was cleared for that sort of information, what level of discussion was authorized in the admiral's reception area?

Miss Dubs reappeared in the doorway: "The admiral is ready to see you now."

Captain Bradford gave Ash a wink and said, "We'll talk later. Good luck with the interview. And relax. Admiral Garrett's a great guy." He winked again. "All we fighter pilots are."

Ash shook the captain's hand and then followed Miss Dubs out of the reception area and into the adjacent space. "This is the outer office," she explained, arms sweeping across the room like a real estate agent showing a home. "That's my desk, there, and that's where you'll sit, over there . . . if you get the job, of course."

What was all this about good luck and interviews and "if you get the job, of course"? What was the deal here? He'd seen his orders, but did he have the job or not?

Miss Dubs paused in Vice Admiral Garrett's doorway and asked, "Are you ready for him, sir?" in a gentle tone, like someone trying to avoid waking a sleeping baby.

"Send him in," a deep voice bellowed in return.

Miss Dubs turned and nodded at Ash. He swallowed hard and stepped into the room. He stood at attention just past the threshold—protocol when calling on senior officers, especially those who wore three stars.

"At ease, Lieutenant," the admiral said, already moving around his huge wooden desk. He was tall, with a thick head of white hair that he styled with a ramrod-straight part on the side—a politician's hairdo. His body was wide at the shoulders and slim at the waist. His khaki uniform was adorned with gold pilot's wings above more rows of ribbons than Ash could count at a glance. "Miss Dubs, will you please close the door behind you?"

"Yes, Admiral. Remember you have to be over at the Chairman's office in a half hour."

"What's that about again?"

"He wants you to review part of his testimony before he briefs the Senate Armed Services Committee tomorrow."

"Oh, yeah. Got it." The admiral shook Ash's hand as Miss Dubs made a quiet exit. "It's a pleasure to meet you. Thanks for getting here on such short notice."

In spite of the stress and gnashing of teeth of the last hours, Ash replied, "No problem, sir."

"Why don't we relax over here and chat for a bit?"

Ash followed Garrett across the office. Once they reached the sitting area, the admiral motioned for him to sit down before taking a seat in a matching leather chair across from him. He organized a few sheets of paper in his lap. "Let me start by asking you a series of questions," the admiral said, glancing at the top sheet. His voice resonated with authority, like an anchorman's. "Why do you want to be my aide?"

Ash wasn't sure whether to speak or laugh. The admiral's expression suggested it was a serious question. In spite of that, Ash wasn't about to fake anything. "Admiral, to be honest, I'm here only because I received orders to be. Nothing personal, sir, but I've never wanted to be an aide."

"Oh," the admiral replied. He ran his finger across the paper for several seconds, and Ash studied him as he did. He didn't look as old as he had to have been by Ash's math—maybe a decade shy of it. The few lines on his face were faint, nearly indistinguishable. His dark brown eyes matched the color of his eyebrows, and his windblown complexion joined both of them in contrasting with his white hair.

The admiral raised his head and said, "Tell me about your previous staff experience."

"I don't have any, sir."

The admiral considered the lieutenant with concern but then relaxed his expression and tossed the papers on a nearby end table. "That's right," he said. "You don't. So why are you here?"

Ash was halfway through a shrug when the admiral continued with, "You're here because I wanted you here. Do you know why I wanted you here?"

"No, sir," he replied as curtly as the setting allowed, eager for the admiral to get on with it.

The admiral paused, nodding as if reconvincing himself of his point. "You're here because I asked for you," he continued. "When I read the mission report from Operation Medusa, and I knew you were custom-made for this job." Ash must have flinched ever so slightly at the mention of the top-secret operation, because the admiral said, "Don't worry, when my office door is shut, this is a secure space."

"But the mission report doesn't have any names in it, sir," Ash noted.

"No, it doesn't. But I made a call to SOCOM and said I needed somebody like the guy profiled in the report." He grew a wry smile. "I got back a pretty short list of candidates."

Garrett got to his feet. Ash moved to stand as well,

but the admiral gestured for him to remain seated. The admiral paced in front of his desk with his arms behind his back. Ash noted the definition of his triceps; he looked to be in very good shape for an old guy.

"I don't need to tell you, Ash, the battle space has changed a lot in the past few years," the admiral said. "Wars now are fought mostly by guys like me and guys like you—tactical aviators and special operators. Have you ever done any forward air-controlling?"

"Yes, sir. In Afghanistan, mostly."

"Then you know what I'm talking about. In every meeting I have with the Secretary, he goes on about how we need to shape the overall force of the future to look more like today's special operators. And I happen to think he's right." The admiral put a hand across his chest. "Obviously, flying is my game. It's been a few years since I was in the cockpit, but I never left the business of developing better ways to project air power."

Garrett jabbed a finger at Ash and said, "Your world is foreign to me, for the most part. I had a SEAL team under me when I was a battle group commander, but they always seemed to be off doing stuff on their own. Plus, that was before 9-11. I'm sure your doctrine has changed significantly since then."

Garrett eased himself back into the chair across from Ash. "The aide to the admiral who had this job before me was a SEAL." He spread his fingers apart, simulating the blossom of an explosion. "So it could be said SEAL aides are almost the standard around here. What do you think?"

"What do *I* think?"

"Yeah, what do you think? Are you up for it?"

Up for it? The admiral suddenly sounded very informal, like a guy trying to convince a buddy to join him for a weekend road trip instead of a flag officer searching for a member of his staff. Was Ash up for it? And what was *it?* His mind fired with hundreds of thoughts, but something his detailer had said registered above the rest of the noise: *I would advise against saying no to a three-star, Ashton.*

"Again, Admiral," Ash said, voice catching. He cleared his throat and continued: "I've never been on an admiral's staff before, and to be honest, I've never thought of myself as an aide type."

"An aide type?" Garrett asked. "What's an aide type?"

Don't get cute here, Ash thought. *Just say yes, and let the pain begin.* "I guess I'm not sure, sir. I've just always associated a certain type with an aide job."

"Am I that type?" *Dammit, boy,* Ash thought to himself. *You're going to get yourself in big trouble.* "I only ask because I was an aide when I was a lieutenant."

The admiral moved from the chair to his desk, picked up a folder there, and slowly stepped back toward the sitting area, flipping through pages as he did. "I see from your record you're a Naval Academy grad."

"Yes, sir."

"Any sports?"

"Yes, sir. Lacrosse."

"What do you know? I played lacrosse at Navy. What position?"

"Midfield."

"This certainly is a small world, isn't it?" the admiral said as he sat down again. "I was a midfielder, too. Then I spent the next twenty-five years flying fighters off aircraft carriers and occasionally dropping bombs on hostile nations."

Ash felt the blood draining from his face.

"I'm not trying to put you on the spot," Garrett continued, somewhat letting him off the hook. "In fact, I felt the same way about being an aide when my detailer *suggested* it to me." The admiral signaled quotes around the word "suggested" as he spoke. "But I'll tell you this: My aide tour was one of the most rewarding jobs I ever had."

"With all due respect, Admiral, being a mission team lead in wartime was the most rewarding job I ever had."

Even as he heard the words coming out, he wanted them back, but Ash was powerless to stop himself. He flashed forward to the court-martial where he'd blame his disrespect and failure to carry out a direct order on posttraumatic stress disorder, combat fatigue, and jet lag.

Garrett sat silent for a time. Ash sensed the tension building along with his heart rate. He'd been more poised in the middle of combat.

Finally, the admiral said, "The 'aide type' is a myth; good officers aren't. And the simple truth is I need a good officer to be my aide. Your record made me think you were a good officer—a good officer with the right kind of background for the times. You still a bachelor?"

"Yes, sir."

"Although Mrs. Garrett would disagree with me, that's a plus from my point of view. We work long hours around here, and we'll be on the road a lot. So, I'll ask again: Are you up for it?"

"I still have no idea what the job entails, sir."

Garrett puffed a deep breath and said, "Your job is to get me to the right place, wearing the right clothes, and saying the right things to the right people. That's all there is to it. Can you handle that?"

Ash offered a shallow nod and asked, "Who am I relieving? Will I be able to get a turnover with the outgoing aide?"

"No, unfortunately not," the admiral said. "Lieutenant Sampson moved on rather quickly. Cancer, you know. He did a great job before he got sick, though."

The admiral drifted off momentarily, eyes unfocused and expression trancelike, but he soon shook himself out of it. "In any case, I think there's an aide turnover binder somewhere around the outer office, and the rest of the staff will help you get up to speed, especially Miss Dubs. She's the corporate knowledge around here; been with me for two years and many other admirals for decades before that. I don't make a move without her, and you shouldn't either."

Garrett stopped himself short. "Listen to me," he said. "Here I am talking like you're the aide, and you haven't even agreed to take the job yet. I'll ask you one more time—with the understanding I never ask anything twice, let alone three times—are you up for it?"

Ash knew there was only one right answer, even without his detailer's sage advice. Plus, if he said no at this point, he'd probably piss off so many people he'd never get good orders again. He'd be sent back to Camp Doha, sure, but he'd be issuing volleyballs from the rec tent instead of leading a team in the field.

"Why not?" Ash said with a shrug.

"That's not *yes*," the admiral shot back.

"I mean, *yes,* sir."

Garrett popped out of his chair and reached for Ash's hand. "Okay, then. Make sure Miss Dubs knows how to get in touch with you."

"When do you want me to start?" Ash asked as they shook.

"Well, let's not get ahead of ourselves," the admiral said. "There are a few other candidates to consider."

"You mean I don't have the job?"

The admiral flashed a palm and said, "Not officially, no. I said SEALs have become the standard, but I still have to interview some front-runners from other communities." He flipped through the sheets on the end table. "There's a submariner, a Marine Harrier pilot, and a Navy helicopter pilot left. We have to give everybody a fair shot, don't we?"

Ash was both embarrassed for his presumption and confused by the idea that he might not get the job. What about his orders? Why would they waste the time and travel money to have him haul ass back from the war?

New emotions crept to the fore. There was a competition in progress, and Ash hated to lose. He turned to leave, but then surprising himself, offered a wholly different sentiment than he'd presented on the front side of the meeting and said, "I hope it works out, Admiral."

Garrett winked. "It always seems to."

Back in the outer office, Miss Dubs greeted Ash with her hands clasped in front of her and asked, "Well, how did it go?" in a cheery singsong.

"Fine, I guess," Ash said. "The admiral told me to make sure you had my number."

"Oh, I've got your number, all right," she said with a gleam in her eye. "We know how to find you. I'm sure you'll be hearing something one way or another very soon."

Miss Dubs gave Ash one last smile and turned her attention to the phone ringing on her desk. Ash suddenly realized that, in spite of the fact that he still had a million questions, there didn't seem to be anyone idle enough to answer them. Captain Bradford and Miss Dubs worked their phones, while Chief Monroe sat at her desk, fingers a blur across her keyboard.

A bald man in a suit poked his head in from the reception room and, with a mawkish, big-toothed smile, asked Miss Dubs, "Is he available for a minute or two?"

"He's almost late for a meeting with the Chairman of the Joint Chiefs," Miss Dubs returned, putting her hand over the phone. She focused on the computer screen. "Today's probably not a good day, Mr. Sullivan. Can I get you to try us toward the end of the week?"

"Ah . . . sure, no problem." He reached under his arm and produced a small ringed binder. "Did I give you one of our new date books, Miss Dubs?"

She pointed at the phone and said, "I've really got to deal with this."

"Of course," the man said apologetically. "I'll just leave it over here."

The man had no sooner walked out than Miss Dubs hung up the phone and mused aloud, "I've got more date books than I know what to do with."

Her phone rang again, and as another man in a suit appeared in the doorway, Ash left to wait for his own phone to ring.

THIRTEEN

Ash stepped back into one of the Pentagon's mazes of hallways. Around two corners and into the E Ring, he passed a Marine who was guarding the most lavishly appointed passageway of all, presumably the one that led to the Secretary of Defense's office. Ash realized, in spite of the primer the Army officer had given him on the airplane, that he had no idea how to get to Wild's office.

"Excuse me, Corporal," Ash said. "Can you tell me how to get to Room 4C312?"

"Are you familiar with the Pentagon's numbering system, sir?" the young Marine asked.

"Sort of."

The corporal reached under the ledge of his station, a podium of sorts, and produced a diagram of the Pentagon sheathed in a sheet of plastic. He ran his finger around the sheet as he spoke: "The floors are numbered one through five. There's a mezzanine and a basement, too, but we'll skip those for now. We're on the second floor, which is the main floor. Five rings labeled A through E. E, the one we're in, is the outermost ring. Cutting across the rings are ten corridors, or 'spokes,' that radiate from the center. Spoke number one is at the south end of the concourse—where the stores are—and they work counterclockwise from there." He looked up from the sheet. "Are you with me so far, sir?"

"Seems straightforward enough," Ash replied with a nod.

The corporal pointed over Ash's shoulder. "To get where you want to go, take that stairwell up two decks then follow the first spoke you come to toward the center of the building until you get to the C ring. Walk clockwise around the ring until you get to the three hundreds, which will be almost halfway around the circle. Three-twelve should be right there."

"Got it," Ash said. "I think I can make it."

"Ever been aboard an aircraft carrier?"

"Yeah?"

"The Pentagon is like five aircraft carriers linked together. Good luck, sir."

Ash made his way to the stairwell, already wondering if the fact that his cell phone hadn't rung yet was a good or bad sign. Up two flights, he stood on the landing looking for the nearest spoke toward the center of the building. He saw nothing but solid wall across from him, so he headed to his left, checking room numbers as he went. Good. He was on the fourth floor and in the E Ring.

Ash walked along the E Ring until he turned into the first spoke he came to. Past the D Ring the corridor grew dark, and although he couldn't read any room numbers, he assumed the next cross passageway was the C Ring. He took a left.

He stepped tentatively through the darkness. He saw outlines of bodies, silhouettes that silently passed him headed in the opposite direction. There was a faint light around the bend that revealed a wall at the end of the passageway he was traveling along. A false ring? Nobody had said anything about those. He cursed under his breath and doubled back.

It seemed darker at the spoke than it had been before, and he felt his way around the corner and along the smooth plaster wall, longing for a pair of NVGs. Somebody bumped into him, and as he offered an "excuse me," he was suddenly blinded by a penlight directed into his eyes.

"Do you know where you are?" a raspy female voice asked.

"Not really," Ash replied.

"Me either." She pushed past him and was gone.

Something dripped onto Ash's face. Water? He wiped it away and brought the tips of his fingers to his nose. No scent. No telling what might be running through the building's old pipes.

There was enough light at the next intersection to make out room numbers, and as he traveled along the C Ring the hallway got progressively brighter. He passed from the four-digit offices to the one hundreds, and figured he'd crossed back to the beginning of the spokes. He was going clockwise. The office numbers were getting bigger. The building was starting to make sense.

But then it abruptly stopped making sense. Ash suddenly found himself wandering among rooms numbered in the four hundreds. What happened to the three hundreds? Dammit. Hadn't the corporal's explanation made the system seem so intuitive, so simple?

Ash hailed an Air Force captain who was passing by: "Do you know where Room 4C312 is?"

The baby-faced captain recoiled a bit and said, "I don't work around here," and scurried off before Ash could ask anything else. An Army major followed, and Ash repeated his question. The tall black officer passed without a word.

Ash tried backtracking, but that only got him more lost. The hallways grew ever smaller and more poorly marked. He pulled out his cell phone to call Wild but couldn't get a signal. As he released another string of profanity under his breath, he was hit by the urge to urinate.

After wandering along another unmarked corridor, Ash happened across a bathroom. Past the double swinging doors stood a dark-skinned man in green coveralls twisting a strip of plastic around the top of an opaque trash bag. Finally, a guide to lead him to his destination. Who would know the building better than a janitor?

"Excuse me, sir," Ash said. "Can you tell me how to get to 4C312?" The man continued to attend to replacing the full trash bag with an empty one without looking up.

Ash had started to repeat the question when the man violently shook his head and mumbled, *"No hablas inglés."* He hurriedly shoved the fresh bag into the metal bin and then wheeled his cart past Ash and through the doors.

Ash stood and relieved himself along the row of urinals and took a number of deep breaths. Over at the sink, Ash studied himself in the mirror, wondering what the admiral's impression might have been as he walked into the office. His uniform looked good adorned with rows of fresh ribbons and a shiny, gold SEAL pin, the largest warfare device on the face of the earth. Higher, he caught a glimpse of something dangling from his nose. A booger? Shit, how long had that been there?

Ash wiped his nose with a paper towel and checked his cell phone again. Still no signal. What if Miss Dubs was trying to call him right now? Would he forfeit the job if he didn't answer his phone?

The clinking of a belt buckle against the tile floor informed Ash he wasn't alone. Without being too obnoxious about it, Ash peered under the line of stalls and spotted a pair of khaki trousers bunched above black shoes. Maybe this guy would know the way to 4C312. Ash didn't get out the first word of his question before he was cut off by a blast of flatulence that reverberated around the restroom for a frighteningly long time. Once the noise stopped, Ash could hear the man snicker and say to himself, "Damn, I'm good."

Ash thought he recognized the voice. "Wild?" he asked tentatively toward the stall.

"Yes?" the man seated in the stall sang back.

"It's Ash."

"Trolling around bathrooms again, huh?"

"I was lost."

"I knew you would be. Give me a second here."

"Don't rush it. I'll be outside."

Ash waited in the hallway, avoiding the glances of the few passersby who were probably wondering what he was doing just standing in front of the bathroom. He heard the toilet flush, and a brief time later Wild appeared, wearing a wide grin, blond as ever, and tanned in spite of the fact that it was late winter.

"Hail to the war hero," Wild said, bending at the waist with his arms raised above his head.

"To be a war hero you have to stick around for the war," Ash returned.

They shook and patted each other on the back. "The building kicked your ass, huh?" Wild asked.

"It's a good thing I ran into you," Ash admitted. "I might never have found my way out."

"I thought you said you knew the system."

"The system," Ash repeated with a derisive laugh. "I've heard the tale a couple of times, but I never believed it until the system swallowed me whole."

Ash followed his old friend around three corners, somewhat relieved that the numbering pattern still made no sense. They came to a steel door, and after Wild punched the keys on the adjacent cipher lock, they entered a large room segmented by cloth-covered partitions. Phones rang incessantly all around. Large monitors lined the far wall, most of them broadcasting views of Iraq in various scales.

Wild raised a big arm and announced: "All right, you

geeks. We've got a real live SEAL war hero here, so I want you to show the proper respect.'' Only a couple of officers reacted with the obligatory parochial banter. The others looked too busy to bother.

Wild waited a few more beats for more ball-busting that didn't come, then threaded through the maze of cubicles with Ash in trail.

"Well, lookie here," the burly SEAL said as he plopped into his padded swivel chair. "Take a shit, get twenty emails."

"That's more detail than I need, Wild," a Marine major with a shaved head said from the opposite side of the horseshoe of six cubicles surrounding a round table ringed by four metal chairs. "But I do thank you for sharing."

Wild spun around in his chair and gestured toward Ash. "Mongo, meet my buddy, Ashton Roberts the fourth."

"The fourth, huh?" Mongo said, getting to his feet.

"It's just 'Ash,' " Ash returned, narrowing his eyes at Wild as he shook Mongo's hand. "Nice to meet you."

"He's a rich kid," Wild said. "His dad owns New York City."

"Really?" Mongo said with his eyebrows arched. "My dad was going to buy that but decided against it once he heard it didn't come with the Yankees."

"His dad owns the Yankees, too," Wild added.

"What the hell are you doing in the Navy, Ash?" Mongo asked.

"Standing here in the Pentagon, I'm not sure I have a good answer for that," Ash said.

"He's here to be an admiral's aide," Wild explained.

"Ouch," Mongo said. "That's one of the few jobs in this building that I wouldn't trade mine for. What made you want to do that?"

"I didn't want it," Ash said.

"Remember the war hero I was telling you about, Mongo?" Wild asked. "This is the guy."

"You're the guy who did the 'snatch and grab' into Baghdad, huh?" Mongo asked.

"For a highly classified mission, it seems to be the worst kept secret in Washington," Ash muttered.

"We work in the current ops cell," Wild said. "It's our job to know things."

Mongo sat back down in his chair and asked, "So you didn't want to be an aide?"

"No," Ash replied.

"But here you are."

"Yes."

"I've never heard of anyone being nominated into an aide job who didn't actively campaign for it."

"Right now I'm not even sure if I've got the job." The discussion prompted Ash to check his cell phone. He still had no signal. "Can I borrow your phone, Wild?"

"Who are you calling?"

"What do you care?"

"You're not calling one of your old girlfriends in the area, are you?"

"What if I was?"

"I'd say bullshit on that. And even if you somehow actually *did* have a girlfriend, I'm taking you out on the town."

"Unfortunately, I don't have any old girlfriends in the area. Can I use the phone or not?"

Wild stepped out of the way and swept both arms toward his desk. "Be my guest."

Ash checked his cell phone log and then dialed. After the second ring, a voice said, "Vice Admiral Garrett's office. This is Miss Dubs."

"Miss Dubs, this is Ash Roberts, the lieutenant who interviewed for the aide job earlier today. My cell phone doesn't appear to be working, and I wanted to make sure I hadn't missed your call."

"You left less than a half hour ago, Ash."

"So you haven't called, yet? I just wanted to make sure."

"No, we still have a few interviews left. I wouldn't expect a call before the close of business."

"Okay. What time does business usually close up around the office?"

"Hard to tell, really. It varies."

"Oh . . ."

There was silence across the line as Ash tried to decide whether he sounded reasonably curious or desperate. He wanted an answer now. And if he hadn't won the job, he wanted to know who had and why. "So, you'll call . . ."

"You'll get a call either way as soon as we have something to tell you."

"If I don't answer it's because my cell phone isn't getting a signal."

"I understand," Miss Dubs said, obviously amused. "Fortunately, this isn't one of those 'must be present to win' things."

Now Ash felt like a complete idiot. Although he knew there was no way to fully recover his dignity, he attempted it anyway: "Okay, then. I'll just wait for word."

"I think that would be best," Miss Dubs said. "Good-bye for now."

"Good-bye. And I'm sorry to bother—" The phone went dead.

"Everything all right, buddy?" Wild asked. "You look like you just got some bad news."

"I'm fine," Ash returned. "I was just checking in with the admiral's office to see if they'd made any decisions yet."

"And?"

"They haven't."

Wild patted Ash on the back and said, "Don't sweat it. They asked for you, you didn't ask for them."

"What admiral are we talking about here?" Mongo asked.

"Vice Admiral Garrett," Ash replied.

"Good man. I sat next to him and his wife at a dinner

a few months back. She's pretty foxy for an older lady. And word has it that he's got a political future after the Navy if he wants it."

"Perfect," Wild intoned, "a political pretty-boy admiral."

A thin Army captain who barely reached Wild's shoulder appeared at the opening in the horseshoe of cubicles and said, "C'mon, you guys. You're keeping the colonel waiting."

Mongo looked at his watch, and with eyes widened, spat, "Oh, shit," and popped out of his chair and pushed past Ash without another word.

"I won't be out of here until six o' clock or so," Wild said with a long exhale as he fished into his pocket and produced a key. "My apartment number is fourteen twelve. Why don't you head over and cool your heels for a few—recharge your batteries. It's Ladies' Night at Club Metro, my friend. You're in for a welcome home celebration like you've never had before."

FOURTEEN

For all of his claims—conscious or otherwise—against being a geek, Wild had a thing about computers. Ash was reminded of that fact as he inspected the high-tech setup that dominated one corner of his buddy's apartment: twin flat-screen monitors, three processing unit towers, surround-sound speakers including a steamer trunk–sized subwoofer, and a host of other peripherals all tucked neatly into black anodized racks. He sat in the padded swivel chair in front of the gear and jiggled the mouse, which brought the right monitor alive. The wallpaper selection was signature Wild: A redheaded beauty wearing nothing but a come-hither expression while kicking her legs to opposite corners of the screen.

Ash checked his watch again: seven-thirty in the evening and he still hadn't received a phone call from the admiral's office. In spite of what Miss Dubs had said, it had to be past the close of business now. Although he'd spent the afternoon reasoning with himself and keeping his concerns at bay, at this point he was convinced someone else had been selected to be Vice Admiral Garrett's aide.

But what did he care if he didn't have to worry about

getting the admiral to the right places at the right time wearing the right uniform and saying the right things? He was a SEAL, dammit, and SEALs never sweated the small shit. He could whine about how he'd been jerked around by his detailer and yanked out of war, or he could make the most of the gratis liberty opportunity he'd been granted.

But somehow the idea of partying didn't ease the sting of how the events of the last few days were playing out. His team was still in the field.

"You're not wearing that shirt, are you?" Wild asked, striding out of his bedroom, rubbing a towel against his hair.

"What's wrong with it?" Ash asked in return.

"It looks like something an old man would wear."

"It's just a standard button-down."

"Exactly. Take it off." Wild threw the towel over the back of a big leather recliner and picked his way across the small living room littered with magazines, DVD cases, computer games, pizza boxes, newspapers, and empty beer bottles until he made it to a mound on the floor. "Here," he said as he balled a bright blue something between his hands then tossed it over to Ash. "Wear this."

Ash held the item up in front of him, a shirt—sort of. "I can't wear this," he said.

"Why not?" Wild returned, incredulous.

"Because I hate stuff like this."

"That's bullshit. You wear that dork shirt you have on right now and people are going to laugh you out of Club Metro."

"What's this thing made of anyway, spandex?"

"It's a Dri-FIT mock tee. That material is space-age. It wicks the sweat away from your body."

"I'm sweating?"

"Only if you're doing it right, my brother." Wild worked an index finger between the shirt Ash was wearing and the one he was holding, and said, "Take that one off and put this on."

Ash paused for a second and then, with some struggling, slipped the new shirt over his head. He stood with his arms out, beseeching reason.

"That's it," Wild proclaimed.

Ash stepped over to the mirror that doubled as the far wall and studied himself from several angles. "This thing is tight as shit."

"Exactly."

"I seriously prefer the other shirt I was wearing."

"Negative, shipmate. That's it. I'm wearing one just like it."

"Both of us wearing the same shirt? Sounds dorkier than me wearing a button-down."

"Not to worry," Wild said, striking a bodybuilder's pose. "On me it'll look like a different shirt. Besides, mine's a different color." Wild moved toward Ash and waved a hand over his head, saying, "Okay, what about your hair?"

"My hair?"

"Yeah, what are you going to do with it?"

"Comb it?"

Wild rolled his eyes. "Follow me."

They picked their ways across the debris-strewn living room into Wild's equally trashed bedroom. They had to inch along sideways to make it past the unmade royal king-size waterbed and into the master bathroom— another model space of slovenly chaos highlighted by a dissipating cloud of steam from Wild's recent shower. Towels lay wadded into two of the corners, and a capless tube of toothpaste on the counter had oozed at least half of its contents into the sink.

"*Voilà,*" Wild said as he opened the medicine cabinet. Ash was surprised and a bit amazed by the sight: Inside the cabinet, hygiene products were lined up like those on the shelves of a drugstore. On closer inspection, Ash could see that Wild had dedicated the top row to deodorants, or "body spray," as half of the bottles were labeled, the middle shelf to aftershaves and colognes, and the bottom shelf to hair care products—shampoos, conditioners, rinses, gels, and mousses.

"Impressive," Ash intoned drily.

Like a doctor studying a patient, Wild narrowed his eyes toward the top of Ash's head then reached into the cabinet and produced a purple canister. "Gush a golf ball–sized amount of this in your palm and spread it through your hair," he said before looking back at Ash's hair. "On second thought, make it two golf balls."

Ash had spent enough time with Wild over the years to know it would be futile to argue with him, so he squirted a small amount of mousse into his palm. After working the white foam through his hair for a time, Ash said, "I need to get my comb."

"No combs," Wild ruled. "Use your fingers to give your hair some texture."

Ash halfheartedly stirred his gooey hair as Wild dove back into the medicine chest. A second later he emerged holding two glass bottles. "I'm wearing this tonight, so why don't you splash this other stuff on?"

"I'm not a big cologne wearer," Ash said.

"You don't seem to appreciate that I'm arming you with the tools for success here."

"There's a not-so-fine line between cool and homosexual, Wild."

Wild ignored the remark and thrust one of the bottles toward Ash. Ash grasped it with limited enthusiasm, opened it, and took a whiff. Satisfied the contents weren't too strong—pleasantly spicy, actually—he spread a few drops across his wrists and neck.

"You still like pizza?" Wild asked.

"Are you kidding me?" Ash said. "I haven't had a decent pie in months."

"There's a great place across the street—New York

style. We'll get some over there, and then head out. What time is it?"

Ash glanced at his watch and said, "Seven forty."

"Still way early. Club Metro doesn't even think about coming alive until nine or so on a weeknight. Go watch a little tube, and I'll be right out."

Ash walked back through Wild's bedroom, stopping along the way to check his appearance in a full-length mirror against one of the walls—a move that left him convinced more than ever that he looked like a complete fool. In the living room, he plopped onto the recliner's matching leather couch and watched one of the myriad twenty-four-hour news stations, marveling at the quality of the picture on Wild's fifty-six-inch plasma television bolted against the wall like a piece of fine art.

STORM IN THE DESERT written in huge block letters dissolved, revealing an attractive blond anchorwoman with exceptionally full lips who smiled pleasantly before reporting that the winds in Iraq were still blowing and that the American advance had stalled as a result. From a podium in Qatar, a general garbed in desert cammies downplayed the notion that supply lines were dangerously strained.

"This weather actually works in our favor," he said.

The report was followed by a segment featuring a retired admiral seated in a television studio who finished his commentary with, "War is never easy."

Ash wondered where his boys were. Had their next mission been scrubbed based on the forecast, or were they bogged down behind enemy lines? Who was leading them, and what did Billy White think of him?

It was a cold March night in Washington, so Wild and Ash slipped fleece pullovers over their Dri-FITs and made their way across the street to Sal's Famous New York Style. In a dark booth toward the back of the place, Wild poured the second round of beer into both glasses and then slurped across the lip of his to keep the growing head of foam from spilling over.

"So tell me about the first mission," Wild said as he wiped his mouth against the forearm of his jacket. "That had to be a blast."

"I'm not sure that's the word I'd use," Ash said.

"Oh, come on, dude. I read the misrep: First the HALO, and then the up-close-and-personal stuff. That was choice all around."

Ash checked the booths around them, then nonchalantly raised an eyebrow and said, "We got in and out without any of the team getting smoked."

"Again with the modesty," Wild said as he folded another slice of pizza in his hand and tilted it so the oil dripped across its tip and onto his paper plate. "But that's not what we're looking for tonight, I'm afraid. The chicks at Club Metro are expecting a balls-out war hero."

Ash narrowed his eyes. "Why would they be expecting that?"

"Like I said, I've given you all the tools for success. Don't blow it like you usually do." Wild lowered an index finger tipped with tomato sauce. "And no phone numbers. Tonight isn't about that."

"What *is* tonight about?"

The blond SEAL spread his arms and said, "Celebrating your return, bro. And when a Navy man celebrates his return, he gets laid. How long has it been for you? Months? Years?"

"A while."

"Sure it has." Having decimated the previous slice in a couple of gulps, Wild reached for another slice of pizza, took several bites, and continued to talk with his mouth full. "So, what are you getting for that mission? A Silver Star?"

"I don't know," Ash replied with a shrug. "Delta never makes a very big deal out of medals, which is fine with me. Plus, that's been the least of my concerns over the last few days."

"I'll bet you get the Silver Star, you fucker. That'll go

nicely with the Bronze Star you've already got." Wild tapped himself on the sternum. "And what's my highest award? A Navy Commendation Medal."

"You were in Albania. . . ."

"Yeah, so what? Unlike you, nothing happened while I was there. I was the goddamn halftime show." Wild shook his head in disgust. "I've got to get over to Iraq before this war ends."

"Have you talked to our detailer, Lieutenant Schoen-whatever?"

"Yeah. The little prick said I had to stay in place because I was in a joint billet."

"I was in a joint billet, but it didn't seem to matter."

"The rules don't apply to you. You had an admiral in the mix. I'm not done trying, though, I'll tell you that. One way or another, I'm going to get over there."

Ash looked at his watch and then checked the display window on his cell phone.

"Still no calls, huh?" Wild asked.

"No," Ash said.

"Well, it's still early."

"Early? It's after eight o'clock."

Wild shook his head. "You really have no clue what you're getting into, do you?"

"I'm not getting into anything, by the looks of things." Ash released a long breath and cradled his chin on a fist. "I hate getting jerked around, you know—and especially getting jerked out of the action."

"At least you had a taste of the action." Wild poured the last of the pitcher into his glass. "Oh, by the way, this crowd we're hooking up with tonight thinks I have orders to go to Iraq, so just go with it, okay?"

"How did they get that impression?" Ash asked with a wry smile.

"It's not a lie, really, since I'm actively seeking orders to Iraq. It could happen."

All routine ball-busting aside, at that moment, Ash knew that Wild needed someone he trusted to share the hope. "Sure, it could happen," Ash said. "They're only one deep over there in most places. They'll be needing replacements before too long."

"Except the whole shooting match might be over soon. Do you think this war will last more than a few days?"

Ash offered a slight nod. "Probably. Regime change is a bit more complicated than pushing an army back across a border."

Wild seemed pleased by Ash's analysis, and he sat for a time with his eyes unfocused, looking toward the silver pizza tray, corners of his mouth curling just upward, perhaps conjuring images of himself thriving under fire. His head jerked as he snapped out of it, turning his attention to the television in a distant corner that broadcast another report on the weather from the front. "Keep blowing, wind," Wild said, "at least until I get over there."

The discussion cued Ash that he had another question for Wild, but before he asked it, he scanned the adjacent booths. Those around them seemed too involved in their own conversations to worry about what Wild and he might be talking about.

Ash leaned forward across the table. "I've got a question about the misrep," he said, quieter than before.

"Shoot," Wild returned, taking Ash's cue and matching the volume of his voice.

"Did the report you read say anything about an industrial site we came across toward the end of the mission?"

Wild mulled over the question and then replied: "I read it kind of quickly. Maybe I missed that part."

"Think hard, now," Ash coaxed. "Did you see anything about a factory and bright lights suddenly shutting down and us winding up in a chase with one of their vehicles?"

"Whose vehicles? Iraqis'?"

"Who else?"

"How close did they get to you?"

"Awful damned close. After exchanging gunfire for awhile, we wound up taking them down with an RPG."

Wild shook his head. "Nope, I didn't read anything about that in the version of the misrep I saw. I would have remembered that action."

"One of my team got a few photos of the complex, but after we turned them over to the intel guys we never saw them again and never got any feedback about what they showed. They were blurry, but still. . . ."

"That's pretty strange."

The conversation abruptly ceased as the waitress walked up and asked, "Can I get you guys anything else? More beer, maybe?"

Wild looked at his watch and replied, "No, thanks. We have places to be and people to meet. All we need is the check."

The waitress nodded and walked off. Wild's eyes followed her as she did. "That chick is doable, for sure."

"She looks kind of young," Ash said.

"*Kind of* young is miles away from *too* young. When's the last time you got busy with a nineteen-year-old?"

"Probably when I was eighteen."

"Oh, I see how it goes," Wild said. "Kidnap one Iraqi official and now you own the high ground, right?"

"Let's keep it down, okay?" Ash said quietly as he motioned for Wild to lower his voice. "That mission is still top-secret."

"Then why did you bring it up?" Wild asked, joining Ash in both the tone of his voice and subtly checking around them. "Besides, I think most of this classification crap is something the intelligence geeks make up to impress one another. The people in here couldn't care less, and those who want to know about it already do."

"Want to know, or *need* to know?"

"What's the diff?"

"Based on the number of people who told me they read the misrep, apparently nothing."

"And what do you care? Look at the attention you're getting. The only time I've ever had an admiral call me is to yell at me for parking in his spot in front of the officers' club." Wild stood, pulled a wad of money out of his pocket, and threw a couple of bills on the table. "I know you're no rookie, but you've got to face the fact that whether you like it or not, that mission has changed things for you."

FIFTEEN

The two SEALs left the pizzeria and rode the Metro to the northwest side of town. The escalator leading up from the tracks was impossibly long, and the angle at which it climbed against the arch of the concrete ceiling overhead gave Ash slight vertigo. He gripped the handrail and scanned across the impassive faces of the people descending into the depths after rush hour, imagining what they did for a living based on how they were dressed. A silver-haired man wearing a tan overcoat over his suit smacked of big money—a lobbyist, most likely. A younger man in a suit without an overcoat had circles under his eyes and mussed hair as if he'd been running his hands through it all day. Ash placed him as an intern slowly being milked of his enthusiasm.

Ash tried to get his bearings as he followed Wild out of the confines of the station and onto the street. He read the streets signs at the first intersection they came to—Wisconsin and M. He knew where they were. In his college days, occasionally unmotivated by the predictability of the haunts around Annapolis, he had traveled to Georgetown in search of girls untainted in their attitudes toward midshipmen.

The two SEALs turned a corner and walked down a hill until they were nearly to the river, then followed a line of trestles that braced the causeway above their heads. Wild's pace increased with each step, and a block later, they were nearly jogging. Without warning—so quickly that Ash had to double back—Wild took a hard right into an alleyway.

At the far end of the narrow path, Ash saw a line of people bathing in the white light of a naked bulb hanging over a black door bordered by a brick wall. After several strides, Ash bumped into a body, and he realized the line was longer than he had thought. Wild didn't queue up but rushed past the fifty or so in the line until he reached the doorman, a huge Samoan with a barbed wire tattoo cresting below the sleeves of his tight T-shirt—Dri-FIT, no doubt—and wearing a headset with a slim boom mike that mirrored the curve of his fat cheek.

"How is it in there, Nui?" Wild asked as the big brown man moved those at the head of the line aside, much to their apparent indignation.

"No worries, bro," the Samoan replied. "You know Kid 500 always brings them out."

"He's the man."

"You not planning on any fights tonight, right, bro?"

"I never *plan* on them. Sometimes they just happen, you know?"

"Well, try not to make one happen tonight, okay? We're light on bouncers right now."

"I'll try . . ."

As they slid through the doorway, Ash asked, "Who's Kid 500?"

"The DJ," Wild replied. "Epic around here."

Lights flickered and dry ice smoke blossomed along the claustrophobic confines of the long entryway. The bass tones from the music inside reverberated and hit Ash with physical force. "Take off the fleece," Wild commanded before feeding his across the counter to the coat-check girl, a raven-haired Latino with nipples on prominent display against the spandex of her tank top.

Past the coat check, the crowd slowed their progress toward wherever Wild was leading them. Across the shoulders of those lining the railing, Ash saw that street level was actually two stories above the dance floor. He marveled at the size of the cavernous club, a much bigger space than he had imagined based on the approach down the alley. The beat of the music thumped from every direction, as if the walls were constructed of nothing but speakers. Tight cylinders of changing colored light washed over those packed on the dance floor. Ash's eyes followed the beams upward until they reached a ceiling lined with exposed girders another three stories above where he stood.

The crowd parted as Wild waded through it. Those caught unawares shot dirty looks over their shoulders but took no issue with the big SEAL's forearm in their backs once they saw who'd given it to them. For his part, Ash struggled to stay close enough to Wild that he didn't get swallowed up once the sea of bodies rejoined in Wild's wake.

They came to an elevator, and Wild produced a plastic card and stuck it into an adjacent slot. The doors opened. Inside the elevator, Ash noted the control panel only had three buttons: DANCE FLOOR, MEZZANINE, and VIP LOUNGE. Wild pushed the VIP LOUNGE button and the doors closed.

As Ash felt the elevator surge upward, Wild turned to him and said, "Remember, you're a war hero."

"If you say so," Ash replied.

"And I'm on my way to be a war hero."

Ash pulled his cell phone out of his pocket and checked to see if anyone had called.

"Stop worrying about that now," Wild said, reaching over to lower Ash's arm holding the phone. "We're here to have fun. This is your homecoming celebration, so don't bum everybody out with any B.S. about your personal problems, okay?"

The doors reopened and revealed a large balcony that overlooked the dance floor, now four stories down. In the middle of the balcony was a sitting area dominated by a long L-shaped sectional couch crowded with people. It took a few moments, but soon the women's faces lit up, and they popped off the couch with their arms in the air and ran over in a wave of tanned skin and flowing hair and grasped Wild in what became a massive group hug.

"Where have you *been?*" a tall blonde wearing bright pink lipstick demanded.

"We thought you might have blown us off," an even taller blonde said from behind the first.

"Come now," Wild said. "Has the Wild Man ever let you down?" He extended his arm. "Ladies, I'd like you to meet my good friend Ashton Roberts the Fourth."

Ash smiled sheepishly and said, "It's just 'Ash.' "

"I like the first version better," the lead blonde said as she took Ash's hand. "It sounds like money."

"It should," Wild said. "He's filthy rich."

The girl pushed several locks of her long hair off her face as she widened her smile and said, "In that case, I'm Melinda."

"I'm not really rich," Ash said.

"He will be once his father dies," Wild countered.

"Tall, handsome, and rich," Melinda said, strengthening her grip on Ash's hand. "Like I said: I'm Melinda."

"He's already forgotten you," the second blonde said, playfully elbowing her way to the front of what had become a receiving line of sorts. "I'm Tina."

Ash managed to release himself from Melinda's grip, and had no sooner taken Tina's hand than she was pushed aside by two identical brunettes. "I'm Fawn," the first of them announced.

"And I'm Fanny," the other said, bypassing the handshake and going right for the hug. Ash attempted to take the gesture in stride, but it wasn't easy. She was warm and smooth against him, and he fought not to get noticeably aroused.

"Fawn and Fanny are twins," Wild informed him.

"I noticed," Ash muttered back.

"Why don't we all have a seat and get acquainted for a bit?" Wild suggested. "And where's the drink guy? We have some catching up to do here."

The girls bounced back to where they'd been seated on the couch as Wild greeted a Rastafarian-looking guy wearing a beehive-sized red, yellow, and green striped stocking cap on his head. A few dreadlocks twisted out from under the cap and tangled in the frames of the sunglasses with blue rectangular lenses he sported at the end of his wide nose.

"When do you start, Kid?" Wild asked.

"Very soon, mon," the Rastafarian returned without rising off the couch. "I just catching a cooler." His Jamaican accent was barely audible over the music, which Ash noticed was at a more reasonable volume than elsewhere in the club.

"If he's up here, who is playing the stuff coming through the speakers now?" Ash asked.

"This is just recorded music, mon. Nothing special. You hear the difference when I get back to the rig."

"Word, dog," Wild said, pulling a couple of chairs from across the lounge to the near side of the marble table.

Kid 500 shifted the black dots of his eyes to Ash and asked, "You just back from over there, then?"

Ash nodded in reply.

Kid 500 still didn't get up but slowly reached across the table like a sovereign greeting a subject. His grip was moist and soft, softer than any of the girls' had been.

Ash sat down as a waiter with a black bow tie and a red dinner jacket came out of nowhere and stood attendant. Before Ash could utter the word "beer," Wild interrupted him, saying, "We'll take two Sprints."

Ash watched the waiter walk smartly away and then looked over at Wild. "What's a Sprint?"

"The house special," Wild replied, "uses one of those energy drinks as the mixer."

"What's wrong with a beer?"

Melinda leaned forward and said, "Tell us about the war, Ash."

"Yeah," Tina said, matching Melinda's posture. "What was it like?"

"I was only there for a few days," Ash said.

"He's too modest, ladies," Wild said as the waiter returned and set the drinks on the table in front of them. "The details of his missions are classified, of course, but let's just say the most action-packed movie you ever saw has got nothing on this guy."

"Did you have to kill anybody?" one of the twins asked.

"I told you that's not something we like to talk about, Fawn," Wild said.

The girl reached across her ample cleavage and tugged on the tube top under her collared silk shirt and said, "Excuse me. I was just wondering."

"I didn't kill anybody," Ash said.

"On that mission, anyway," Wild added before downing his first Sprint—fluorescent green in color, like antifreeze—in a single tip of his head. He made a circular motion with an index finger toward the waiter, and the man nodded and hurried off again. "Will you be going back soon?" Melinda asked.

"I don't know," Ash replied as he took another look at his cell phone. "I'm not sure what I'm doing, to be honest."

The blonde leaned even closer to him and purred, "You expecting a call from somebody?"

"No," he said with a shrug. "Not anymore, anyway."

"Girl trouble?"

Ash grinned and shook his head. "To have girl trouble you have to have a girl."

"Girls aren't always trouble, you know," she said with a smile that quickened his pulse.

"Wild's going over to Iraq," Tina said, breaking Ash and Melinda out of their brief aside. "Right, Wild?"

"That's what they tell me," Wild said. "I just hope there's plenty of ass left to kick by the time I get there."

"Ever thought about joining the Army, Kid?" Fawn asked across her twin sister.

"Navy," Wild said. "Don't insult the man."

Kid 500 took a long draw on his glass and then asked, "Would they let me have my smoke?"

"Sure," Ash said. "I know a lot of guys who smoke."

"Wrong kind of smoke, shipmate," Wild said. "Besides, Kid's mad skills are needed stateside. Morale on the home front is an important element in victory. Just look at what happened during Vietnam."

The waiter delivered another round of glasses filled with the green glow. Before Wild disposed of the second as quickly as he had the first, he looked at the two full glasses in front of Ash and said, "You're already falling behind."

Ash considered the growing collection of empty glasses on the table and surrounding floor. He glanced down at the readout on his cell phone once again and saw that he hadn't missed any calls in the last thirty seconds. *Screw it.* It was time to celebrate.

He brought one of the two glasses before him to his face, mesmerized by the bright color of the contents. "Hey, doctor," Wild chided. "It's not a lab experiment. Drink the damn thing." He held his own glass up. "Actually, maybe it *is* a lab experiment." Wild threw his head back again and made short work of his third drink.

Ash put the glass to his lips and took a cautious sip. The drink was carbonated and not as sweet as he thought it would be. Whatever alcohol was in it was tasteless. He took a bigger sip, then another. Soon the first drink was gone, and he moved on to the second, downing it as Wild had, in a single gulp. When he lowered the second empty glass, a line of smiles greeted him from across the table.

"Now you're getting it," Wild said.

"Let the games begin, mon," Kid 500 said with a sinister laugh.

Ash soon felt his head starting to spin. Whether he could taste it or not, a Sprint contained alcohol—a lot of it. The music suddenly had new depth—bass pulsating, cymbals searing into his consciousness. The surrounding lights blazed. The shadows were darker. The conversations at once were pointed and unintelligible. The girls' teeth and eyes were bright white. Their arms and long legs were all a perfect shade of light brown, to his eye achingly smooth but very real, and it took great effort not to reach across the table and run his hands across them.

More drinks appeared and more again. Even with his waning senses, he could see that he was not alone in his journey to a less focused point of view. The volume of the chatter grew; the laughter was free and boisterous. The twins got off the couch and perched themselves on each one of Wild's big knees. Kid 500 slouched cool as ever, nodding in time to the heavy beat. Melinda and Tina moved to the edge of the marble table. Their perfumes blended into a delightful brew that filled Ash's nostrils.

"Where do you work?" Ash asked, forcing himself to speak more deliberately now.

"Pentagon," Melinda said. She gestured toward Tina. "She works there, too."

"Is that where you met?"

"No, we met here," Tina said, pointing to the carpet between her spiked heels.

"This is where everybody meets," Melinda added.

Kid 500 rose from the couch and stood taller than Ash pictured he would based on how he looked sitting down. The black man spread his arms out from his sides and proclaimed: "Dance time, it is."

The girls squealed and clapped their hands in front of them like cheerleaders along a sideline. After joining the rest of the group in finishing off what was left of their Sprints, Wild and Ash followed the others walking slightly wobbly paths onto the elevator. Kid 500 pushed the DANCE FLOOR button and the doors closed.

Ash expected the crowd on the dance floor to meet them once the doors opened, but instead they stepped into a black tunnel much like the one inside the club entrance. About halfway along the tunnel, Kid 500 stopped and worked the knob on a door marked PRIVATE with the key hanging from a lanyard around his neck. Before he shut the door behind him, he said, "You give the Kid your best now, boys and girls."

There was a door at the end of the tunnel that Wild unlocked with the same key that had allowed him onto the VIP elevator. Now they were among the crowd on the dance floor, awash in the spotlights, moving to the loud beat. Tina and Melinda each took one of Ash's hands while the twins did the same to Wild. They bounced off dancers without a care, loving the contact, the heat, the energy. Once satisfied they were near the center, Wild and the girls began dancing while Ash just sort of shuffled his feet, watching the movement around him.

"What are you grinning at?" Melinda asked, working to be heard over the music.

"You're a good dancer," Ash shouted back.

"Don't just stand there," Wild said over his shoulder. "Dance!"

"I am dancing," Ash returned.

"That's not dancing. *This* is dancing." Wild went into a series of moves—fluid one moment, frozen the next— as the girls cheered him on.

The music suddenly stopped and the spotlights went black. "Washington, are you ready?" a voice boomed over the PA, sounding a lot like an arena announcer introducing the home team. Those on the floor roared in response.

"Are you ready?" the voice asked again. A louder roar followed. "All right, then. Please join me in welcoming the mix master general, the slammer, the jammer. From the Caribbean to your hearts and minds, please put your hands together for one of the top DJs in the country, *Kid 500!*"

A heavy beat thudded across the club, more resonant than what had come through the speakers before. At the same time, a spotlight hit Kid 500 standing in a circular booth just above head level over the dance floor. He waved an arm over his head in time with the rhythm, and most of those on the floor mirrored him. Then he focused on the turntables, knobs, and slides before him, coaxing all kinds of sounds, musical and otherwise, out of his gear and mixing them with the relentless backbeat. Ash had always thought of DJs as guys who simply cued up songs, but that didn't fully describe what Kid 500 was doing. He may not have been a musician, but with his hands moving about and his attention a dozen places at once, he seemed as focused as a concert pianist.

Ash's own focus was diverted as Melinda straddled one of his legs and Tina saddled in from behind, repeatedly banging her ass against him as he did his best not to look like a spastic white boy. Over the years of pretending to enjoy himself on the dance floor he'd developed one rule of thumb: Don't repeat the same move twice in a row.

But Ash was past keeping track of things like that. The culture shock of his sudden reëmersion in Western civilization, or the end of it, was gone. Now he was everything at once—motion and energy and desire. At the hands of Kid 500, one tune blended into another and time ceased to exist. Ash's only gauge for how long he'd been dancing was his Dri-FIT shirt, wetter with sweat by the minute but keeping him cool. In what was left of his cognitive mind, he thanked Wild for making him wear the damn thing. The button-down would have been an anchor around his neck by now.

Song after song, the girls showed no interest in leaving

the floor. Their dance moves grew increasingly overt in their sexuality, and they fueled his enthusiasm. They danced with him and with each other. At one point, they stopped dancing to engage in a lengthy soul kiss that caused the men around them to ignore their own partners momentarily and applaud.

Then, without warning and as if on cue, Wild and the girls grabbed one anothers' hands and headed for the side of the dance floor opposite the way they'd come in. Ash was almost swallowed up by the surrounding crowd, but right as he was sure he'd lost them, Melinda reached out and grabbed his arm.

The group stayed together for the journey through the storm-tossed sea of dancers and shortly found themselves in the drink line for one of the myriad bars that dotted the club. Wild was standing still, looking across the room with a dorky grin on his face.

"What?" Ash asked.

"Look at that guy," Wild said, pointing toward Kid 500, now bathing in a red spotlight. "He owns this crowd. They'd do anything for him."

"They're just dancing and having a good time."

Wild moved his face closer to Ash's and repeated, "They'd do *anything* for him."

"All right, fine," Ash said, sloppily throwing his palms up. "Whatever you say."

"He's got *cred.*"

"Really . . ."

"Yeah, really. He's the real deal. Those dreadlocks are *real,* dude. People respond to that. *Chicks* respond to that." He looked toward the spotlights and mused, "I've got to get into this war."

"You don't look like you're having trouble with chicks to me," Ash offered. "And you were sure busting a move on the dance floor."

Wild shook his head. "No, my shtick is wearing thin by the day. I can tell by how the girls are reacting to you. You've got the cred; I don't."

"Are Melinda and Tina bi or something?"

"No, they just do that kissing thing for the shock effect, although it doesn't seem to have the impact it used to."

Two glasses crossed Wild's shoulder. He took one and handed the other to Ash.

"I'm feeling pretty damned good for a guy fighting jet lag," Ash observed after swallowing a healthy portion of his newly arrived drink.

"It's the Sprints, bro," Wild said. "I told you they'd do you right."

Drinks finished, they were back on the floor, paired off like before. Whatever inhibitions Ash had retained during the first dance session were gone now, and he moved with abandon, touching and being touched by his partners. Then Kid 500 said something about setting the mood, and the lights went low and the beat slowed. Melinda immediately pulled herself close to Ash. Tina shrugged and slinked away, the loser in some unspoken game of positioning.

Melinda simmered, the sweat running down her neck and across her shoulders, soaking Ash's already drenched top. As they swayed in time, she nuzzled into him and ran her tongue along his neck while he dragged his fingers lightly down her spine and stroked the small of her back. He felt her nipples stiffen against him. She moved her hands lower, and he did some stiffening of his own. He had an inkling to fight it, but as her scent wafted up and her hair brushed his cheek, the inkling passed. Now she could strip him naked if she wanted. Why didn't they all get naked? An orgy seemed like the logical next step in the hedonistic atmosphere of the club.

Melinda manipulated him through his khakis, stroking him while she continued to work her crotch against his thigh. He cupped her ass and held on for dear life. Soon, he was ready to unload in his pants—at once a joy and a bummer. In any case, at that point he was powerless to do anything but revel in the building ecstasy of it.

The song suddenly stopped, and the lights grew bright again. The urgent beat returned, and the people around them started dancing. "Oh, no," Ash uttered involuntarily as bliss began to morph into pain.

Instead of dancing, Melinda smiled and took his hand and led him through the chaos. Ash wasn't sure where they were going, but assumed they were headed to the bar for another Sprint. He hoped that would douse the fire that consumed him. But they bypassed the line and went straight for a door labeled UNISEX.

Behind the door the air was choked with a thick cloud of cigarette smoke. Through it Ash saw a column of men and women pushed against a line of sinks, concentrating on themselves in a long mirror along the black tile wall. Around the corner were dozens of stalls. Melinda put her shoulder into several stall doors without success, a move that flashed Ash momentarily back to when his team smashed through the door to that house in Baghdad. After the third attempt, one flung open.

She balled her fist into his Dri-FIT and shoved him into the stall before threading her way in behind him and latching the door. The look in her eyes was no longer sweet but manic; she was all business. She tore off her silk shirt and yanked her tube top down, revealing the full globes of her tanned breasts and her rigid pink nipples. He reached out to touch her, but before he could, she pulled close and kissed him hard. Her tongue worked aggressively around his mouth, and he tried to match her with everything his current physical state would allow.

Melinda pulled back and considered him with a devilish grin. "How selfish of me," she said as her hands began working his belt buckle. "I completely forgot about your problem."

Ash momentarily wondered which of his problems she was talking about, but soon got his answer as she tugged the zipper to his khakis down and deftly threaded him into the outside world—no easy chore, considering how primed he was. Without a word she dropped to her knees and took him into her mouth. She began bobbing her head back and forth with a porn star's enthusiasm. Ash braced himself, one hand hooked across the top of the shiny black stall partition and the other cradling the back of her head.

Life was good—not necessarily romantic, but good. Ash moaned quietly in pleasure, which caused Melinda to intensify her pace. He wanted it to last, but after months in the field and her prepping on the dance floor, there was little hope of that. Would she follow him back to Wild's apartment? This brief encounter in the bathroom was going to be a release, sure; but he wanted to take his time studying every inch of her gorgeous body, tasting her in return, feeling her all over him.

There was a momentary buzzing just below his hip, a sensation that hit him several more times before his carnal fog lifted and he realized that his cell phone was ringing. *It couldn't be,* he thought. *It's too late.* He was tempted to ignore it, but on the fourth vibration he fumbled for it, hoping to avoid distracting Melinda in the process.

"Hello?" Ash said, voice catching a bit.

"Lieutenant Roberts?" a female said on the other end.

"Yes?"

"This is Vice Admiral Garrett's office calling. Please hold the line for the admiral."

The voice sounded too young to be Miss Dubs, and Miss Dubs probably would have identified herself. He figured it was Chief Monroe. *Unfuckingbelievable.* Ash checked his watch: ten p.m. Gently—and very reluctantly—he urged Melinda to stop her efforts, explaining, "I have to take this call. It shouldn't be too long."

Admiral Garrett jumped on the line: "Ash, I hope I didn't wake you."

"No, Admiral, I'm definitely up."

"Well, that's good. Did you get a chance to get out and have a nice dinner or something? I always looked forward to a nice dinner on my first night back from deployment. And Washington's got some great restaurants."

"Oh, yes, sir. A nice dinner . . ."

"Good, good. Look, Ash, I won't waste your time here. I've conducted all of the interviews for the aide job, and I wanted to let you know how things came out. I have to tell you competition was very stiff. I continue to be amazed by the quality of the junior officers in our fleet today."

I didn't get it, Ash thought.

"And you've got to remember that only the best officers from every community are allowed to even put their hats in the ring," the admiral continued. "So, long story short, I just wanted to say . . ."

So sorry? It sucks to be you? Get your ass out of the bar and back to the war?

". . . congratulations. You're my new aide."

Ash's brain spun in neutral for a few beats. He wasn't sure what to say, so he just said, "Thank you, Admiral."

"I'll let Mary fill you in on the administrative details. Good night."

Chief Monroe returned to the phone. "Welcome to the team, sir."

"Thank you, Chief."

"We'll see you here tomorrow at six."

"Six . . . in the morning?"

"Yes, sir. That's when Captain Bradford runs the first staff meeting of the day. Then we have a stand-up with the admiral at six-thirty. Then the admiral has to be down to the Secretary's office for the daily situation brief—" She stopped herself. "I'll let Miss Dubs fill you in on everything tomorrow. Good night, sir." The chief cut the connection without waiting for his response.

Ash folded his phone and looked at Melinda, now off her knees with her tube top back in place. The fire was gone from her eyes. "Sorry about that," he said.

Melinda lowered her stare and offered a slight smile. Ash gazed down and saw that his dick was hanging out, limp—a shadow of its recent self. He looked back at the girl. "I guess the moment has passed, huh?"

"I guess," Melinda returned.

"Melinda!" someone shouted. "Melinda, are you in here?"

"Yes, I'm in here," Melinda answered, pulling her shirt across her shoulders.

"Melinda, it's Tina."

"Of course it is."

"Is Ash in there with you?"

Ash felt himself blush as Melinda matter-of-factly replied: "Yeah, he's here."

"You guys need to get outside quick," Tina said. "Wild's in another fight."

Ash stuffed himself back into his pants and followed the two girls out of the bathroom. They forced their way through the crowd, cutting a path along the edge of the dance floor and down the long tunnel that led to the main entrance. In the dim light of the alleyway, Ash saw a ring of people surrounding Wild standing a few feet in front of a guy Ash had never seen before. The stranger was at least as big as Wild, with a goatee, a shaved head, and a diamond stud in the lobe of his left ear. He wore a hooded sweatshirt with GOT PUSSY? emblazoned across the front of it.

Ash pushed his way past a handful of people to the innermost layer of the ring. "What's up, shipmate," he threw out to his friend.

"No problem, amigo," Wild returned. "This joker just needs a quick attitude adjustment."

"Fuck you, dipshit," the guy spat. "Nobody runs into me on the dance floor but my lady."

"See what I mean?" Wild said.

"You don't want to do this, man," Ash said to Wild's opponent.

"And why is that?" the guy asked without taking his eyes from Wild.

"Because the dude you're about to fight is a Navy SEAL."

"Ooohhh," he crowed sarcastically. "I'm really scared now." A few of those around the circle laughed.

Nui, the Samoan bouncer, pushed his way next to Ash and said, "All right, knock this off. Nobody gets hurt and the cops don't show up."

"Chill, Nui," the guy said, "Let us settle this."

"Don't do it, Seth."

"I said chill. Besides, this tool ain't a Navy SEAL. If he was, he'd be over in Iraq."

Ash saw Wild's eyes narrow ever so slightly. He relaxed his posture and looked over at Nui and shrugged, a move his opponent mistakenly took as an opening—exactly what Wild had intended. Seth, as Nui had called him, attempted a roundhouse to the side of Wild's jaw, but the SEAL dodged it with a quick arch of his back. With a complete absence of effort to the untrained observer and an expression that belied any stress, Wild put Seth to the ground. Before the civilian could stand fully erect again, Wild swept a leg behind him and caught the other behind the knee. The sound of cartilage snapping was buried beneath the man's scream as he crumpled.

Before the first man was fully down, two others leapt from the crowd and onto Wild's back. With a quick twist of his torso, Wild threw one of them off, but the other one was firmly attached, having wrapped his arm tightly around Wild's thick neck. Ash split his attention between scanning the rest of the crowd around the circle, making sure the first two guys stayed down, and watching Wild deal with his situation.

Wild judo-flipped the man off his back and, holding the arm, used his free fist to strike a series of rapid-fire blows to the nose, sounding a martial arts type of cry with each jab. Blood gushed, and the man flopped across the asphalt. Nobody else came forward. The crowd stood in stunned silence, amazed by the efficiency with which Wild had dealt with his adversaries.

With a nod of acknowledgment in response to a smattering of applause, Wild took each one of the twins by the hand, and started back through the circle of spectators. Melinda took Ash's hand and together they followed the others.

Nui grabbed Wild's biceps, and with his single thick eyebrow knit asked, "Where do you think you're going?"

"Back into the club," Wild replied. "We've got a lot of partying left to do."

"Maybe you should think about calling it a night, bro."

"Bullshit, Nui. We're going inside."

"We don't want any more trouble, dammit."

Wild pointed to the big motionless lump in the alley. "Then keep assholes like him out of the place."

"You can get yourself blackballed. If Sammy puts you on the list, you'll never get back into Club Metro."

"Whatever, bro," Wild said with a flick of his fingers and a step toward the entrance. He immediately stopped and cut his eyes back to the bouncer. "My days around here are numbered, anyway. There's a war going on, you know?"

SIXTEEN

Awan Assayd crouched on a rooftop, gripping his rifle and thinking about his life. It wasn't like him to look back; he seldom had the impulse for reflection, but on this dark night, his mind wandered freely. Perhaps it was the sudden stillness in the streets of Najaf, a stark contrast to the relentless thunder of bombs dropped from American jets that had surrounded them for the last few days, even through the sandstorm that had ended only hours before. Or maybe it was a simple by-product of the adrenaline flowing through his veins.

Assayd thought about how his business had developed, how he'd managed to survive if not thrive under tough conditions. His family in Baghdad had always been well taken care of. The stipends kept the secret police from asking too many questions or poking around in warehouses of which they were best ignorant. He knew how to use a rifle—that had served him well, no doubt—and had managed to avoid directly aligning himself with the Baathists. For those attributes, some American organization—CIA or Army intelligence, probably—had labeled him as a "good Iraqi." On the eve of war he'd been whisked away to a desert training base—he wasn't even sure in what country it had been—and, after several days of target practice and push-ups, he was told he was in charge of part of the new Iraqi militia.

And now Americans in his midst. He reminded himself of the arrogance demonstrated by the American instructors over those days. "We're bringing freedom to Iraq," they'd proclaimed, "but you're going to have to keep it." Fools. What was Iraq but a collection of nomads who had feuded for centuries? Did they honestly think that those years of hatred would be forgotten with one man's removal from power? What had led them to believe the lines between good and evil were so clearcut? These Americans were naive, living in a storybook world. Besides, even under Saddam, Assayd was as free as any of them, maybe more so, and the constant flow of currency and goods would keep it that way.

Even now, the irony of his selection caused him to chuckle quietly. And hadn't he played well his role of the good Iraqi, he who had never really considered himself exceptionally Iraqi at all? Of course, his arrival into the mix hadn't been the work of the Americans. They'd had help—the so-called *Les Affreux*—but Assayd knew not to speak of them or ask too many questions. Only once had he heard a colleague say the name in plain conversation just before disappearing forever. It didn't matter. Assayd didn't trouble himself with labels. Whatever they were called, they paid well.

The vehicles were approaching. He could hear the roar of motors. He gripped his AK-47 a bit tighter as he swung the barrel from side to side and sighted through the night scope. He saw the Delta team in place across the street. The noise grew louder; the vehicles were coming fast. But still his mind raced with thoughts.

Several days ago, he'd received his tasking over the phone. "It is going to take more than one mission to deal with this," the voice had said. "You aren't the only one."

The mission was a sweep for a handful of "bad Iraqis"

on which the Americans supposedly had a line. He'd looked at their list, nodded, and failed to mention that he knew the men they were looking for had left Iraq and were now cooling their heels in Saudi Arabia. And even if he'd told them, would they have believed him?

While warning Assayd and his men of the complexities of this mission, the members of this so-called Delta Force had poorly muted their doubt that their newfound allies could handle such things. Assayd was at once insulted and impressed by their absence of trust. But it remained his job to earn their trust. He'd gone so far as to say a prayer aloud in the presence of the Americans following the final mission brief, thanking Allah for the first steps in bringing peace to this troubled but hopeful country. He saw the Americans smile at each other in self-congratulations.

"Anything could happen," the officer in charge had said as a final thought. And he was correct. Anything could happen in the fog of war. And Assayd was going to ensure it did. It wasn't betrayal. Betrayal demanded a shift in allegiance. Assayd's allegiance had always been solely with the course of action that was best for business. French, Russian, American, or Iraqi—what did it matter?

Now he saw the first flash of gunfire from the bed of the lead truck as it came around the final corner. With cool detachment, he aimed his rifle toward the other side of the street.

SEVENTEEN

"Wakey, wakey."

Ash's head hurt. It had been awhile since he'd last suffered a hangover. Through bleary eyes he saw Wild leaning over him, already fully dressed in his khaki uniform.

"What time is it?" Ash asked with a mouth that wasn't quite working yet.

"Five o'clock," Wild replied. "You'd better get moving. Didn't you say you have to be at the office at six?"

"Yeah." Ash tossed the down comforter off and sat up on the couch he'd used as a bed. Slowly, he stood, and as he did, the pain in his skull intensified. "What time did we get in?"

"Just after two, I think," Wild said just before crunching into a brown block of something—some sort of energy bar, no doubt. He didn't seem to be suffering any ill effects from the night before. His movements were sharp; his eyes were bright; his blond mane was combed.

"Aren't you hurting at all?" Ash asked as he stumbled over to the window and looked into the darkness outside.

"No. Why, are you?"

"Badly," Ash replied, wishing he could sleep until the sun came up, at least. "You got any aspirin?"

"Nobody uses aspirin anymore, dude. Take some two-twenty-twos instead. You know: caffeine, codeine, and ibuprofen. Just look in the medicine chest in my bathroom."

"Would you mind if I took a shower while I'm in there?"

"Stop asking shit like that," Wild replied. "Like I said: *Mi casa es su casa, comprende?*"

"Comprende." Something caught Ash's eye across the room, something he'd missed the day before. "What the hell is that?"

"What?"

"That flesh-colored ceramic object on the shelf over there. It looks like a—"

"Rock-hard dick? Right, that's what it is."

"Whose is it?"

"Mine, of course. You don't think I'd have somebody else's dick on display in my crib, do you? That would be *très* homo."

"How the hell did you have it made?"

"It was a gift from this chick I was dating a while back. She was into pottery, what can I say? I think it turned out pretty good."

"That's fucking bizarre. Even for *you* that's fucking bizarre."

"No, my friend. That's fucking art. Look, I've got to take off. I have to get ready to brief my part of the daily ops update. Call me once things settle down on your end. Maybe we can do lunch."

"Will do."

"Oh, and keep it down when you walk through my bedroom. Some people are still sleeping in there."

"People?"

Wild grew a broad grin and signaled for Ash to follow him. Through the doorway, Ash could see two women sprawled across either side of Wild's gigantic waterbed.

The one on the near side was laying face down wearing only a pair of pink panties that barely covered the crack of her tanned ass. The other was on her back, completely nude, breasts rising like identical monuments along a wondrous horizon. Focusing on what he could see of their faces, Ash recognized the two as the twins, Fanny and Fawn.

"Beautiful sight, huh?" Wild said.

"Beats waking up buried in a hole in the desert."

"So how did you do?"

"Not as well as you, apparently."

"What about Melinda?"

"What about her?"

"Last I saw, you guys were on the couch together."

"We were?"

Wild looked at his big watch and said, "I've got to boogie. Check you later." He threw on a black uniform jacket, tossed a small backpack across his shoulder, and slipped out of the apartment. Ash watched the door close behind him, and then stood for a time watching the girls sleep and trying to remember what had happened between Melinda and him. His throbbing brain was a blank on the topic.

He stepped lightly past the bed and into the bathroom. Once the door was shut, he hauled down his gym shorts and inspected himself, using every bit of evidence—or the absence of it—available. He found nothing definitive except that the pain that had gripped his balls following last night's *fellatus interruptus* was gone. But did that mean he'd sealed the deal with Melinda? Damn those Sprints.

Ash considered himself in the mirror, noting the circles under his eyes and the solid red of his eyeballs. He wondered what the rest of the admiral's staff was going to think, not to mention Vice Admiral Garrett himself. He needed to rally. He steeled himself with the notion that, although his body clock was totally out of whack, he had just come from a place where it was early afternoon now. Ash opened the medicine cabinet and searched for eyedrops along with two-two-twos. He found both. Obviously Wild wasn't new to this drill.

Ash dragged a razor across his face and then jumped into the shower. After months of standing under a trickle—if he was allowed to shower at all—the stream of hot water delivered at a decent velocity was sheer pleasure and did much to both ease his pain and wake him up.

He heard someone open the bathroom door and then put the toilet seat down. "Why didn't you wake me up, Willie?" a female voice whined. "I have to go to work, too, you know?"

"It's Ash," he replied.

"Oh," she said. "In that case, don't come out until I finish peeing."

"Uh, okay . . ."

"Are you almost done in there?"

"Just about, I guess."

The shower curtain was pulled back, and through a face covered with soap, Ash saw one of the twins step across the edge of the tub. "I'm in a hurry," she explained. "Keep your eyes above neck level, please."

"I'll do my best," Ash said just before he put his face into the column of water and vigorously worked his hands against his face and through his hair. After a few more seconds of letting the water beat against him, he turned back to her and politely said, "It's all yours."

Ash slipped past her and out of the shower, trying his best not to bump against her naked frame, although his impulse was to do just that. Standing on the tile trying his best to keep from leaving any puddles, he caught a glimpse of the digital clock on the nightstand next to Wild's bed. He was running short on time. The last thing he wanted to do on his first day—besides showing up with a hangover—was to show up late.

He noticed the other twin was still asleep, so as he toweled himself off he asked, "Does your sister need to get up?"

"She starts work at eight, lucky bitch. She works at one of the normal offices of the Pentagon."

"What's a normal office?"

"One that lets its people show up at eight instead of six-thirty."

Ash rapidly worked a comb through his wet hair while chewing on his toothbrush. After gathering his effects, he bid his bathroom companion farewell. "I'm taking off," he said. "Have a good day."

He heard her spit water before she replied, "Okay. I'm sure I'll see you tonight."

"What's going on tonight?"

"The same thing that goes on every night: Club Metro."

The words made his head ache, and he had a thought unlike anything that had come to him under fire: *I might not survive this.*

Miss Dubs had already shown Ash where to line up among the handful of staffers strung across the thick blue carpet when Captain Bradford entered the outer office. The idle chatter ceased as they spotted him; postures stiffened. He moved in front, focusing all the while on the screen of the Blackberry in his hand.

"It's another busy day in Garrett Village," the captain said, still without looking up. Ash tried to ignore his rising nausea by counting the freckles visible under his thin layer of red hair. "Highlights beyond the usual meeting cycle are a follow-up office call with SECNAV to review yesterday's testimony before the Senate Armed Services Committee, a luncheon downtown with defense industry reps, and then a dinner tonight at the House." Captain Bradford scanned the line until he found Ash, then extended his hand while looking across the others. "This is Lieutenant Roberts, the new aide. Tell us a little about yourself, Lieutenant."

Ash, a bit thrown by suddenly having the floor, said, "Ah, well, I'm not sure . . . there's not a whole lot to say really . . ."

"He just got back from the war in Iraq yesterday, so I'm sure he's still getting acclimated," Captain Bradford said. "He's new at this staff game and is going to need every bit of help each one of you can offer."

"Maybe we should start by introducing ourselves," Miss Dubs suggested.

The captain nodded and put a palm to his chest. "I'm Captain Bill Bradford, the admiral's executive assistant. We met yesterday."

"Do you know what the executive assistant does, Ash?" Miss Dubs asked.

"No, not exactly," Ash replied.

Miss Dubs looked back to the captain and said, "Perhaps each of us should briefly explain our roles as we introduce ourselves."

The captain nodded again, a bit stiffly this time, and said, "The EA is the admiral's senior staff member." He pointed to Chief Monroe.

"I'm Chief Mary Monroe, the admiral's flag writer," she said, leaning forward and looking down the line to Ash. "As I told you yesterday, sir, I'm basically Miss Dubs' assistant the deputy secretary, I guess." She smiled a bleached-toothed smile and fell back into the lineup.

Captain Bradford looked to the next person, a short female lieutenant with a round face and spiky brown hair. Ash caught a quick glimpse of the surface warfare pin atop the ribbons over the right pocket of her khakis. "I'm Lieutenant Molly Dubois," she said. "I'm the flag secretary, which is confusing, I know, because I'm not really a secretary. I handle the administrative work for the staff."

Captain Bradford's index finger moved down the line again, and a thin, prematurely balding sailor wearing working blues craned around the others to make eye contact with the lieutenant. "I'm Yeoman Second Class Burt Peabody," he said. "I'm the admiral's driver." He raised an index finger. "But I do paperwork, too." The others chuckled—an inside joke, apparently.

"And of course you met Miss Dubs yesterday," Captain Bradford said just after looking at his watch with concern. "She's the admiral's secretary."

"*Executive* secretary," Miss Dubs added. "I'll fill you in on my details later, Ash. And don't forget about Joe."

"Right," the captain said, eyes returning to Ash. "Chief Wildhorse works over at the residence in the Navy Yard. He's the steward; sort of like the admiral's butler. You'll meet him tonight at the admiral's reception."

Before Ash had any time to wonder what his own role would be at the reception, Vice Admiral Garrett slipped behind the line of staffers and continued into his office without a word. Captain Bradford followed him. With Ash taking up the rear, the line of staffers queued up in the doorway until the captain signaled them to enter the office. Ash noted he was the only one in khakis not wearing an aiguillette, and wondered if he was supposed to bring his own. Was there a uniform shop on the concourse, and would they carry something as rare to the fleet as an aiguillette? There were so many details to worry about all of a sudden—trivial details, the kind most SEALs didn't give a shit about and would be proud never to.

The admiral was seated behind his desk, thumbing through a short stack of papers as Captain Bradford gave him his initial greeting for the day: "It's another fine Navy day, Admiral."

The admiral looked up and smiled, saying, "It certainly is, isn't it, Bill?"

"Yes, sir," the captain said back. "We've got a busy

day on tap, Admiral. After your meeting with the joint chiefs, you've got a meeting with SECNAV."

"Why are we doing that one?" Garrett asked.

"I'm not sure," Captain Bradford replied.

"The Secretary wasn't happy with the presentation or the committee's overall response to some of the issues," Miss Dubs said.

"Our part of the presentation?" the admiral asked.

"No, not our part, but he wants to meet with the entire group anyway."

"Okay." The admiral looked back toward Captain Bradford. "What else?"

"You've got the luncheon with the defense execs at Crawford's at noon."

Garrett opened a ringed binder on his desk and asked, "Are their bios in the daybook?"

"Yes, sir," Miss Dubs replied.

"Do you want the new aide to go with you?" Captain Bradford asked.

The admiral focused on Ash—the first time he'd acknowledged his presence that morning—and smiled. "Sure. That'd be good experience for him."

"And then you're hosting the NATO flag officers tonight at the residence."

"Are we ready for that?"

"We're tying up some last-minute details," Miss Dubs said.

"This would be another good learning opportunity for Ash," the admiral said. "Does he have time to get over to the house this afternoon?"

"Yes," Miss Dubs said.

"All right. What else?"

"You've got the Panama trip tomorrow," Captain Bradford said.

"That's right," the admiral said. "I almost forgot about that. Is the itinerary finalized?"

"Not quite," Miss Dubs said. "I'm waiting to hear from the general's executive secretary to fill in a few of the blanks. We should know everything by this afternoon at the latest."

The admiral pointed toward Ash and asked, "Is he going with me?"

"He should," Captain Bradford said.

"You ready to go on a trip?" the admiral asked.

Ash's head was mush; the meeting was a blur. "Yes, Admiral," he replied.

Garrett looked at Miss Dubs and said, "Sit down with him and make sure he's up to speed on how to do one of these."

"Yes, Admiral," she said. "I've got a lot to review with him in addition to the trip."

"Okay, what else?"

"That's it, Admiral, unless you've got something for us," Captain Bradford said.

"I do have something, actually." Garrett removed something from the center drawer of his desk before getting to his feet. "Ash, I want to make your status as my aide official by giving you this." He held aloft an aiguillette. "This is your loop. Wear it well." The admiral slipped the rig up Ash's left arm and then pinned it to the shoulder of his uniform along the seam at the sleeve. Once he was done, the admiral shook Ash's hand as the others clapped.

Garrett checked his watch and said, "I've got about fifteen minutes here. Let me talk to Ash for a bit."

The admiral retook his seat as the others filed out without delay. Ash was left standing alone in front of the admiral's desk. Garrett gestured for him to sit and said, "Welcome aboard, Lieutenant."

"Thank you, sir," Ash replied.

"Do you feel overwhelmed yet?"

"Sort of."

"You should. There's no such thing as a new aide. There's only an aide. The tasks are going to come at you fast and furious. But I know you're up to it, right?"

Ash fought off a wave of nausea as he replied, "I'll do my best, sir."

"Are you all right? You don't look so good."

"Slight bug, maybe," Ash said. "I'll be fine, sir."

"I'm sure Miss Dubs has an aspirin if you need it."

"I took something earlier. I'll be fine."

"I hope so. Life without an aide is not good around here." Garrett leaned back in his chair. "Like I said yesterday, your job is to have me in the right place at the right time, wearing the right uniform, and saying the right things. My motto is 'no surprises.' Anywhere I go, I need to know who it is I'm talking to and what they intend to say to me. If they want something, I need to know what it is. That's why I have this daybook. It tells me the who, what, where, when, and how of my day. No surprises. The other advice I want to give you up front is always work through Miss Dubs. She's the corporate knowledge, the brain trust, everything, really—" One of the phones behind the admiral's desk rang. "That's the direct line," he explained. "I'd better answer that."

"Should I leave, sir?"

"No. You're the aide, Ash, a trusted agent in every way. Stick around." He plucked the receiver from the cradle and answered with a simple "Garrett . . ."

The admiral listened for a time, eyes focused on the daybook, before his expression turned dour. "Oh, no," he said. He listened for a bit longer, scribbled something on a notepad, then said, "I'll let him know. Appreciate the call, Hank," and hung up.

Garrett propped his elbows on his desk and rubbed both hands across the length of his face. "This is not the way I wanted to start our working relationship, Ash, but I'm afraid I have some bad news." Ash felt his face go white. Admiral Garrett pursed his lips and shifted in his chair. "That phone call was from General Hank Lee in the SOCOM offices here in the building. There has been a tragedy . . . in Iraq." He read from the notepad. "Staff Sergeant Renaldo Hidalgo and Petty Officer Brent Stephens . . . were both killed in action just a few hours ago." The admiral paused briefly and then offered, "I know how it feels to lose men who served under you. I'm sorry."

Ash fought to contain his emotions in front of his new boss. Who'd led the mission and what poor execution had allowed this to happen? And why had he accepted these orders without more of a fight?

He wanted to kill. He needed a rifle or a knife now. No, with his bare hands he'd feed the bastards their black innards. Ash's adrenaline was flowing; his heart pounded in his chest. He felt a trickle of cold sweat trickle down his back as the nausea came at him once again, more intensely this time. He tried a few deep breaths while gripped by the out-of-body realization that there would be no containing the oncoming tide in his current physical and emotional state. He leaned into the trashcan next to the admiral's desk and heaved.

EIGHTEEN

It felt good to work out. Vice Admiral Garrett had ordered Ash to go home and take it easy for a while, but when Ash got back to Wild's apartment, he was in no mood to sleep. Wild had made a passing reference to a health club in the building, so Ash changed out of his khakis, threw on a pair of shorts and a T-shirt, and set out to work up a good sweat.

Ash was happy to have the space to himself. He lay along the weight bench and repeatedly pushed the steel bar to arm's length, welcoming the burn, working to turn the adrenaline that coursed through his body into something more productive. Halfway up the wall in one corner a TV broadcast the news from Iraq. He was tempted to change the channel if not turn it off altogether, but felt guilty about the impulse. He wasn't in the field anymore. The least he could do was try to keep in touch with what was going on.

But he was in touch, painfully so. Some of his men had made the ultimate sacrifice. His men; his friends. The anger welled up again. He pushed the bar over and over. The burn would cleanse.

Ash had just seated himself on a curling bench to

work his biceps when he heard his cell phone go off from inside the small cloth bag he'd used to carry a towel and bottle of water. As he picked the phone up, he noted that the caller ID read UNKNOWN, but he figured it was probably Wild checking in from a covered line in the Pentagon.

"Ash is up," he said, dabbing his forehead with the towel as he spoke.

The voice on the line was distant and laced with static; he could just make out the words: "Lieutenant, it's Senior Chief Billy White. Can you hear me?"

"Just barely, Billy," Ash replied, voice raised now. "Can you hear me?"

"I can hear you fine, sir." Senior Chief White slowed himself down.

"Can you say where you are?"

"I'm in the TOC. I snuck onto one of the bat phones. If I drop off the line real quick you'll know I was busted by one of the intel weenies around here."

"It's good to hear your voice."

"Same here, sir, but I'm afraid I have some bad news. I've never been good at this, so I'll just say it: Go-man and Steve-O were smoked during the last op."

"Yeah, I heard. My new boss just gave me the word about an hour ago."

"Oh, all right then. I just wanted to make sure you knew."

"I appreciate the effort, Billy. I needed to hear it from you. They were good warriors. Good men."

"They were."

"Were you on that one?"

"No."

"Heard anything?"

"Plenty. I got to tell you, Lieutenant, not all of it adds up."

"What do you mean?"

"I mean that they were working with Iraqis on this

one; you know, good Iraqis, Shiites that hate the regime worse than we do."

"Okay, and?"

"And they just vanished after the mission. I tell you it—"

There was a burst of static through the line and then the phone went dead. Ash sat at the weight bench with the cell phone poised in front of his face for a few minutes, waiting for Billy White to call back. The call didn't come.

NINETEEN

Nobody makes eye contact, Ash thought as he made his way back to the admiral's office after his second shower of the day and the short Metro ride from Pentagon City. The pace of those walking the long corridors of the Pentagon wasn't fast necessarily, but there seemed to be an underlying sense of purpose in their expressions and body language. For his part, he was just happy that he wasn't lost. He hoped three trips would be enough to figure out how to get from the front door to his workplace.

But for that short observation, his mind was on Iraq. He wanted to know more about the circumstances surrounding the deaths of Steve-O and Go-man; he wanted to know who had led the operation. Vice Admiral Garrett certainly had the means to call that part of the world. Ash resolved to attempt a call back to the SOCOM headquarters building when time allowed.

The lieutenant had arrived at the top of the long ramp past the concourse when he heard a female voice calling his name: "Ash? Ash, hello. Wait a second."

He turned and saw a young woman dressed in a dark

blue business suit. Her blonde hair was pulled back and she wore dark-rimmed glasses—a very professional look, he thought. But who was it, and how did she know his name? Closer, the mystery wasn't solved.

"Hi," she said with a smile.

"Hi," he returned, mind working to place her. She was attractive, no doubt—pretty and tall.

Ash obviously didn't do very well in hiding his confusion. "You don't recognize me, do you?" She splayed a hand across her chest. "I'm Melinda, from last night."

He tried a recovery: "I knew it was you. It's just you look a little . . ."

"Different?" she offered.

"Yeah, different."

"Less like a bimbo?"

"I didn't say that," he said with an emphatic shake of his head. "You looked good last night."

They stood in awkward silence until Ash asked, "Where do you work here?"

"Downstairs," she answered.

"What's down there?"

"My office. I work with Fawn. You met her last night, too."

"Oh, right."

Before he had a chance to wonder, Melinda said, "You also took a shower with her this morning."

As he felt the blood rushing to his face, she said, "I had a great time last night."

"Same here," he replied.

"Are you going with Wild to Club Metro tonight? It's another big night there, you know?"

"Yeah, I heard. I don't think I can make it. I have to help my admiral host a reception at his house over in the Navy Yard."

"What time is it over?"

"I'm not sure. This'll be my first one of these."

"What about the next night?"

"I think I'm going to Panama."

"Panama, huh?" She looked to the toes of her shoes. "That's a new one."

"No, really, I'm going to Panama, or so they tell me, anyway." He puffed a bemused chuckle. "Listen to me. I don't have a clue what I'm doing around here."

"I'm sure you'll get the hang of it," she said, allowing another smile.

He took a long look into her tanned face while trying to conjure up images from the night before, but couldn't remember anything past leaving Club Metro and jumping into a cab. The driver was Pakistani. Any of the details after that were blurs at best. He glanced at his watch. "I'd better get going. They wanted me back by eleven."

"I guess we'll see you later . . . or maybe not."

Ash touched her arm. "Can I call you once things settle down a little for me?"

"Wild knows how to get in touch with me."

"I promise I'll call you soon." Ash turned to go, but then stopped himself. He couldn't let this chance meeting pass without getting an answer to The Question. "Melinda, hold on a sec."

"Yes?"

"Did we . . . I mean, did anything . . ."

"Happen between us?"

"Yeah."

"Besides the unfinished blow job in the bathroom?"

Ash saw a few heads around them turn with the words "blow job," so he lowered his voice a little. "Yeah, I was just curious whether—"

"No, we didn't," she interrupted, apparently more disappointed than angered by the question. "And I promise you, if we ever do sleep together you'll never forget it, no matter how many Sprints you drink." Melinda flashed her eyes and walked away with a strut that belied the conservative style of her outfit. He fought the stirring and hoped the trip to Panama would be a quick one.

* * *

"The daybook is the admiral's bible," Miss Dubs said, reaching across her desk and orienting the three-ringed binder so it faced Ash. The cover featured a picture of an F-18 landing on an aircraft carrier under the title ADMIRAL'S DAYBOOK. "We've tried getting him into the twenty-first century; you know, getting him to use one of those hand-helds, but he just wants to read everything on good old-fashioned pieces of paper."

She opened the binder and tapped an index finger against the thin film of plastic that sheathed the first page. "The daybook starts with the schedules: daily, weekly, monthly. Anything beyond three months is a guess, so we don't worry about that except for really big events like an inauguration or an aircraft carrier commissioning, things like that." She flipped through a couple of pages. "If you look at the monthly calendar, you'd think there wasn't much going on, but once you start getting into the weekly schedules it always fills up. And Admiral Garrett doesn't know how to say no. That's where I come in."

Miss Dubs looked up to make her next point. "Rule number one is only the executive secretary can add or subtract things from the admiral's calendar. Do you understand that?"

Ash nodded.

"Do you understand?" she repeated, jabbing a finger toward him.

"Yes, ma'am," he said.

"Don't call me ma'am." She turned several more pages. "I'm sure the admiral has already given you the 'in the right place at the right time saying the right things' speech, right?"

"Yes, he has."

"This is a big part of that. You can see here that the admiral never walks into a situation where he doesn't already have a good idea of who's going to be there and what they're going to say. Take today's luncheon, for example: Here are the bios for each of the attendees along with a summation of the pitch they intend to give."

"So you get all of that for him?" Ash asked.

"Yes. I'll take care of the daybook. You just make sure it's executed. You and I have to work closely together to keep the system functioning the right way. The admiral might make a request to you or meet somebody on the road that I don't know about, so you have to make sure I get that information. That's the only way. Otherwise we wind up signing him up to be two places at once or miss getting him where he's supposed to be. And a man like Admiral Brooks Garrett doesn't like to miss an appointment. Nothing upsets him more than making people unhappy. Got it so far?"

"Yes. Could we walk through today's events?"

"Sure. I'll be right back." Miss Dubs pushed away from her desk and walked out of the outer office without any further explanation.

Ash paged through the daybook, stopping on the monthly calendar and reviewing the myriad meetings, receptions, speeches, and trips. It seemed unlikely he would be hooking up with Melinda any time soon. Then he skimmed the bios of the defense industry reps the admiral would be having lunch with. He studied their photos as he'd studied the photo of Deputy Minister Hassid and felt some comfort. Gathering and using intelligence was something about which he knew a thing or two. Perhaps some of his skills would come into play, after all.

Ash heard someone enter the room. He turned expecting to find Miss Dubs behind him but instead saw a man in a dark suit with white hair a lot like Admiral Garrett's. The man smiled widely as he approached with his arm extended.

"Hello, there, Lieutenant," he said, words coming rapid-fire as he enthusiastically pumped Ash's hand. "I don't remember seeing you in the office before. Have we met?"

"I doubt it, sir," Ash returned. "I just got here."

"Oh, you're the admiral's new aide. That's great. I'm Bill Freemont. I work in Congress. Hey, is that a SEAL pin on your uniform?"

"Yes, sir."

"Another SEAL aide, huh? That's great." Ash watched the man's eyes work away from him, toward the admiral's office. "Do you know the last aide, Lieutenant Sampson?"

"No, sir."

"He was a SEAL, too. In fact, if I remember correctly, the aide before him was a SEAL. That was with a different admiral, of course. Where were you before here?"

"Iraq."

"Iraq, huh? Wow, that's impressive. Say, I see the boss is in. Would you mind if I had a quick word with him?"

Before Ash could respond, the man slipped past Miss Dubs' desk, and following a friendly series of raps on the doorframe, he was in with Garrett. At the same time, Miss Dubs returned from wherever she'd been. She was about to refocus on the daybook when she heard laughter coming from the admiral's office. She peered through the doorway and scowled.

"Who is that?" she asked.

"That's Congressman Freemont," Ash said.

"That's not *Congressman* Freemont," she seethed. "That's *Bill* Freemont. How did he get in there?"

"He sort of let himself in," Ash attempted to explain.

"He's a lobbyist," Miss Dubs said as she ran a finger along the daily schedule in the daybook then checked the bejeweled watch around her delicate wrist. "The admiral needs to be prepping for his luncheon, not talking to that guy." She took a deep breath and calmly moved to the doorway. "Excuse me, Admiral," she said sweetly, composure instantly regained—an impressive shift of moods. "We need to get you to the car for the trip downtown."

"Where are you headed?" Freemont asked the admiral.

"I have a luncheon," Garrett replied.

"Oh, yeah? Who with?"

"I'm sorry, Mr. Freemont," Miss Dubs said, voice dripping with regret, as if the disappointment was all hers. "The admiral really needs to go."

Freemont gave her a wave as he continued to focus on Garrett. "Have you seen the results of that interoperability think tank?"

"Which one?" the admiral asked back.

"The one you guys commissioned a few months back."

"I don't remember that."

"I don't think you're going to like the findings, quite frankly, but we're here to help, if you want."

"Mr. Freemont, please," Miss Dubs said, a bit more forcefully this time. Freemont attempted another wave of his hand, but Miss Dubs stepped over and took him by the elbow, blocking his line to the admiral in the process.

"You're looking good, by the way," Freemont said over his shoulder as Miss Dubs led him to the door. "Been working out?"

Garrett patted his stomach and said, "When I can. My secret is never having time to eat."

Freemont let out a hearty laugh and said, "We're overdue for that round of golf, by the way. Are you free this weekend?"

Miss Dubs shut the door behind Freemont before the admiral got his answer out. "I'm sorry, Mr. Freemont," she said, "but we've got a lot on our plate today."

"How does he look for golf, say, Saturday?" Freemont asked.

"Not good, I'm afraid," she replied.

"Sunday?"

Miss Dubs shook her head.

Freemont pointed toward the monitor on her desk. "Should we take a look at the calendar?"

"That won't be necessary," she said with a smile. "Why don't you have your office call us, and we'll see what we might be able to work out in the future. Have a good day."

"Hey, aren't you and your husband baseball fans?" he asked. "Season's coming up fast, you know, and we've got a corporate box right behind the home dugout at Camden Yards. Orioles are supposed to be good this year."

"We're not really baseball fans," Miss Dubs returned. "Again, have a good day."

Freemont cut his eyes toward Ash: "How about you, Lieutenant?"

"I like baseball, I guess," Ash said.

"Of course you do," Freemont said. "What red-blooded American doesn't? You let me know when you want to go, and I'll make it happen. Heck, bring a couple of buddies with you. Baltimore's a great town. Good nightlife, too."

"Okay, thanks."

"Don't mention it. We like to support our war fighters anyway we can. Isn't that right, Miss Dubs?"

"Have a good day, Mr. Freemont," she intoned.

"I'll have my secretary call you," he said and then slipped out of the outer office.

Miss Dubs emitted a long exhale as she retook her seat behind her desk. She drummed her fingers against the daybook, eyebrows knit. Eventually her expression relaxed, and she offered Ash a gentle smile. "What's rule number one?" she asked maternally.

"Only you can add to or subtract from the admiral's calendar," Ash said.

"Very good," she said. "Here's rule number two: Nobody gets in to see the admiral unless I let him or her in."

"You weren't here, and—"

Her smile widened as she closed her eyes and nodded slowly. "Nobody gets in to see the admiral unless I let him or her in."

"Yes, ma'am."

Miss Dubs reached across the desk and patted his hand. "Don't call me ma'am. Oh, and we never accept gifts, *period,* even irresistible baseball tickets." Ash nodded his understanding, happy that she was talented at wrapping her corrections or instructions in a muted encouragement that kept him from screaming, "Fuck this!" and sprinting out of the Pentagon. Miss Dubs grabbed the binder from her desk and held it up. "Here, take the daybook. The admiral can study it in the car on the way to the luncheon." She jabbed a thumb over her shoulder toward the closed door to the admiral's office. "Don't be late, now. Remember: in the right place at the right time . . ."

TWENTY

It was sponge time. Ash put his best intelligence techniques to work the moment he spotted the beaming businessmen standing attentively around a banquet table that ran nearly the length of the upscale restaurant's far wall. The facts would come quickly.

Vice Admiral Garrett worked his way around the table, pumping hands and patting backs. The admiral was at ease in the presence of the group, coolly muting the mawkish enthusiasm, the buddy-buddy tone of each of their greetings with his calm aura, his command presence. Once fully around, he pointed toward Ash and said, "Gentlemen, you probably don't recognize this guy. In fact, the only people who've seen Lieutenant Ash Roberts lately are Iraqi, and many of them aren't with us anymore. He's my new aide, so go easy on him."

"You can trust us, Admiral," a bald guy with red cheeks and bad teeth said with a hearty laugh before he reached over. "Hello, Ash. I'm Chuck Devlin of General Fabric Solutions."

"I'm Poppy Barksdale of Go Tech International," another, less bald man said. "I was a fighter pilot, but you won't hold that against me, will you?" They all laughed. There was a lot of laughing going on.

And around they went. Names, positions, companies— Ash processed it all, topping each mental file with the face. He was sure he'd be seeing them again, as sure as he hadn't seen the last of Bill Freemont. These were the new players in his life, and he needed to know where they fit—and fast. He wasn't about to get caught flat-footed again. No more drive-bys. And, hopefully, no more lectures from Miss Dubs, nice as she was.

They sat, and lunch was quickly served, which was good, because the last thing Miss Dubs had said before he left was that the admiral definitely needed to be on time for his pop-up one-thirty appointment with the Chief of Staff of the Air Force. The waiter had just finished filling Ash's glass with a second helping of iced tea when Chuck Devlin leaned his shiny melon across the table and asked, "You're a Republican, right?"

"What kind of question is that to ask, Chuck?" Poppy Barksdale said from Ash's right. "Of course he's Republican. Have you ever met an officer who was a Democrat?"

"Sure I have."

"Really? Who?"

"Felix Carchow, for one."

"That doesn't count. He started life as a Republican; he only became a Democrat when the party convinced him that he might be able to win his district back home if he switched over."

"Okay, then: Bob Sikes."

"I'm not sure I'd call him a Democrat."

"What would you call him then?"

"A moderate."

"You know, Ash, like I said, I'm a former fighter pilot," Barksdale said, waving his glass of iced tea about the air like he was proposing a toast. "I flew Phantoms in Vietnam for the Marine Corps, but you want to know the best thing about you boys in special operations? You guys don't have to wait for the normal procurement process to happen. You can just go out and get what you need without all the hassle. Isn't that right?"

"I really don't know, sir," Ash replied.

"Boy, what I wouldn't give to make that the standard for all the warfare specialties, huh, Chuck?"

"Sure would make life easier, wouldn't it?"

"Don't you think that's how it should be for everybody, Ash? War fighters should be able to come to us with a wish list that we'd fill right away. No middlemen. No delays."

"Sounds like a good idea to me," Ash said.

"Hey, Admiral," Devlin said, mouth now full of venison and caramelized onions, "your aide agrees that we need to streamline the procurement process."

Garrett raised an eyebrow and said, "He does, huh? What part of it does he think we should get rid of?"

The bald man looked to Ash as if he expected him to have an opinion on the matter. Ash shrugged and said, "Honestly, I really don't know anything about the procurement system, sir."

He smiled in return and said, "I'm just kidding. Hey, by the way, I need to get on the admiral's calendar in the next day or so. Can you make that happen for me?"

"You need to talk to Miss Dubs about that, sir."

"Really? When did you guys start doing business that way? The old aide used to get me on the calendar himself."

"What about this war, Admiral?" Frank Bonita of Air Systems, Incorporated, asked boisterously from across the table, cradling a cup of coffee just under the flesh roll of his second chin.

"What about it, Frank?" Garrett returned.

"Well, how's it all going to turn out?"

"We're going to win."

"Of *course* we're going to win. But what is it going to show? What's it going to change?"

"It's going to change the government of Iraq to one

that supports democracy, hopefully," the admiral said without any hesitation.

"Okay, but do our forces have the right equipment in place right now to get the job done?"

"I think so, yes. The results over the first few days of the war are encouraging. Now if we could only control the weather."

"We can arrange that," the bald man said with a sly smile. "For a price, of course."

"Let's ask the aide," Devlin said. "Are you happy with the gear you've been given?"

Ash mulled over the question for a second and then said, "Every time I ever pulled a trigger, bullets came out of the barrel." The executives each nodded toward the other, seemingly impressed with the bottom-line warrior's practicality of his answer.

"That's the kind of feedback we like," the corpulent Bonita said before refocusing on Garrett. "Sir, our brave fighting men and women should always be able to say exactly what your aide just said, whether they're talking about bullets or bombs or missiles or whatever."

"I agree," the admiral returned with a nod.

"Of course. But I'm afraid—we're all afraid—that the cost of current operations may take away from the commitment to the future."

Vice Admiral Garrett waved his hand like he wanted a pass from the blackjack dealer and, sitting up a bit, said, "Not to worry, gentlemen. From what I can see, the administration remains committed to keeping our military ready to fight this war and the next one. Both sides of the aisle now understand the need for a strong national defense. I know it will come as no disappointment to any of you when I say your future is bright."

Ash sensed Barksdale moving toward him and he fought jerking away as the man whispered into his right ear: "Your boss has quite a future ahead of him, you know. The party has already earmarked him for greatness." Ash turned to make eye contact as the exec leaned back into his chair and winked. "Stick with this guy, son. You'll like soldiering for a while, but ultimately you'll discover there's no money in it."

Ash felt the blood rush to his face. Suddenly the fat cats were smothering him. Why was he here? Why was he being forced to learn this moronic Washington game with a war in progress? He'd long ago bypassed the pursuit of money for its own sake. In his mind's eye he saw Steve-O and Go-man, and with that picture came a wave of guilt. His men needed him.

Ash threw a twenty-dollar bill on the table and pushed his chair back. He bent over the admiral and quietly asked, "Sir, would it be a problem if I waited in the car for you?"

Vice Admiral Garrett studied him with concern. "You're not sick, are you?"

"No, sir. I just need to make a few phone calls."

"Do what you've got to do, Lieutenant. You don't need my permission. Did you get enough to eat?"

"Yes, sir. I did."

"Beats MREs, right?" said Frank Bonita. "Oh, Admiral, that reminds me: We've got a subvendor who can provide chow hall facilities for a lot less than what I think the government is paying now. . . ."

Ash tried to keep a low profile as he wandered out of the restaurant and across the sidewalk. He slid into the plain blue sedan's passenger seat next to Petty Officer Peabody, who sat behind the wheel reading an issue of *Men's Health*.

"Lunch over?" Peabody asked as Ash pulled out his PDA and began looking for the listing for "Schoenstein," the last name of the goddamn detailer who'd assigned him to this stupid job.

"No," Ash replied without lifting his head.

"Aren't you supposed to pay the admiral's bill?"

Peabody was right. This was another idiosyncrasy of the aide job that Miss Dubs had tried to shove into Ash's already overworked brain. Apparently it was bad form for Admiral Garrett to ever reach for his wallet in public. Ash was to pick up all the tabs and somehow he'd get reimbursed later. Just how remained unclear.

Ash found the number he wanted, but as he cradled the cell phone, he couldn't bring his fingers to mash the buttons. He let out a long breath and folded the phone back up and went back into the restaurant to pay for the admiral's lunch.

TWENTY-ONE

Chief Joe Wildhorse looked nothing like a steward, or at least nothing like the image Ash had conjured up when he'd first heard Captain Bradford use the term to describe him. Ash had had some experience with hired help around the house during his formative years. Butlers, gardeners, maids, and chauffeurs had swarmed the main Roberts compound in Old Greenwich, Connecticut, appearing out of nowhere when there was a shirt to be pressed, a plant to be watered, or an errand to be run.

But Wildhorse didn't fit the mold of those who had made careers out of going unnoticed. For one, he was huge. Dressed in a crisp white smock and black pants, he nearly filled the doorway as he stood between the kitchen and the dining room.

The chief's copper face was impassively fixed, with heavy-lidded eyes closely bracketing his long, wide nose capped at the bridge by a single thick brow. His coarse hair was jet-black and jutted across his wide forehead in a rough approximation of bangs. His demeanor was businesslike, just short of humorless.

"Are you wearing your loop that way for a reason, Lieutenant?" Wildhorse asked, pointing toward the formal aiguillette that adorned the left sleeve of Ash's mess dress uniform—the Navy officer's version of a dinner jacket, complete with bow tie.

Ash looked across to the gold braid pinned under his left shoulder board, thicker and longer than the aiguillette that he'd worn with his khakis earlier in the day. "I have no idea how to wear it, Chief," he said. "Miss Dubs handed it to me as I was on my way out to change before coming over here. I'm just happy I had all the parts that make up the rest of this uniform. It's been years since I wore mess dress."

"If I may, sir?" The chief adjusted the gold braid about Ash's uniform, taking the end of it from where the lieutenant had twisted it under his left shoulder board and hooking it over one of the buttons. "It is confusing."

"I'm confused about a lot of things, Chief," Ash said, "including what I'm supposed to do here."

"Only one mission around the house," Chief Wild-horse said. "Keep Mrs. Garrett happy." His voice dropped to a loud whisper with the sound of high heels clacking across the hardwood floor in the next room. "At these sort of receptions, that's not always easy."

Through the small part of the doorway the chief's body didn't block, Ash caught a glimpse of Mrs. Garrett entering the dining room, her white-blond hair flowing straight back and flipping up just above her shoulders. She wore a conservative knee-length dress that nevertheless showed she had managed to keep her figure into middle age. Her movements were jerky, harried. She studied the arrangement of hors d'oeuvres spread across the white tablecloth, brow furrowed as if something wasn't quite right. "Where's the melted Brie, Joe?" she asked.

"It's still in the oven," the chief replied. "It has a few minutes to go."

"And the artichoke soufflé?"

"It's out there already."

"Where?"

"Next to the crackers."

"Okay, okay." She brought both index fingers to her bright red lips as she looked over at the clock. "People are going to start arriving any minute."

"What can I do, Mrs. Garrett?" Ash asked.

She narrowed her eyes and said, "Mrs. Garrett is Brooks' mother, Ash. I'm Dottie."

"Is the admiral still upstairs, ma'am?" Chief Wildhorse asked.

"Yes. I think he's more worried about the trip to Panama tomorrow than this party tonight."

"What's he worried about?" the chief said as he pulled the oven door open, filling the kitchen with the smell of warm cheese. "I've already got him packed." He looked over to Ash and explained, "I'm responsible for getting the admiral ready for trips, getting his uniforms dry-cleaned and prepped, and packing his bags—things along those lines. You and I need to work together to make sure he has what he needs—ribbons, medals, gloves, whatever. And if I don't pack it, not only am I in trouble, you're in trouble."

The deep bong of the doorbell resonated through the entryway, and Mrs. Garrett drew a long, cleansing breath. "Ash, why don't you work the front door? If they have any coats, stick them in the front closet on the left side of the hallway. After they come in, direct them to Molly so she can check them off the list and give them their name tags."

Ash moved for the front door, tugging his jacket down and picking a few bits of lint off his pants as he went. Around the corner from the dining room into the entryway he ran headlong into Vice Admiral Garrett coming the other way. The admiral cut an impressive figure with his solid gold shoulder boards and array of miniature medals adorning the lapel of his mess dress uniform.

"Excuse me, sir," Ash said as he stepped aside, barely avoiding a collision.

"It looks like we're all in a hurry around here," the admiral returned. "Did Dottie assign you the front door?"

"Yes, sir."

"Okay. I'm off to the kitchen to get my instructions." He grasped Ash at the biceps. "Again, I'm sorry about the loss of your men. Are you holding up all right?"

"Yes, sir. I'm fine. I apologize for throwing up in your trashcan. That's more than a little embarrassing."

"Don't give it a second thought. Couldn't be helped."

It could have if I hadn't stayed out all night partying, Ash thought.

"We'll have some time to talk on the airplane tomorrow," the admiral continued as the doorbell rang again, "but now, we'd better get to our places."

Garrett headed the opposite direction while Ash rushed across the hardwood of the entryway, passing Lieutenant Molly Dubois standing behind a card table covered with name tags. "Send them to you, right?" he asked.

"Right," she returned. Her hair looked even spikier than it had earlier in the day, wet and untouchable. She was a fireplug of a woman, and Ash wondered how well she usually performed on the semiannual physical fitness test, remembering how much trouble some of his similarly built female classmates had had with it back at the Academy.

A few steps from the door, Ash caught a quick glimpse of the magnificent glass chandelier that hung from the plaster ceiling high above, and it struck him the residence was as much a museum as it was a house. The house he'd grown up in was big, no doubt, but it had still retained the elements of a normal dwelling—albeit one with a six-car garage. But this was like living in a piece of American history. Was it really possible for the admiral and Dottie to be comfortable here? And what did their two sons think each time they returned from college? Was this stately mansion considered home to them?

Ash pulled the door open in time to catch a tall, thin man reaching for the doorbell a third time. The man sported a beard that made him look like a college professor.

"Sorry about that," Ash said. "I was all the way back in the kitchen. Please come in, sir."

The man stepped across the threshold and scanned the entryway. "Am I the first one here?" he asked in a mild panic.

"You are, but you're not early," Ash said, extending an arm toward Molly. "Lieutenant Dubois will sign you in and get you a name tag."

The man reluctantly shuffled over toward Molly, who momentarily added to his consternation by not being able to find his name on the guest list. But after figuring out he was listed as "Burt Charles" instead of "Charles Burt," he was issued a backup name tag with his name scrawled on it in black marker instead of the elegant cursive type of the premade ones.

The guests were coming quickly now, a parade of politicians, high-ranking military officers, and dignitaries, real and imagined, of all stripes. None of them seemed to care that they'd never seen Ash before, either accepting his dress aiguillette at face value or blowing by him undeterred in their quest to cozy up to the Garretts. For his part, he was happy that the temperature on this early spring evening was moderate so that few people wore coats. He also tried to listen as each checked in with Molly, hoping to match faces with names from the guest list he'd quickly reviewed that afternoon.

By half past the hour, the flow of guests through the front door had all but stopped. Ash saw that Molly had abandoned her post, so he wandered through the dense crowd gathered around the dining room table and into the kitchen to find Chief Wildhorse for guidance on what he should do next. He found the chief in full flurry, slamming oven doors and stirring steaming pots.

"Chief, what can I do for you?" Ash asked.

Chief Wildhorse looked up, momentarily perplexed by the question, then said, "Check with the bartenders and see what they need."

"Where are they?"

"All around. There are three of them."

Ash nodded and spun on his heel out of the kitchen and back into the crowd. He excused his way past the guests, making further note along the way of name tags and faces, building his corporate file. At one point, his eyes went from the lapel of an Armani suit to what had to rank near the top of the list of the most amazing cleavages he'd ever seen. He realized he was staring, and as he lifted his gaze it was met by an intensely white smile under a nose sharp enough to cut paper. Higher, her too-blue eyes bordered by too-long lashes seized him. She wasn't young—late forties, he guessed—but had done a laudable job of holding onto her looks.

"Paula Lemont," she said, extending a well-sculpted arm—a product of frequent workouts at some upscale health club, no doubt.

"Lieutenant Roberts, ma'am," Ash replied.

"What's your first name?" she cooed.

"Ash."

"Ash . . . is that short for something?"

"Ashton."

Her smile brightened, almost blinding now. "I like that. Say, can you do me a favor? Can you get me a glass of Chablis?"

From war fighter to waiter, he thought. *How the mighty have fallen.* He took her glass with the chagrined smile that follows the realization that one is more servant than suitor, and went in search of the nearest drink station. In the far corner of the massive living room he found it.

"Can I get you anything?" he asked the young black

man dressed in the same white-smock-and-black-pant outfit Chief Wildhorse wore.

"I need ice," he replied, holding up a silver bucket. "Where should I get it?"

He pointed across the entryway into the sitting room on the other side and said, "See if Petty Officer Simons has some I can bum off him."

Silver bucket in one hand, Chablis glass in the other, Ash set off again. He hadn't gone ten steps when he was stopped again, this time by a thirtysomething gent with slicked-back hair and a double-breasted blazer that made him look like a yacht club commodore.

"Could I trouble you for a gin and tonic?" he asked, waving his tumbler like a dice cup.

Ash started to explain that he wasn't a waiter but saw in the man's expectant expression that he probably didn't care. Besides, Ash wasn't sure that schlepping drinks *wasn't* part of his role. He consolidated the ice bucket and Chablis glass in one hand and took the tumbler with the other. "With a twist," the slick-haired commodore called across Ash's shoulder.

In the sitting room Ash was happy to find, along with Chablis and the makings for a gin and tonic, that the pudgy petty officer with the shaved head had an abundance of ice he was willing to share. Ash carefully cradled his burden, but before walking off asked, "Where is the other bar?"

The fat petty officer pointed and said, "In the corner of the living room."

"Yeah, I know about that one. Where's the other one?"

"The third one is on the patio, believe it or not. We got lucky with the weather."

Ash tracked down the commodore in short order, returned the ice bucket to the black bartender, and found Ms. Lemont, the buxom wine drinker, behind a line of attentive male guests. Closer, he saw they weren't fo-

cused entirely on her but primarily on the man with
whom she was holding hands—a square-jawed fellow
with a bad comb-over whose name tag read SENATOR
PAUL LEMONT. Before he got beyond earshot, Ash heard
the senator pronounce that although his name was of
French derivation, he was the first to introduce "freedom
fry" legislation to the Senate floor.

Ash passed outside through one of the pair of massive
glass doors that ran nearly to the ceiling. Down a half
dozen stone steps he saw that the crowd on the patio
was densely packed, penned in by the waist-high hedges
that bordered the large brick semicircle. He paused on
the periphery, hoping to avoid any more drink orders as
he continued his search for the third bartender. The only
way around was across the manicured lawn, but noting
the complete absence of traffic across it, he wondered if
it wasn't some sort of faux pas to leave the prepared
surfaces, the walkways and such.

So he stood in place and admired the view beyond
the crowd, across the rolling lawn punctuated in the middle by a well-lit fountain to the Anacostia River. Down
the private pier he watched a group of guests boarding
the admiral's gig for a quick spin around the river. It
was amazing how much elegance could be jammed into
an urban setting like the one that surrounded the Navy
Yard.

The moon was rising, leaving a bright streak that
danced across the calm water of the river. The air was
sweet and still, and the stars were numerous. Summer
was coming, and that notion buoyed Ash's spirits. Out-
door concerts and sunshine and lazy days. Would this
new role allow him to enjoy the season? And could he
enjoy it with thoughts of the war constantly gnawing at
his guts?

Female companionship would help. Melinda suddenly
popped into his head. Perhaps he'd be in a mood to
catch up with Wild and the gang after the reception
ended, whenever that was. Probably not. He was headed

to Panama tomorrow—and clueless about it. He wanted to be one hundred percent. Life was easier that way.

"Beautiful evening, isn't it?"

Ash turned to see an older man standing behind him. "Good evening, Lieutenant," the man said as he extended his hand. "I don't think we've met, have we?"

"I don't think so, sir," Ash replied. "I'm pretty new around here."

"Well, then, let me be among the first to welcome you to Washington. I'm Murdo Edeema."

"Ash Roberts."

"Ash Roberts?" the man repeated. "That name's familiar, for some reason. Are you sure we haven't met before?"

"No, I don't think so."

The man's eyes went to Ash's lapel. "SEAL, huh? Did you just come from one of the teams?"

"No, I was in a joint job."

"Joint? Delta Force?"

Ash demurred in spite of the fact he was pleased to be recognized as something other than a waiter. For all the movies and TV shows about Delta Force, the Department of Defense remained reticent about its existence.

"Relax," Edeema continued before Ash could fully wear his poker face. "We do a lot of work with the department. Your secrets are our secrets." He looked over his shoulder toward the far end of the patio. "It looks like the line for the bar has gone down. Can I get you a drink?"

"I don't know if I'm allowed to drink on the job," Ash said.

"Of course you are," Edeema returned. "It would be uncivilized to prohibit that. Follow me; I'll get you one."

As they threaded through the crowd, Ash asked, "Which company do you work for?"

"The Huntington Group," Edeema replied.

"The Huntington Group?"

"We're a consultant firm."

"What sort of consulting do you do?"

"We do a little bit of everything, really. Whatever needs to be done."

"That doesn't sound like much of a specialty."

"Ah, but we do specialize."

"In what?"

"Whatever specialty is required." Edeema reached the bar. "What can I get you?"

"I'm still not sure—"

"Come on now, Lieutenant. I'm a guest at this reception, and you're supposed to make me feel welcome. I feel most welcome when I'm joined in a drink."

Ash shot a furtive glance over his shoulder and said, "Fine. I'll take a beer."

"A beer and a glass of white wine," Edeema said to the bartender before turning back to Ash. "You must hate being over here while the war is going on."

"Actually, I just came from there," Ash explained. "One day I'm in the field, the next day I get a call from my detailer saying I'm a by-name call to be Vice Admiral Garrett's new aide."

"Well, we're glad you're here," Edeema said. He handed Ash a glass of beer and then held his own glass up in a toast: "To new friends."

"New friends," Ash echoed.

Edeema looked across Ash's shoulder and raised his eyebrows in recognition. "Come with me, Ash. I'd like to introduce you to someone."

The older man grabbed the lieutenant by the sleeve of his mess dress and led him through the crowd until they stood at the feet of a handsome couple—one Ash had already come across that evening.

"Senator Lemont, how good to see you," Edeema said.

"Murdo," the senator returned. "What a great surprise. Paula, look who it is."

"Murdo!" the woman sang out before throwing her arms around him. "How is Andromeda?"

"She's doing well," Edeema said. "She's going to be so mad that I ran into you and she wasn't here."

"Well, why isn't she here?"

"You know her, always busy with something or other on her own."

"Well, do be sure and tell her hello for us."

"Of course." Edeema directed Ash in front of him. "Senator, I'd like you to meet a friend of mine. This is Lieutenant Ash Roberts."

"Very nice to meet you, Ash. How do you know Murdo?"

"Actually—"

"Ash is Brooks' aide," Edeema said. "He just got back from Iraq."

"Iraq, huh?" The senator turned to his wife, which allowed Ash to shoot a quick glance at her cleavage. "Dear, this handsome young gentleman just returned from Iraq."

The woman took his hand and, oozing with bleached-tooth sincerity, said, "Let me thank you on behalf of all Americans everywhere for what you do to protect our freedoms."

The woman showed no sense that she'd ever laid eyes on Ash before, and his first impulse in the face of her patriotic fervor was to ask if he could freshen up her wine. Instead he simply said, "America's support is what keeps—" But before he was able to finish the thought, the Lemonts moved on, having spotted someone more worthy of their time across the terrace.

"Senator Lemont is a good man for you to know," Edeema said. "He's on the Appropriations Committee. Come on, I've got some other people you need to meet."

And so they were off, once again motoring determinedly through the crowd. Over the next half hour, Edeema introduced Ash to no less than twenty-five people, each of a standing rivaling if not bettering the last. They were not just surgeons but deans of colleges of surgery. They were not just lawyers but district attorneys and judges. They were foreign diplomats and TV pundits and Pulitzer Prize–winning newspaper writers and even the quarterback from the Washington Redskins' glory days, who had seemingly perfected the art of flashing his Super Bowl rings. Edeema seemed to be good friends with them all.

"One thing you need to understand right up front, Ash," Edeema counseled as Ash waited behind him in line for another drink. "This town is not about what you can do, it's about who you know. Natural talent, can-do spirit, great work ethic—everybody's got those things, so none of that matters here. The X-factor is who you know." He spread his arms out and smiled. "So now you know some people. And not just slugs, either—*important* people."

"That was interesting," Ash said.

"Interesting? It wasn't just interesting. It was fundamental toward your success in Washington. That's what I'm telling you, my friend."

Ash wasn't sure what to say, so he said, "Thanks."

Edeema handed Ash another glass of beer. "No thanks required. In the crunch, let's just make sure we remember each other, deal?"

Ash shook his hand and said, "Deal," because it seemed like the friendly, polite thing to do, even if he had no idea what Edeema was talking about.

Edeema shot a glance at his big, silver watch and said, "If you'll excuse me, I have a dog to let out. It was a pleasure meeting you, Ash."

"Yes, sir. Thanks for showing me around."

"I'm sure it'll be the other way around very soon. You strike me as a guy who catches on pretty quick. Do you have a card, by chance?"

"As a matter of fact, I do," Ash said proudly. He reached into one of the inside pockets of his mess dress jacket and produced a card. "These are fresh off the press, courtesy of our executive secretary."

"I deal with outer office staff all the time, and I'll tell you: Miss Dubs is one of the best. She'll keep you out of trouble."

"She's already well into that with me. Like I said, I'm new to this staff work."

"If you're patient, the rewards can be great," Edeema said as he handed Ash one of his cards in return. "You may not know it yet, but you've been given access to something very special—magical, even. Now you work behind the curtain of power. You wouldn't be the first guy who couldn't go back to the other world after this."

"The other world?"

"One of my specialties is making aides' lives easier, Ash. Are you interested?"

"Easier?"

Edeema's focus went toward the house. "I see that Dottie Garrett is free. Let me say good-bye to her. We'll talk again soon, Ash. In the meantime, remember this: Life has a natural order that we don't always understand. Be true to the natural order." He disappeared into the crowd and then reappeared walking back up the steps into the house. Ash watched him, unsure quite what to make of the man. Be true to the natural order? What the hell did that mean?

One fact stood out in the SEAL's mind, however: Murdo Edeema was the first guy that day who—over the course of a conversation—hadn't asked him for office time with the admiral.

TWENTY-TWO

It was just after one-thirty in the morning before Ash urged the rental car along the curve of the on-ramp and started southbound on I-395 for the short ride back to Wild's condo. It had been a long day; tomorrow was going to be even longer. The flight for Panama was leaving from Andrews Air Force Base at six a.m. But before that he was going to have to go by the office to grab the updated daybook and get his final orders from Captain Bradford, then grab the driver, Yeoman Second Class Peabody, for the trip along the outskirts of town to pick up Vice Admiral Garrett at the Navy Yard.

Ash wondered if he'd ever feel rested again. He hadn't had a decent night's sleep since several weeks before the snatch-and-grab mission on the first night of the war. The prospects looked dim. He'd make it, though. He was trained to make it. From his earliest days at Basic Underwater Demolition School in Coronado he'd learned that sleep was optional for a SEAL. "I'm tired" was not on a SEAL's excuse matrix.

Before reaching the bridge across the Potomac, in spite of the draw of a warm bed, Ash considered turning toward Georgetown and Club Metro. Mess dress wouldn't be wholly inappropriate there; in fact, the sartorial impact might be just what the doctor ordered. Melinda would be unable to contain her desire, and there'd be only one way to settle that.

Ash's cell phone buzzed. If it was Wild calling, he was done for. That would be the push off the fence, the one that would ensure he'd forgo the possibility of even the slightest amount of sleep. He did the math in his head: Sprints, dancing, and the opportunity for the great sex he imagined based on last night's interrupted blow job and today's chance encounter or a flight to Panama without fighting the urge to vomit every ten minutes. *Goddamn you, Wild . . .*

But Ash read UNKNOWN on the ID window of his cell phone and knew it wasn't Wild on the other end, at least not Wild calling from his cell phone. "Ash is up."

"L.T., it's Senior Chief White again. Can you hear me, sir?"

"Yeah, I've got you, Billy. How do you read me?"

"I've got you, sir. We were cut off earlier today."

"Any idea why?"

"Gremlins, intel geeks, who knows?"

"Any more word on what happened to Steve-O and Go-man?"

"No, sir. I'm afraid I've got more bad news: Tang and Mac got it last night."

Ash jerked his car to the shoulder and skidded to a halt. His heart thumped, threatening to explode through his muscular chest. "Killed?"

"Yes, sir."

Ash banged his fists against the wheel. "*Goddamn,* Billy. How?"

"Drove a Humvee over a mine."

Dead air followed. Ash sat in the rental car on the side of the bridge, trying to process the information. "What kind of a mission was it?" he asked, balancing his attempt to compose himself with the fear that they had limited time before the call was cut off again.

"They were on their way to scout an area for an infantry battalion. They had a civilian escort they were following, some foreigner."

"Foreigner? What country?"

"Most of the contractors who have suddenly descended on the place sound French to me, but I don't know, exactly. This guy was supposedly an expert on where the mines were in that area."

"Some fucking expert. What did he say after the mission?"

"Nothing. He's gone."

"Where did he go?"

"Nobody around this place knows. He just vanished just like the Iraqis who vanished after Steve-O and Goman got killed."

"What the hell is going on over there?" Ash asked.

"That's what I'm wondering, sir. I know this is a war and people get smoked and all, but this shit is tingling the hairs on the back of my neck. And I've learned to trust those hairs; they've kept me alive."

Ash thought for another second and then asked, "Did those four do any other missions together after the one they did with us?"

"Negative."

"And had they ever worked together before they were with us?"

"No. We were all strangers, remember?"

"Yeah, I remember." The moment of their first meeting at Fort Bragg appeared in his mind's eye, which gave rise to another question: "Has that Army intel captain given you any feedback from that night, Billy?"

"No, sir."

"Nothing? Nothing on the photos we took? No word on what that place was that we stumbled over?"

"No, sir. Nothing. And I've hit him up a couple of times since you left."

Again there was silence across the thousands of miles

that separated them. Ash heard a sharp burst of static and feared they'd been cut off. "Billy?"

"I'm still here, L.T.," the senior chief said. "So, what do you think we should do?"

"I don't know," Ash replied. "Maybe we're making something out of nothing here. Maybe it's just a strange coincidence that those four got killed."

"All the same, I'll be keeping my eyes open. I respectfully recommend you do the same."

"Good advice."

"I'll be in touch, sir." There was a click, another burst of static, and then the line went dead.

TWENTY-THREE

Vice Admiral Garrett leaned across the table in the P-3 Orion's galley and spooned the last bit of chili from a Styrofoam cup into his mouth. "That's good stuff," he declared over the din of the four turboprops to the hulking lieutenant with the thick mustache whose flight-suited name tag read, appropriately enough, WALRUS.

The lieutenant turned from the sonar console he'd been staring into and said, "Thank you, Admiral. Eat as much as you want, sir. We'll keep that crock-pot fired up for the duration of this trip. The squadron is known wing-wide for its chili."

"Well, it's good to be known for something, I guess," Garrett said in return.

Ash saw the big lieutenant's brow furrow during his attempt to figure out whether or not he'd just taken a flag officer's verbal arrow in the chest. In the meantime, the admiral shifted his focus to his new aide. "Grab a seat over here, Ash," he said, pointing to the bench seat opposite the one he occupied at the rectangular table. "You got the daybook?"

"Right here, sir," Ash replied. Until very recently he

had carried a weapon; now he was drawing a daybook from his satchel.

"Unless you're already up to speed, before we go over the details of this visit, I'd like to give you a little background on what it is I'm responsible for. Or would that be a waste of time?"

"No, sir. I'm pretty clueless about that."

"I am the Joint Chief's Assistant Chief of Staff for International Relations. Fancy title, right? So what does it mean? Basically, I am the Pentagon's business development representative. I'm responsible for both ensuring the defense climate remains healthy for our existing allies, and seeking out new opportunities worldwide." The admiral's voice grew increasingly animated; a few words later, he sounded like he was addressing an auditorium full of people instead of a single lieutenant across a P-3's galley table. "I don't have to tell you, we live in uncertain times, times of remarkable and drastic change. My job is a perfect example: I'm only the third admiral to hold my billet. If you had told me a few years ago we'd have a flag officer involved in business development, I would have said, 'no way.'

"But the Department of Defense doesn't look like it used to. We're smaller, and shrinking by the day. But we've still got commitments—more than ever, in fact. The War on Terror isn't going away anytime soon. So we've started outsourcing. Now jobs that were traditionally performed by uniformed personnel are being done by the private sector. It's not good or bad; it's just different.

"My job is to make sure that the private sector stays aligned with the Defense Department's mission. The fact that we have contractors in the mix should be transparent to the nation. We're all one team headed for a safe and prosperous United States of America."

"That explains the lunch with the defense industry reps yesterday," Ash said.

"I have to maintain a productive relationship with our industry partners. A healthy defense industrial base is vital to our war effort. At the same time, I have to make sure they don't go off on some tangent. Like I said, I have to ensure alignment." Vice Admiral Garrett slapped his palms against the linoleum tabletop. "That's the quick and dirty version. Any questions at this point?"

"Why are we going to Panama?"

"Because Miss Dubs told us to, and I do whatever she says." The admiral waited a beat and then laughed. "No, we're going to Panama for an update on what they're doing to Howard Air Force Base. This is valuable real estate, four thousand acres' worth, and just because we turned it over to the Panamanians back in ninety-nine doesn't mean we don't have a stake in how it's developed. This place has all kinds of potential: industrial zones, residential communities, urban developments, even a third set of locks for the Panama Canal and a new port facility. So, we're not here, but we *are* here, if you get my meaning."

"Yes, sir. I think so."

"Well, if you're going to be my aide, you might as well have some idea about what it is I do." The admiral flipped the daybook open to the trip itinerary. "All right, let's see what we've got here. Is this land time in Panama local time?"

Ash had no idea—another function of having next to nothing to do with the planning for this trip. He'd never been so unprepared, even during his days as a boot ensign—even as a plebe at the Naval Academy, for that matter. "I'm not sure, sir."

The admiral was unfazed. He calmly checked his watch and did the math aloud: "Four hour time difference, five and a half hour flight. It must be local time." He flipped the page. "I see we're being met by the Naval Attaché and the Southern Command's SAO rep."

"SAO?"

"Security Assistance Organization. Southern Command used to have its headquarters in Panama. Once we handed the canal over to the locals, the powers that be decided that maintaining the level of presence there was too expensive for what we were getting out of it, so they moved back to Miami." He concentrated on the daybook again. "Have you ever met either of these guys?"

"No, sir."

"I'm not a big fan of either of them." He tapped on the attaché's photo. "Captain Keeler here has deluded himself with the idea that he's headed places, and Captain Fogerty hasn't met a superior officer's butt that he wasn't willing to kiss." The admiral looked up from the daybook and raised his eyebrows expectantly, gauging Ash's reaction to the information. Ash, slightly taken aback by the admiral's sudden shift in tone, tried to appear unmoved, as if a flag officer's offering him candid impressions was an everyday occurrence.

"When it's just me and you, Ash, you'll get nothing but straight, unfiltered talk," Garrett continued. "I hope that's okay."

Ash nodded, a bit stiffly, and said, "That's fine, sir."

"Good." He flipped another page. "It looks like we hit the ground running: Tour of power plant; tour of communications center; windshield tour of Panama City; dinner at ambassador's residence. Another easy day, huh?"

Ash chuckled politely as the admiral scanned the fuselage above their heads. "These P-3s aren't the fastest airplanes in the inventory, but they sure are solid. I'm glad my Hornet buddies can't see me, though. If they saw how much time I was spending riding around in prop jobs, I'd be thrown out of the jet drivers' club. Oh, well. The price for a ticket was right. You flown much?"

"Some," Ash said. "I've jumped out of a bunch of them."

"Oh, yeah, your last mission in Iraq, right?"

"Actually, my last mission didn't involve a jump. I had one more after the one you saw the misrep for."

"What was that one about?"

"Lying buried in the sand counting enemy tanks for two days. Not quite as exciting as the one before it."

"I guess not."

There was a lull in the conversation, and Ash used it as an opportunity to shift the discussion slightly: "Speaking of that mission, Admiral, I was wondering if I could discuss something with you."

Admiral Garrett nodded and said, "What's on your mind?"

Ash furtively glanced over his shoulder. Walrus was oblivious to everything except the blips and squiggles on his screen. "Something happened toward the end of that mission," Ash said, leaning into his forearms against the table. "Something kind of weird."

The admiral cut his eyes toward the front of the cabin and then back again. "What?"

"On the way out of Baghdad, our primary egress route was bombed out, so we had to divert to the north. We wound up coming across an industrial site in the middle of the desert, nowhere near anything else, really. The place was lit up like a stadium. There was all kinds of activity going on: cranes, trucks, towers, smokestacks. As we got closer the lights shut down and a pickup truck started after us, firing at us with a high-powered semiautomatic rifle. We eventually took it out with an RPG one of my guys had."

"What was it?"

"That's just it, sir; I don't know."

"What did intel say?"

"Nothing. The captain at the operations center said he'd check it out, but he never got back to us with anything."

Garrett's eyes narrowed. "What did you give him at the debrief?"

"The entire team gave a thorough recounting of what we'd seen. We also managed to take some digital pictures."

"Did you pass them the latitude and longitude of the site? It seems like with that they could cross-check against national source imagery and see what's there."

Ash shook his head. "No, sir, we didn't get that—not an exact location, anyway. Our GPS and comms gear died as we got in the vicinity."

"All of it?"

"Yes, sir."

"Still . . . you knew the general area you were in, right?"

"Plus or minus five miles, I'd say."

"And the intel guys said they couldn't find anything there?"

"No, sir. They didn't say *anything*. That's the problem."

Garrett pressed the tips of his fingers together. "Sometimes analysis takes time. I've always been impressed by the intelligence community."

"There's more," Ash returned. "My number-two man, a senior chief, called from the theater last night and told me that two more guys who'd been with us on that mission had been killed."

"Killed? How?"

"They drove over a mine with their Humvee."

"Damn, it never ends, does it?" the admiral muttered. "I'm sorry. Do you feel all right?"

"I'm fine, sir."

"As I told you before, I know how hard it is to lose men." His eyes momentarily lost focus as he thought aloud: "I wonder why SOCOM didn't call me."

"I got the call from Senior Chief White, my number-two man on that mission, late last night."

"Oh, sure," the admiral said with a wave of his hand. "Well, all that matters is that you got the word. Again, I'm sorry."

"Four of the six on that mission are dead now, Admiral."

"It doesn't seem fair, does it? But war's like that sometimes."

Ash paused. The admiral was missing his point, apparently. It was early in their relationship, and he didn't want to come off as too intense. He needed to build a measured case even if all he had at the moment was gut instinct. He took a deep breath and said, "The reason I bring it up is I thought you might know someone on the intelligence side who could help in getting some feedback on the photos we took on that mission. Those may be sitting in somebody's in-box, for all I know."

"An industrial site in the middle of the desert, you say?" Garrett asked, running his palm along the line of his jaw.

"Yes, sir. And I'm no expert, but if anything ever reeked of a smoking gun it was this place."

The admiral's eyes widened. "You've got to be careful here, Ash," he said. "This might be information that best resides above all of our pay grades, mine included. You just might not have a need-to-know on this one. Trust the system, son. I always have, and I've gone pretty far in the organization."

"It was *my* mission."

"And I'm sure your nation appreciates your efforts. I know I do; heck, that's why I hired you."

"Maybe if I hadn't left none of this would have happened."

"There's no use blaming yourself for something you had no part in, Lieutenant. I know this is a heartbreaker, but, sad to say, we've got a war going on over there." Garrett refocused on the daybook. "Now if you're up for it, I'd like to get back to reviewing this itinerary. . . ."

TWENTY-FOUR

As the last of the Orion's four propellers ground to a halt, one of the enlisted aircrewmen cranked a handle and pushed the side hatch open. Bright light streamed into the cabin along with a burst of hot, humid air. Through a small observation bubble on the left side of the aircraft, Ash could see a contingent gathered at the base of the boarding ladder. He noted that of the dozen or so huddled there, only one was in uniform.

"You know, I actually landed an A-7 here years ago when I was a lieutenant," Vice Admiral Garrett said as he stood and smoothed his khakis along the line of his belt. "We were doing an exercise in the Gulf of Mexico, and I had a hydraulic failure that forced me to divert here. That's back when this was Howard Air Force Base, of course. Not sure what it's called now."

Ash shoved the daybook into his nylon satchel and followed the admiral forward along the aisle. The pilots were waiting by the door just like they do on a commercial airliner, all hearty handshakes and bright smiles for Garrett as he passed into the intense sunlight and oppressive heat and started down the ladder. The pilots' cheery disposition faded as Ash reached them.

"Twelve o'clock sharp tomorrow, right?" the taller of them, a full commander, asked.

Ash dug for the daybook and said, "I think so, yes, sir."

"You think so? Let's make sure, shall we?"

Ash produced the daybook and said, "The itinerary shows twelve o'clock."

"Don't be early," the pilot warned. "And if you are, give us a call. Do we have your cell phone number?"

"I don't think my cell phone works in Panama," Ash said.

"Didn't you arrange for a local one?"

"I didn't but maybe somebody else on the staff did."

The commander turned to the other pilot and asked, "Does he have our number?"

"I gave it to the secretary a few days ago," the other pilot, a lieutenant commander, explained.

The commander shifted his attention back to Ash. "What are you, new or something?"

"Actually, I am," Ash admitted. "This is my second day on the job."

The commander's posture relaxed. "I was an aide a few years back. It's not so bad once you get the hang of it."

Ash nodded and shoved the daybook back into the bag. He slipped a pair of desert-spec sunglasses on and stepped through the door to rejoin Vice Admiral Garrett.

The pilot called after him with, "I'm serious, though. Find a phone and give us a call if the admiral wants to launch before noon."

The greeting party had engulfed Garrett by the time Ash's feet hit the tarmac. The lieutenant stood patiently, unnoticed for a time, and he used the opportunity to scan the surroundings. Just beyond the group was a line of vehicles, two sedans led by a pickup. A few hundred yards past the convoy was a series of round-roofed hangars and, behind them, a collection of symmetrical buildings that Ash figured were once the nerve center of a busy American Air Force base. In the distance, tall verdant hills reached into the blue sky dotted by white clouds that passed quickly overhead as they rode the hot Pacific breeze.

Ash turned a slow circle and noted the dense jungle that bordered the airfield on all sides. *This place would be a bitch to defend,* he thought. He tried to recount what he'd heard about Operation Just Cause, the short war that had been waged there in 1990. He did remember that some SEALs had been killed, but he couldn't recall the exact circumstance. What was Panama now, anyway? A democracy? A benevolent dictatorship? And what had ever happened to the ousted dictator? Was he still in jail in Florida somewhere? Ash felt a twinge of guilt: Here he was walking on Panamanian soil, and he didn't know shit about the current state of the place.

One of those on the outer edge of the greeting party moved toward him, a man about his age, trim, tanned, jet-black hair slicked straight back. He wore khaki slacks with black crosstrainers and a white polo shirt with UGS embroidered across the left breast. "Kurt Montana," the man said as they shook. "I'm a member of the security team covering the admiral's visit."

"I'm Ash Roberts, the admiral's aide."

"I figured that from the loop," Montana said, pointing at Ash's aiguillette. "I also see you're a SEAL."

"I am."

"I was too before I got out a couple of years back."

"Really? What team?"

"West Coast guy. How about you?"

"East mostly, although I just came off a joint assignment."

Montana narrowed his eyes and nodded. "See anything?"

"A bit on the first night. But I was yanked out of there to do this job pretty much right after that."

"That sucks, huh? Did you want to be an aide?"

"Are you kidding me?"

"I don't know. Some guys are motivated that way."

Another guy—bespectacled, bald, and jumpy—rushed up and shook Ash's hand. "Lieutenant, I'm Captain Todd Fogerty, Southern Command's SAO rep. We're going to start the admiral's visit with a quick tour of the telecommunications facility on the other side of the base. After that we'll swing by Captain Keeler's office so you and the admiral can change into civvies before we go out into town for the office call with the ambassador. How's that sound?" The captain hurried off without waiting for an answer, not that Ash had any objection to the plan.

Montana gestured over his shoulder and said, "Why don't you jump in with me for now?"

Ash started to throw the admiral's rolling suitcase into the bed of the pickup along with his own hanging bag, but Montana stopped him. "Here, let me take that one," he said. "We're paid to do that sort of thing for the admiral." He lifted the bag and eased it into the bed as if he thought the admiral was carrying eggs instead of underwear.

Ash had no sooner shut the passenger door than they were off at a good clip, leading the two sedans across the tarmac toward the hangars.

"What is UGS?" Ash asked.

"UGS?" Montana parroted.

"Yeah, it's on your shirt and the door of your pickup."

"Oh, yeah, of course. Unified Global Strategies. That's the company I work for."

"What is it, a private security firm?"

"It's a lot of things."

Ash started to ask another question but cut himself off as Montana stepped on the brakes, hard enough that Ash feared the sedan behind them might rear-end the pickup. Montana threw his door open and announced, "I need to get the rest of the security team before we start the admiral's tour. This will only take a second."

Ash climbed out of the cab and followed Montana across the concrete flight line toward the bay of one of the massive hangars. Ash noted the only aircraft parked in the hangar was a small helicopter wedged deep into one of the corners. The helicopter was also adorned with the UGS logo. At the center of the bay was a group of men—locals by the look of their brown skin and black hair—dressed in brown T-shirts and green fatigue trousers. Closer, Ash saw the group was ringed around a large padded mat upon which two men were squared off. One of the men looked much like any of those around him but the other looked quite different, tall with fair skin and close-cropped white-blond hair that ran down the side of his face in bright sideburns that extended to the bottom of his ears. Instead of a T-shirt, he wore one with a collar, light brown in color, like a safari shirt, with two big pockets on the front. The shirt was soaked with sweat; sleeves were rolled tight against his biceps.

"Kaas, the admiral is here," Montana called across those along the edge of the mat.

"Ja," the tall man shot back without taking his eyes off his opponent. *"Eine minute."*

The two men on the mat moved in a clockwise circle. The smaller man made a few feints, moves by which Ash gave him the speed advantage between the two.

"Come on, Kaas," Montana said, irritation growing. "We don't want to keep the admiral waiting."

The big man glared at Montana for just a second, but it was long enough to give his opponent the idea that he'd let his guard down. The smaller man lunged toward the other's torso—a great move, Ash thought, but the big blond moved aside faster than his large frame suggested he could. The aggressor hit the mat face-first with a loud splat, and before he could react, Kaas put a knee into the prostrate man's back between his shoulder blades, grabbed his hair, and drew an imaginary knife across his throat.

The blond man stood and barked the lesson to those around him as the man on the mat let out a just-audible moan: "Never make a move unless you are prepared to see it through. Now set Security Condition Alpha. Get to your posts!"

The recently vanquished trainee slowly got to his feet as the rest dispersed in all directions. The blond man threw a towel around his neck and stepped toward Montana and Ash.

"Ash, I'd like you to meet my associate, Kaas Leeuwendijk," Montana said. "Kaas, this is Lieutenant Ash Roberts. He's the admiral's aide."

Leeuwendijk shook Ash's hand and muttered a simple, "Hello."

"Kaas, was it?" Ash asked. "What is that, Dutch?"

"Afrikaans," Leeuwendijk replied. The ornament on Ash's uniform caught his eye. "You are a SEAL, eh? I should have let you have a go with some of the men . . ." He cut his piercing blue eyes toward Montana. ". . . although we are trying to keep them from developing bad habits."

Ash smiled politely and said, "You have a special operations background?"

"South African paratroopers."

"Is that a spec ops unit?"

"Yes."

"I don't think I've ever heard of them."

"That is the way we like it. Unlike the U.S. Navy SEALs, we do not want our pretty faces all over the cinema screens and videogames."

Ash sensed an intensity in the South African beyond simple parochial ball-busting, and at the moment he didn't feel like measuring dicks, so he changed the subject. "Are you with UGS, too?"

"In a way," he replied without offering any additional explanation.

Montana tapped on his watch and said, "Maybe you guys could continue this conversation in the pickup. Ash,

why don't you jump in the lead with Kaas? Kaas, let me
have the keys to your pickup and I'll follow behind the
two sedans."

Ash slammed the passenger door and Leeuwendijk
pushed the accelerator down. The convoy rapidly
wended its way through the hangar complex and onto
what looked to be one of the main roads through the
base. Leeuwendijk rode in silence, eyes glued through
the front windshield.

"It's hot down here," Ash said, both as a way to break
the awkward silence and to figure out who the hell this
guy was.

"Yes," Leeuwendijk said.

"I guess it's always hot here."

"Yes."

Ash hummed a nonexistent tune for a time, then
asked, "So, who were those guys, part of the Panamanian army?"

"If you can call it an army."

"Do they guard the airport?"

"They do what we tell them to do."

"Isn't this their airport now?"

Leeuwendijk negotiated the pickup through a turn before replying, "This airport is too important to leave to
them, just like the canal. What we let them think and
what is going on are two quite different things."

"Who do you mean when you say 'we'? The United
States?"

"The United States?" Leeuwendijk asked back, blond
brow furrowed. "I am from South Africa, *ja*?" He pulled
a cell phone out of his shirt pocket and mashed his
thumb against one of the keys. "If you have a cell phone,
you need to turn it off now."

"I don't have one," Ash said. "Is that a security
precaution?"

"Actually, it is so the phone is not damaged." Leeuwendijk pointed over the steering wheel to the thick
green jungle that surrounded them. "You can see how

close the tree line is to the buildings on this side of the base. We have a very sensitive motion-detection system in place around certain buildings. It will shut down most electronic gear: cell phones, radios—"

"Handheld GPS."

"*Ja,* exactly." Leeuwendijk focused back to the road in front of them. "Are you familiar with this system?"

"You said electronic gear, so I just figured—"

"Of course you are not familiar with this system," Leeuwendijk said. "The technology is proprietary."

The convoy entered a large parking lot and came to a stop. By the time Ash climbed out and walked over to where the admiral was standing, Captain Keeler had already commenced the tour: "This is a state-of-the-art fiber optic telecommunications center that interconnects all former and present military installations in Panama— a capability they didn't have during the Noriega regime."

Ash feigned interest in the captain's words, but his mind was miles away, back to the night in the desert. It had been less than a week, but it seemed like a few years now. He remembered how the SATCOM phone had fried, and how Billy's laptop and his GPS had gone screwy. Ash's eyes wandered along with his mind, and he was snapped out of his reverie by the cold gaze of Kaas Leeuwendijk on the opposite side of the group around Vice Admiral Garrett. Ash attempted to mask his transition back to the present; to hide how hard the wheels in his head had just been turning. He gave the South African a subtle nod, a friendly, insouciant gesture. Leeuwendijk nodded back, but the manner in which he did struck Ash as having little to do with being friendly.

The interior of the building was, as the admiral quipped, "cold enough to store meat." Captain Keeler explained that the temperature was kept very low because of the sensitive electronic gear throughout the facility. Past the check-in booth the group came to stainless steel double doors. The captain put his hand against an adjacent touch pad, and the doors swung open.

Inside was an expansive control room that reminded Ash of something NASA would have dreamed up. The far wall was covered by three large-screen displays, each highlighting various regions of Central America and northern South America. Red dots flashed at various spots about the map.

"This part of the tour is classified Secret," Captain Keeler said. "I don't have to tell you what parts of the world you're looking at on these screens. Our interests here in Panama extend down through Colombia and some parts beyond that occasionally. The red dots show the location of our teams."

"Teams?" the admiral asked.

"We call our field units 'response teams.' We currently have half a dozen teams in the field."

"What's their composition?"

"Each team has ten members, special operators of all flavors. A few locals are interspersed." The captain produced a laser pen and directed the beam against the center screen. "One of the teams, Team Foxtrot, here, is bigger because of the nature of the mission it's engaged in."

"What's that?"

"I'm sorry, Admiral, but I can't say. I could have you read in, if you wanted, but I doubt we have time for that with everything else we're trying to show you during your short visit."

"Don't bother. I guess if I needed to know about it, I would."

"Roger that, sir. Now I'll show you our mission watch officer station. It's very state-of-the-art. Remember the suite of gear you had at your disposal aboard the aircraft carrier when you were a battle group commander?"

"I do. In fact, my carrier was the first with a fully integrated digital tactical force command center."

"Well, imagine that command center on steroids."

Captain Keeler extended his arm. "This way please, Admiral."

Ash was in the procession between Montana and Leeuwendijk. As they threaded their way past the row of consoles manned by civilians wearing jackets with the UGS logo across the breast pocket, Ash drew closer to Montana and said, "What nationality are these guys?"

"It varies," Montana replied.

"So, who's managing this effort?"

"A private firm."

"*Your* firm?"

"A firm that my firm deals with."

"I see," Ash said, although the only thing he was beginning to see was that straight answers were hard to get from these guys at times. "Can I ask you about that motion sensor system we passed through on the way over here?"

"Extremely effective," Montana said.

"That's what Kaas was saying. Who's it proprietary to?"

"To the company that made it, I guess. Details beyond that start to hurt my brain." The former SEAL stopped and faced Ash. "I like what your admiral said: 'I guess if I needed to know about it, I would.' "

TWENTY-FIVE

Murdo Edeema put his hand to the touch pad next to the SCAR's door and waited to hear the click of the lock as the bolt moved out of the way. He pulled the heavy door open and, slipping into the space, was surprised to find Ned Reynolds seated at the conference table. No music played.

"Hold on, Paris," Reynolds said toward the speaker in the middle of the table. "Murdo just walked in." He considered Edeema with poorly muted irritation. "Can I help you with something?"

"I was looking for the file on that thing in Sri Lanka," Edeema said. "I thought I had it in my office but I can't find it. I figured I'd check the computer in here."

"Is it a classified report?"

"No."

"Then I doubt it's in here."

Edeema shrugged. "I just thought I'd check." He turned for the door but immediately twisted back toward Reynolds. "Do you need me to sit in on this call?"

"No, I've got it, thanks," Reynolds said.

"Who are you talking to?"

Reynolds gestured toward the phone, saying, "Please,

Murdo, I need to get back to this. I'll catch up with you later."

Edeema nodded and started to make his way out, but stopped himself as something on the conference table caught his eye. Under Reynolds' right elbow was a wrinkled sheet of paper, pressed flat. On the paper was handwriting, some of it lined through.

Reynolds noted Edeema's focus and methodically folded the paper in half.

"Is that Paris on the line?" Edeema asked.

"It's an operations call," Reynolds said.

"I'd like to sit in, Ned. You know it's the accepted practice for both of us to sit in on discussions at that level." Edeema pulled a chair away from the table and took a seat.

"This is really just a routine operation meeting," Reynolds said.

"That's fine. Don't mind me."

Reynolds directed his voice toward the speaker, saying, "Murdo is joining us, Paris."

The speaker was silent, and then someone with a French accent said, "We are done on this end, Washington, unless you have something else."

"No, I think I'm complete here." Reynolds reached over and disconnected the call. Without a word, he gathered his things and slid out of the SCAR, leaving Edeema alone.

TWENTY-SIX

The convoy was down to a single vehicle by the time Vice Admiral Garrett left the grounds of the former American Air Force base. Now the admiral was seated in the backseat of the armored Mercedes—the "hard car," as it was known—along with his aide, with Kaas Leeuwendijk behind the wheel and Kurt Montana in the passenger seat next to him. The sedan hugged the winding road across the north face of the foothills above Panama City, passing beat-up Chevys and donkey-drawn carts along the way.

The Mercedes crested the final hill, revealing the skyline of Panama City and the deep blue of the Pacific Ocean. "So, what does the ambassador want to tell me, fellas?" Garrett asked into the front seat.

Montana twisted to face the admiral and replied, "He's not happy with the funding levels for the effort down here."

"He has to understand the focus is elsewhere right now," the admiral said.

"I don't think he wants to understand."

"I thought it was your job to make him understand,

Kurt," the admiral snapped. "I mean, isn't that what we're paying you guys for?"

Ash tried to read between the lines of the exchange. Montana had said he was a security specialist, but there was more to his role—and presumably Leeuwendijk's—than simply guarding the admiral. The SEAL continued to listen while pretending to concentrate out the window on the line of roadside vendors standing before crumbling wooden stands. But however sly or unnoticed he thought he was with his feigned inattention, something about his body language cued the admiral to offer an explanation.

"I apologize, Ash," he said. "I know a lot of this has got to be confusing for you." He faced the front seat again. "I want you guys to know, Ash is fresh from the war."

"Yes, sir," Montana said. "We had a chance to talk a bit earlier."

"Good, good. You need to get to know these guys, Ash. They may be a product of outsourcing, but they're as close to teammates as you'll have in this job—as long as their contract gets renewed, anyway." The admiral snapped his fingers. "I've got an idea, Kurt: Why don't you guys host Ash tonight? It would give you a chance to get to know one another."

Montana nodded and said, "That's a great idea. Ash, you could come up to my place overlooking the city. It's a great spot to solve all the world's problems. We'll pick you up at the hotel when the admiral heads for the reception."

"What about the reception, sir?" Ash asked. "Don't you need me there for that?"

"No, I'll be fine," the admiral replied. "Those things are pretty boring unless you're talking shop or schmoozing the official party. Let them show you the town."

Ash cut his eyes toward Montana and asked, "Don't you two have to work?"

"We're not the only guys down here," Montana explained. "This is our night off, so to speak."

"Go on, enjoy yourself, Ash." The admiral turned to the others and laughed. "I can't believe I'm begging a junior officer to go on liberty, especially one who's just come back from a war."

"All right," Ash said. "Meet me out front at, what, seven or so?"

"Seven it is," Montana said.

"That's more like it," Vice Admiral Garrett said as he gave the lieutenant a wink. "I got a feeling you're going to enjoy getting to know these two."

Kurt Montana's villa was nestled into the southern side of a steep hill that afforded a breathtaking view through the two-canopy vegetation, across the high-rises of Panama City to the Pacific Ocean. The water was still and alight with a bright moon. Cooled by a slight breeze off the water, Ash took a sip of the margarita that Montana had concocted and did his best to decompress.

"Not a bad life, huh?" Kurt Montana said, threading his fingers behind his head and leaning back in one of the handful of overstuffed rocking chairs that dotted the expansive wooden porch.

"I wouldn't complain," Ash said. He glanced at his watch. "What time do you think the ambassador's reception will break up?"

"Not for a while yet," Montana replied. "Don't worry. You saw from the drive up here that the hotel is pretty close. We'll get you there in time to tuck the admiral in." He pointed to Kaas Leeuwendijk, nestled into another of the rockers on the other side of Ash. "You need to model yourself after that guy, learn how to relax."

"*Ja,* learn how to relax," Leeuwendijk repeated mechanically, the orange light from the torches around the edge of the porch flickering off his angular face.

"So who's got the security detail right now?" Ash asked.

Montana plucked a walkie-talkie off the table next to his chair. "They'll let us know if anything's going on."

Ash watched the ceiling fan spin above his head and asked, "How long have you been out of the Navy, Kurt?"

"Two years."

"Only two years and you live in a place like this?"

"UGS takes care of its employees, even entry-level employees."

"I guess you made a good choice."

"You could say that."

Ash lolled his head toward the South African. "Do you have a place around here, Kaas?"

"Nee," Leeuwendijk returned.

"Where do you live?"

"A lot of places."

"His schedule is brutal," Montana said. "It makes mine look tame."

"I'd like to settle down once I get out," Ash mused. "A little stability might be nice for a change."

"Overrated," Montana said. "You're a SEAL, Ash. Stability isn't what floats your rubber raft."

"Oh, yeah?"

"Yeah. Guys like you and me need anything but stability. We thrive on change and unpredictability. As soon as life becomes routine, we're on to something else. That's why this job is custom-made for us. Last night I'm kicking it in Cabo Saint Lucas, tonight I'm chilling with you dudes, having a cocktail and enjoying the best view in the hemisphere." He finished his drink before continuing. "Tomorrow? I don't know yet. Maybe I'll take a road trip to Costa Rica; maybe I'll jump on a plane back to Los Angeles; maybe I'll hang out in Panama for a few weeks. I've actually got a smoking local senorita who might appreciate that."

"How is the social life around here?"

"Impressive, as long as you stay along the resort strip down there. Outside of that it can get pretty sporty."

"Like what?"

"What you saw today was the nicer side of Panamanian life. There's a dark underbelly beneath the lush tropic exterior, things the high mucky-muck handlers would never let most visitors see. A lot of Noriega's former crowd are still around, Dignity Battalion alumni, dudes like that. Throw in a Colombian or two and you've got all kinds of things going on: drug trafficking, money laundering, bogus labor disputes, you name it. That's why we're here, though, to make sure those boys keep their noses out of our customer's interests."

"How do you do that?"

"Just like the old SEAL days: We do whatever the situation calls for." He paused, mouth twisted as he rocked back and forth in his chair a few times. "You know what's funny? You guys in the American special operations community pride yourselves on innovation, on not being bogged down by bureaucracy. I remember it well; it was a source of my pride as a SEAL. But the way you do business is a joke compared to what I'm doing now. Imagine a world where you could immediately get any weapon you needed, where all the latest technologies were at your disposal the minute they were manufactured. And imagine a world unburdened by the narrow limits of national interest. Complete and utter mission focus, man. That's where I operate every day."

"Aren't your customers aligned with national interests?"

"Usually, when that alignment is in synch with their efforts, of course." Montana shook a finger toward Ash. "I can see the wheels turning in your head. Let me ask you a basic question: Are you an American?"

Ash shrugged and replied, "Yes, of course."

"Well, there you go. Already limits creep in."

"Aren't you an American?"

"Who's asking?"

"Me."

"Then color me red, white, and blue."

The walkie-talkie crackled with static and a man's voice passed, "The reception is ending."

Montana reached over and grabbed the brick-sized device and replied, "Got it. Be right there." He lolled his head toward Leeuwendijk. "Kaas?"

The South African got to his feet and said, "*Ja,* on the way."

Montana rose as well, and shook Ash's hand. "It was great getting to know you better, Ash."

"You're not coming down to the hotel with us?" Ash asked.

"No, I've got some things to finish up here. Kaas will drive you down."

"So, we'll see you tomorrow at the airplane?"

"Ah . . . yeah. That's the plan, anyway; tomorrow at the airplane."

Ash nodded and swept an arm about the porch. "Again, this is quite a place you have here."

"No complaints. And good luck."

"With what?"

Montana paused, obviously a bit thrown with the need to put a finer point on his salutation. "Ah, with everything . . . you know, the aide job and all."

"Thanks."

"That job can be a springboard, you know. Opportunities might come your way."

"Opportunities?"

"Yeah." Montana sprouted a cocky grin, a SEAL's grin. "But don't waste any effort looking for them. You don't find these sorts of opportunities, Ash. They find you."

TWENTY-SEVEN

The Mercedes turned out of Kurt Montana's long drive-way and onto Avi Blanco, the street that wound down the hill toward Panama City's resort area. Behind the wheel of the car, Kaas Leeuwendijk remained as silent as he'd been during the hour he'd spent on Montana's porch. Ash had long since figured out that Leeuwendijk was a man of few words, but that didn't make the silence any less awkward. Plus, the day had left him with some unanswered questions.

"You get to Panama a lot, Kaas?" he asked.

"A lot? *Nee.*"

"How about South Africa? You get home much?"

"Sometimes."

"I've never been there, but heard it's pretty nice." Ash waited a moment or two before shifting the topic: "Hey, you know that motion sensor system around the communications center? Do you know what company makes that?"

Leeuwendijk brought his focus from the road to Ash then back again. "I work security."

"Yeah, I know. That's why I asked. I thought you might know."

"I do not."

"Are you happy with the system?"

"*Ja,* it works, if that is what you are asking." As they reached the base of the hill, Leeuwendijk pulled the pickup to the side of the road and parked. "We can walk from here."

Ash tossed his blazer across his forearm and grabbed his nylon bag. On the street the air was sticky; the hotels blocked the breeze that had made Montana's porch a comfortable place. Leeuwendijk's long legs set an insistent pace, which was fine with Ash in spite of the fact that he didn't want to soak with sweat the only civilian collared shirt he'd packed. The last thing he needed on his first trip was to be labeled a slob by his well-groomed boss.

Without any warning or explanation, Leeuwendijk crossed the street and turned into an alley between two of the high-rises.

"Where are we headed, Kaas?" Ash asked.

"Shortcut to the hotel," Leeuwendijk returned.

The alley reminded Ash of the one outside Club Metro in the Georgetown section of D.C. and that, in turn, brought Melinda to mind. Was it just the need for sex or was there a spark beyond that between them? Did she blow all of her boyfriends on the first date, or in his case had it been simple appreciation for his military service?

Ash's thoughts were interrupted when he was suddenly bumped from behind, and as somebody passed him in a sprint, his nylon bag was yanked off his shoulder.

"Hey!" Ash shouted to the silhouette rapidly moving away. "Give that back."

Leeuwendijk reached to the small of his back and produced a pistol. "What is in the bag?" he asked.

"Nothing, really, except the admiral's daybook and some other papers," Ash said.

"Wait here. These *straat jougens* do not play around."

Leeuwendijk ran off with his pistol poised, screaming, *"La parada, tengo una pistola!"* toward the heedless street urchin who disappeared around the first corner. Ash stood in the alleyway, watching the South African run away, feeling somewhat like a child unable to fight his own battles. He would've felt better with a pistol of his own.

Tires squealed from behind, and Ash looked over his shoulder into the headlights of a car bearing down on him at high speed. He tried to flag it down, but as he did, the car didn't stop but accelerated toward him, sparks flying as the quarter-panels on either side scraped against the bricks of the buildings. The alley was too narrow to attempt a dodge to the side, so he started to sprint for the same corner Leeuwendijk had just rounded. A second later, he shot a glimpse backward; he wasn't going to make it.

Ash faced the car and readied himself for impact. His training told him that the best way to absorb a vehicular assault was to jump above the line of the hood and try to roll across the windshield and down the trunk. Once he hit the ground, he knew, regardless of his injuries, he would have to get back to his feet and be ready to do the same move again going the other way when the car tried to back over him. Above all else he had to stay out from underneath the car.

One last option occurred to him. Ash looked up and saw a possibility: a fire escape ladder hanging down from the building on his left. But could he make it? In the split second before the car reached him, he leapt for all he was worth. His fingers were barely able to grasp the bottom rung, and he held on tight. Before he could draw his legs up, the roof of the car grazed his heels, sending him swinging about the ladder like a gymnast doing an uneven parallel bar routine.

Ash was relieved to see the car keep on going, but at the same time he feared the driver might be circling around for another pass. He pulled himself up the ladder until he reached the fire escape's first landing above the alleyway and then stood on the metal grating and leaned against the railing. He took measured breaths and tried to make sense of what had just happened.

A minute later, Leeuwendijk appeared from around the corner. Ash watched him from above for a time, gauging his reaction. The South African didn't seem overly confused or concerned by Ash's disappearance, but then again, Leeuwendijk wasn't much for overt emotions. He scanned the street to either side and then worked his attention higher until he finally caught sight of Ash and hailed, "What are you doing up there?"

"Dodging cars," Ash called back as he started down the ladder.

"Dodging cars?"

Ash hung from the bottom rung for a few beats and then dropped onto the cracked asphalt. "Yeah. You didn't see a sedan come hauling ass down the alleyway a few minutes ago?"

The American watched the other's eyes; he didn't flinch. "*Nee.* Where did he come from?"

Ash pointed over his shoulder. "From that way."

"Did he see you?"

"I don't know how he could've missed me. I was standing in the middle of the alley waving at him until it was obvious he wasn't going to stop."

"*Got verdammin,*" Leeuwendijk seethed. "The drivers here are very bad, I think. Perhaps we should make a report to the police. Did you get the license number?"

Ash let out a sarcastic chuckle and said, "Believe it or not, Kaas, I was too busy trying to avoid getting run over."

"Could you make out what kind of car it was?"

"Like I said, a sedan, older American car, Olds or Chevy, I guess."

"There are many of those around here."

Ash shrugged and said, "Let's just get to the hotel."

"*Ja,* follow me. It is just this way." Leeuwendijk took

a step and then stopped again and held out his arm. "Oh, here is your bag."

Ash took the bag and surveyed the contents. "Where did the guy go?"

"He dropped the bag and ran away."

"Ran away? Didn't you have a gun on him?"

"*Nee,* not really. He was just a young boy."

Ash momentarily studied the South African's expression but got nothing from it. There was silence between them for the rest of the walk to the hotel.

TWENTY-EIGHT

Murdo Edeema sat in his office sipping his second cup of coffee and reading the morning edition of the *Washington Post*. The war coverage was generally sanguine, at least more so than it had been over the last few days between the weather and the strained supply chain. Now the advance was on, a modern-day blitzkrieg of sorts. He searched beyond the headlines for some mention of weapons of mass destruction or "smoking guns," but only found a single line stating that nothing of the sort had been found. Then he read the list of the fallen. He'd been a player in a crazy world his entire life, but this conflict was going to take it to a new level, he feared.

Out of the corner of his eye he caught movement in the doorway, and he looked over and saw Ned Reynolds. "You were looking for me?" Reynolds said.

"Yes, Ned, come in, please," Edeema replied, throwing the paper on a nearby table and hopping to his feet. "Have a seat over here. Can I get you some coffee or something?"

"No, I'm fine."

"Have you had breakfast? I can have Allison get us some bagels or something."

"Bagels, huh?" Reynolds said, managing a weak smile. "This must be serious. You've never offered me bagels before."

Edeema shook his head and said, "No, it's not serious. I'm just a little curious about something, that's all." He shut the door behind Reynolds and sat facing him across a coffee table covered with papers and trade journals. "Look, Ned," he started, "you and I have worked together for some time now. We've done a lot together, a lot that benefited the company—the whole organization, for that matter."

"Yes, we have."

"Yes . . . we have. And I think a lot of what we've been able to accomplish is a function of how we work together, how we communicate. Would you agree?"

Reynolds curled his lower lip and said, "Sure."

"Well, I feel like we've stopped communicating."

"Really?"

"Come on, Ned. Secret phone calls, whispers in the night. We never used to do business that way. I know we don't agree on everything, but executives at our level should be able to express different points of view, don't you think?"

"Sure, Murdo."

Edeema's expression turned dour. "I refuse to be in the dark around here."

"Settle down, Murdo. Like I told you before: This situation is an operations issue."

"We're peers, Ned. Don't forget that."

"What's that supposed to mean?"

"It means I won't—"

There was a knock on the door. Allison, the receptionist, stuck her head in and said, "Ned, you have a call in your office. It's Paris." Reynolds acknowledged her with a quick nod and moved for the door.

"We should only head in one direction at a time, Ned," Edeema said to Reynolds' back.

Reynolds stopped in the doorway, and then turned and said, "We *are* only headed in one direction, Murdo. Which way are you going?"

TWENTY-NINE

As the P-3 Orion cruised northeast-bound at 30,000 feet over the Caribbean, Garrett pulled off the headset and climbed out of the co-pilot seat. He shook hands with the real co-pilot as the younger man passed on his way to retake his place in the cockpit and said, "Thanks for the stick time."

"No problem, Admiral," the lieutenant commander returned, threading his legs under the yoke. "You're still as smooth as ever, sir."

Garrett beamed and slapped him on the back. "It's like riding a bike, I guess."

The pilot-in-command called over his right shoulder: "We'll be on deck in Norfolk in just over four hours, Admiral."

"All right, Commander," the admiral returned. "I'll have to see if I can't polish off the chili by then. Mrs. Garrett will be loving me after these two days." Both of the P-3 pilots laughed and slapped the glare shield in front of them.

Ash waited at the crew station across the aisle from what was normally the mission commander's station but on this trip had become the admiral's desk. Once the admiral seated himself and got settled, Ash handed him a stack of papers.

"I went hard copy with a couple of messages that Captain Bradford forwarded to you, sir," Ash said. "And I also printed out the latest Pentagon news clips."

Admiral Garrett winked and said, "You just might get the hang of this aide stuff." The admiral put on his reading glasses and shuffled through the stack, then turned back to Ash. "So, what did you wind up doing last night?"

"We went to Kurt Montana's house."

"That's a good connection for you to have. He was a SEAL, you know."

"Yes, sir, he mentioned that."

"Had you met him before?"

"Before this trip? No, sir."

"Was Leeuwendijk there?"

"Yes, sir."

"Both good men, I think. You can rest assured if those two are around nothing bad is going to happen."

Ash narrowed his eyes. "I'm not sure that's true, sir." The admiral twisted his face in confusion as the SEAL continued: "Last night I barely missed getting run over by a car."

"Run over? Where?"

"In an alley near the hotel."

"Were you by yourself?"

"No, Kaas Leeuwendijk was with me, although he wasn't there when the car came by."

"Where was he?"

"He was chasing down a local street kid who stole my bag."

Admiral Garrett's face evinced the confusion that Ash heard himself inducing even before he'd finished his last sentence. "Did the driver see you?" the admiral asked.

"I'm pretty sure he did."

"What did you do? How did you get out of the way?"

"I pulled myself onto a fire escape above the alley-way."

The admiral leaned into the aisle, resting his elbows against his knees. "You've got to watch yourself in these countries sometimes. Thank God you weren't hurt."

Ash swung his legs around so he was facing his boss. "Admiral, part of the reason you hired me is because I'm a SEAL, right?"

"That's right, sure."

"Well, over time I've learned which hunches to ignore and which ones to honor. There are things going on that don't feel right."

"I know about honoring a hunch," Garrett said as he gave the top of Ash's leg a friendly whack. "Remember, son, I flew jets for a living for twenty-five years. Naval aviators appreciate the wisdom of trusting a hunch."

"I'd like your help in finding out what happened to the photos my team took that night in the desert," Ash said.

The admiral thought for a moment, and then said, "I could make a call or two on that."

"Also, I need to be issued a weapon for these trips."

"What kind of weapon?"

"Nothing huge. A pistol."

"An aide with a gun, huh? Never heard of that before."

"Well, Admiral, if I may say so, times have changed for all of us."

"I wouldn't even know how to get a pistol."

"I'll take care of it, sir. I may need you to sign some authorization forms, but that'll be it."

"You wouldn't carry it in the Pentagon. . . ."

"No, sir. Only when we're out of the country."

"Let me think about it. Is that it?"

"One more thing: We need another guy like me when we go on the road."

"Another aide?"

"No, sir, somebody who can watch my back—and therefore yours, of course—if things get interesting. I'm talking about another special operations type, preferably a SEAL. Perhaps you could call the personnel bureau and make somebody else a by-name call. You were able to get me easy enough."

"That's true, but to make a by-name call I have to have a name. Do you have anyone in mind?"

A wry smile spread across Ash's face. "As a matter of fact, Admiral, I do."

THIRTY

Ash was low on razors and deodorant, so he took advantage of a lull in the midmorning action and made a trip down to the shops along the Pentagon's concourse. On his way back to the office, somebody called him from behind: "Hey, sailor, can I buy you a cup of coffee?" He turned and saw a well-dressed older man approaching with a smile. A few steps closer, Ash placed the face.

"Hello, Mr. Edeema."

Edeema smiled and said, "Impressive. I usually have to bribe people to get them to remember my name. Got a second?"

They moved to one of the chest-high circular tables next to a nearby kiosk, where Edeema asked, "Regular coffee?"

"I'll get it."

"No, no, my treat."

"Black, please."

"Of course, black. I apologize for even asking. I've been hanging around with Air Force guys too much lately, I'm afraid."

A minute later Edeema was back with two large paper

cups sheathed in brown cardboard. "So, what brings you to the Pentagon?" Ash asked.

"Just making the rounds," Edeema said. "Boring stuff, really. Nothing a young man of action like yourself would find very interesting." He peeled the plastic lid off his cup and asked, "How about you? How's life in the puzzle palace going?"

"I'm barely treading water," Ash said. "Just got back from Panama last night."

"Really? Good trip?"

"I guess."

"Meet the ambassador?"

"Briefly."

"He's a good man."

"You know him?"

"Very well. We did some work together in the early days of Homeland Defense."

"You know everybody, don't you?"

"No," he said with a smile, "but I'm working on it." He tasted his coffee before dumping in another packet of artificial sweetener. "Anybody else interesting down there?"

"Not really. I spent a lot of the time just hanging out with the security guys."

"Military?"

"No, they worked for a private company."

"Now that sounds like a fun job. I understand they do pretty well salary-wise."

"From the look of this one guy's place, I'd have to agree."

"This War on Terror is an opportunity-rich environment for folks with your skill set. Ever thought of taking to the private sector?"

"Not really."

"Yeah, why would you? Your Navy career is going great, obviously. Only the best get the opportunity to be an admiral's aide, not to mention a three-star's aide."

"If you say so."

"I *know* so. All the same, you might want to keep your options open. Like I told you at the admiral's house, if you're interested, I can help."

"I haven't had time to think about what I'm interested in. These last few days have been a blur of riding in planes and dodging cars."

"Dodging cars?"

"I nearly got run over in an alley in Panama City."

"Run over? By what?"

"A beat-up Chevy or something."

"Did they see you?"

"I don't know how they could have missed me."

"Was anyone else with you?"

"Not at the time. The security guy had just run after a local kid who snatched my bag."

"*Damn . . .*" Edeema trained his eyes toward the clock above Ash's head. "I've got to go. I've got a meeting across town." He finished the last swallow of coffee and shook Ash's hand. "I have your card; in the meantime, be careful."

Ash watched Murdo Edeema rush away again, and as he did, he realized that he still had no idea what the man actually did for a living.

THIRTY-ONE

Miss Dubs studied the day's menu card as the elderly black waiter stood attendant, hands clasped in front of him. She was having trouble making up her mind. The movement of her penciled-on eyebrows told a tale of indecision—elegant indecision, but indecision, nonetheless.

"Is this the normal navy bean soup?" she asked.

"Yes, ma'am. It's real good," the waiter said.

"Is there ham in it?"

"Yes, ma'am, of course."

"What kind of ham is it?"

"Virginia ham. That's the only kind Marvin uses in his recipes."

"It's not too salty, is it?"

"I don't think so, no. I had a bowl myself today."

She tapped a narrow finger against her thin red lips. "Okay, I'll take a cup of that, but make sure there's not too much ham in it, please, Jensen. And then I'll have a house salad with chicken strips."

"Yes, ma'am, very good. And you, sir?"

"I'll just have a hamburger."

"Very good, sir."

Jensen walked away, and Ash took in his un-Pentagon-like surroundings. The burnished wood paneling, heavy drapes, and silk tablecloths gave the room a feel similar to the restaurant in downtown D.C. where the admiral had joined the defense industry reps. Had that really been just two days ago? It seemed like a week or two.

"This is a nice place," Ash said.

"The Flag Mess?" Miss Dubs returned. "Yes, it is nice, isn't it? This is definitely one of the perks we have for the hectic life we lead on the admiral's staff."

Ash reached for the carafe of iced tea at the center of the table and charged both glasses. "So how long have you been working here?"

"At the Pentagon?"

"Yes."

"Oh, well, let me think." Her eyes went to the ceiling. "I started working here about twenty-five years ago. My first job, believe it or not, was working for the Navy as a budget analyst, which is one of the reasons I'm partial to Navy people. Anyway, after working the money side for a few years I had an opportunity to fill in on an admiral's staff for a person who was out sick for a few weeks, and that was that. I've been working on flag staffs ever since."

"Do you enjoy it?"

"I doubt I'd still be at it if I didn't. Of course some days are better than others, but usually it's a very rewarding job."

"I know Vice Admiral Garrett appreciates what you do. He's constantly saying he does whatever you tell him, and half the time I'm not sure he's kidding."

Miss Dubs chuckled. "That's very kind of him. He's a good man. And he enjoys traveling, which is one of the keys to success in that job. Some of those before him didn't take to it as well."

"How many admirals have you worked for in this job?"

"Well, the billet has been restructured and renamed a few times, but the basic answer to your question is ten."

Ash shook his head. "You really are the corporate knowledge."

"I've seen a thing or two, that's for sure. I've also seen the bosses learn some lessons along the way that I'd prefer the next one doesn't repeat."

Jensen delivered Miss Dubs' navy bean soup, and she stirred the cup's contents with a spoon as she continued to speak: "Have you heard the expression 'war is too important to be left to the generals'?"

"I guess I have somewhere or other."

"Well, there you go." Miss Dubs blew across the first spoonful of soup before putting it into her mouth. She dabbed her dimples with a napkin and said, "Listen to me. I'm just a secretary, for pete's sake."

" 'Just a secretary'?" Ash said. "From what I've seen so far, the office couldn't function without you. I know *I* couldn't."

"Well, grooming aides is a big part of what I do, I guess. I certainly enjoy watching your progress as you go along after you leave. This job is quite a stepping stone, you know."

"I have been told by more than one person that having an aide tour under your belt is great for a military career," Ash said. "In fact, Vice Admiral Garrett mentioned that he was an aide."

"That's true, but from what I hear, the billet you're in now can lead to success out of uniform, as well."

"Oh, yeah? Doing what?"

"Oh, I don't know. Any number of things, I guess. Getting a job in the civilian world is mostly about who you know, and after a few months as the aide, you'll get to know a lot of people. With the right amount of drive and ambition, there's no telling where those sorts of contacts can take you."

"I've got pretty good connections through my family already."

"Really? What business?"

"Shipping and finance."

"That sounds quite lucrative."

"Sure. But the idea of working in an office, especially an office in the heart of Manhattan, just doesn't do it for me."

"Who says being a civilian means you have to work in an office? I'm sure there are jobs that would suit your need for adventure plus reward you with a healthy salary. It seems to me that more and more, the government is privatizing things the military used to do. Depending on your point of view, a young man like you might find that rather exciting."

Miss Dubs' statement reminded Ash of a conversation he'd had a few hours earlier. "Have you ever met a man named Murdo Edeema?" he asked.

"Murdo Edeema? Of course. Everyone knows Murdo."

"What is it that he does, exactly?"

"He's a consultant."

"Right, but what does that mean?"

Miss Dubs pursed her lips and stirred her soup again. "It means he consults. Washington's full of them. But Murdo's different than most, I must say. He's a dear man." Miss Dubs grabbed a package of crackers from a wicker basket at the center of the table and tore it open. "I hate to change the subject, but we should probably talk about your trip tomorrow."

"What trip?"

"The one to the Congo."

"The Congo? The African country, the Congo?"

"That's the one. It'll be a great experience for you. By the time you get back from that one, you'll know a lot about how those things go."

"The Congo? Tomorrow? I didn't see that on the calendar."

"No, you didn't. It was just added on."

Ash shook his head in disbelief. "A no-notice trip to Africa, huh? Why are we going to the Congo?"

"Because I said so. That's why the admiral does everything, remember?" Miss Dubs kept a straight face for a few seconds but then smiled. "No, it's because the admiral has been tasked by the Secretary to go over there. They're afraid the war on terror might shift from the Middle East to Africa if they're not careful. Apparently there's been a recent intelligence finding about a uranium mine over there or something." She shot a furtive glance over each shoulder. "Oh, my. I'd better watch what I talk about in here." She ran her thumb and forefinger along the line of her mouth and then made a twisting motion at her dimple. "Mum's the word."

"Great, another trip where I'm going to have no clue. The admiral's going to love me." Another thought hit Ash: "I wonder if we're going to be able to incorporate the changes I requested in time for this trip?"

"Changes?" Miss Dubs asked in return, eyebrows forming dual arches across her forehead.

"I wanted to add a guy to our traveling roster," Ash explained. "Another SEAL I know. I also need to carry a weapon of some sort during these trips."

Ash saw Miss Dubs' complexion quickly grow red through her white pancake. "Why these changes?"

"It's a long story, but the bottom line is the admiral was okay with the requests."

"The admiral agreed?"

"Yes, he did. I gave him a name to ask the Bureau about—a friend of mine who's on the Joint Staff."

"He didn't say anything to me about this," Miss Dubs snapped. "We work as a team around here. Lieutenant Dubois has to write the travel orders, and I have to process them with the travel request. I don't have this new person on there, and they won't be happy on the other end if someone shows up they didn't know about. And you can't just go carrying guns around. This isn't Iraq, you know." She dropped her fork, pushed away from the table, and stood up. "Excuse me, but I've got some more work to do now." She checked her bejeweled watch. "And don't forget you have to get the admiral over to the Army-Navy club for that Navy League speech in an hour."

"I already have the forms for the pistol," Ash offered, but she was already on her way out of the mess. Ash took a bite of his hamburger, in spite of the fact that his appetite had just left him. He felt guilty as he watched the diminutive woman stride purposefully away. The last thing he'd intended with his requests to the admiral was to frustrate the person who was arguably the most important member of the staff.

He polished off the last of the iced tea and then sat chomping on a piece of ice, eyes unfocused, mind adrift. He pondered how long it would take for him to grasp the complexities of life in the Pentagon and how many other people he'd piss off before he did.

THIRTY-TWO

Ash had just managed to remove Melinda's thong when a heavy knock rattled the door to Wild's apartment. Melinda bolted off the couch, covered herself with a large throw pillow that had been kicked onto the floor, and said, "I thought you said Wild was working late."

Ash considered his now-dying erection under his gym shorts and moaned, "He was supposed to be." He ran a hand through his mussed mop of hair and pointed to his left. "Why don't you wait in the bedroom and I'll see who it is." She nodded and dropped the pillow. He watched her shapely ass disappear into the adjacent room, then threw on a T-shirt and stomped over to the door and peered through the peephole.

In the fish-eye view he saw a well-groomed white man in a suit, holding a clipboard. Ash cracked the door to the length of the locking chain and asked, "What can I do for you?"

"Hello, sir. How are you this evening?" the man asked with a nasal whine. He was thinner than he'd appeared through the lens, skeletal, even.

"Busy," Ash replied.

"Of course, sir. I work with the management company for the building here. Can I come in for a second?"

Ash shrugged and removed the chain. The man ambled into the apartment. In the light of the apartment his pallor shined pasty-white, nearly translucent. He wore too much sickly sweet cologne. Ash gestured toward the lounge and then took a seat on the couch he'd just shared with Melinda in passionate embrace.

The man settled his gaunt self into the chair and looked over his shoulder toward the kitchen. "Do you have any coffee?"

"I'm not sure where it is, if there is any. This isn't my apartment."

"Oh, you're not the tenant?"

"No, Willie Weldon is the tenant. I'm staying with him for a few days."

"Oh, fine then. I'll try to come back when he's in. Do you know when that might be?"

"No. He works pretty long hours over at the Pentagon. There's no telling."

"Fine." The man's eyes walked around the apartment, and Ash saw them lock on the ceramic hard-on perched on the shelf. The thin man grew a sheepish grin and said, "Impressive. You?"

"No," Ash returned, doing his best to ward off the creepy vibe that had suddenly blanketed the room. "I've really got to—"

"Well, I'll tell you what. As long as I'm here, could I ask you a few questions?" He reached under one of the lapels of his suit coat.

"How long will this take?"

"Not long." There was a thump from the bedroom. "What was that?" he asked as he withdrew his hand from his coat.

"My girlfriend's in the bedroom," Ash explained. "She's asleep."

"It doesn't sound like she's asleep." The man got to

his feet and stepped quickly to the door. "I'm sorry to have bothered you, sir. I'll come back another time."

Without any more chitchat, the man left. Ash peered through the fish-eye and watched him disappear down the hallway without stopping at any of the other apartments. He stood behind the door contemplating the quick visit until he remembered Melinda was waiting in Wild's bedroom. He hurried across the apartment and found Melinda supine on Wild's bed, naked and inviting.

"Who was that?" she asked.

"Some guy from the apartment management company," Ash replied.

"What did he want?"

"I'm not really sure."

"Is there a problem?"

"I have no idea. Now, where were we?"

With that Ash ran his tongue along the inside of her thigh until he reached her downy mound and buried his face into her. He felt her writhing beneath him, lifting her ass off the bed as she bucked with pleasure. She was obviously as ready as he was; the fireworks were going to be incredible, perhaps record-breaking.

There was another rap on the front door. He stopped moving but didn't draw back. Maybe whoever it was would get the hint and go away. The rapping turned into banging.

"You have absolutely got to be shitting me," Ash said as he sat up on the end of the bed.

"I guess it just wasn't meant to be," Melinda said, hands behind her head, sexy body remaining on full display.

"No, that is not true," he said with a raised index finger. "It *will* be. Just give me a second to get rid of whoever it is."

Again he waited a moment for his erection to descend before traipsing across the room to answer the door. Another view through the peephole revealed no one. "Who is it?" he asked through the door.

"It's Wild," a voice called back. "Open up, asshole; I forgot my key."

Ash called back to the bedroom: "Melissa, it's Wild." He undid the chain, and as he twisted the doorknob, the bigger SEAL burst through the door and tackled Ash, throwing him against the carpet. Wild straddled Ash's rib cage and wrapped both hands tightly around his throat.

"I got one question for you, motherfucker," Wild bellowed, nose nearly touching Ash's. "Why the fuck am I going to Africa tomorrow?"

THIRTY-THREE

Not only was the C-9 Skytrain faster, quieter, and smoother ridewise, the sleek jet had better creature comforts than the P-3 Orion. This particular Navy version of a commercial airliner was fitted with what the crew had called an "Alpha package"—a special configuration in the forward half of the cabin with a handful of captain's chairs, a conference table, several desks including an executive desk for the admiral, and even a bed. The back half of the jet was loaded with the traditional economy-class array of seats, which were dotted by a dozen or so sailors and Marines hitching a ride to Lajes, Azores, where the Skytrain was gassing up before continuing to the Congo.

Ash lounged in one of the captain's chairs and opened the daybook, but before he started reading, he stared out the window, down at the Atlantic Ocean more than 30,000 feet below, growing darker by the minute as the sun disappeared below the horizon behind them. Across the cabin in another captain's chair, Wild sat fast asleep with the tiny headphones from his MP3 player tucked into his ears.

"This is a little better, huh?" Vice Admiral Garrett

said, startling Ash a bit as he came unannounced from behind him. "I do miss the chili, though."

"No chili, but I'm sure the food will be better, too, sir," Ash said.

"We'll see. In any case, as far as your ongoing aide education goes, these first two trips are good examples of what the Assistant Chief of Staff for International Relations does. It boils down basically to two things: I need to keep an eye on places we've already attacked to make sure they don't reemerge as problems, and I need to assess places we might be forced to attack in the future if things get out of hand. Make sense?"

"Yes, sir," Ash returned with a nod.

"This isn't just window dressing we're doing, either. In spite of what critics are saying, our president has established what we're calling the 'Global Peace Operations Initiative.' " The inflection in the admiral's voice had suddenly changed again, as it did every time he began to wax big picture. He was now testifying before Congress or perhaps working the wonks on the convention floor. "This five-year plan has a six hundred and sixty million dollar budget to train seventy-five thousand peacekeepers."

The statesman's spirit left Vice Admiral Garrett as quickly as it had arrived. He plucked the daybook from Ash's grasp and began paging through it. "So, what the hell are we doing over the next day or so in this place we might be forced to attack in the future?"

"I really haven't had a chance to—"

"You know much about this area of the world?"

"No, sir, not really."

"Never operated there, huh?" The admiral tossed a thumb over his shoulder toward Wild. "What about him?"

"I don't think so. I'm sure he would've told me about it if he had."

The admiral sat down on the edge of the conference table. "Well, I'll tell you what I know about the place.

For starters, most people don't realize that the Congo is actually two countries: the Republic of the Congo and the *Democratic* Republic of the Congo. You know which one we're going to, right?"

A no-notice quiz on a no-notice trip. Perfect. Ash didn't know the answer, and just like the flight into Panama, he was struck by how much he didn't know about the region he was about to descend upon. He had a fifty percent shot to get it right—worth a guess, he figured. Well, given the choice they'd certainly visit a place where democracy was part of the program. "The Democratic Republic?" he said, unintentionally in the form of a question.

"Nice guess, Lieutenant. Here's question number two: What did the Democratic Republic of the Congo used to be called?"

Damn, no multiple choice this time. Ash wanted to explain to the boss that he'd been highly trained as a Middle East specialist and that training had come at the expense of knowledge of other parts of the world, especially non-Arabic-speaking, non-Muslim parts. But the admiral stood expectant; he wanted an answer to question number two.

"Uh . . . just plain Congo?" Ash guessed.

"*Uuuurrrrrnnnnt!*" the admiral grunted, doing his best imitation of a game show buzzer. "Zaire. And do you know the bottom line behind why are we going there?"

"Because Miss Dubs told us to?" Ash said, hoping that humor might end the examination.

"You learn well," Garrett said before quickly losing the smile. "No, really." So much for humor.

Ash took a breath and said, "She did mention something about a uranium mine and SECDEF's fears about terrorists getting their hands on the stuff."

"Bingo." The admiral pushed off the table and paced up and down the aisle as he spoke: "You see, this is what's going on today, Ash: We're tying up the loose ends caused by years of neglect and ignorance in our foreign policy. Look at where the problems are: all the areas we didn't pay attention to after the Cold War ended. And when you're talking about terrorists instead of conventional militaries, it gets even tougher because these organizations can grow and flourish in places that even our best intelligence sources can miss."

Garrett turned another page of the daybook. He rubbed his brow and said, "Touring an abandoned uranium mine, huh? And it looks like we're flying a bush hopper across the country and spending the night in a camp. This really will be an adventure. Did we pack for this?"

"Chief Wildhorse knew the itinerary," Ash said. "I reminded him to pack some cammies for you."

"Did you pack some for yourself?"

"Yes, sir."

"I guess they'll have whatever else we might need out there. I'm always up for an adventure, but I don't know about getting too close to uranium. I hope I don't grow a third eye on the way home or anything."

Ash chuckled politely as Admiral Garrett focused on the sleeping Wild. "You know, I caught holy hell from Miss Dubs over this guy," the admiral said. "She really loses it when we bypass the normal procedures."

"I appreciate the effort, sir."

"No problem. Sorry we weren't able to get your gun request approved. There just wasn't enough time."

The admiral started to move away, but Ash stopped him, saying, "Sir, were you able to find anything out about that matter we talked about on the plane back from Panama?"

"What matter?"

"The intelligence feedback from my mission in Iraq."

"Oh, yeah. No, I haven't had time to make any calls on that yet. I will though, I promise." He pointed toward the back of the cabin. "Now if you'll excuse me, I'm going aft for a few minutes to talk to some of the troops back there. I like to see what's on their minds."

Admiral Garrett handed the daybook back and walked down the aisle toward the denser seating in the back of the jet.

Ash watched the boss stride aft and greet the first sailor he came to. They shook hands and began to chat—the admiral animated and cheerful, his manner putting the junior man at ease. Soon they were both laughing. Garrett performed a similar feat with the next man and the one in the seat behind him and so on, until the back half of the airplane was alive with new warmth. For the time being, the troops had stopped moping about those they'd left behind. At that moment they were special, respected and appreciated for their sacrifices and talents. With everything Vice Admiral Garrett had on his plate as one of the front men in the war on terror, he hadn't lost sight of what was really going to get the job done once the orders came. It was an impressive display of leadership; the kind Ash wouldn't have given most flag officers credit for.

Ash reopened the daybook and skimmed the itinerary and the bios for the cast of characters who were about to enter their lives. Behind the bios was a State Department write-up on the Democratic Republic of Congo, not to be confused with the Republic of Congo, as he now knew. Along with the requisite statistics regarding population, acreage, commerce, and agriculture, the report contained the most recent classified assessment of the military and the political landscape. The historical overview read like a Mario Puzo novel with a uniquely African twist—colonialism, overthrows, crime, corruption, betrayal, assassinations, and wars between tribes, rebel gangs, or both. Fun place, no doubt. He was happy to have Wild along.

THIRTY-FOUR

Senior Chief Billy White sat in the backseat of the Humvee and wondered where all the helicopters had gone. He preferred the speed and agility of a terrain-following helo insert—zorching along at one hundred and forty knots fifty feet off the deck. Riding overland to get to an op cold sucked. It was too slow, and it gave a guy too much time to think.

And not only did a helo get him there faster, if it crashed along the way it would have been a quick death. That wasn't the case on the ground, especially not in the company of regular Army. Anything could happen in a convoy lumbering along at forty miles an hour—on civilian roads, no less, with civilian cars zooming by occasionally as if the American military descending on Baghdad was an everyday occurrence.

"Are we there yet, Micro?" White called to his Delta Force teammate, who was riding shotgun.

Micro yawned and straightened his legs, pushing himself into the seat while stretching his short arms along the Humvee's canvas roof. "At least it's daylight," he returned. "This is the first mission I've been on in a while where even part of it was during the day."

"That's a good point. I guess I should just sit back and enjoy the scenery, right?"

"Right, just sit back, relax, and enjoy this beautiful countryside." Micro pointed across the Humvee's door. "There's a dirt hut, and there's another one, and another one. And look, over there is a tree."

Sit back and relax. Great idea, except that once he crossed into Iraq, Senior Chief White knew better than to let his guard down, regardless of how smoothly things seemed to be going. Too many buddies had died of late; too many questions were left unanswered.

"Actually, parts of this country are really beautiful," the driver, who looked old enough to be any of their grandfathers, said.

"Really?" Micro said, a bit shocked that after three hours of driving the man finally had spoken. "You been here before?"

"No, of course not." The driver raised his sunglasses and wiped the dust out of his eyes with a red bandanna tied to his flak jacket. "So how long are you guys riding with us?"

"Just up the road a piece," the senior chief replied.

"Oh, I get it," the driver said. "Classified stuff. You snake eaters are always doing ops you can't talk about, right?"

"Something like that."

"That explains why the convoy master was being such an exacting prick before we started on the roll this time. 'You're number four in the line,' he kept telling me, like I'm some sort of idiot or something. 'Make sure you keep your position.' "

"This guy in your unit?"

"No, he's a contractor."

"Are the convoy masters always contractors?"

"It's been about half and half since the war started. I guess it depends on what we're hauling and where we're going."

"Was this contractor American?"

"He didn't sound like it—had some kind of an accent."

"French?"

"No . . . well, maybe. But what do I know? I'm just a lowly reservist."

"You're a reservist, huh?" Micro said. "What do you do in the real world?"

"Orthodontist."

"No shit. For real?"

"Yep. Last year I bought out both of my old partners and started my own practice."

"Hell, son, what are you doing over here, then?"

"That's kind of a long story, but let me just say that an ortho doesn't make as much as you might think. I also needed a steady stream of income, however little it might be, when I was getting the new business going."

"What do you mean orthodontists don't make as much as we think? Didn't you do braces?"

"Of course."

Micro pointed toward his mouth. "You see these teeth? The missus swore our kids wouldn't have these teeth, so I paid for back-to-back brace jobs. Cost me a goddam fortune."

"Boys or girls?"

"Girls."

"Then you saved a fortune; in fact, you didn't just save money, you made money—maybe as much as fifty thousand dollars a year."

Micro leaned forward in his seat and winced. "Fifty thousand dollars? What the fuck are you talking about, doc?"

The driver's eyes were distant and unfocused as he mused, "Doc, huh? I like the sound of that. It seems like a long time since anyone called me that."

"Never mind that. How am I going to make fifty thousand bucks a year?"

"Easy. Rich guys don't marry girls with buck teeth."

"That doesn't matter to Micro's daughters," White said. "They're both headed for the convent."

"Damn straight," Micro said. "Hey, I've got another question for you, doc. What is that big long thing sticking off the front of the lead truck in the convoy?"

"Wire cutter," the driver replied.

"Wire cutter?"

"Yeah. A couple of the first convoys moving north discovered a little trick the local like to pull: They bury a wire cable in the sand and hide on either side of the road until just before the convoy drives up and then pull the cable taut at driver's head level. We've already lost a couple of guys that way. A few days ago, some of our guys broke out the welding gear and stuck those wire cutters on the front of the lead vehicles."

"Smart move."

"So how old are you, doc?" the senior chief asked.

The driver looked over his shoulder and asked, "How old do I look?"

"Oh, no," Micro said. "We ain't playing that shit. We've still got to ride together for a while."

"I'm fifty-one," the driver said.

"Damn . . ."

"Is that 'damn, he looks good for that age' or 'damn, I would have guessed older'?"

"I told you, we ain't playing that shit."

As Senior Chief White laughed and shook his head, he noticed movement out the right side of the Humvee. Across the ditch that lined the road and beyond several hundred yards of parched earth, a white pickup emerged from a grove of palm trees. He stuck the barrel of his M-4 out the window and asked, "Micro, you see that guy?"

"Got him," Micro returned.

Even at long range, Senior Chief White could see that the pickup was too cherry to have been in country for very long. "Doc, get on the radio and tell your fifty cals to watch this white pickup to the right."

"Will do," the driver said. He plucked the radio handset from where it hung against the dashboard and transmitted: "Potato Lead, this is Potato Four, over; Potato Lead, this is Potato Four, over."

"Go ahead, Potato Four," somebody replied.

"Potato Lead, Potato Four's passengers want to know if you see the pickup to the right of us."

There was a slight pause and then, "We see the pickup. What about it?"

The driver shot a glance over his shoulder and echoed: "What about it?"

"Get your gunners to put eyes on and be ready to fire if need be," Senior Chief White said, trying not to lose his temper with the nonchalance of the others.

"He wants you to watch him," the driver passed into the handset.

"Will do," the voice said back.

"What do you got, Chief?" another voice asked, a voice White recognized with a grimace. The mission lead didn't strike him as the sharpest tool in Delta Force's box. Among other things, the Green Beret captain had consistently refused to make the distinction between chief and senior chief. White yearned for the likes of Lieutenant Roberts to rejoin their elite ranks.

The senior chief leaned between the front seats and gestured for the driver to hand him the mike. "White pickup east of us just came out of the trees, Captain. Want to keep an eye on him."

"Roger that."

The pickup paralleled their path for a time, kicking up a trail of dust. Then, without warning, the vehicle sped up and made a hard left.

"He's crossing the berm," the captain said over the radio. "Take him out."

Gunfire erupted all around them, with both the senior chief and Micro adding to the hail of bullets flying at the pickup. White saw several shots ricochet. Amazingly, the windshield remained intact and the tires stayed round. Closer, he saw that a whip antenna had been mounted just behind the cab.

"There's nobody driving the damn thing," another voice reported over the radio.

Remote control? Who was controlling it and where was he? "Aim for the motor," the captain commanded. But the bullets skimmed off the hood like flat rocks across a pond. Senior Chief White quickly judged the closure between the unmanned pickup and the Humvee he was riding in, and he wasn't happy with the results: The two were on a collision course.

There was no time to stop or swerve. The radio crackled with something unintelligible. The occupants of Potato Four only had one option left.

"Bail out!" Senior Chief White shouted. He hugged his rifle to his chest and dove over the left side of the Humvee. He hit the ground hard and started tumbling. Everything was a blur; there was a bright orange flash. The senior chief's last sensation before the lights went out was a searing blast of heat against the back of his neck.

THIRTY-FIVE

The Skytrain finally came to rest after taxiing for what had seemed like miles, and Ash spotted the first indication of where they were—a sign mounted on the face of a modest, if not rundown, terminal that read BIENVENUE À N'DJILI AÉROPORT INTERNATIONALE. It was just after six in the morning local time, and in the low light Ash could see baggage handlers and a couple of soldiers with automatic rifles slung over their shoulders moving across the tarmac around the jet.

The second leg of the flight after the fuel stop in the Azores had been just over three hours long, and Ash had joined the admiral and Wild—the sole remaining passengers aboard—in getting some sleep as the jet hurtled through the night. When the aircraft commander announced they had started their final descent into the Democratic Republic of the Congo, Ash looked out his window, unable to tell if they'd crossed the African coastline; the absence of cultural lighting below made it impossible to differentiate the continent from the ocean.

Now Ash stood up in the aisle and ran his thumbs along the top of his belt line, straightening the wrinkles of his khaki shirt. He grabbed the black bag and started to follow Vice Admiral Garrett out of the jet when he noticed that Wild was still slumped in his captain's chair, fast asleep.

"We're here, Wild."

The big SEAL jerked upright, slinging a chain of drool as he did, and said, "I'm good. Let's get to work."

Again, the pilots faced Ash on his way out of the jet, but this time he was ready. Daybook in hand, he announced, "We'll meet you here tomorrow, five o'clock p.m. local." He handed the senior pilot a card. "This has got all of our contact information during our time here on it. If you have any concerns, you can reach me at either or both of those numbers." Each pilot looked at the card and then they looked at each other and nodded their understanding.

It was not yet unbearably hot outside but it was already oppressively humid. At the base of the roll-away stairs was a contingent nearly twice as large as the one that had met them in Panama, made up mostly of men with coal-black skin dressed in suits and ties. Several had bright-colored sashes across their chests. The man in front, who also happened to be the widest among them, greeted the admiral as he stepped to the ground.

"*Bonjour,* Admiral Garrett," he said, "and welcome to the Democratic Republic of the Congo. I am Joseph Kuma, DR Congo's deputy foreign minister."

"Yes, of course, Deputy Minister Kuma," the admiral returned as they shared an extended and vigorous handshake. "I'm honored to meet you and very pleased to finally have the chance to visit your great nation."

Deputy Minister Kuma gestured toward the gaunt, white-haired white man to his right: "This is Mr. Oogalong, a representative from the United Nations' International Atomic Energy Agency."

Ash didn't remember a Mr. Oogalong among the biographies in the daybook, but the admiral seemed unfazed. "Certainly, Mr. Oogalong," he said. "And may I begin by passing on our president's keen desire to assist the U.N. as together we work tirelessly to make the world a safer place."

"Hear, Hear," Oogalong added in a high-pitched voice. "We are especially thankful that you could make it during a time when your country is engaged in combat actions elsewhere."

"Well, you know, Mr. Oogalong, better now with notebooks than later with tanks."

A line of vehicles pulled up—two black Mercedes sedans bracketed by white pickups with the UGS logo on the doors. Behind the wheel of the lead vehicle was a now-familiar face.

"Kaas Leeuwendijk . . ." Ash muttered under his breath.

"Who?" Wild asked from over Ash's shoulder.

"I met him in Panama. He's a private security guy from South Africa."

"Good dude?"

"More like *mysterious*."

Leeuwendijk climbed out of the pickup and made his way over to Ash. He was dressed exactly as he had been in Panama, right down to the baggy shorts. His hair looked blonder than before, nearly white, perhaps because he also looked more tanned than he had a couple of days ago.

Without a handshake or pleasantries of any kind, the South African said, "You ride *met* me; the rest can get in the hard cars. Put the admiral in the second one." He spun on his heel and started back for the pickup.

Ash saw the lead pickup had an extended cab, so he pointed over his shoulder and asked, "Can he ride with us?"

Leeuwendijk turned back around. "Who is he?"

Wild extended a big arm from behind Ash and said, "Lieutenant Willie Weldon. Friends call me 'Wild Willie' or just 'Wild.'"

Leeuwendijk shook Wild's hand but looked over at Ash and said, "What is he for?"

"He's helping me with force protection."

"Now it takes *two* of you to do the job, huh?" the South African said with a laugh. "Okay, he can ride *met* us." He waved an arm toward a black soldier standing behind the official party and shouted, *"Venez!"*

Ash and Wild started to schlep the parties' bags from the jet to the pickup, but Leeuwendijk stopped them just as Montana had stopped Ash in Panama. "We must carry the luggage," the South African said. "It is in the contract. The locals get very upset if we violate the contract."

Ash raised his arms and said, "Be my guest. I'd hate to be the one to violate any contracts." Leeuwendijk hailed a couple of the baggage handlers, and the men scurried over and snatched the bags off the tarmac and hauled them the fifty yards between the jet and the bed of the pickup.

The core of the official party split up between the two sedans, Vice Admiral Garrett climbing into the second one as Leeuwendijk had directed. Ash figured the front seat of the pickup had more legroom, so he slid into the backseat. Wild slammed the door shut, and they were off.

After being waved through two security checkpoints they took a right on a four-lane labeled with a large sign as the BOULEVARD LUMUMBA. Besides the occasional rusty truck or decrepit bus crowded with people inside and out, there was no traffic along the road dotted with little but unsightly palm trees. Leeuwendijk set a fast pace as he led the convoy down the left lane.

"Well, Kaas, you sure are making the rounds, aren't you?" Ash said.

Leeuwendijk attempted eye contact using the rearview mirror and asked, "What do you mean?"

"I mean you have covered a lot of miles in the last few days."

"So have you."

"I know, but I go wherever Vice Admiral Garrett goes."

"And I go wherever my contracts tell me to go."

Thoughts of Leeuwendijk's contracts reminded Ash of the other security guy he'd met on the last trip. "Did Kurt Montana make it for this one?"

"Nee."

"Where is he?"

"I do not know."

"So how far is it to . . . Kinshasha?" Wild asked.

"Kinsha-*sa*. Twenty-five kilometers. The Grand Hotel is on this side of the capital, so it will not take too long to get there."

Ash pulled the daybook out of his bag and flipped it open. "The Grand Hotel, did you say? I thought we were staying at the Kinshasa Regent."

"Rebels set fire to the Regent two days ago. There was quite a bit of damage. The Grand Hotel is better anyway."

"Are rebels a problem here?" Wild asked.

"You could say that, *ja*," Leeuwendijk replied. "You are not very familiar with the recent history of this country, are you?"

"No, not really. Our focus has been on another part of the world for the last few years."

"That is a mistake you Americans always make, *ja*? Focus on one place and ignore the rest of the world?"

"That's not true," Wild shot back. "It's a matter of priorities and assets."

"Actually, it is a matter of racism and resources. These people have black skin and no oil. Why would you have any interest in them?"

"Oh, that's beautiful: a South African white guy lecturing me about racism?"

Ash suddenly felt compelled to act as an intermediary between the front seat occupants. The last thing he needed was for his by-name call to get in a fight with the head of the security detail two minutes out of the airport. The admiral certainly wouldn't have been impressed with that sort of international engagement.

"Okay, Kaas, we're ignorant," Ash said, which caused Wild to shoot an angry look over his shoulder at him. "So how about giving us a quick and dirty overview of the situation here?"

"Overview, eh?" Leeuwendijk said. He was silent behind the wheel for a time. Ash could see the wheels turning in his blond head. He delivered a body of facts in his typical no-nonsense fashion. "Refugees come here in 1994 from Rwanda and Burundi. Political power shifts. Tribes fight. Marxist dictator is overthrown. Surrounding countries—Angola, Chad, and others—attack the new government. President is assassinated. His son takes over. And here we are."

It was the longest single statement Ash had heard Leeuwendijk make in the short time he'd known him.

"Is the civil war over?" Ash asked.

"The situation is unstable."

"What about this uranium mine we're touring today?"

"What about it?"

"Is it closed up, or what?"

"It is closed up, and my company has been hired by Oogalong's people to ensure that it stays that way."

"What's with all this private hiring stuff?" Wild asked. "What happened to governments protecting their interests?"

"The government cannot even provide security for visiting dignitaries; you think they could manage to keep a uranium mine shut?"

"I'm not just talking about here; I'm talking about everywhere. Even America is hiring companies to do work government employees or the military used to do."

"I do not see that as a problem. These companies are getting the job done."

"So, what are we looking for in terms of threats to the admiral?" Ash asked, hoping to change the subject.

The South African paused again before offering his answer: "Anything is possible."

"Oh, good. That narrows it down," Wild said.

"Well, let me put it this way, Kaas," Ash said. "Who might have a problem with an American admiral around here?"

Leeuwendijk looked in the rearview mirror again. "Are Americans liked anywhere these days?"

Without slowing down or offering a warning of any kind, the driver took a hard right turn onto a narrow dirt road bordered by tall grass, tangle bushes, and groves of palm trees. They bounced down the road at a hurried pace, and Ash looked out the back window and saw that the hard cars were eating dust but in position. He wondered how smooth the rides were in the Mercedes sedans across the unprepared surface and how the admiral was faring in the backseat of the second one.

"You think we ought to ease the pace a smidge?" Ash asked.

"Speed is the best way to avoid an ambush," Leeuwendijk replied. "UGS drivers are well trained. They will keep up."

"Is this the way to the hotel?" Wild asked, one hand against the roof to keep from bumping his head.

"No, this is the way to the school," Leeuwendijk said.

"What school?" Ash asked.

"The school we are visiting."

"I didn't see anything about a school visit on the itinerary."

"This was a last-minute decision. Mr. Oogalong wanted the admiral to see one of our projects. Besides, deviating from the published itinerary is a good security measure."

The convoy came to a clearing and slowed down. On the other side of the open area was a compound of some sort—a couple of two-story buildings with a covered walkway between them. The architecture of the buildings was unique—thin pillars stood vertically along the outside every ten feet or so, and small windows dotted

the upper quarter of each floor. The upper balcony
stretched across the length of the building, and railings
ran the full height of the story, giving the structure the
look of a prison. The roofs, including those over the
walkways, were dense thatch.

Once the vehicles came to a complete stop and the
dust cleared, Ash could see a stream of children pouring
out of doorways at each end of the buildings, running
toward them for all they were worth. They were dressed
in what he assumed was the school uniform: boys in blue
shorts and girls in blue skirts. All wore white collared
shirts that looked even whiter against their dark skin. A
handful of them were missing legs below their knees.
Land mines, no doubt.

Leeuwendijk jumped out of the cab to greet all of
them like a father back from a long voyage, extending
his arms wrapped around as many as he could manage
with each embrace. Ash was surprised to see such ten-
derness from the South African. The children began to
chant "Kaas, Kaas," in unison, waving their little fists
like supporters at a political rally.

"Kaas has done great work with these children," Oogalong said as he escorted the admiral and the rest of
the party to where Ash and Wild stood watching the
scene. "As you can see, they have really taken to him."

"What is this?" Garrett asked. "A private school or
something?"

"No, Admiral," Oogalong said, raising his soprano
voice to be heard as the children closed on the group.
"This is an orphanage. All of these children lost their
parents to either war or AIDS."

Leeuwendijk raised an arm and all around him fell
silent. He began to clap out a beat that reminded Ash
of the song "We Will Rock You." The children enthusiastically followed his lead for a few measures and then
began to sing in French. As they sang, Ash studied the
South African's beaming smile. He looked like a differ-

ent man, relaxed, gentle. The song ended, and they all cheered.

The children suddenly grew quiet as a man with a string of animals' teeth around his neck and a cheetah pelt around his waist waded among them. In his right hand he held a long, intricately carved walking stick. In the man's company were half a dozen soldiers cradling AK-47s.

"Mfuma ya ntoto," Oogalong said to the man, greeting him with a handshake and a quick peck on either cheek. "Admiral, this is the village chief."

Garrett hesitated for a second; Ash sensed he was wondering whether he was supposed to kiss the chief as well. The chief eased the tension by simply extending his hand and saying in perfect English, "Thank you for coming, Admiral. The children and I appreciate you taking the time to see us."

Ash saw the admiral's eyes dart as they shook; he still wasn't sure why they were there. "Sure," the admiral said, tentatively. "No problem."

A wave of guilt washed over Ash. He was still new at the aide job, but he was sure this was the sort of awkward circumstance he was supposed to prevent. "The right place, at the right time, wearing the right uniform, and *saying the right things* . . ."

"The chief is many things to the people of this region," Oogalong explained. "He is the judge of civil matters and the protector of ancestral lands."

"Really?" the admiral said, obviously still fumbling for something to say. "How did you get the job?" Ash tried not to wince.

"I know people," the chief deadpanned.

Oogalong laughed and said to Garrett, "We wanted you to get a full appreciation for the range of our efforts in this country. These Kenyan soldiers are part of the U.N. peacekeeping force and are supplemented by private security where required throughout the region. In this case, the same firm that supplies the private security built the school, hired the teachers, and provided everything they needed to get started—books, sports equipment, everything." Oogalong swept an arm in a broad arc. "We have the full support of the Congolese government. The idea is to give the next generation here more hope than their parents had."

"Very noble, Mr. Oogalong," the admiral said. "Very noble, indeed."

THIRTY-SIX

Reynolds didn't bother looking away from the computer screen as Edeema approached him in the SCAR, which allowed Edeema to study the wrinkled piece of paper sticking out of Ned Reynolds' effects on the other side of the conference table. Edeema thought he'd seen the paper before. He leaned across the table and snatched it from between a manila envelope and a leather portfolio and kept one eye on Reynolds as he brought the sheet closer to his face.

A single column of six handwritten items, four of them lined out. The fifth was circled. The handwriting was a scrawl worthy of a doctor—incredibly hard to read.

"What the hell do you think you're doing, Murdo?" Reynolds asked.

"There are six names on this list," Edeema said.

"What makes you think you can root through my papers?"

"I made a simple request, Ned," Edeema said, waving the sheet in front of him. "Leave the officer alone"

"I have no idea what you're talking about."

"Bullshit. *Les Affreux* tried to run him down in Panama a few days ago."

"I don't know anything about that."

"Sure you don't. I don't like being lied to, Ned."

"And I don't like being badgered by a has-been smuggler."

Edeema felt the anger welling up inside of him. He worked to keep himself calm as he moved across the SCAR toward Reynolds, but by the time he reached him, he couldn't help but yield to his impulse. Exclaiming, "You little bastard," Edeema reached down and balled his fists into the other man's oxford shirt, yanking him out of the chair and to his feet.

"Take your hands off of me," Reynolds seethed as he grabbed Edeema's wrists.

"I deserve a little respect around here," Edeema said, squeezing harder. "I've given my life to this company. I've earned my place."

Reynolds grew a twisted smile as he pulled Edeema's hands free. "That may have been true once, but times are changing, Murdo. Besides, word has it your lieutenant would never be a good fit for us."

"That's impossible to say at this point. I've just started working with him."

"The organization is changing, too, Murdo. All of your glad-handing and schmoozing—what does it get us?"

"Access. Talent."

"Really?" Reynolds held up the wrinkled sheet of paper. "I got these and I didn't have to attend a single reception. Your methods are dated."

"And throwing large sums of money at informants is something anybody could do."

The two men squared off, a tense silence hovering between them. Finally, Reynolds worked his palms along the front of his shirt in an attempt to smooth it and then stepped away, wrinkled sheet in hand. Across the room, he tacked the paper to the wall with a pushpin and stepped out the door without another word.

Edeema sat motionless, and then walked to the wall

and stared blankly at the wrinkled sheet of paper. He snorted a sad chuckle to himself. Obviously, a lot had gone on without his input—too much. Such a binary business, winners and losers. But he'd already resolved that he wasn't going down without a fight. He had a trump card that would either see Reynolds destroyed or take the organization down altogether. And perhaps that was the better option. Killing was coming too easily now. Legal or not, the business used to have elegance about it, a moral conscience.

Edeema pulled a business card from his wallet and dialed his cell phone. No answer, so he left a message: "Lieutenant Roberts, this is Murdo Edeema. I need to talk to you as soon as possible."

THIRTY-SEVEN

Closer to the city, a river appeared, bordering the highway to the north. Several miles later the river widened into a bay, and across the bay Ash could see a skyline. "What city is that?" he asked, pointing out the right side of the pickup.

"Brazzaville," Leeuwendijk replied. "The capital of the Republic of the Congo."

"What's the difference between here and there?" Wild asked.

"They have oil."

"Oil? How much?"

"Not as much as the Middle East—otherwise I am sure your president would have already ordered an invasion."

Ash saw Wild's head jerk with the comment, and he subtly reached over and tapped his friend's shoulder and shook his head at him. Wild's expression in return told of a man ready for a battle of ideologies, but he yielded to Ash's judgment. All the same, Ash was already concerned about the chemistry between the two. Wild wasn't one to suffer anti-American sentiments without a fight. Actually, Wild didn't suffer much of anything without a fight. Ash had a quick flashback to the day Wild had single-handedly dispersed a crowd of protesters as they attempted to burn an American flag in front of the Coronado Amphibious Base's main gate. The dozen-plus assault charges against him in the wake of the event had nearly sidelined his SEAL career before it had even started, but cooler heads and a high-priced attorney had prevailed.

The streets narrowed and the buildings closed in as the convoy reached the heart of Kinshasa. The city was rumpled but not dirty, destitute but attempting pride. The buildings were unremarkable, plain structures—flat-roofed and earth-toned. Bare spots outnumbered patches of grass in the squares. There were a lot of trees, the majority of them palms.

As they crossed intersections, Ash caught glimpses of the River Congo at the end of the streets, and, on the other side of the water, the skyline of Brazzaville, hazy now in the distance. People shuffled in front of the modest shops marked with amateurish hand-painted signs along either side of the street without paying much, if any, attention to the convoy as it passed. Most looked down at the ground in front of their feet. No one smiled.

Around the next corner Ash spotted the Grand Hotel's entrance. Leeuwendijk turned into a narrow lane lined with manicured hedges and brought the pickup to a quick halt in front of another gatehouse, albeit more upscale than those at the airport, save for the sandbags stacked up around the base of it. The South African exchanged some French with the guard and flashed a paper, and the guard shouted to another, who hefted the red-and-white striped pole up from across the lane.

At the entrance they were greeted by a platoon of bellhops in short pants and top hats, which looked strange and reminded Ash of the way the midshipmen used to dress up for pep rallies. The bellhops lined up in a row and stood at attention, like an honor guard. Leeuwendijk peered into the rearview mirror, waiting for the last car to stop before he climbed out of the cab.

Outside of the pickup, the thick air offered a Third World potpourri of scents, most of them unpleasant—brackish water, rotting fish, and animal dung. But beyond the odors, the hotel compound was a world away. The grass on the median and the center of the roundabout in front of the hotel was as lush and manicured as that on the fairways of a private country club. There was an abundance of trees, none of them palms. Gold trimmed every surface.

Ash started to reach for the bags in the bed of the pickup, but again Leeuwendijk stopped him. "These bellboys get even more upset than the baggage handlers if someone else carries the luggage. In the Congo it is an insult if someone does your work for you."

Ash backed away and watched two of the black men in top hats unload the bags. Vice Admiral Garrett came up behind him and said, "Is that a pool I see beyond those hedges? I wouldn't mind an hour or so to cool my heels."

Ash started to move for the daybook, which was stuck in the nylon bag near the rest of the luggage, but before he could reach it, Leeuwendijk stepped over, armed with room keys, and said, "We are short on time, gentlemen. Your bags will be brought to your rooms right away. I need you to change into your cammies and meet me back in the lobby in ten minutes."

"Where are we going?" Ash asked.

"To the uranium mine."

"Already?"

Leeuwendijk tapped his wrist and said, "They expect us in four hours. We should not be late."

The South African showed the party through the large revolving door at the hotel entrance and into the lobby. Ash had expected animal skins on the floor and tribal shields against every wall, but the expansive space showed nothing that might have distinguished it from the inside of any other luxury hotel he'd seen. It was clean, ornate, and upscale, but the decor didn't make any attempt at local flavor. And maybe that was the point.

The group was waiting for one of the three elevators to reach them when Ash realized he still didn't have the daybook with him. On the other side of the lobby he saw the bellhops stacking the luggage on a dolly, so he went over to find his black nylon bag. Halfway across the marble floor, he watched one of them wheel the dolly into a room behind the front desk and shut the door.

Ash reached the door and opened it after rapping a quick set of courtesy knocks. The bellhop was crouched on the floor and looked up, obviously startled. In his hand was a silver object, a bent pipe of some sort with industrial-sized bolts around either end of it. Without a word, the bellhop stood and pushed the door shut in Ash's face.

Ash was about to knock again when a hand clamped down across his shoulder. "The elevator is here," Leeuwendijk said. "Everyone is waiting for you."

"I just wanted to get the daybook," Ash explained.

"Daybook?"

"The book with all the information in it."

The door reopened and the dolly with their luggage rolled into view. "Be my guest," Leeuwendijk said with a sweep of his arm.

As Ash dug for his black nylon bag, he noticed that one of the pouches to the admiral's bag was unzipped. He furtively glanced over his right shoulder and, seeing that Leeuwendijk's focus was momentarily elsewhere, he pulled the pouch open and peered inside. There was something resting against the bottom of it, a copper-colored ring.

With another look behind him, Ash snaked his hand into the pouch and grabbed the ring. It was too big for his hand to completely cover, but he managed to transfer it to his nylon bag without drawing anyone's attention, including Leeuwendijk's. In turn, Ash removed the daybook from the bag and, with a smile, waved it in the South African's direction, saying, "Here it is."

THIRTY-EIGHT

The twin-engined turboprop barely cleared the trees at the departure end of the dirt runway as it launched from the remote airfield beyond the city limits north of Kinshasa. "This thing could use a little more giddy-up, eh, Kaas?" Vice Admiral Garrett said, doing his best not to evince concern as he looked down to the ground across his right shoulder pressed against the front passenger door.

"Not a problem," Leeuwendijk replied, urging the yoke forward, further decreasing the aircraft's rate of climb.

"I didn't realize you were a pilot, too." The admiral twisted around and asked his aide, "Do you know how to fly, Ash?"

"No, sir," Ash replied.

"This Kaas is the total package, huh? So where exactly are we going?"

"Shinkolobwe, in the Katanga Province, near the border with Zambia," Leeuwendijk said.

"How far is that?"

Leeuwendijk punched a button on the GPS duct-taped

to the instrument panel and said, "Just over five hundred miles to the southeast."

"I guess we're going to log some flight time, then."

"Not that much." The South African patted the black plastic glare shield. "She is faster than she looks."

"Good," Wild called from the third row, the aft-most pair of seats. "I'm not a big fan of little planes."

"Little? We're carrying five people plus luggage and equipment."

"I hate to break it to you, total-package dude: This is a little plane."

The admiral looked over his shoulder and said, "Now, Mr. Oogalong—"

"Please, Admiral, call me Boga."

"Boga . . . what does that mean?"

"It doesn't mean anything. Boga is my first name."

"Boga Oogalong, huh? What kind of name is that?"

"What kind?"

"Where are you from?"

"Norway."

"Oogalong doesn't sound Norwegian. It sounds Australian or something."

"I promise you it's Norwegian, sir. In fact, there are quite a few of us around Vest Fiord."

"Boga Oogalong," the admiral repeated.

"What is the name of your organization?" Ash asked.

"The United Nations," Oogalong replied.

"No, not that. The deputy minister mentioned something about an agency when he introduced you at the airport."

"You mean the International Atomic Energy Agency."

"That's it. What exactly is that?"

"The I.A.E.A. is the U.N.'s nuclear watchdog organization. We're involved in stopping uranium trafficking worldwide."

The plane suddenly banked hard to the left, and Leeuwendijk directed the passengers' attention out the left side. "Look, down there."

"Ah, yes," Oogalong said as he braced himself against the side of the fuselage. "You see that clearing down there? This time last year that was thick jungle."

"What happened to it?"

"Refugees." Leeuwendijk returned the airplane to level flight as Oogalong continued: "Since 1998 the wars have spawned nearly two million refugees."

"Man, look how they've torn it up down there," Wild said. "They're like locusts."

"Those are human beings, lieutenant," Oogalong said over his shoulder. "And they need our help."

"Right. That's what I meant."

With that, the conversation died. For the next few hours Wild slept, Vice Admiral Garrett paged through the daybook, and Ash occupied himself by splitting his focus between the GPS taped in front of Leeuwendijk and the vast wilderness below. The dark green of the multicanopy jungle didn't look like a place he'd want to jump into except where it was punctuated by the occasional brown clearing. Mountains grew east of the central basin foothills, and as Leeuwendijk dropped the nose to commence the approach, Ash wondered where on the rugged terrain they intended to set down. To his eye, there didn't seem to be any suitable place to land between where they were and the horizon in any direction.

Leeuwendijk banked, climbed, and dove as he worked to hug the rises and falls of the mountains. The aircraft was more maneuverable than Ash would have given it credit for. "We're impressed, Kaas," Wild said, turning green in the back row. "You can stop anytime."

"I am not trying to impress you," Leeuwendijk returned. "This is how we keep from getting shot down by rebel forces."

"In that case, turn harder."

The turboprop followed a stream for a few miles, carving through the valley well below the ridgelines to either side of them. Ash checked the GPS and noted the range readout was down to single digits. Around the next bend a runway materialized—short, crowned, and carved through the thick vegetation at an awkward angle against the side of a mountain.

"That's not where we're landing, is it?" Vice Admiral Garrett asked, index finger against the front windscreen. Leeuwendijk replied by lowering the gear and flaps. "Seriously, Kaas, we're not—"

The plane crossed the tree line, and Leeuwendijk bunted the nose hard enough to cause them all to go light in their seats. He followed the rapid descent by chopping the throttle and bringing the nose up sharply for landing. The back wheels hit the dirt a handful of times before the plane touched down for good. They bounced along the crooked runway with Leeuwendijk taxiing around the large potholes—traps that Ash figured could only be avoided by someone who had landed at the remote strip many times before.

"And I thought landing on the aircraft carrier was hairy," Garrett said with a long exhale.

A platoon of soldiers had formed a perimeter around the aircraft even before the propellers stopped spinning. At first Ash thought they may have been an honor guard of some sort, but when they made no effort to acknowledge the admiral as he climbed out of the plane, he knew they were serving a much more serious purpose. This wasn't a place of ceremony; this was a potentially rebel-filled jungle.

"I'd feel better with my own AK-47," Wild quipped to Ash.

"I know what you mean," Ash returned. "Keep your eyes open."

"Always."

It was hotter and considerably more humid than Kinshasa had been. In spite of the insect repellent Leeuwendijk had provided, bugs instantly swarmed around exposed areas of skin. Ash saw Wild rolling down the sleeves to his cammie shirt, and although Ash was already sweating through his uniform, he elected to do the same.

"All right," Leeuwendijk bellowed as he finished buttoning up the airplane. "Get in the back of the second troop transport over there. We need to hurry if we're going to tour the mine before sunset; we do not want to have to travel the road back to camp after dark."

Ash couldn't tell what make the transports were, but they were very European looking, olive drab with big tires and a narrow wheelbase. As he got closer, he noted UGS stenciled on the doors in black. Ash hopped in, and then Wild and he assisted the admiral, although Garrett groused that he didn't need any help. The back of the transport smelled of mildew, probably from the weathered canvas top pulled across the ribs that arched over the troop benches. One of the soldiers slid into the driver's seat while two others joined Leeuwendijk in climbing in behind the official party. The soldiers pulled the tailgate closed, and with a lurch, they were off.

THIRTY-NINE

The path through the jungle was narrow but the parallel ruts were too wide and deep to have been created by simple oxen-drawn carts. As the two-vehicle convoy bounced along and the driver noisily ground the gears, Ash watched for signs of impending ambush. The soldiers at the tailgate would get hit first. Hopefully they'd fall where they sat and not tumble out the back of the transport.

Wild leaned forward toward Ash and asked, "Are we bailing or sticking with the truck if we get hit?" Their minds were working along the same lines.

"How much faster do you think the vehicles could go down this road?" Ash asked quietly back.

Wild looked across the other passengers to the jungle palm fronds meandering by. "We're already maxed out."

"Then we're bailing into the jungle. I've got the admiral; you grab the rifles."

"Right."

But the rhythm of the jungle remained steady. Ash cut his eyes toward the admiral occasionally for a read on how the boss was dealing with the austerity. He didn't look angry or uncomfortable; in fact, each bump that slammed him against the troop bench brought a smile to his face. In his bright eyes Ash could see that, for all of his stars and standing, Garrett still considered himself an operator at heart.

"How long ago was this mine shut down?" the admiral asked the U.N. official across from him as both of them continued their struggles to stay planted on the troop bench.

"The Belgians originally shut it down in 1960," Oogalong said. "But small-scale miners had been working it off and on since then."

"So what shut *them* down?"

"International pressure has mounted in the last few years, obviously. The idea of uranium flowing across borders unchecked was a concern. I know it certainly didn't sit well with the United States."

"Didn't Norway think unchecked uranium was a big deal?"

"Of course they did, but Norway doesn't have the same sort of influence that the United States does, now does it?"

The transport stopped and the soldiers dropped the tailgate and jumped to the ground. By the time Ash's boots hit the dirt, the soldiers had fanned out and formed another perimeter around the edge of the clearing. "Are those soldiers UGS employees, Kaas?" he asked.

"Why do you ask?" Leeuwendijk returned.

"I'm just curious."

"Does it matter?"

"I was just wondering."

"You wonder about too much." The South African strode away, headed toward an opening in the trees, a trail of some sort.

Wild came up behind Ash and said, "Maybe if you clapped and sang a little French song he might be nicer to you."

Leeuwendijk waved for the group to join him on the

far side of the clearing. At his feet was a box, and as
they neared him he repeatedly reached into it and produced neatly tied bundles that he tossed to each. "These
are anti-exposure suits," he explained. "We'll put these
on once we get closer to the mine. For now, just carry
them."

"Anti-exposure suits?" Vice Admiral Garrett said.
"How much radiation is there?"

"There's more radiation aboard your nuclear-powered
ships," Oogalong said. "This is just a precaution."

"You're positive, right? I don't want to grow a third
eye on the way home."

Leeuwendijk pointed to his waist and said, "I have a
dosimeter on my belt, Admiral, just to be sure. But as
Mr. Oogalong said, there is nothing to worry about. We
would not bring you here if it was not safe."

Garrett scanned the soldiers around him and quipped,
"I can see that."

After a mile hike uphill along the narrow trail, flanked
by the soldiers and surrounded by flies, they came to an
overlook. Beneath them was a verdant valley covered in
elephant grass and dotted with short-trunked palms and
other knotty, tangled trees. In the center of the valley
was an earthen mound that looked like the burrow of a
gigantic animal.

Leeuwendijk grabbed a walkie-talkie from one of the
soldiers and transmitted, *"Nous arrivons."* The response
that came back over the radio threw Ash off a bit as he
could've sworn the voice said, *"Hasanan"*—the Arabic
word for "okay." Ash feigned inattention but furtively
watched Leeuwendijk hold the radio to his face and
calmly say, *"Seulement français, s'il vous plaît."*

Handing the radio back to the soldier, Leeuwendijk's
eyes passed over Ash. The SEAL made sure his expression said nothing. Whatever his curiosity, he was done
asking the South African questions.

"Put your anti-exposure suits on now," Leeuwendijk

commanded. They all undid the strings around their bundles and slipped on the one-piece outfit, complete with booties.

"Don't we need gloves?" Wild asked.

"Do not touch anything," Leeuwendijk replied.

"What about a hood and mask?"

"Do not lick anything, either."

One-by-one each member of the group picked his way down a primitive staircase carved into the face of the bluff. The booties provided poor traction against the dried clay, and each stair was shaped differently than the last. Worse still, the spacing between the stairs was uneven, as many of them had crumbled into oblivion.

Oogalong, who had presumably made the trip before, hissed through his teeth and whined about how he was going to fall with each step. Near the bottom of the one hundred foot descent, the U.N. official's oft-repeated prophesy came true, and Ash managed to collar him before he rolled out of reach on the way by. Ash balled the sleeves of Oogalong's anti-exposure suit into each of his fists and walked him like a marionette for the dozen remaining steps.

After the last one in the line made it off the rudimentary stairway, a soldier led the group through the elephant grass for several hundred yards until they reached the base of the earthen mound where more soldiers stood, automatic weapons slung over their shoulders. All looked to be locals.

"This is a mine?" Wild asked. "It just looks like a big pile of dirt."

"I assure you, Lieutenant, this is a mine," Oogalong returned, dignity apparently regained now that they were back on relatively level ground. "Or it *was* a mine until we shut it down. You know, Admiral, this mine has an important place in American history."

"Oh, yeah?" the admiral returned.

"In 1945, forty shiploads of uranium ore were shipped

from Shinkolobwe to the United States for use in the atomic weapons that were dropped on Hiroshima and Nagasaki."

"Really? Very interesting."

"I find it ironic."

"Ironic? What's ironic about it?"

"Well, now you are here because your government fears proliferation."

"Don't you fear proliferation?" Wild asked.

"Of course, but . . ." Oogalong shook his head. "Admiral, the Shinkolobwe mine is a perfect example of what your government wanted you to see. Before we shut it down a few years ago, six thousand tons of ore was being hauled across the border each month."

"Six thousand tons?" Wild said. "Damn. So how many nuclear weapons could be made from that?"

"The number would vary depending on what process was used to get the uranium to weapons grade. It wouldn't take much to make something like a dirty bomb, though. One pound of uranium yields as much energy as three million pounds of coal."

"Never heard of a coal bomb."

"I just use that as a basis for comparison."

Oogalong led the party halfway around the circumference of the mound, where they came to a large hole filled with concrete. "This was the main entrance," he explained. "This area is also rich in cobalt and nickel, but the real money is in uranium. Workers would go in with crowbars, pickaxes, shovels—whatever—and haul the ore out in buckets. A good miner might have been able to produce up to twenty buckets a day. Six thousand tons of ore went out of here every month." He pointed toward another line cut through the jungle. "A light rail system used to run in that direction, south to Zambia. The rails were removed, but you can still see some of the ties along the ground."

"Quite an operation," Garrett said.

"Yes, it was. But as you can see, there's no getting through now."

"I guess they were in a hurry when they filled it in, huh?" Wild said as he ran his hand lightly across the rough surface of the plug. "You could cut your hand on this."

"Intentional and effective," Oogalong said.

For the next twenty minutes, they strolled around the perimeter of the mine, passing two more concrete plugs—both smaller than the first—before returning to where they'd started. "Well, it looks closed up to me," the admiral said in sum.

"Very much so," Oogalong said. He gestured toward the line of soldiers ringing the full way around the mound. "And as you can also see, it is very well patrolled."

Leeuwendijk pointed to the ball of sun just touching the tree line. "We should start for the camp. Darkness comes quickly here."

"That's it?" Wild asked. "That's the tour we came all the way out here for?"

"What did you expect?" Leeuwendijk asked in return. "You saw that it was closed, and that is it. There is nothing else to see."

"And this isn't a place you want to be after dark," Oogalong said. He wiped his forehead with the sleeve of his anti-exposure suit and considered the bluff rising out of the elephant grass a quarter mile away. "I just wish there was another way up."

FORTY

The party ringed a wood fire at the center of the campsite, seated cross-legged with wooden plates of warm food in their laps. An hour earlier a dozen tribesmen had wandered out of the foliage and into the flickering orange light, scaring the hell out of everyone but Leeuwendijk, who greeted them like old friends. Two of the tribesmen had shared the task of carrying a dead antelope that they flopped onto the ground and quickly carved into steaks. The meat was skewered with sticks, and the sticks were then jabbed into the dirt near the fire. Other tribesmen produced small sacks of rice and pots that they perched on top of makeshift stoves. Before too long, a surprisingly delightful aroma joined the inviting sounds of cooking. Ash sipped on his canteen and watched the attentive grillmaster twist the sticks every few minutes and brush the meat with a thick marinade from a clay bowl.

"It's amazing these men are still able to smile," Oogalong said as he looked across the fire between bites. "The Mangbetu-Azande tribe was nearly decimated by the ethnic fighting. I'm sure these men have seen all manner of atrocities committed before their very eyes."

"There's a lesson there for all of us," Garrett said, without adding what the lesson actually was.

"Admiral, I know it's a touchy subject, but how do you think the war is going to go?" Oogalong asked.

"I thought you said the war was over."

"No, I'm not talking about here; I mean Iraq."

"What's touchy about the war in Iraq?"

Oogalong laid his plate aside and shifted how he was sitting so he was facing the admiral. "I just mean I know it's hard for a military man to talk about an ongoing operation."

"It's not hard to talk about. How do *you* think it's going to go?"

Having the question thrown back at him momentarily nonplussed the Norwegian, and after a few awkward moments of silence he said, "I'm really not qualified to answer that."

"Really? I only ask because it seems to me that most of your questions are really statements. You think we weren't justified in going in there, were we?"

"I guess that would depend on your definition of 'imminent threat.' You see, I've seen intelligence reports that counter what your Secretary of State presented to—"

Drums suddenly pounded a wild beat and a handful of the tribesmen began a synchronized dance, leaping into the air and high-stepping with their knees nearly touching their chests. They formed a circle and chanted for a while, then snaked their way around the fire to where Garrett was seated. Two of them urged him to his feet, and after the obligatory prodding, he attempted to join the dance. The tribesmen shared broad toothless smiles and nodded their approval as they continued their frenetic moves.

Wild leaned over to Ash and whispered into his ear: "More proof that white men can't dance."

The dance continued for several minutes, and Ash could see the admiral was determined to go the distance.

His smile gave way to a determined look; rivulets of sweat glistened in the firelight as they trickled down his face. The dark patches on his T-shirt widened.

The drumming stopped abruptly and the tribesmen faded back into the jungle as quickly as they had appeared. Garrett, winded but happy, waved into the night and asked, "Where did they go?"

"Their village is some distance away," Leeuwendijk explained.

"What fun. I wish I could have thanked them for the meal."

"They saw you finish it. In their world, that's appreciation enough."

"All the same, I feel like I need to give them something in return." He turned to Ash and asked, "Do you have any of those pens left?"

"A few," Ash replied. He walked the few steps to his tent and dug into the black nylon bag. "Here you go, sir."

The admiral caught the pen and handed it to Leeuwendijk, saying, "You'll probably see them again before I do. Please tell them this is a token of my thanks."

"I am sure they will appreciate it," Leeuwendijk returned.

"Maybe they'll even use it to write with," Wild mumbled under his breath. Ash shot him a look.

Leeuwendijk gathered the wooden plates and wrapped them in a plastic bag, explaining, "We do not want to attract animals."

"What kind of animals are there around here?" the admiral asked.

"Jungle animals."

"Snakes?"

"Some, yes."

"I hate snakes."

"If you close your tent and stay on your cot, you will be fine." Leeuwendijk's face glowed aqua momentarily from the light in his watch. "We return to the airplane before sunrise. I recommend we try to get some sleep now." He gestured across the fire. "Do not worry. The soldiers will be at their posts all night. You are quite safe here."

The group dispersed, and the last thing Ash heard the admiral say before he disappeared inside his tent was, "I *really* hate snakes."

FORTY-ONE

Ash was lying facedown on his cot, peering through the opening in the tent flap. He watched the fire slowly die off, occasionally spraying a hail of embers into the night. Beyond the fire, he saw slow movement, a lone soldier strolling back and forth.

"Are you awake?" Wild asked.

"Yeah," Ash said quietly back.

"What time is it?"

"Just past one-thirty."

Wild rolled onto his back and said, "Damn, it's a good thing I don't need much sleep. I wonder what's going on at Club Metro tonight?"

"It's the middle of the afternoon there."

"Okay, smart guy. I wonder what's *going to go on* at Club Metro tonight. Oh, and I want to thank you for bringing me on this great trip, too. Three days and thousands of miles to see the world's biggest mud pie. I shudder to think I might have missed this."

Ash sat up, facing the other cot. "What did you notice about the soldiers guarding the mine?"

"What did I notice? Uh, they lacked diversity in their ranks?"

"They weren't wearing anti-exposure suits."

"Maybe Congo's defense budget sucks."

"They're not government troops. They're on the U.N.'s payroll."

"Maybe the U.N.'s budget sucks."

"No, it just doesn't add up. The whole thing was too staged."

"I agree with that. Here we fly halfway around the world and then all the way across the Congo and the tour lasts, what, a half hour?"

"Even the railroad ties looked like they'd just been thrown into place. Did you check the condition of that wood?"

"No."

"It was pretty fresh—too fresh to have been lying on the ground for very long." Ash dug into the side pocket of his cammies and pulled out the flat metallic ring. "And check this out." He handed it across the tent to Wild.

"What is it?"

"I don't know. I found it in one of the pockets of the admiral's bag. I walked in on the bellhops at the hotel when I was looking for the daybook, and you would've thought I'd nailed them smoking dope or something. I think they accidentally left this behind."

As Ash reached over to take the ring back, he caught movement out of the corner of his eye. He flopped onto his stomach along his cot and through the opening in the tent flap saw Leeuwendijk surveying the area in front of his own tent.

"Why are we the only guys with a two-man tent?" Wild whispered, which Ash answered with a wave of his arm, a petition for silence.

Leeuwendijk confabbed with one of the soldiers, lighting the man's smoke and nodding occasionally. After a minute, the soldier moved on and the South African strolled down the main trail away from the camp.

"Get your boots on," Ash said to the other SEAL.

"What?"

"We're going for a walk."

"Where?"

Ash pointed toward Leeuwendijk, just now disappearing into the darkness. "Wherever he goes."

They slid on their boots, and with a quick scan to make sure the soldiers on patrol weren't watching, they slinked out of the tent and hurried with the hushed feet of trained warriors down the trail behind Leeuwendijk, careful to keep their distance. They could just see him up ahead, barely distinguishable against the opening through the trees. Two hundred yards later he came to one of the military troop transports nestled in the foliage. Without pause, Leeuwendijk climbed behind the wheel and started the vehicle.

"Run for it," Ash said in a loud whisper, just audible over the transport's idling engine. They took off running. Ash saw the truck's taillights come on just as it started to roll. He picked up the pace, in a full sprint now. He heard Wild puffing behind him.

The transport was accelerating. If Leeuwendijk dropped it into second gear, there was no way they were going to catch up. The angry grinding of gears split the night, and the vehicle lurched, which was all the two SEALs needed to step onto the thick bumper and scamper over the tailgate.

Ash and Wild laid flat against the steel bed between the troop benches, catching their breath and listening as Leeuwendijk found his rhythm with the gears. Wild turned his head to face Ash and asked, "Now what?"

"Now we go for a ride."

"Oh, good. I was afraid you didn't have a plan."

"This isn't just a pop-up trip for him, you know. This is why he had the solders park so far away from the campsite."

"So where is he going?"

"We'll find out, I guess."

They bounced along for another half hour, doing their

best to avoid landing on each other or having the wind knocked out of their lungs as they slammed against the bed. Light began to flicker through the cracks in the side panels, and the transport came to a halt. They heard Leeuwendijk slam the driver's door and call out in a foreign tongue. Someone answered in kind.

"I knew it," Ash said in a hushed voice. "They're speaking Arabic."

"Why would they be speaking Arabic?"

"Great question. What say we try and figure it out?"

Slowly, each one of the SEALs parted the canvas cover over the back of the troop transport and eyeballed his surroundings. The place was awash in stadium lights much like the ones that had circled the site Ash's team had come across in the Iraqi desert. About fifty feet away from the troop transport, Leeuwendijk spoke with two brown-skinned men sporting thick black mustaches. Each of the men wore a lab coat and safety glasses. Beyond those three, other men, locals by their looks, shuffled past wearing helmets with lights attached to the front of them—miners' helmets. Their bodies were covered in a silver-gray coating that made them look like zombies in a low-budget horror flick. Several of them were much shorter than the others—children, judging by their gaits.

Ash and Wild watched the procession of workers head for a massive opening in the side of a hill. The opening was perfectly square and braced around the edges by wide steel girders. Inside a string of acetylene lights danced, creating eerie shadows against the rough, pock-marked surface of the wall.

Slowly, a rumble began to shake the earth, accompanied by a high-pitched metallic screech. From inside the opening a single headlight shone, making silhouettes of the miners as they parted to either side. The headlight grew wider and brighter until it passed through the opening and into the artificially lit night, revealing a low-slung box of a tractor pulling a train of wheeled containers overflowing with ore. The tractor drove up an elevated ramp without delay and tipped its burden into a waiting dump truck.

"Now *that's* a mine," Wild said.

"Funny how we skipped this vein on the tour," Ash said. "We need to get a closer look."

The pair slinked out of the back of the transport and edged their way to the dark side of the vehicle. "Let's follow the jungle around to the other side," Ash said before crouching down and moving swiftly into the trees.

The noise of machinery and the shouting of orders kept the SEALs from being heard as they crunched through the jungle. A few minutes later, they had positioned themselves as close to the mine entrance as the jungle cover would allow, close enough that the dust from the loading zone burned in their nostrils. They fought not to sneeze.

"Look at that," Wild whispered. "They're covered in it. Shouldn't those guys be wearing suits?"

"Probably. I doubt UGS has much of a health plan."

There was yelling from inside the mine, then two miners appeared dragging a third between them. They called in French over to Leeuwendijk, who was still talking with the two Arab technicians. The South African stepped over and, arms crossed, listened to the story offered by the miner on his left. As the man spoke, he reached into the pocket of the miner next to him and pulled out a fist that he opened, allowing small rocks to fall to the dirt. The miner in the middle shook his head and struggled against the two holding him as one of his captors said, *"Regardez, commandant."*

Without a word in return, Leeuwendijk reached to the small of his back and produced a pistol. He put the weapon to the black man's temple and pulled the trigger. The back half of the miner's skull blew off in a cloud of mist that showed very red in the light. The two other miners recoiled as if they hadn't expected such a drastic measure.

"Jeezus," Wild mumbled with a wince. "That guy's fucking bipolar."

"Maintenant, travail!" Leeuwendijk shouted. "Anyone else caught poaching will see the same end." The miners hurried back into the mine while the others compliantly went about their business.

"Do you have your GPS with you?" Ash asked.

Wild dug into the left leg of his cammies and said, "No good SEAL goes anywhere without one. What's your excuse?"

"I have you. Save the lat and long for this place. I think we might be doing a little intel work when we get back."

"What about the admiral? Should we tell him about this?"

"I'm not sure yet. Let me worry about that."

Leeuwendijk said something else to the Arabs and walked toward the transport. "Shit, we're going to miss our ride home," Wild said.

"Time to haul ass."

Ash and Wild sprinted through the jungle. They slipped out of the tree line on the backside of the transport, blocked from the view of those near the mine, and in rapid succession swung in between the troop benches.

Once they caught their breath, Ash rolled over toward his friend and said, "What's going on at Club Metro has nothing on what's going on here."

FORTY-TWO

Murdo Edeema was awakened by the tinkling of silverware coming from the dining room directly beneath the master bedroom. He sat up in bed and cocked his head to one side, trying to listen closer, making sure his weary ears weren't playing tricks on him. Again, the same sound. He looked over at the clock: 2:34 a.m. His wife was fast asleep.

Edeema slipped out of the bedroom and crept along the hallway, hugging the wall in an attempt to avoid the creaky parts of the floor. As he got to the top of the circular staircase, he heard more noises—drawers opening and chairs sliding across the hardwood floor. Someone was definitely down there and not exactly being sneaky—a sign of criminal arrogance or a bad burglar. The intruder certainly had tripped the security alarm, but how long would it take for the police to show up?

He reached the landing at the base of the stairs accompanied by still louder noises from the dining room, the snap of a plastic garbage bag followed by the crash of silverware being dumped into it. Edeema slipped into his study and removed a cricket bat signed by the members of the 1978 West Indies national team from the hooks that held it against the wall. Then, step by tentative step, he padded across the landing and peered around the doorway to the dining room. The figure, standing by the prone and unmoving body of Edeema's Borzoi, was busy dumping the contents of drawers into the garbage bag. Enough light from the walkway lantern outside streamed through the picture window to allow him to see the intruder's face.

"Kurt?" Edeema called into the room as he came around the corner. "Kurt Montana, is that you?"

"Yes, it's me, Murdo," Montana returned without any hint of fear or surprise in his voice. "I didn't think you'd ever wake up."

"What the hell are you doing with that silverware?"

"I'm stealing it."

Edeema raised his hands and said, "This isn't funny, Kurt."

Montana laughed and trained the pistol on Edeema. "I'm not trying to be funny, Murdo. *Les Affreux* has little interest in humor."

"*Les Affreux?* This is your so-called security work?"

"You're quick, Murdo. Word had it you didn't even know about us until a few days ago."

"Why are you here, Kurt?"

Montana held his arm out, revealing a large handgun fitted with a silencer. "I bring you a message from Paris: Your services are no longer required at Huntington."

Edeema slowly raised his hands and said, "*Me,* Kurt? After all I've done for you?"

"This isn't about me and you. This is about *you.* You should have just let us take care of Roberts."

"I'm grooming him . . . like I groomed you."

"You're not the judge of character you once were, Murdo. I've met him, you know. He'd never see it our way."

"Our way?" Edeema extended his arms and started a slow walk toward Montana. "Look at what you've become, Kurt. Did you set out to be an assassin?"

"Don't move, Murdo."

"It doesn't have to be this way. You could help me chart a new course for the company, for the entire organization. We could make the business profitable and legit. I know how to do it."

"I said stop moving!"

"I know you're a good man; you just wound up with the wrong arm of the organization. What do you say, Kurt?"

Montana laughed. "You have no clue just how out of touch you've become, do you?"

Edeema realized the soft sell wasn't going to work. "Get out of my house immediately!" he shouted, posture stiffening. "You've already set off the alarm. The police will be here any minute."

Montana laughed again, harder this time. "The police? I know you're not a security specialist like I am, so let me explain how your company-financed system works. When somebody trips the alarm, the police aren't notified; *we* are. And I'm pleased to report that your system is working fine; in fact, it's better than fine: I was here at the precise moment the alarm went off. How's that for response time?"

Murdo put his hands to his chest and took another step toward Montana, saying, "This is how you repay me? You were an aide. You came through my process. I made you."

"You made me?" Montana said, sweetening his aim. "Well, then, you did a damn fine job."

Montana squeezed the trigger twice. The first bullet shattered Edeema's collarbone; the second just missed his heart before piercing his lung and lodging against one of his ribs along his back. He fell onto the floor in shock and disbelief, waiting for the pain to hit him. He felt nothing; he figured he might already be dead.

"Don't worry," Montana said. "I know Ned will take care of the office for you. And you'll be pleased to know that I intend to pay special attention to Allison." He leaned over his victim. "Can you still hear me? Are you dead yet?"

"Rot in hell, bastard," Edeema spat in return.

"After you." Montana trained his pistol on Edeema's chest again and discharged another round. With a dark chuckle, he threw the garbage bag over his shoulder and walked out.

Laboring to breathe, Edeema slid across the floor and propped himself against the wall. He reached up and flicked the switch above his head, which brought the small chandelier over the dining room table alive. He tried to call out to his wife but couldn't raise his voice loud enough to be heard. He coughed and tasted blood. He was dying fast, and to his surprise, that realization blanketed him in soothing clarity. His mind was bright, maybe brighter than ever, like a lightbulb intensely aglow just before it burns out.

Edeema had never been a religious man, but now it struck him that this fate was the price of his sins. His had been an exciting life, an unorthodox one, but for all his attempts at window dressing in recent years, ultimately he had served an evil master. But would evil win? Could he manage a final gesture that could possibly prevent it? And might that change the closeout calculus of his life?

He snaked an arm around the edge of the doorway, into the entryway, and grabbed his cell phone from a marble-topped curio table there. He opened up the device and searched the call history for a recent entry. Finding it, he hit SEND, and with nearly the last of his energy, he put the phone to his ear.

FORTY-THREE

After snoozing for the first six hours of the trip home, Wild and Ash huddled in the last row of regular seats in the back of the Skytrain, well aft of the VIP configured portion of the airplane, where Vice Admiral Garrett currently slept. There were a few other passengers who'd joined them in the Azores, but they were spread out enough that the two SEALs could speak freely, albeit quietly.

"So . . . what?" Wild asked. "You think the admiral's involved?"

"Maybe," Ash said. "He's seemed pretty comfortable with Leeuwendijk and the other UGS guys during the two trips I've been on."

"What about the U.N. dude? They just argued the whole time."

"I don't know. Maybe that was just a show for us, or maybe Mr. Oogalong isn't part of it."

"And what is *it*? Are they shipping uranium, making weapons-grade stuff, or what?"

"I don't know. I saw what you saw. For starters, I need to figure out what this thing is I found in the admiral's bag."

"Give it to me."

"What?"

"I know an intelligence analyst, one of the best. And he'll give me answers without asking a lot of questions in return."

As Ash reached down to retrieve the black nylon bag he'd stashed under the seat in front of him, a pair of brown shoes appeared in the aisle. He worked his eyes up, along the khaki trousers and across the shirt adorned with dozens of ribbons and gold pilot's wings, to Vice Admiral Garrett's face.

"Why are you guys sitting back here?" the admiral asked.

"Change of scenery, I guess," Ash replied, trying to avoid appearing surprised. "Plus, we didn't want to disturb you."

"Don't worry about disturbing me. When you've lived on as many aircraft carriers as I have, you learn to sleep through anything." He put his foot on the armrest of the aisle seat across from where the two SEALs were seated. "So, what were you two talking about?"

"The uranium mine." Ash could sense Wild cringing next to him.

The admiral's head jerked slightly. "What about it?"

"Nothing specific, really. We just thought it was kind of interesting."

Ash sensed intensity in the admiral beyond that of a man simply chewing the fat with subordinates. "Interesting, huh? What was interesting about it?"

The SEAL thought for a few seconds before offering, "I don't know . . . how they closed it up. How many guards they had around it. Those sorts of things."

"I'm just glad I'll be able to report to SECDEF that it's out of commission."

Ash looked at Wild, and both nodded, and then Ash said, "I'm sure the Secretary will be pleased to hear that, sir."

*   *   *

A cold wind whipped across the flight line on the Navy side of Andrews Air Force Base as Ash and Wild followed Vice Admiral Garrett off the Skytrain and across the concrete. Although it was technically spring on the calendar, it still felt very much like winter around Washington, D.C. The admiral tugged on the fur collar of his leather flight jacket and rushed though the double doors into base operations.

Ash scanned the space for Yeoman Peabody, but the driver was nowhere to be found. Ash grabbed his cell phone out of his bag and dialed the Pentagon. A woman answered on the second ring: "Vice Admiral Garrett's office, Miss Dubs speaking."

"Miss Dubs, it's Ash. We're back."

"Oh, good," she said. "How was your trip?"

"Fine. There's no driver here, though."

"Yes, I know. Burt called from the car about ten minutes ago. There's a traffic jam on the outer loop of the Beltway. He's going to be there a little late."

"How late?"

"A few minutes. Is there a fax machine nearby?"

"I'm sure there is."

"Get the number and call me back. While you're waiting, we might as well get the admiral up to speed a bit."

"Okay. Let me go ask this guy where the fax machine is. I'll call you back."

When Ash folded the phone shut, he noticed he had a couple of voice mails. Melinda, maybe? Walking toward the service counter, he dialed his access code and put the phone back to his ear.

"Lieutenant Roberts, this is Murdo Edeema. I need to talk to you as soon as possible."

Ash made a mental note and erased the message. The second voice mail started with someone coughing followed by a tired voice: "Lieutenant Roberts?" More coughing, deep and wet. Painful to hear. "This is . . . M-Murdo . . . Murdo Edeema." The coughing continued; he wasn't well. "My building . . . in the . . . s-scar. Go . . .

there. You . . . you'll n-need my h-hand." One last long cough and then a gurgling sound and then nothing.

A female sailor walked up to the counter, and Ash lowered the cell phone and asked, "Do you have a fax machine that our office could use to send Vice Admiral Garrett a few things while we wait for our car to show up?"

She nodded and wrote the number on a Post-it note. Ash called Miss Dubs back, and as he waited for the fax machine to start belching paper, he called Wild over and held the cell phone to his ear. "Listen to this," Ash said. "Tell me what you think."

Wild listened to the voice mail then proclaimed, "Whoever it is, he's shit-faced."

"Shit-faced?"

"The dude's totally bombed. Who is it?"

"Murdo Edeema."

"Who?"

"Murdo Edeema. He's a consultant I met at the admiral's house last week."

"A boozing consultant, huh? Sounds like your kind of guy."

As Ash listened to the message again, he thought Edeema sounded more sick than drunk.

Yeoman Peabody flew through the double doors from the front parking lot. The sailor hurried over, saying, "I'm sorry I'm late, sir. The traffic was bad."

"I heard. How is it going the other way?"

"Bad, but less bad, I think."

"Grab a couple of the bags over there and let's go." He called over to the other SEAL: "Wild, tell the admiral we're going." Wild gave a wave and started to walk over to the admiral, who had his own cell phone against the side of his head.

Ash wasn't sure what Miss Dubs was faxing, but he was certain it would be best if the material didn't sit in a fax machine waiting to be read by whomever happened to wander by. He redialed Miss Dubs, who had just finished organizing a stack of things she intended to fax, and told her that Yeoman Peabody had arrived and that they were on their way back to the office.

Peabody ran back out to the sedan he'd left running at the curb and opened the rear door for Vice Admiral Garrett, who climbed into the back with his cell phone still at his ear, deep in heated conversation with someone he kept referring to as Smitty. Once he made sure they'd loaded all the bags, Wild jumped in the back next to the admiral, and Ash slid in the front.

Through Andrews' main gate and onto the slow crawl of the Beltway's inner loop, Peabody glanced into the rearview mirror and saw the admiral was still on the phone. He looked at Ash and pointed to the newspaper folded next to him. "Got the evening edition of the *Post* here, sir."

"Thanks, Burt," Ash replied. He picked up the main section and skimmed the headlines. Steady progress in Iraq. Baghdad in three weeks, tops. The editorial page had one analyst predicting democracy six months after that. The other side of the congressional aisle was wary but supportive of the administration. Everyone supported the troops, even the rock stars.

Behind the front page, a local section headline caught his eye: NORTHERN VIRGINIA BUSINESS LEADER GUNNED DOWN IN HERNDON HOME. He started the article with passing interest, but finished it with his heart racing like he'd just jumped out of a Talon:

Prominent local businessman Murdo Edeema, VP of the Huntington Group, a consulting firm that specializes in defense work, was shot and killed in his home located in the affluent Hillsdale Estates neighborhood in Herndon, Virginia, sometime early today. The Herndon Sheriff's Department reported that after receiving a 9-1-1 call from an unknown source, they found Edeema dead on the floor of his dining room. An official who spoke on condition of anonymity said that Edeema had been shot three times in the chest at close range. The official also said that a nearby silverware drawer was empty, which has led investigators to believe that robbery may have been the motive for the crime.

Former coworkers were in shock at the Huntington Group offices in Crystal City as the workday started this morning. "This is a terrible tragedy," said Ned Reynolds, corporate vice president in charge of the firm's Washington operations. "Murdo was a great leader and mentor to all. His loss will be felt by the company and the community for many years to come. We all hope the murderer will be caught and punished to the full extent of the law very soon."

Edeema was born and raised in the Netherlands, where he lived until accepting a position with the Huntington Group in 1987. He became an American citizen the following year. Edeema was also very active with civic groups, most notably the Washington Council for the Arts, where he led a program designed to introduce inner-city youths to classical music. The upscale home was equipped with an alarm system, but it was unknown at press time whether or not it had functioned properly. This is the first murder in Herndon since a drug dealer gunned down a popular high school football star in 1998.

Edeema is survived by his wife, Andromeda, who was unavailable for comment. Memorial services will be held at Breedon Brothers Funeral Home in Arlington.

Ash passed the paper over his right shoulder and said out of the corner of his mouth: "That guy wasn't drunk when he called. Read this."

Wild wiped his eyes, skimmed the article, and then shrugged. "So why did he call you?"

"I'm not sure. And why would he say I needed his hand?"

"I hate to break it to you, shipmate, but if you need his hand for something, you're sucking."

FORTY-FOUR

Miss Dubs wandered over to Ash's desk in the admiral's outer office and asked, "Do you have the receipts from the trip? I want to submit the admiral's travel claim right away."

Ash fished through his black bag as he explained, "There's only one receipt."

"You're lucky. These first two trips were pretty straightforward as far as transportation goes. No commercial airliners. No rental cars. No tollbooths. No parking."

"Lucky, huh? Why don't you ask the admiral how his butt feels after bouncing over the trails of the Congo for two days?"

"I think I'll pass on that, thank you."

"Speaking of trips: I don't see any on the calendar right now. When's our next one?"

"I haven't decided yet."

Miss Dubs tittered and turned for the other side of the office, and before she reached her desk, Ash asked, "You heard about Murdo Edeema?"

"Yes. What a tragedy." Her phone rang, and she quickly answered it.

Vice Admiral Garrett walked out of his office, spinning a coffee mug around his finger. It was time for his late afternoon caffeine fix, not to be confused with the handful of other caffeine fixes he executed over the course of a long day. He grabbed the pot from where it was perched atop a small cabinet near Chief Monroe's desk and charged his mug with the bitter, black stuff he favored.

Garrett strolled over and plopped himself in the plain wooden chair next to Ash's desk. "So, did you guys enjoy the trip?"

"Yes, sir," Ash replied, wearing his best poker face. "Very interesting place."

"Interesting? I guess that's one way to put it." The admiral took a long draw from his mug and then worked his eyes across Ash's desk. "Did you make a note of everyone we owe thank-you letters to?"

"Yes, sir. Chief Monroe is working on them."

"Good." Garrett put the mug to his mouth again and swallowed loudly.

Although Ash feared he already knew too much, he had one burning question that wouldn't tip his hand. "Can I ask you something, sir?"

"Shoot."

"Why did you select me?"

Garrett jerked his head back as if Ash had rabbit-punched him. "I selected you because you were the best officer for the job."

"What job, sir? Riding herd on thank-you letters?"

"Of course not. I need your expertise and counsel on important matters. You're one of my most trusted advisors, or I'm sure you will be once we really get to know each other a little better." Garrett leaned forward in the chair. "Do we need to talk about something, Ash?"

Ash shook his head and intoned, "No, sir."

The admiral stood up and said, "Like I said on day one, Lieutenant: If we don't have trust between us, we don't have anything. You'll let me know if there's a problem, right?"

"Certainly, sir."

"We've had a long day. Hell, we started the day halfway around the world, for crying out loud. Why don't you finish up whatever you're working on and head on home?" Garrett snatched his mug from Ash's desk and headed back to his office.

"Admiral," Ash called to his back, "have you found anything out about what we talked about on the airplane a few days ago—you know, during the flight back from Panama?"

Garrett searched his memory, winced, and then said, "Oh, that . . . ah, no. Not yet. I will though, I promise." Ash's phone rang. "You'd better get that."

Ash picked up the phone as he watched the admiral disappear into his office: "Lieutenant Roberts . . ."

"It's Wild. Meet me in the basement."

"What?"

"I've arranged a small conference for us."

"A conference? What are you talking about? And what basement?"

"Damn, just meet me in my office. Do you remember how to get over here?"

"Not really."

"Just start walking down the E Ring and I'll meet you along the way. They're expecting us in ten minutes."

"Who are *they*?"

"Get going." Wild hung up without any further explanation.

Ash tried to tell Miss Dubs he'd be out for a few minutes, but she was too busy with the phone to her ear—fielding requests and adjusting the admiral's calendar—to notice him as he passed. He slipped out of the outer office, through the waiting area, and across the shiny floor of the E-Ring. Half a dozen spokes later, he ran into Wild, who wordlessly led him down the nearest stairwell. Two floors down, the stairs narrowed and the lighting dimmed until Ash could barely make out the other SEAL in front of him. They exited the stairwell and followed an unmarked hallway for several hundred feet.

"Where are we going?" Ash asked.

Wild didn't answer but stopped at a steel door outlined with industrial-sized rivets. At eye level, the door hosted a thick piece of glass with wire mesh running through it. Wild pushed a button next to the door, and a female voice crackled through the adjacent intercom: "Can I help you?"

"We're here," Wild said.

The latch buzzed, and Wild pushed the door open. Ash followed his friend along another long, dark corridor, around a corner, and into a spartanly appointed space that reminded Ash of an interrogation room from a cop show on TV. A woman was seated at the head of the sole table in the room, and on second glance, Ash realized he knew her—rather well, by some standards.

"Melinda," he said.

"Hello, Ash," she replied.

Wild could see the confusion in his friend's face, so he offered an explanation: "Melinda works as an analyst in one of the Joint Chief's intelligence cells."

Melinda shrugged and said, "I'm as much a librarian as an analyst." She pointed past the two SEALs. "And from what Wild told me on the phone, I think we need that guy."

Ash and Wild turned to discover that a tall black man sporting dreadlocks had silently materialized in the doorway behind them. He extended his hand toward Ash without speaking.

"Kid 500?" Ash asked as they shook.

"Jeremy," the man replied without any traces of a Jamaican accent.

"I'm sorry," Ash said, looking over at Wild for confirmation. "You look a lot like someone else."

"Why don't you guys sit down and we'll take a look at the item in question?" Melinda suggested. "Jeremy has got a lot on his plate with the war going on, and so do I." Ash noted there was nothing come-hither about her demeanor; she was all business.

Before sitting down in one of the metal chairs around the table, Wild undid two buttons on his uniform shirt and pulled out the oblong washer Ash had found in the admiral's luggage during the African trip. He handed it across the table to Jeremy.

The black man ran the tips of his fingers along the surface of the washer. "Titanium . . . specially machined." He held it up. "You see the shape of this? That's harder to manufacture than it looks."

"What would it be used for?" Ash asked.

"A seal, most likely—a seal between two other titanium parts. Now, the fact it's titanium indicates primarily that it's designed to be used in high-temperature and high-pressure environments. It could be used in any high-flow-rate application, but looking at the size and shape of this, my guess might point to a more specific use."

"What?"

"A nuclear still."

"A nuclear *what*?" Wild asked.

"Still. We've come across schematics for homemade refineries that can enrich uranium—turn raw uranium into near weapons-grade, close enough for a dirty bomb, at least. This is a little different than anything I've seen, but it generally looks like it could be a component in that sort of miniature plant, maybe part of a centrifuge." He handed the washer back to Wild and checked his watch. "Anything else?"

"How do you guys do with GPS coordinates?" Ash asked.

"You give us somewhere to look, we can tell you everything that can be currently known about that point on the planet," Jeremy replied.

Ash reached into his wallet and produced a tattered briefing card. "I've written two sets of coordinates on the back of this card. One is in Iraq, about thirty miles due west of Baghdad, the other is in the easternmost part of the Democratic Republic of the Congo."

Melinda intercepted the card as Ash was handing it to Jeremy, saying, "Let me take care of this." She studied both sides of the card and asked, "What was this card originally used for?"

"A mission brief," Ash said.

"A mission in Iraq?"

"You know I can't answer that unless you have a need to know."

"Do I?"

Ash balanced his chair on the back two legs, withdrew a long breath, and said, "Why not? I'm not getting answers from anyone else." He rocked forward and leaned his elbows against the table. "I jumped into Iraq on the first night of the war with five other guys and an SUV. Our mission was to take the Deputy Minister of Information into protective custody."

"Kidnap him?" Melinda said.

"Protective custody," Ash repeated. "Anyway, on our way out of Baghdad we had to deviate to the north because the damn Airdales blew the road up during the first wave of Shock and Awe. Just before we reached our C-130 pickup point, we came across some activity— a factory, or something—some sort of industrial effort. We took a few pictures in a hurry because we got chased down by a vehicle that we wound up neutralizing."

"Did you turn the pictures over to the intelligence debriefers at the TOC?" Melinda asked.

"Yes."

"And?"

"And nothing. I never got any feedback on what the pictures showed. Meanwhile while I've been over here babysitting Vice Admiral Garrett, four of my men have been killed."

"In action?" Jeremy asked.

"Presumably," Ash said.

"And you think all of this is related somehow?"

"I'm trying not to think anything right now. I'm in data-gathering and fact-finding mode. All I know is a lot of weird shit has been going on over the past week or so, and I need some answers, quick."

"Did you use a standard ruggedized laptop on that mission?" Melinda asked.

"Yes."

"Did you write the serial number down on this briefing card?"

"It should be on the front near the top," Ash said as he leaned over toward her. "Yeah, there it is."

"Good. I can use that to go into the database and see what's on file for that mission."

"How much detail would be in the file?"

"It varies."

"Photos?"

"If they were part of the debrief, they should be in there. Anything else?"

"That's enough. I don't want to bog you down with what might turn out to be nothing but my wild imagination."

"That mine wasn't your imagination," Wild said. "I saw it, too."

"How long do think it will take for you to come up with anything?" Ash asked.

"Referencing GPS coordinates is easy," Melinda said. "The mission stuff will depend on how well it was filed."

"This is just between us for now, right? At least give me a chance to put the pieces together before we broadcast anything to the rest of the world."

"We don't know anything until you tell us we know it."

"We need to get back to our offices before our bosses notice we're gone," Wild said. "Why don't we catch up later at, say, *Club Metro*?" Melinda looked at Ash and bit her lip to suppress a smile.

Jeremy stood and, sounding fresh from the Caribbean, shook his dreadlocks and said, "No worries, mon. We see you dere."

FORTY-FIVE

Ash would've preferred a good night's sleep, but Melinda's expression as he was on his way out of the Pentagon's basement was more than he could ignore. There was a deal to be closed, and as his brother SEALs had always said, "Sleep when you're dead." In the meantime, he surfed the Web for information on dirty bombs and nuclear stills while waiting for Wild to return from the Pentagon. The links brought up articles and think tank documents that were frustratingly general in their level of detail. He combed the text and racked his brain for the exact sequence of events with the bellhops at the hotel in Kinshasa. His cell phone rattled against the coffee table—a number he didn't recognize.

"Ash is up . . ."

"Lieutenant Ash Roberts?" a male voice asked.

"Speaking."

"This is Captain Ben Tudor calling from Wiesbaden, Germany. Can you hear me?"

"I can."

"I'm a doctor in the Army Medical Center here. I'm calling to let you know the condition of Senior Chief William White."

Ash bolted upright. "Billy? Is he all right?"

"He's stable now. He was medevaced here yesterday."

"What happened?"

"I don't have all the details, I'm afraid. I do know that he was in a convoy that was attacked by a radio-controlled SUV full of explosives."

"Did you say 'radio-controlled'?"

"Yes, that's what I was told, anyway."

"How the hell does a radio-controlled—"

"Lieutenant, I've told you what I know about that. I'm simply calling to let you know that he is out of the woods now from a first-response standpoint. There is significant scarring from flash burns along the back of his body, and it will take some rehab for him to regain the full use of his legs, but he's alive. He requested that we tell you."

"Is he there? Let me talk to him."

"No, he's out at the moment. He's in a lot of pain, so we keep him under as much as possible." Ash heard another voice in the background. "Lieutenant, I've got to go. We have quite a few wounded rolling in here, as you can imagine. I'll tell William that we got through to you."

"When can I talk to—" The doctor hung up. Ash dropped the cell phone and sunk into the couch. The thought of Billy alone in a hospital room, probably bandaged head to toe, was a painful one. But he was alive. Of course he was: Senior Chief Billy White was never going to die, certainly not at the hands of an enemy. That's more than could be said for the rest of Task Force Bravo. And what of this trend? Tragic coincidence in a time of war, like those five Irish brothers killed during World War II, or something else—something beyond the pale of normal warfare? His temples pounded as he continued to wrestle with the elements before him: the attrition of Task Force Bravo; the activities of UGS and Kaas Leeuwendijk; the admiral as a nuclear component mule, unwitting or otherwise; Kid 500 and Melinda as

Pentagon analysts—none of it made sense at a glance. And why had he been picked to be the aide? That was the question he wanted answered over all others.

Western Tennessee was an hour behind the East Coast. The guy might still be at work. Ash dug into his wallet and pulled out a scrap of notepaper upon which he'd written a number he thought he might need eventually. He dialed his cell phone and listened to it ring three times on the other end before a voice came over the line.

"Bureau of Naval Personnel, Lieutenant Schoenstein. How may I help you, sir?"

"Lieutenant Schoenstein, this is Lieutenant Ash Roberts." Silence from the other end. "New aide to Vice Admiral Garrett . . ."

"Oh, yeah, of course," Schoenstein returned. "How's it going over there?"

"I want to know who asked for me?"

"I'm sorry?"

"Who actually called you and asked for me? Was it the admiral?"

"I assume so. I was just given a note that you were a by-name call."

"So you didn't actually speak to the admiral yourself?"

"Me? Of course not. I'm just a lowly detailer. Admirals talk to other admirals, not to me."

"So there's a chance the admiral didn't actually ask for me."

"No, you were definitely a by-name call."

"But could someone else have made me a by-name call on the admiral's behalf."

"I guess so, but I assume they'd be calling with the admiral's concurrence. You're a staff guy now. What do you think?"

Ash didn't answer the question but instead asked, "How hard would it be to get orders back in-theater?"

"For regular people or for you?"

"Just in theory."

"It's very easy unless you have an admiral who says, 'No can do.' "

"Thanks. That's all I needed to know."

"So, how's it going? Are you having fun being around the power brokers?"

"Oh, yeah. It's a blast."

"Good, good," Schoenstein said, oblivious to Ash's sarcasm. "Okay, I have to take another call here. Don't hesitate to call. I'm here for you." The detailer hung up.

There was a knock on the front door. Ash tossed the cell phone aside and stepped across the room. Through the peephole he saw the strange thin man from the complex's management company who'd come by before the trip to Africa. The man was holding a clipboard, just like the last time he'd knocked on the door.

Ash undid the chain and pulled the door well open, which allowed the man's pungent cologne to waft into the apartment and turn the SEAL's stomach.

"Hello, sir. How are you this evening?" the man asked with the same nasal whine he'd used to irritate Ash during his last visit.

"Not too good, actually," Ash replied.

"Very good, sir. I work with the management company for the building here."

"I know. We met the last time you came around."

"Of course. It's good to see you again, sir. Can I come in for a second?"

"This isn't a good time. The owner still isn't here. Maybe tomorrow."

"Oh . . . well, actually, that's okay. I'm not here to see the owner. I'm here to see you, Lieutenant Roberts."

The man moved the clipboard and revealed a large pistol with a silencer. Ash tried to slam the door, but the skinny man was much stronger than he looked. He threw the door open, knocking Ash backward in the process. The SEAL rolled over Wild's coffee table, which was lucky because the wood was thick enough that it stopped the initial burst of shots from the pistol.

The splinters continued to fly as Ash dove behind the couch.

This was it; Ash had cornered himself. Either the man was going to run out of ammo, or he was going to reach behind the couch and perform an execution gangland-style. Ash had time to wonder how ugly the head wound would be after taking a round at point-blank range. He moved his hands up to cover his head, and as he did, one of them bumped against something under the couch. He wrapped his fingers around the object and brought it in front of his face. Even in the poor light there was no mistaking what it was: Wild's ceramic hard-on.

Without taking the time to wonder how the clay member had made its way from the shelf to under the couch, Ash stood up and hurled it, much like one might throw a knife, where he thought the man's head would be. In his stress-fueled mind, the roughly nine-inch statuette seemed to take forever to reach its target, traveling in slow motion as it tumbled end over end, circumcised tip over balls. There was a flash of light from the end of the pistol and the muffled swoosh of another bullet through the silencer. Plaster peppered the side of Ash's face as the bullet hit the wall beside his head, followed a millisecond later by the erotic pottery catching the man squarely against his nose.

It was an absolute bull's-eye, the kind of shot Ash could have attempted with several truckloads of decorative genitalia and not repeated. The dick shattered, and the man's nose exploded in twin streams of blood. He let out a wail and clutched his face, but held on to the pistol. Before Ash could spring from behind the couch, the neutralized assailant ran out of the apartment. Ash knew he had the advantage now, even unarmed, so he went after him.

The SEAL used his best house-to-house techniques to quickly but cautiously advance down the hallway. He pushed his way into the stairwell and stuck his head over the banister, looking both up and down. His attacker had escaped without leaving even trace amounts of blood, which was a feat considering how his face had erupted.

Ash walked back into the apartment, careful not to step on the ceramic shards that littered the floor at his feet. The coffee table had three large bullet holes in it; the wall behind the couch hosted two more.

Ash heard movement from behind, and he turned, poised for a fight. "Easy there, big guy," Wild said, wiping his face with a towel. His mouth fell open as his eyes scanned the apartment. "What the fuck, over?"

"You didn't happen to see a guy with a bloody nose waving a pistol run by on your way in, did you?" Ash said.

Wild fetched one of the shards from the carpet. "Oh, no. Not the dick. NOT THE DICK!"

"Don't worry, Wild. I'm fine. Thanks for your concern."

Ash spotted something gold among the white pieces of fired clay—a bullet shell. He picked it up and studied the end of it under the nearest light. Etched there were four letters: APLP.

"This guy used armor-piercing, limited-penetration bullets," Ash mused aloud.

"And look at this coffee table," Wild moaned as he continued to survey the damage.

Ash pointed toward the corner. "Lock the door tight and get on the computer, Wild."

"Have you called the cops yet?"

"No cops. We've got to work this one starting right now."

"*We,* huh?" Wild said with a dark chuckle. "Which *we* are you talking about?"

"You and me—and no cops."

Wild flashed his palms at Ash. "Oh, no. You're not dragging me into your sorry little program here, warhero boy. I've already helped." He counted his recent accomplishments on his fingers. "I went to the Congo with you. I got you access to the Pentagon intelligence analysts. Just call the cops."

"By the time they broke themselves away from the coffeemaker I'd be dead."

"I've got orders coming. I'm headed for Iraq, and you and all of your three-star buddies aren't going to stop me."

"Nobody's stopping anything," Ash returned. "Now, please, just grab a seat over here."

Wild sat down at his computer workstation, shook his head, and resignedly said, "Give me a keyword."

"A keyword . . ."

"Come on. You were just on this computer. Act like you know what the hell you're doing. Give me something to type in the search engine buffer; you know, like 'uranium dealers,' or 'people trying to kill Ash Roberts,' or your favorite: 'co-eds with big tits.' "

"APLP."

"APLP? Remind me what that stands for?"

"Armor piercing, limited penetration."

Wild's fingers were a momentary blur. "Okay, we've got a butt-load of entries here."

"Try that one," Ash said, reaching across Wild's shoulder and tapping on the screen.

"Don't touch the screen," Wild protested. "Fingerprints are a bitch to get off."

"Sorry."

"You've been touching this screen, haven't you?"

"No, I haven't."

"Bullshit." Wild clicked on the link and began to read aloud: "Company showcases nonstandard ammo at annual shoot-out expo."

"Jump ahead."

"Okay, okay. *Blah, blah, blah.* Oh, check this out: 'The frangible APLP round will bore through steel and other hard targets but will not pass through a human torso, an eight-inch-thick block of artist's clay or even several layer of drywall. Instead of passing through a body, it shatters, creating 'untreatable wounds.' "

"Does it say what company makes it?"

"Looking . . . looking . . . ah, here we go: APLP bullets are made by Robertson of San Antonio and distributed by Letourneau, Ltd., of Baton Rouge, Louisiana. Both companies are subsidiaries of Monde Internationale, a multinational conglomerate with headquarters in Paris."

"New search," Ash commanded. "Type in 'Monde Internationale.' "

Another flurry across the keyboard. "Bingo," Wild sang. "The first link looks like money."

On the screen a globe appeared. A second later, MONDE began orbiting the globe in big block letters. Wild clicked on the ENTRER link and another screen materialized with a language option. Wild selected ENGLISH and then continued reading aloud: "Monde offers clients a global vision. How can we help you? Please click on any of the links below for more details on our companies and services."

Ash scanned the list of links along the left edge of the homepage, and, careful not to touch the screen, pointed across Wild's shoulder again and said, "Click on 'Find a Global Partner.' "

Wild complied with the request, and the screen featured a map of the world punctuated with small red dots. Wild ran the cursor around the map and said, "Damn, these guys are all over the place: Helsinki, Auckland, Kuala Lumpur, Johannesburg—"

"Johannesburg, South Africa?"

"Yeah."

"What company is that?"

"Hold on." Wild double-clicked on the southern tip of the African continent and said, "Unified Global Strategies."

"That's Leeuwendijk's company."

"It is?"

"Of course it is. Don't you remember seeing 'UGS' written on everything over there?"

"Yeah, but I just figured that was the abbreviation for the country, you know, like 'USA.' "

"We were in the Democratic Republic of the Congo, Wild. What would 'UGS' stand for?"

"United G-string of States, or something? Fuck, I don't know."

"Is there an Internet link?"

Wild nodded and brought up a new screen, a black background with plain white type across the center of it. This time Ash assumed the narrator's role: " 'UGS specializes in security services for a dynamic range of situations using the latest technologies and techniques to guarantee desired customer outcomes.' Are there any links from that page?"

"I don't see any," Wild returned.

"Is there any way to figure out who created that website?"

"Sure. First we click on VIEW, then we click on SOURCE. *Boom.* There's your HTML readout for the page."

Ash scanned the dense collection of letters and symbols, unable to make anything of it. "What the hell am I looking at here?"

"That's the computer code that determines what goes on with the website." He leaned closer to the screen. "Let me see if I can find the webmaster in this alphabet soup." Wild's index finger hovered just above the screen as it moved horizontally following what appeared to Ash's eye as the lines of nonsense. "Ah, here it is," Wild said. "The Huntington Group IT Services."

"The Huntington Group?"

"Yeah, ever heard of them?"

"Murdo Edeema's outfit was called the Huntington Group. I wonder if it's the same company?"

"Let's see if we can figure it out." Wild returned to

the search engine's homepage and typed "The Huntington Group" in the buffer. Again, he selected the first option among a long list of links, and a new Web page jumped onto the screen, featuring an American flag waving in the background. " 'Welcome to the Huntington Group: Your gateway to the Beltway,' " he read aloud before scanning the page and reporting, "Yep, it looks like they've got an IT branch. This might be your boy's company—or former company, rather."

Ash pulled Edeema's business card out of his wallet and asked, "Do they list an address?"

"Crystal Gateway Seven in Crystal City."

"That's it."

"Okay, let's try a little varsity work here." Wild furrowed his brow and took to the keyboard and the mouse like a man possessed. "I've made it through the first firewall. Now I need a password. How did your dead buddy spell his name?"

Ash looked at the card. "First name: M-U-R-D-O. Last name: E-D-E-E-M-A. And just for the record, I wouldn't really call him a buddy. I barely knew him."

"Whatever. Let me try a couple of basic passwords. Sometimes people keep things real simple." Wild punched the keyboard some more and declared, "That's not going to work." He rolled his chair back and pulled a disc out of the computer table's center drawer. "Now I have to start breaking things, cyberwise, that is."

"What does that do?"

"This is a bootable floppy that wipes out user names and passwords. At this point they're going to know we're here. Hopefully they don't have a computer administrator up and running after hours." Wild typed in a flurry and clicked the mouse like a Morse code operator, but a few expletive-filled minutes later he threw his hands up and said, "I've hit some pretty serious roadblocks here. They must have a database worth guarding."

"We need to get to it. Are you out of tricks?"

"I am unless I can get my hands on one of their computers."

Ash smiled and said, "How about a trip over to Crystal City?"

FORTY-SIX

The security guard looked up from his fast-food meal as Ash and Wild pushed through Crystal Gateway Seven's massive glass revolving door of an entrance. Without making eye contact, the SEALs walked straight for the elevators like they knew what they were doing. "You know what floor we're going to?" Wild asked under his breath.

"Business card says Suite 409, so I'm guessing the fourth," Ash said.

"Works for me."

Wild pushed the UP button, which cued the guard to call to them: "Can I help you, gentlemen?"

"No, we're just going up for a sec," Wild returned.

"Where are you headed?"

"The Huntington Group," Ash said.

"Do they know you're coming?"

"Yes."

"I doubt it. They're all gone for the day."

Ash walked over to the guard's post in the center of the lobby, focusing on the man's name tag as he drew close enough to read it. "Are you sure about that, Mr. Henderson?"

The white-haired guard dropped his hamburger onto

its spread wrapper and dusted his hands together as he said, "Yep."

"Even Mr. Ferntree?"

"Mr. Ferntree?" He scanned a laminated list tacked to his desk, straining to read it. "Never heard of him."

"That doesn't surprise me, sir. He just started working there."

"He did, huh?"

"Yeah, he's Mr. Edeema's replacement."

"Oh, right. That was a tragedy what happened to him."

"It was—a real tragedy."

"You knew him?"

"Yes, I did."

"And they already hired somebody?"

"Sure did. Mr. Ferntree."

The guard reached for the phone at his elbow and said, "I'll just let him know you're coming up. I assume he's working in Mr. Edeema's old office?"

"Please don't do that, sir." Ash removed his wallet from the back pocket of his jeans and flashed the guard his military ID card. "The two of us are lieutenants in the U.S. Navy. Commander Ferntree was our commanding officer before he retired. We just got back from Iraq, and we'd like to surprise him."

The guard's face lit up. "Oh, I got it. I was a military man myself. I know how strong the bonds can be." He put a clipboard on the counter that ringed his station. "Can I at least get you to sign in?"

"Sure. Can I sign both of us in?"

"That will be fine."

Ash scrawled unreadable signatures on two lines while scanning the guard's station to see what technology he had at his disposal. Views of hallways changed every few seconds on two television screens behind him. That was fine. He knew they were in the building, plus he was too busy eating to turn around and stare at the screens for any length of time.

"Huntington is still on the fourth floor, right?" Ash asked as he started back for the elevators.

"Yep."

A minute later, the elevator doors opened on the fourth floor, revealing THE HUNTINGTON GROUP in three-dimensional silver letters against the opposite wall. Carefully, they stepped into the lobby, trying to look like two innocent officers looking for their former commanding officer. Ash noted the red light on a camera mounted high against one wall blink and then go out. The subdued lighting over the reception area told of an abandoned suite. They heard nothing. Past the receptionist's station, Ash pointed to a doorway shrouded in bouquets of flowers. "I'll bet that was his office." Closer, they directed penlights across the nameplate mounted halfway up the wall.

"Murdo Edeema—Huntington Group vice president for manpower," Ash read aloud.

Wild handed Ash a pair of surgical gloves before donning his own pair. He worked the knob to the office door and announced, "It's open."

After they entered the dark office, Ash plucked a frame picture from one of the shelves and said, "Obviously Mrs. Edeema hasn't been through here, yet."

Wild focused his light on another photograph perched on the window ledge. "Damn, she's hot. I don't think she'll have any trouble landing on her feet."

Ash began rifling through drawers. "Let's keep moving, Wild. That security guard might just figure out we bullshitted him and call the cops. Get on the computer."

Ash's cell phone vibrated at his hip. He snatched it from his belt and read the incoming number. The admiral was calling on his personal line. That meant he had actually dialed the phone for himself, which, in turn, meant there was probably a hot topic to discuss. Ash had to answer it. He waved a hand to get Wild to stop tapping on the keyboard and said, "Yes, Admiral?"

"Good evening, loop," Garrett said, using the collo-
quial slang for an aide—a reference to the aiguillette. "I
hope I didn't disturb you."

"No, sir. Wild and I are on our way to grab a bite
to eat."

"Oh, good. Where are you guys headed?"

"We were thinking of someplace near Crystal City."

"That's not exactly the restaurant district, but there
are a couple of decent places around there. Look, Ash,
I don't want to waste your time, so I'll get right to the
point: I've been thinking about your question today and
I'm afraid I've been negligent. I want to apologize and
do my best to keep us on the right track. I've told Miss
Dubs to clear my calendar tomorrow night, and Dottie
and I would like to invite you over for a dinner—just
us. How's that sound?"

The admiral wasn't calling to give him information on
Task Force Bravo's mission. Ash forced his enthusiasm
as he replied, "That would be great, sir."

"Do you have a lady friend you could invite?"

"Perhaps."

"Well, give her a call. And if she's got any special
dietary needs just call Chief Wildhorse. In fact, why
don't you pick the menu? Whatever you'd like—except
swordfish. I'm sick of that."

"No swordfish. Got it, sir."

"This'll give us a chance to get to know each other a
bit better. Things have been so hectic since you signed
on, we've barely had time to say 'boo' to each other. I
told you I wanted to talk special operations, and I meant
it. Hell, we haven't even talked about lacrosse yet."

"What time would you like us to come over,
Admiral?"

"Six or seven, I guess. Ask Miss Dubs in the morning.
I'm not sure what time she picked. Okay, I'll let you
guys get your dinner. You like steak?"

"Sure."

"Of course you do. What red-blooded American doesn't? Morton's Steak House is right there in Crystal City. It's a bit pricey, but very good."

"We'll check it out."

"If you need me I'll be at this phone for a while. I'm catching up on a few things."

"Okay, sir. I'll call you there if anything comes up."

"See you in the morning. And one more thought: Whatever doubts you have, I remain convinced you are the right man for this job."

"I guess time will tell, sir."

"Good night, Ash."

"Good night, Admiral."

As Ash returned his cell phone to his belt, Wild tossed his hands up and said, "This computer has been slicked. There's nothing on it."

"I think this whole office has been slicked. Besides his personal effects there's nothing here: no folders, no in-box, no nothing. Let's look around some more."

The two SEALs stopped at the door to the adjacent office. " 'Ned Reynolds—Huntington Group Vice President for Operations,' " Wild said. "Operations might be money."

The door was locked. Wild leaned over and studied the knob and then dug through the pouch around his waist. He pulled out a credit card-sized piece of plastic attached to a small screen by a coiled wire. He stuck the plastic into the slot above the knob, pushed the READ button below the screen and focused on the presentation. As the card emitted a series of inaudible sonic pulses, a picture shaped on the screen—a series of dashed lines scattered about that showed where the tumblers in the magnetic lock were relative to each other. Wild pressed the OPEN button, and the dashes lined up horizontally across the screen. Slowly, tentatively, he twisted the knob. The door opened.

Wild went straight for the desk, powering up the computer and pulling the bootable disc out of his shirt. "We don't need no stinking passwords," he declared as Ash noted a complete absence of any personal touches in the office.

"Not a whole lot in his desktop files," Wild reported. "A flier for the company spring picnic, the corporate policy document on sexual harassment. I guess that shit's everywhere, huh?"

"Can you get into his email?" Ash asked.

"Hold on." Wild pursed his lips and slapped the keys like an airline ticket agent for a time. "Servers . . . email exchange . . . okay, I'm in. Looks like he's got a lot of emails from the same guy: velanges@monde. international.co.fr."

Ash walked around the desk and studied the monitor's screen over Wild's shoulder. "Monde International was UGS's parent company, remember? Read the first one."

"All right. Hold on . . . 'Ned: Although this is not the most pressing issue at the moment, we should not lose track of Murdo's efforts at the Pentagon. Did he keep a file of these potential hires? All I can remember is that he was partial to admiral's aides. Call me, Bertrand.' "

Ash leaned closer and read the item himself. "Was that the offer he was talking about?"

"What?"

"Murdo left me an earlier voice mail where he said something about an offer."

"An offer to work here?"

"Maybe. Pull up another email."

"Okay, let's check this: 'Ned: Concerned that the contract didn't fully address the terms of an abrupt exit. Folks here are going to be upset if we wind up paying for something we had no control over. Call me as soon as possible on this, Bertrand.' "

"Contract, huh?" Ash said. "Any contract files on his computer?"

"Let me do a file search." Several seconds later Wild

said, "Nothing with the word 'contract' in it; like I said, there aren't many files on this hard drive at all. This puppy is plain vanilla."

Before Ash re-entered the hallway, he snuck a glance around the door frame toward the camera in the lobby. If Mr. Henderson had been paying attention, he would've noticed by now that the SEALs' movement around the Huntington space was not that of two guys visiting their old skipper. The camera light was out. Quickly, Wild and he slipped out of the office and down the hall to the left. Past a kitchenette with a handful of cabinets, a refrigerator, and a microwave, they came to a heavy metal door with an AUTHORIZED PERSONNEL ONLY sign posted on the center of it. Next to the door was a black square—a touch pad.

"My magnetic lock buster ain't going to work on this bitch," Wild said, digging through his pouch again. "But I do have a small stick of C4."

"Are you shitting me?" Ash returned. "Look at the size of that door. It would take the whole stick of plastic explosive to open it, and you'd probably blow out the building wall in the process."

"I'm out of tricks, then."

"You need my hand," Ash muttered.

"What?" Wild asked as he continued to study the pad at close range.

"Remember the voice mail? Edeema said, 'You need my hand.'" Ash pointed toward the door. "This is what he meant. We need his hand to be able to get in there."

"He's dead," Wild intoned. "How the hell are we going to get his hand?"

Ash didn't answer but jogged down the hallway to the waiting area near the receptionist's desk. He found a copy of the day's newspaper lying on the coffee table and tore through the local section until he came to the obituaries page.

"Breedon Brothers Funeral Home in Arlington," Ash said before pointing to the receptionist's desk. "Wild, see if there's a phone book on the desk. Look up Breedon Brothers."

Wild paged through the thick book and asked, "What should I look under?"

"Funeral homes? Shit, I don't know. Just look."

"Here it is: Breedon Brothers Funeral Home. 'Let us ease your burden.' "

"Now look up 'taxis.' "

FORTY-SEVEN

Although the front parking lot for Breedon Brothers Funeral Home was empty, Ash had the taxi driver continue down Glebe Road for another hundred yards. "You can let us off here," he said, pointing toward a convenience store.

"You had me drive you all the way over here so you could go to a convenience store?" the turban-wearing driver asked. "We passed many of these along the way."

"Not like this one," Ash said. "This is the best. Chili dogs like you only read about." He checked the meter and threw thirty dollars at the man. "Keep it."

"Thank you, sir. You are most generous."

"Let's keep that between us, okay"—he read the name on the license tacked to the dashboard—"Kamil?"

"Okay, sir. Should I pick you up later?"

"Got a card?"

"Right here." The driver opened the glove compartment and handed Ash a business card.

"We'll call you in a bit."

The two SEALs got out of the cab and stood in front of the convenience store like a couple of teens waiting for someone to buy them a six-pack. Once the taxi sped away, they hurried into an adjacent line of evergreens and crouched down to study the floodlit exterior of the funeral home.

"It looks closed," Wild observed.

"We're not exactly walking up to the owner and asking if we can borrow Mr. Edeema's hand for a few hours, now are we?" Ash said.

"You ever been in one of these?"

"A funeral home? Of course. Haven't you?"

"Negative. Where do they keep the bodies?"

"Fuck if I know. I didn't say I'd *worked* at a funeral home."

"There must be a storage room somewhere. You know that TV show about that family of funeral people? They're always fixing up the bodies in a room that looks like a laboratory. I'll bet it's in the basement."

They stepped out of the woods and, noting no security cameras on the facade, followed a driveway that ran downhill to another parking lot behind the building. Once around the back, hugging the side brick wall to stay in the shadows, they peered through the small windows at their feet. In the glow of a single fluorescent bulb over a sink they could see the room was filled with stainless steel appointments—shiny countertops and industrial-sized storage cabinets. Beakers and jars lined one of the plain white walls.

Ash went over to a nearby dumpster and removed a wadded newspaper. He wrapped the newspaper around his hand and then picked up a large chunk of cracked asphalt from the edge of the parking lot. "The clock starts now. We've got to hurry." He tapped the chunk against the window, and the glass shattered.

After removing the shards from the windowpane, Ash undid the latch and slid into the building. Wild followed close behind. The odor of chemicals burned their nostrils as they quickly redonned their surgical gloves.

"I don't see any bodies," Wild said.

Ash scanned the room and pointed toward a stainless steel door. "I'll bet they're in there."

Ash tugged the latch and was hit by a wave of cool air. Inside the refrigerated room were four wheeled tables, each hosting a lump covered with a white sheet. He moved to the first table, pulled back the sheet, and said, "This isn't him."

"Damn, this one's a woman," Wild announced from the first table across the room. "And she doesn't look that old, either."

"A little reverence, please, Wild," Ash said as he stepped to the next body. "Here he is. This is Edeema."

Wild tugged the sheet further back, revealing his chest. "Three shots, huh? I don't know how he managed to call you. He must've been a tough cookie."

Ash reached across the body and sized up both hands. "Which one do we need?"

"Which what?"

"We're not carrying the whole body around, Wild. Which hand do we need?"

"You're not . . ."

"The touch pad was on the left, so I'm guessing we need the left hand." Ash wheeled the table into the adjacent lab. "Grab that saw hanging on the wall over there."

"You're serious? You're going to cut his hand off?"

"No, *you're* going to cut his hand off. I'm going to keep him still."

"I'm pretty sure this is illegal."

"So is breaking and entering. We're running out of time, Wild. Grab the saw."

Wild was about to go to work just above the dead man's wrist when Ash stopped him, saying, "We need something to carry the hand in."

"Like what?"

"A Baggie or plastic wrap, something like that."

Wild pulled open a handful of drawers while Ash

searched a small refrigerator. "Somebody didn't eat his yogurt today," he said as he held up a plastic grocery bag. "This'll work."

Ash held the arm in place while Wild went to work, a bit tentatively at first, but soon with the grit of a seasoned woodsman. The saw was mercifully sharp, and as it sliced through the last layer of skin, Ash was struck by the absence of blood. He slipped the hand into the grocery bag.

The lieutenants wheeled the table back into the refrigerator room and then did what they could to make the place look untouched before climbing out the basement window. They were pleased not to see any flashing lights in the parking lot. Ash produced his cell phone and the business card the taxi driver had just given him. He dialed while they walked up the drive to the convenience store to wait for Kamil to return them to Crystal City.

FORTY-EIGHT

Ash was fully prepared to bullshit his way back to the fourth floor of Crystal Gateway Seven, but this time as Wild and he pushed through the revolving door, they were greeted by the sound of snoring. Henderson, the security guard, was fast asleep at his post, slouched in his chair with his head tilted back and mouth wide open.

"That guy's seriously out," Wild whispered.

"We don't want to risk the elevator bell waking him up," Ash said. "Let's take the stairs."

The lieutenants slipped past the security desk and into the stairwell. After a four-flight sprint, they were back in the Huntington Group offices. Wild removed the grocery bag from the front pocket of his hooded sweatshirt and gingerly unwrapped the hand. He let the bag fall to the floor and stood holding the body part like a child holding a writhing crab. "Now what?"

"Give it here," Ash said. He slapped the palm of the hand against the touch pad, but nothing happened. He pulled the hand away, worked to straighten a couple of the fingers, and then put it against the pad again. No click. No buzz. Nothing.

"That was a stupid idea, my friend," Wild said.

"Maybe we could get back to the funeral home and sew the hand back on and nobody would notice."

"It needs to be warm," Ash pronounced. "That's the problem. That pad probably senses temperature along with reading the handprint."

Ash zipped back down the hall and into the kitchenette, where he searched through the cabinets until he found a stack of paper plates. "What are you doing?" Wild asked.

"What would you say the setting would be for normal body temperature?" Ash asked back as he popped open the microwave.

"What?"

"The hand isn't opening the door because it's cadaver cold. How long do you think we should cook it to get it to normal body temperature?"

"Shit, I don't know. Twenty seconds?"

Ash studied the keys on the appliance. "What would you call this—a potato, a casserole, or a dinner plate?"

"It's meat. Don't boil the damn thing. Is there a setting for steak?"

Ash looked closer. "Yeah."

"Then select STEAK and zap it for twenty seconds."

Ash slid the plate in the microwave and watched through the window as the hand spun around, paying particular attention to the skin at the stump to make sure it didn't start to bubble. At the bell, he opened the door and felt the hand, as Wild stood by anxiously awaiting a ruling. "Still too cold," Ash decreed. "Ten more seconds."

Ten seconds or so later, they both agreed the hand was ready. Ash removed the plate from the microwave and hustled back down the hall like a waiter schlepping the daily special. With a grimace of doubtful anticipation, he carefully put the hand back against the touch pad. The latch translated with a loud click. Ash dropped the hand back into the grocery bag and pulled the heavy door open.

"Nice place," Wild said once his eyes adjusted from the dark hallway to the room's bright fluorescent light. "That plasma screen alone is probably worth over twenty thousand dollars. And look at this stereo."

"I'll go through those filing cabinets over there," Ash said. "You get on this computer."

Wild pulled one of the leather chairs back and sat in front of the computer, running his hands around the edges of it. "Give me the hand," he said. "This thing has got a fingerprint scanner for a power switch."

Ash slid the grocery bag across the shiny wooden conference table. Wild removed the hand and worked the index finger of it into the scanner. "It's gone cold already."

"Steak, thirty seconds," Ash advised.

Wild plopped the hand back onto the paper plate and ran out of the room as Ash pulled the top drawer of the first cabinet open. The drawer was stuffed full of files, neat, orderly, but labeled in a way that made no sense—"XSV5-2e" and "3V-2000." He dug in, pulled out an armload, and spread it across the conference table.

The first few files were routine paperwork—pay records for the administrative staff and accounting data for office supplies. But halfway through the stack, about the time Wild rushed back into the room with the newly warmed hand, Ash came to a folder—"S34aR56"—containing a collection of flag officers' official biographies. Several of the bios, including Vice Admiral Garrett's, had "aide placed" handwritten at the top of them.

Underneath the bio folder was a folder full of forms and other documents Ash immediately recognized: Navy officer personnel records. A few pages into the folder, a name caught his eye: "Lieutenant Kurt Montana."

"Okay, I'm in," Wild announced, working to balance Edeema's hand on his knee while shoving his bootable floppy into the computer processing unit. "Hopefully this system isn't any more complex than the ones in the offices."

"Kurt Montana was an aide," Ash said, holding one of the pages aloft. "And he was dishonorably discharged."

"Who's Kurt Montana?"

"I met him down in Panama. He works for UGS as a security guy along with Leeuwendijk."

"What got him dishonorably discharged?"

Ash read from the record: " 'Lieutenant Montana misused his access to official documents and other predecisional information to curry favor with a private consulting firm. As a result of this ethical breech, the board unanimously recommends his commission be rescinded and his discharge be characterized as dishonorable.' "

"What's that written on the back of the sheet?"

Ash flipped the page over and again read aloud: " 'Ned, we owe this guy. Murdo.' " He looked back to Wild—whose focus had returned to the screen—and said, "That's how he got the job."

Wild waved his hand in an attempt to avoid distraction and said, "I'm into the network directory files. I'm going to follow Reynolds' branch and see what I come up with."

Ash flipped through a few more officer records until he came to another name he recognized: his own. It was all there—page after page of fitness reports, weapons qualifications, warfare training diplomas, medal citations, even his Naval Academy transcript. Certain things had been marked with a yellow highlighter; the margins had annotations like "We could use this" and "Impressive" written in them in pencil. At the bottom of the last sheet was scrawled, "See 'Medusa' file."

"Does that computer have a file labeled 'Medusa'?" Ash asked.

"Hold on," Wild said. "I hit another password roadblock here. I'm going to have to reboot."

"We need to hurry," Ash said, pointing to the corner. "We're on candid camera."

"I'm going as fast as I can. If you want to change places, just let me know."

"You're the computer geek."

"That's right, so chill out and let me do my thing."

"Okay, go ahead and do your thing. Just do it faster."

Wild rushed out to rewarm the hand. Ash put the officer records to the side and tore through the balance of folders. Finding nothing of interest, he tossed them on the floor and went back to the filing cabinet for another armload.

A few folders into the second stack, Ash came across a series of documents on United Nations letterhead. He skimmed the subject lines and saw that each outlined a different U.N. sanction. The word "Iraq" jumped out at him on a couple of pages, and he read closer.

"I'm not sure how much more microwave action this thing can take," Wild said as he re-entered the SCAR with the hand held out for Ash to inspect.

"Damn, it's swelled up twice as big as it was," Ash observed.

"And it's cracking around the edges, too. Oh, well. I should only need it one more time. If I hit another dead end this time, we're pretty much S.O.L."

Wild went through the balancing act of re-booting the computer while Ash concentrated on a document dated June of 1988. The first paragraph contained a reference to the original U.N. sanctions following the first Gulf War and a general statement regarding the intent of all of the sanctions. It went on to list prohibited military-related equipment: radar and microwave technology; spare parts for aircraft, tanks, vehicles, and air defense systems; and missile engines and motors. Stapled behind the sanction document were several dozen pages on Le Monde Internationale letterhead—contracts, some in English, some in French.

"These guys are all over the place," Ash mused as he skimmed the contracts. "Poland, Bulgaria, Romania, the Ukraine. And they're not just working security: They're supplying engines, guidance components for surface-to-air missiles, radio-control kits." He slapped the table. "Shit, that's what got the senior chief: a radio-controlled pickup truck." He set that contract aside, along with another one written in French that repeatedly mentioned the *Démocratique République de Congo* and uranium.

"Medusa, right?" Wild asked.

"What?"

"Medusa, wasn't that the name of your mission? Operation Medusa?"

"Yeah . . ."

"Reynolds has a folder on here called 'Medusa.' "

"Open it up."

Wild shot Ash a bemused look around the side of the monitor and quipped, "You really are the brains of the outfit, aren't you?"

Ash watched intently as the other SEAL stared at the monitor, face aglow, hands a blur of motion. A few long seconds later, Wild smiled and said, "Jack-fucking-pot. Come check this out."

Ash dropped the papers he was holding and sped to the other side of the table. Once Ash was behind him, Wild ran the cursor over the files. "Which one do you want to start with?"

"How about that PowerPoint file titled 'JCS Brief'?"

Wild double-clicked on the file and a security warning popped onto the screen: THIS BRIEF IS CLASSIFIED TOP SECRET. He called up the subsequent pages and peered over his shoulder, asking, "Does this look familiar?"

"Holy shit," Ash said. "That's the executive mission brief for Operation Medusa. How the hell did they get their hands on that?"

"What else is in this folder?" Wild asked as he exited the brief and studied the other options.

Ash shot an arm over Wild's shoulder and asked, "What are those PDF files?"

Another double-click brought up detailed five-by-seven-inch cards, some with handwritten notes scrawled in what little white space there was. "You've got to be shitting me," Ash said. "Those are the team's briefing cards."

"I don't see yours," Wild said.

"That's 'cause I kept mine, remember? That's what I gave to Melinda a few hours ago."

Wild opened the next PDF file and asked, "Who's Captain Seymour?"

"He was the debriefer at the TOC in Kuwait," Ash replied as he leaned closer to the screen. "This is the misrep he supposedly sent to Qatar. No wonder we never got any feedback. These bastards intercepted all the data."

"All that's left in this folder are these JPEG files," Wild said as he selected the first among a handful of them. A dark, blurred image popped on the screen.

"That's it!" Ash exclaimed. "That's the site we came across. That's one of Sergeant Tangredi's pictures."

"What the hell are we looking at?"

"I can't tell from that view. Open up another JPEG file."

The next digital image was a bit less blurry, but it still wasn't obvious what it showed. The next three were no better.

"Go back to the third one," Ash requested. The image returned to the screen. "Can you zoom in on this part right here, this silver part?"

"Are these high resolution images?" Wild asked as he centered a blinking box around the crescent shape Ash had pointed out.

"I think so."

The box grew to the full size of the monitor's screen. "What is that?"

"A radome," Ash said. "The nose of an airplane." He tapped on the screen. "Go back to the big view." Wild complied. "Now zoom in on that shape right there." Again, Wild accommodated the request. "That's an engine nozzle," Ash observed. "And that looks like the top of a vertical stabilizer. How's your jet recognition?"

"Rusty, but my guess would be that's a MiG of some sort."

"A MiG, huh?" Ash bounced back to the other side of the conference table and sifted through the pile of sanctions and contracts. "Here we go. I knew I saw something about MiGs in this stuff." He held one of the documents in front of his face and read aloud: " '*Agrément pour manufacturer les avions MiG-25.*' " Ash threw the pages on top of the other contracts he'd laid aside. "That's what they were doing in the desert. They were upgrading Iraqi jet fighters. And they've been murdering members of my team to keep anyone from finding out that they were violating U.N. sanctions." Ash scanned the room. "Is that computer mapped to the printer over there?"

Wild clicked the mouse a couple of times and said, "It looks like it."

"Print all those files out, including the photos." Ash pulled his cell phone off his belt and saw he didn't have a signal. "I'm going to the receptionist's desk to make a phone call."

"Who are you calling?"

"Melinda."

Ash heard the printer coming alive behind him as he walked out of the room. He ran down the hallway to the lobby and dialed the first phone he came to. Melinda answered on the second ring: "Hello?" He could barely hear her over the music.

"Melinda, it's Ash. Can you hear me?"

"Hold on for a second," she said. "Let me move away from the balcony." A few seconds later, it was much quieter. "Are you guys coming down here?"

"Maybe in a bit. Did you find anything out?"

"I was going to tell you in person once you got here."

"Tell me now."

"This isn't a secure line."

"Tell me anyway."

There were a few beats of silence, and then she said, "The Department of Defense outsourced the intelligence courier service between Kuwait and Qatar to a private company."

"Which one?"

"Unified Global Strategies. I've never heard of them; have you?"

"As a matter of fact, I have."

"In any case, there's no record of your mission in the Army's database."

"What about the GPS coordinates?"

"I pulled the satellite imagery for both places. There was something weird about the photos, something I've never seen before. The photos were distorted, but only over those positions—like there was some kind of light refractor on top of them."

"It must be those proprietary motion detectors," Ash mused.

"Those *what*?"

"I'll explain later. Could you make anything out at all?"

"No, but I fused the Iraqi location against the most recent intelligence reports from the war and I came up with an interesting match. A platoon of recon Marines just captured that area, and you won't believe what they found buried in the sand there."

"Jet fighters?"

"How did you know?"

"I've got to go, Melinda. Thanks for the work. I owe you big time."

"My pleasure, Lieutenant. I hope we can hook up later."

"Not as much as I do. Keep your phone on."

Ash hung up and returned to the secure conference room, where he scooped up the stack of contracts. He shook his head in the direction of the printer and said,

"Grab those printouts, Wild. And don't forget Mr. Edeema's hand."

"Where are we going?"

"To your apartment to get that nuclear fitting before driving over to the Navy Yard."

"The Navy Yard?"

"We're going to pay Vice Admiral Garrett a little visit."

Wild reared back as he said, "Garrett? What the hell are you thinking about? We need to get this stuff to the authorities, and not the local boys, either. This is international shit."

Ash shook his head. "We start with the admiral. I want to put all of this in front of him and see the look in his eyes. One look and I'll know whether he's involved or not. But I've got to see it, not the cops."

"One look, huh?"

"His hands might be dirty, but he's still a naval officer. His eyes will say it all."

Ash had taken two steps for the door when he noticed something else—a wrinkled piece of paper tacked to the wall. He studied the sheet at close range. Six items scrawled in a column, four of them lined out. The fifth one had a question mark next to it. The sixth item was unmarked, and as he scrutinized it, the scribbling transformed into a familiar name: his own. "Bastards," he muttered. "Absolute fucking bastards."

Ash snatched the paper from the wall and held it with a trembling hand. A laundry list of murders committed in the name of greed. He felt his rage threatening to overtake him, but he managed to suppress it as he had a number of times under fire. It wasn't time for a rant; it was time for pointed action. He slipped the paper between two of the folders he was holding and asked, "You wanted a war, right, Wild?"

"Hell yeah," Wild returned.

"Well, it looks like I've got one for you."

FORTY-NINE

The fact that it was nearly midnight was no guarantee that a three-star workaholic wasn't still at work, so Ash used his free hand to dial Garrett's personal line as he steered the rental car northbound across the Potomac River. Six rings and no answer. The admiral had to be at the residence by now.

In the passenger seat, Wild reached between his feet and opened the hard-shell plastic case he'd grabbed during the quick dash through his apartment. He removed two large bowie knives and two nine-millimeter pistols. He strapped the knife to his calf, and then slapped magazines into the pistols. He stuck one of the pistols inside the belt line of his jeans and placed the remaining knife and pistol on the armrest between the seats, saying, "Safety's on."

"Roger," Ash returned. "I'm just curious: Do you have a permit for these?"

"I've got a dead guy's hand in my freezer, and you're worried about a gun permit?"

Ash matched Wild's body placement for both weapons while doing his best to keep his eyes on the road. Wild reached back into the case and produced the titanium washer and asked, "How much do you think this bitch is worth?"

"A couple thousand, at least," Ash replied.

"I'll bet it's more like twenty or thirty thousand. And I'll bet the going rate for transporting stuff like this is right around ten percent of the item's value. Think about it: Two or three thousand dollars a trip; the admiral has made two trips in five or six days. He could probably do four or five trips a month. That's as much as fifteen thousand dollars a month, which would be, what, one hundred and eighty thousand dollars a year? I don't care how much the man's pulling down as an admiral. One hundred and eighty thousand dollars a year is enough to get anyone's attention."

"I still find it hard to believe the admiral is involved," Ash said.

"Believe it. How many times did you ask him to help you pull down the intel from your mission?"

"At least three."

"There you go. This guy's got the world at his fingertips. Why wouldn't he make a phone call or two to help his new aide out? His new aide, who's fresh from the war, I might add."

"Because he's busy?"

"Bullshit. Everybody's busy. He's on the take. Hell, I wouldn't be surprised if half the flag officers in the military were doing the same sort of thing. Think about it: It's the perfect cover. They travel on their own most of the time. Nobody touches their stuff customs-wise on either end. And they've got a lot of connections. It's actually pure genius when you think about it."

"What about all the talk about the admiral's political future? Why would he do something like this and screw it up?"

"Maybe this is what's creating his political future."

"Smuggling illegal goods and violating U.N. sanctions?"

"What do you and I know about how business is really done? At the end of the day, we're just well-trained

chumps who do what we're told." Wild raised his
sweatshirt and pointed to the pistol tucked into his
pants. "Not that I'm complaining, of course. I don't have
to run the planet. Just give me a mission and I'll be a
happy boy."

Ash tried to suppress the thoughts, but his mind raced,
locking on words like "sanctions" and "mission" and
threatening to deconstruct them. As he wrestled to remain focused, he caught sight of the Capitol between
the rows of office buildings on the left side of the interstate. The dome was brilliantly lit—a beacon of . . .
what? A grand lie?

The speedometer nibbled at ninety, and Ash eased the
adrenaline-fueled pressure on the accelerator. It would
have been the wrong time to get nailed for speeding. A
quarter mile later, they were off the interstate and
stopped at a red light, two blocks from the front gate of
the Navy Yard.

Ash felt his cell phone vibrating at his hip; he didn't
recognize the number—an international area code. Another doctor calling with an update on Senior Chief
White's condition, perhaps? "Ash is up . . ."

"Lieutenant Roberts. It has been too long." The accent was unmistakable.

"What do you want, Kaas?" Ash asked.

"You have some things that do not belong to you,"
Leeuwendijk returned. "I want them."

"Oh, you do, huh? Well, I'll just zip over to Africa
and give them to you."

Leeuwendijk laughed. "I'm closer than that, Lieutenant. I came back from Africa right behind you. You
see, we studied the surveillance tapes from the infrared
cameras we placed around the mine. We know what you
saw there."

"Then you also know I'm bringing you down."

"I would not be so sure about that. You see that parking lot on the other side of the intersection?"

"What about it?"

"Pull into it and park. Then wait for my instructions."

"I don't think so."

"Oh, I think so. Look at the back of your friend's head. Only my compassion for fellow special operators is keeping both of you alive."

Ash turned and saw a tiny red laser dot dancing across Wild's blond hair.

"All right, Kaas. Be cool here."

The second mention of his name caused Wild to look over, and the dot moved to his temple. The stoplight was still red, but traffic along the cross street was light. They could make it. Ash figured Leeuwendijk was somewhere behind them based on how the laser spot was hitting Wild's head.

Ash shouted, "Duck," and slammed the accelerator to the floor before flopping across Wild to get his head beneath the level of the seat back, twisting the wheel side-to-side as the car picked up speed. Several bullets ticked though the rear windshield, and then it exploded—a noise that momentarily flashed Ash back to the night of Operation Medusa.

The shooting stopped, and as the two SEALs sat back up, they were looking into a pair of headlights coming right at them. Ash jerked the wheel and swerved back into the right lane, but not before driving the other car over the curb. With a quick glance into the driver's-side mirror, Ash saw the sedan slam into a bus stop. A second later he took another look and saw the driver waving his fist at him.

"Anyone behind us?" Ash asked.

Wild twisted around and said, "No. We're clear."

Ash skidded into a right turn followed by an immediate left onto the narrow one-way street that led to the main gate. "Keep the guns hidden," he said as he reached for his wallet. "I'm going to tell the guard to watch for Leeuwendijk." But two blocks from the gate, a black sedan flew out of the side street and skidded to a halt, blocking the roadway. Ash slammed on the brakes, and joined Wild in drawing his pistol. As the rental car came to a stop, Ash was surprised to see Yeoman Second Class Burt Peabody behind the wheel of the other car, now just over a dozen yards away.

Before Ash could shout anything to the petty officer, the rear doors of the other car flew open. On one side Leeuwendijk appeared, arm lowered as he took a bead on Ash. On the other side, another familiar face pointed a gun at Wild.

"You're willing to shoot a fellow SEAL, huh, Kurt?" Ash called out the side window, gun aimed at the South African. "I guess you really are the scumbag your record says you are."

"You're cute, Roberts," Montana said. "No wonder Edeema liked you. Now drop the gun so we don't have to kill you."

"Like you killed Edeema?"

Montana shrugged and said, "Whatever. Drop the guns."

"Looks like a standoff."

"Three to two is not a standoff, *jongen,*" Leeuwendijk replied. With that Ash saw that Peabody also had a pistol pointed at them.

"Okay, now what?" Wild muttered.

"Bash and dash," Ash muttered back. "You ready?"

"Guys like you are why rental cars rates are so high."

"Are you ready?"

"Why not? On three?"

"On three. But first grab the titanium fitting." Wild quickly fished through the plastic case as Ash reached back between the seats and found the contracts folder with his free hand before counting under his breath: "One . . . two . . . *three.*"

Both SEALs threw their doors open, and Ash used the full reach of his outstretched leg to hit the accelerator as he fell to the street. The rental slid neatly out from under him, but he still hit the asphalt hard. He stopped rolling in time to see Leeuwendijk and Montana jump in opposite directions. The two cars collided with a loud crash, causing the driver's airbag to blow up into Peabody's face.

Amid the chaos, Ash tucked the folder into his jeans at the small of his back and the gun into his left front pocket. Using his sweatshirt for protection against the barbed wire, he led Wild in a dash up and over the Navy Yard's wall. Gunshots rang out as Wild jumped to the grass on the other side, but he hit the ground unscathed, save that the barbed wire had ripped his sweatshirt nearly the length of one sleeve.

The two SEALs pulled their guns out and aimed for the top of the wall in the general vicinity of where they'd just crossed, but no one appeared. "They're not that stupid," Ash said. "Let's keep moving."

They ran down an alleyway between two brick buildings and crouched behind a dumpster, sneaking glances in the direction they'd just come from. "There's no way they're giving up that easily," Wild said.

"We have to get to the admiral's house before they do. If he's one of them, they'll help him escape."

"So lead the way."

Ash looked over his shoulder toward the other end of the alley. "I've only been on this base three times, and all three times I went to one place and only one place."

"Let's find somebody and ask."

"You see anybody? Not a whole lot of folks walking around the Navy Yard at midnight."

"Then let's go back out there and have a good old-fashioned gunfight with those assholes."

"It's three to two, remember?"

"How good a shot could Peabody be? He's just a yeoman, for chrissakes."

"Is he? I'm not sure what the hell he is."

"Whatever. Anything beats getting shot in the back."

Ash's head jerked a little as an idea hit him. "The river," he said. "I know I could find the house if we followed the river."

"Which way to the river?"

Ash shut his eyes in an attempt to orient himself. "East on the interstate . . . exit south . . . right then left . . . over the wall . . . *left*. We need to go out that way and to the left. The river is south of here."

The SEALs hugged the building as they quietly moved to the end of the alley. Suddenly, the opposite wall was awash in red and blue. Ash motioned for Wild to halt and then peered around the corner.

"Base police by the perimeter," Ash reported over his shoulder. "I don't know if they saw us jump over the wall, but I'm sure the gunshots got their attention."

"Not to mention the car crash. Maybe we should go tell them what's going on."

Ash turned and looked Wild square in the eye. "No way. I told you before: This is my mission. You can bail if you want, but I'm finishing it."

"Who said anything about bailing?" Wild replied defensively. "I just thought maybe we could use an ally or two, not to mention a little more firepower."

"Every second we delay, the advantage shifts to the other guys." Ash pointed past Wild. "Let's try the other end of the alley."

They threaded their way through a narrow opening between the buildings. It was pitch black. Mud grabbed their shoes and made it impossible to walk quietly.

"Are you sure this doesn't dead-end?" Wild asked.

"Keep going," Ash said. "It's got to come out somewhere."

"Yeah, but where?"

Finally they emerged from between the buildings and found themselves in the middle of a thick row of hedges. Ash fell to his knees and pushed his way through the dense tangle of branches. As his head popped out of the other side, he was pleased to see light from the far shore dancing off the wavelets of the Anacostia River.

After sprinting across another stretch of well-manicured grass, they came to the water's edge. "We'll just follow the seawall that way," Ash said, arm extended to the east. "Eventually we'll run into the admiral's house."

"Sounds like a plan—"

A bullet sparked against the concrete in front of them, followed by the report of a pistol. The sharp crack of another shot echoed off the buildings, followed by two more. Ash and Wild ran crouched along the seawall and then jumped onto the first pier they came to. At the end of the pier were four identical boats lashed to pilings side-by-side—admirals' gigs.

"Every driven one of those?" Ash asked.

"Yeah," Wild replied. "I commandeered one in the Med once coming back to the ship from some all-world liberty. I didn't tell you that story?"

"Later."

They jumped aboard the last one in line. Wild flipped the battery switch on and cleared the fuel line with the blower as Ash untied the mooring lines while staying as close to the deck as possible. Wild pushed the starters and the twin diesels came alive with a throaty bellow.

"Are we free?" Wild asked.

"Go! Go!" Ash returned.

Wild shoved the throttles forward and the boat started to move. A second later they were clear of the pier. Wild pushed the levers to their limits and steered for open water while Ash scanned the seawall behind them.

"How far up is the admiral's house?" Wild called over the wind and engines as he stretched to see over the pulpit.

"You see that destroyer pier on the point up there? Once we get past that we should be able to see the house."

"What does it look like?"

"It's big and white, just like the houses on either side of it."

"I'll show you big and white." Wild cut his eyes toward Ash but quickly lost his sly smile as he spotted movement in the distance behind them. "We've got company on the river here."

Another gig was just pulling away from the pier, a good quarter mile away now. "Keep the speed up and we should get to the house way ahead of them," Ash said.

Wild continued to focus down their wake as he said, "I'm not so sure about that."

Ash looked aft again and realized that the other gig was rapidly closing on them. "Are you at full power?"

Wild pushed on the throttles to make sure they were all the way forward and said, "Figures we picked the pig of the fleet."

"They're going to catch us," Ash said. "Head for the north shore."

Gunfire flashed from the other boat, although they seemed out of range. Ash braced himself against the transom and fired a couple of rounds in return, if only for effect. The other boat swerved but continued to close quickly. Soon, the faster craft was only a few hundred feet away.

Without warning, Wild spun the wheel counterclockwise, throwing the gig into a hard left turn. "This running shit ain't going to hack it," he said. "Get up on the bow and be ready to take some forward quarter shots as we pass."

Ash threw the folder full of damning papers below decks and positioned himself up front along the side of the cabin. Wild kept the turn in until the other boat was directly in front of them, saying, "I'm going to try and take him down the port side."

Ash stretched his arm across the cabin and took aim. A second later, the approaching gig erupted with gunfire. Ash tried to make out shapes—heads, torsos, anything—but couldn't, so he simply fired at the flashes. Wild did the same thing from behind the wheel.

The two boats passed close aboard in a hail of bullets.

Ash felt flecks of fiberglass hit his face, but when the shooting stopped, he was unhurt. "You okay, Wild?"

"I'm good. How's your ammo?"

"How many round clips do I have?"

"Ten."

"Then I've got four shots left."

"Here, keep this handy," Wild said, tossing another magazine to Ash across the windscreen. "Stand by. We're going around again."

Wild threw the gig into another hard left turn while watching the other gig do the same thing over his left shoulder. The other boat's speed advantage also gave it a leg up maneuverability-wise. Wild was only three-quarters of the way through his turn as their opponents came nose-on to them.

Wild worked to minimize the lateral separation between the boats, but the other gig had already started an aggressive turn to a parallel course. The second time they passed in another fusillade, there was only a ninety-degree difference in headings between the boats. Wild turned the wheel as far as it would go, but it wasn't going to be enough.

The two SEALs crouched down as the other gig moved into a rendezvous position amid crackling small arms fire. "You do not have to die, *jongens,*" Leeuwendijk hailed. "Just give us what you took from the SCAR, and we will let you go safely."

"Don't be fools," Montana added. "You're out of options." Based on the proximity of their voices, Ash figured the American was at the helm.

"The first time the boats hit, we light them up," Wild said.

"I've got the bow; you take the driver," Ash returned.

The two gigs bumped gunwales, and the SEALs used the distraction to try and get a jump on their opponents. They sprang out of their hiding places, firing in the directions they'd agreed upon as rapidly as their trigger fingers would allow, but their enemy was ready. Leeuwendijk stood forward of where Ash had projected he'd be, and Montana wasn't at the helm but crouched on the port side near the stern.

The SEALs' split-second gauging of aim points was all the others needed to regain the advantage. As the bullets flew, Ash saw Wild grab his biceps and tumble forward into the cockpit of the other gig. At the same time, Leeuwendijk jumped into Ash's gig and took the helm while firing a handful of shots toward the bow.

Ash crawled across the bow in front of the cabin, returning fire without looking up, just to keep Leeuwendijk in check. Out of the corner of his eye, he saw the other gig turn away, and a second later, he recoiled as it erupted into a ball of orange and yellow flame. Streaks of fire arced across the black sky, followed by debris splashing the river all around them.

How had the blast happened? And had it killed Wild? Ash wanted to go over and help, but at the moment there was no time to despair over a friend's fate or assist in a rescue. Ash was in a fight for his own survival. He looked back to the cockpit and saw that the explosion had knocked Leeuwendijk over, so he leapt across the windshield and landed with his knee against the South African's wrist, knocking the pistol out of his hand and across the deck. Ash put his own gun against Leeuwendijk's temple and said, "Freeze, *raja*."

Leeuwendijk smiled and said, "Oh, you speak Arabic, yes?"

"I know much more about you than just what I uncovered at the Huntington Group, Kaas."

"*Ja?* Three of six. Did you know that?"

"What?"

"After I kill you, that will make three of the six."

"I should just kill you right now, *asshole*," Ash said, pushing the gun harder against Leeuwendijk's head.

"But you cannot. You are out of bullets."

Leeuwendijk was right. Ash had already gone through

the second magazine Wild had given him. His bluff hadn't worked, and before he could pin the other man's free arm, Leeuwendijk knocked him across the deck with a roundhouse to the jaw. Ash strained to see through the stars in his eyes and flailed both arms across the smooth surface of the deck in a desperate sweep for Leeuwendijk's loose pistol.

With the South African flying toward him, Ash flopped onto his back and tucked his knees into his chest. Leeuwendijk landed with his belt line against the soles of Ash's feet, and Ash used the momentum to straighten his legs and throw the bigger man across the stern and into the river.

Ash watched Leeuwendijk flounder in the wake, and just then saw how close the gig had gotten to the river's south shore during the confusion. He moved to grab the helm, but before he could, the boat ran aground, going from a ten-knot clip to a dead stop in the blink of an eye. Ash was thrown violently forward across the foredeck, and through the pulpit into the water.

The river was cold but shallow near the bank. Ash stood waist-deep and took stock of his condition while a dozen yards away the gig roared at full power, firmly wedged into the mucky bottom. A few steps back toward the boat, both of Ash's cross-trainers had been sucked from his feet. He figured it might be faster to swim than wade, even wearing the anchor that was his wet sweatshirt. Two strokes later, he felt something wrap around his legs—Leeuwendijk's arms.

With crushing force, the South African bound Ash's knees together, and thrusting rapidly upward, Leeuwendijk toppled the SEAL. Ash's head was driven under the water and into the muck. He struggled against the bigger man, pounding his fist into whatever parts of Leeuwendijk he could reach. In return, Leeuwendijk kicked Ash in the stomach, knocking out what little air was left in his lungs, and then pinned him to the bottom with his foot.

Ash saw the lights going out. He had a surreally peaceful notion that this might be how he was going to die, and in that same moment he remembered something. He had one more chance. With the last of his air-deprived strength, he took both hands and shoved Leeuwendijk's foot from his chest, then swiftly bent upwards at the waist. In a single sweep of his arm, Ash unsheathed the bowie knife strapped to his ankle and jammed the blade deep into Leeuwendijk's thigh.

After Leeuwendijk's arms went slack, Ash broke the surface with the knife drawn back for the final blow, but instead of being caught off-guard, Leeuwendijk met the SEAL with a fist to the cheek that knocked Ash back underwater. By the time he surfaced again, Leeuwendijk was gone. Ash readied himself for another subsurface charge, but it didn't come.

He heard a splashing, and then in the dim light he saw the reeds along the riverbank part. Although Ash could have simply hopped into the gig and headed for the admiral's residence, he wasn't going to let Leeuwendijk go. He couldn't. Regardless of whether or not he was able to take down the organization, he knew that the South African would eventually return with a vengeance. Besides, Leeuwendijk had as much admitted to two of the Task Force Bravo murders, and there was only one pure way for warriors to settle that score. Ash Roberts knew it; he also knew that Kaas Leeuwendijk knew it.

Ash kept the bowie knife at the ready as he slogged through the muck and chilly water. At the reeds, he slowed his pace, cautiously threading his way through the tall plants, trying to stay quiet, trying to avoid walking into a trap. It was too dark to pick up blood trails or bent stalks. His sole advantage over his foe was the fact that he hadn't been stabbed. Ash was cold and getting colder, but he'd long since developed the mental stamina to ignore that sort of irritation. He wasn't bleeding; Leeuwendijk was, and as a result had to be growing weaker by the minute.

The reed field seemed to go on forever. The water was only ankle-deep now, but the pungent muck still grabbed his feet and made the notion of moving smoothly laughable. He stopped to listen and heard the trampling of gravel. Hustling to the landward edge of the reeds, he looked over the bulkhead and saw Leeuwendijk shuffling toward the road, dragging his right leg behind him.

Ash was able to take Leeuwendijk by surprise, knocking him on his back in the middle of the road and pinning him with the bowie knife against his throat. "No need for bullets this time," Ash said.

The two men were suddenly awash in the lights of an approaching car. A second later the quick whoop of a siren was joined by red and blue lights spinning atop the car. "Drop the weapon and get off him," the officer instructed through the PA system mounted behind his cruiser's grill.

"You don't understand," Ash shouted back. "I'm—"

"He is trying to kill me," Leeuwendijk screamed. "Please, sir, do not let him do it."

The officer opened his door and stood outside the car, saying, "I said drop the weapon. Don't make me use force."

"Officer, you're making a huge mistake," Ash said.

"I was just jogging and he attacked me," Leeuwendijk screamed.

"Drop the knife and put your hands up," the policeman said.

"Look, I'm a lieutenant in the Navy," Ash tried to explain. "This guy is guilty of murder and all kinds of other things that I don't have time to explain to you right now."

"I am a tourist," Leeuwendijk said. "I have no idea what he is talking about."

The man fired a single shot over their heads. "I'm done fooling around here. Drop the knife and raise your hands over your head . . . *now*!"

Ash complied with the order. "Now stand up," the officer said. Again, Ash complied, saying, "You've got the gun on the wrong man."

"Well, then, let's figure it out," the officer returned.

Leeuwendijk slowly got up and hobbled over toward the car, palms pressed together as if in prayer as the policeman continued to train his gun on Ash. "Thank you, sir," Leeuwendijk said once he was closer. "How can I repay your kindness?"

"I need you to stay where you are, sir," the policeman said, trying to keep his eye on Ash as he flashed a palm toward Leeuwendijk.

"I was just jogging and he attacked me," Leeuwendijk said, still gimping toward the police car. "As you can see, he has wounded me quite severely."

"Stay where you are, sir," the officer repeated. "We'll get an ambulance here as soon as possible."

"Watch that guy, Officer," Ash said.

"Please just let me shake your hand," Leeuwendijk said. "I owe you my life."

"Just stay in place for now, sir," the policeman said.

But Leeuwendijk didn't stop. And before the policeman could react, the South African ripped the pistol from his hand and shot him in the head. The policeman crumpled where he stood, and Leeuwendijk jumped behind the wheel of the cruiser.

Leeuwendijk gunned the police car toward Ash. The SEAL leapt out of the way but not before the right quarter panel caught him on the thigh, spinning him to the ground. The cruiser continued past in a cloud of dust, and as Ash struggled to get back to his feet, he saw in the light of the headlights—along with Leeuwendijk—that the road was a dead end.

The South African steered off the right side of the road and threw the car into a left-hand power slide, showering the air with rocks and then screeching across the asphalt. As the cruiser steadied out of the turn, Ash sensed Leeuwendijk had lost track of him while fighting to keep the car under control. Before the car regained full traction, Ash pounced toward the driver's side, using the knife to slash the South African across the wrist of his pistol-wielding arm. The gun fell to the street and disappeared among the gravel.

Ash ducked his chin and took the wheel as Leeuwendijk administered a handful of blows to his face. Ash endured the punches long enough to steer into the first utility pole. Although the cruiser was only traveling at fifteen miles per hour when it hit, the crash sent the SEAL flying a dozen yards or more into the high grass that bordered the south side of the road.

Ash dusted himself off in time to see Leeuwendijk limp back across the road and dive headlong into the reeds. Had he picked his gun back up? Ash projected a line between the open door of the crashed car and where Leeuwendijk had disappeared into the swamp and figured he hadn't. There hadn't been time. Ash didn't have time to look for it, either. The knife would remain his advantage.

Ash stood on the bulkhead and listened. He heard slow, tentative trampling to his right. Cautiously, silently, Ash sidestepped across the bulkhead until he was lined up with the noise. He leapt into the reeds with the knife raised over his head and landed in the muck straddling a large muskrat. The rodent squealed and darted away before Ash could do anything other than chuckle to himself.

Suddenly something solid crashed against Ash's back, sending him facedown between the reeds. He flipped over, and in the glow of a distant streetlight caught sight of Leeuwendijk holding a discarded piece of wood—a long two-by-four. His arms were raised high over his head as he prepared to bring the board crashing down on Ash's face like some sort of mutant lumberjack.

Ash sat up, flipped the knife in his hand so he was

holding the blade instead of the handle, and flung it at his opponent as hard as his awkward position would allow. The knife split Leeuwendijk's breastbone and buried nearly to the hilt. He writhed in silence for a brief moment, clutching at the weapon before toppling backward with a splat.

Ash stood over the South African, whose face was now awash in scum, blue eyes open and colder than ever. Ash reached down to retrieve the knife, but it was so deeply embedded he couldn't pull it out. He put his knee against Leeuwendijk's chest and repeatedly yanked on the handle, but the knife wouldn't budge.

Ash raised his arms and shook his hands to get the blood flowing through them again, and as he leaned forward to re-grip the knife, Leeuwendijk's hand shot from under the water and clamped on Ash's windpipe. Ash tore at his wrist then pounded on his thick biceps, but Leeuwendijk refused to release his hold. A second later the lights were going out again.

Ash reached down and wrapped both hands around the handle of the knife and shook it with everything he had left. Something cracked in Leeuwendijk's chest—his rib cage, maybe—and the knife came loose. Ash pounded the knife between the man's ribs half a dozen times, but Leeuwendijk only twitched a smile and tightened his grip.

Darkness was creeping into the edges of Ash's vision. He had to try something else. In one last desperate flail of his arm, he caught Leeuwendijk across the throat, and with that, the South African's body went permanently limp.

Ash stood over his foe, coughing, trying to get his breath while keeping an eye on Leeuwendijk, somehow not trusting that the man was dead. But the drone of the boat's motors informed there was still work to be done. Ash pushed his way back through the reeds to the water.

He jumped into the gig and shifted the engines into

reverse, and by the time he was at full power, the craft still hadn't budged. Leaving the power up, he threaded his way through the pulpit and into the water, careful not to lose his grip on the boat. He put his shoulder against the bow and pushed, but all he managed to do was sink his legs deep into the mud. He needed something to brace himself against—a wide piece of wood, perhaps.

Ash splashed his way back into the reeds. Next to Leeuwendijk's body was the two-by-four he'd intended to use to crush Ash's skull. He picked it up and soon was reattempting to float the gig, only this time bracing his legs against the board, which gave him just enough purchase on the second surge to free the boat from the grips of the muddy bottom. As the gig began to move, Ash grabbed the pulpit and pulled himself onto the deck.

The other gig remained aflame in the middle of the river, so Ash steered to it to see if he could find Wild, fighting a sinking feeling that he might indeed find him. But as he circled the other boat several times, he saw no one. The damage to the boat was severe; the middle of the vessel was mostly blown away and the rest was nearly burned to the waterline. The chances for human survival looked slim.

As Ash rounded the destroyer pier and caught sight of Vice Admiral Garrett's residence, he stored whatever hope he was clinging to. The mission wasn't over.

FIFTY

After grabbing the Huntington Group folder from the cabin and Leeuwendijk's pistol from the deck near the stern, Ash tossed a mooring line around a cleat on the admiral's finger pier and sprinted toward the house. He could see the residence was dark save a couple of lights—one glowing through the French doors that led to the porch and one made opaque by the bedroom curtains upstairs. Maybe the admiral was still downstairs. That would make things easier. He wanted to keep Mrs. Garrett out of it, if he could. Or was she part of the operation?

As his feet slapped against the smooth stones of the patio, Ash decided to remove his sopping and filthy socks before entering the house. He was fully prepared to kick in the French doors at their wood frames using his bare feet, but they were unlocked. Inside, he crept through the dining room and around the corner into the sitting room. He saw no one. He backtracked into the kitchen. Empty.

Ash heard a loud thump on the ceiling. Something heavy had hit the floor upstairs. Swiftly, quietly, he slinked through the sitting room and across the entryway. Another thump and then the sound of someone hurrying down the stairs. Ash hugged the wall and waited to see who appeared, holding his pistol at his side out of view.

A man came around the ornate banister like a skier passing by a slalom gate, so fast it took Ash a second to register who it was. "Chief Wildhorse?"

The chief's eyes widened as he stopped dead in his tracks. "What are you doing here?"

"That's a long story," Ash said. "Where's the admiral?"

"He's not home from the Pentagon yet."

Ash shot a glance at his watch. "Damn, it's past midnight. Have you tried calling his cell phone?"

"No, sir."

"Where's Dottie?"

"She's visiting her mother in New York."

Ash nodded. "I'll add that to the list of things I should have known lately. What are you still doing here, anyway? This is kind of a late night for you, isn't it?"

"Not really."

Ash noticed Wildhorse was carrying a piece of the admiral's luggage, but before he had a chance to ask the steward about it, the front door opened behind them. Vice Admiral Garrett entered the house, pulling his leather flight jacket off and throwing it across the back of a nearby chair before noticing the two men standing silently across from him in the entryway.

"Jesus, guys," Garrett said. "You scared the hell out of me."

"I was just leaving," Wildhorse said.

"Hold on, Chief," Ash said. "Are you going somewhere?"

"I'm going home."

"What's in the bag?"

"Nothing." Wildhorse started for the front door.

"Stop," Ash said firmly. "I'd like to see what's in the bag."

Wildhorse looked pleadingly at the admiral, who said,

"Is this necessary, Ash? The chief has obviously had a long day."

"He's not leaving until we see what's in the bag," Ash said calmly.

With the pistol behind his back, Ash took a step toward Wildhorse, and as he did, the chief shoved a hand inside one of his coat pockets. "Freeze!" Ash commanded, but Wildhorse was quick, much quicker than the SEAL thought he could be. A shot rang out; Garrett yelped and jumped in place. Ash dove to the hardwood, unaware that the bullet had hit him. Somewhere during his first roll he raised his pistol and put a single round into Wildhorse's thigh. Wildhorse collapsed, but his arm kept moving. He labored to get a bead, but before he could, Ash scrambled over and kicked him hard in the face. The pistol dropped as the chief fell back, bloodied and unconscious. A dark pool began to expand under his leg.

Ash recovered the weapon from the floor, then, folder under one arm, directed both pistols toward the admiral. "Have you lost your mind, Lieutenant?" Garrett said, hands now above his head. "We need to call an ambulance."

"We're not making any phone calls until you tell me what's going on," Ash returned.

"You're shot, too."

Ash searched himself, and then considered where the bullet had grazed his upper arm. The shirt, already wet and muddy, was now sticky with blood. "I'm fine."

"I'm sure someone heard the shots. The base police will be here any minute."

"Tell me what's going on, Admiral."

"What are you talking about?"

With one eye on Garrett, Ash unzipped the side pocket of the bag Wildhorse had been carrying. Two rings similar to the one he'd found in the Congo rolled out. "Do you know what these are?"

"No."

"I think you're lying. You've been lying to me from

the beginning. I know all about what you're doing. I just can't figure out why."

"What the *hell* are you talking about?" Garrett asked, pleading now.

"Why was the chief about to shoot me, Admiral?"

"How would I know?"

"And what about our friend Kaas Leeuwendijk?"

"What about him?"

"He tried to kill me, too. I had to leave him dead in the swamp across the river about a half hour ago." Ash nodded toward the folder under his arm. "I have a pretty good idea why he wanted to kill me. And I think you do, too."

"I don't—"

"Stop the bullshit! I want some answers. Now." Ash urged Garrett back to the dining room. One by one, the SEAL spread the contents of the folder across the dining room table, asking, "Ever see any of this before?"

"No."

"These contracts?"

"No, I have no idea what those are."

Ash snatched another sheet from the table and waved it in front of the admiral's face, peering into Garrett's eyes. "What about these pictures?"

"I don't know what those are, either."

"I'll tell you what these are: These are the pictures my team took on the first night of the war." Ash tapped a finger against one of the contracts on the table. "The same company that Kaas Leeuwendijk worked for was violating U.N. sanctions by rebuilding MiGs in the Iraqi desert. But you already knew that, didn't you? That's why you blew me off when I asked if you could find out about my mission."

"I tried to find out about that mission," Garrett returned.

"Yeah, sure. You didn't have to find anything out for me because you already knew everything. You're one of

them. You work for the same company that Leeuwendijk did, the company that stole part of my mission debrief instead of delivering it to Qatar like they were
hired to; the same company that is actively mining uranium in the Democratic Republic of the Congo."

"The uranium mine is closed. You saw that with your
own eyes."

"I also saw your private security chief managing an
active mine after he thought we were all asleep. And
what about those titanium washers in your luggage?
What about the one I found in Kinshasa? Look me in
the eye and tell me you knew nothing about those."

The admiral glowered across the table and said, "I
repeat: I have absolutely no idea what you're talking
about, son. And I'd watch my tone, if I were you."

Ash studied Garrett's expression but got no read from
it. Whatever discrimination he anticipated he'd have at
that moment was absent. In its place was a combination
of fatigue, injury, frustration, and anger. He felt the
blood trickling from his shoulder as he scanned the papers. His eyes were having trouble focusing.

"Four of my men are dead, Admiral," Ash said. He
heard himself slurring the words but could do nothing
about it as he continued to speak. "Another lies in a
hospital, severely wounded. Three attempts have been
made on my life in the last few days." He steadied himself against one of the dining room chairs. "I need to
know one thing, something you've never really answered
for me. And forget the crap about best qualified and
special operations advisor and all that. Give me the
truth. Why did you pick me to be your aide?" Vice
Admiral Garrett stood speechless, brow furrowed, so
Ash went on: "Was this just a ploy to isolate me, or
what? What did you want from me?"

The admiral was about to say something when he was interrupted by a sharp rapping on the front door. It opened,
and a female voice hailed, "Hello? Anybody home?"

"Miss Dubs, thank God you're here," the admiral emoted as he rushed over to her.

"I got a call on my cell phone, Admiral," Miss Dubs said. "They said something about gunfire from inside your house. I happened to be on the interstate just short of the Navy Yard."

The admiral pointed toward Wildhorse still unconscious on the floor and said, "Lieutenant Roberts shot Chief Wildhorse."

"Oh, good heavens," she replied, hands against her cheeks. "Why on earth did you do that?"

Ash ran his fingers along his arm and displayed the blood. "He shot me first."

"And the lieutenant here thinks I had something to do with why his men were killed in Iraq," Garrett said. He led Miss Dubs in to the dining room table and held up several of the contracts. "He thinks I was smuggling illegal goods during my trips. Tell him I don't know anything about that sort of thing."

"Now, let's just all calm down here," Miss Dubs said. "Has anyone called the base police?"

"No," Garrett said. "He won't let me. He's lost his mind."

"Nobody's making any phone calls until I get some answers," Ash said.

"Answers, huh?" Miss Dubs mused as she worked her way around the dining room table, picking up documents and studying them at close range. "What are these things?"

"U.N. sanction–violating contracts with Iraq," Ash said.

"And what are these . . . pictures?"

"Those photos were taken by one of my men the night of my first mission in Iraq. Along with showing more sanction violations, they also help explain why some of my teammates were murdered."

"What makes you think the admiral was involved in any of this?"

"Plenty. I found a nuclear component in his bag when we got to the hotel in Kinshasa—a component just like the ones I just discovered in the bag Chief Wildhorse was about to sneak off with. Obviously, the chief was helping the admiral smuggle goods for a company called UGS."

"That's absolutely insane," Garrett said. "I have no clue what you're talking about."

"Sure, Admiral. What about the UGS security specialists? What about Kaas Leeuwendijk and Kurt Montana? They tried to kill Wild and me tonight after we searched Murdo Edeema's offices and headed over here with those papers. They're both dead now. It looks like Wild might be, too. I couldn't find him."

"So much killing," Miss Dubs intoned.

"Too much," Ash replied. "But now the admiral needs to answer my question."

"What question?"

"Why did he pick me to be the aide?"

"He picked you because you were—"

"Hold it," Garrett said, cutting Miss Dubs off with a flash of his palm. He paused, momentarily lost in thought, and then his eyes narrowed. "I just realized something: I didn't pick you," he said before pointing to the diminutive woman. "She did."

Miss Dubs nodded and continued to scan the papers as she slowly made her way around the table. Ash watched her closely, his pistol at the ready. Her expression and body language remained unchanged; she could've been walking around the jewelry counter at Bloomingdales as easily as the admiral's dining room table covered with illegal documents.

"That's right," Miss Dubs said, now standing next to the admiral. "I pick all the aides. But this time I obviously made a mistake." With that, a small derringer suddenly materialized in her hand, and before Ash could react she pointed it at Garrett's head. "Drop the gun, Lieutenant, or he's dead."

Ash kept his pistol trained on her until the admiral raised his hands and stammered, "Do as she says, Ash."

Without losing eye contact with Miss Dubs, Ash let the gun fall to the hardwood floor.

"Now I'm going to be on my way," Miss Dubs said, "and I'm taking the admiral with me, for the first part of the trip, anyway. If you make a move, he's dead."

Miss Dubs reached up and wrapped her forearm around the admiral's neck while holding the pistol against his temple. Dragging him with her, she started backward through the sitting room and toward the front door. Ash's tired mind worked in overdrive. If he lost sight of her, she might be gone forever. He needed to buy some time, even a few seconds.

"Whatever Miss Dubs says," Ash thought aloud. "It all makes sense now. You arranged the trips. You had Chief Wildhorse pack the bags."

Miss Dubs stopped backing up as she jabbed the gun against the side of the admiral's head and said, "He's a smart one, isn't he?"

"But why did you do it?" Ash asked.

"Why?" Miss Dubs asked back. "A better question is, 'Why not?' You think you're doing the right thing now, but in reality you've thrown away the opportunity of a lifetime."

"I'd never had much interest in being a criminal."

"Really? Kidnapping isn't a crime? Dressing up like a local civilian isn't against the Geneva Convention? Yeah, that's right. I know all about you, Ashton Roberts. I studied you, just like I studied all the other aides I placed over the years. I knew what made them tick. You know Kurt Montana? He was going to run the Huntington Group. I thought you were from the same mold. I thought I knew what made you tick, but I was wrong."

"Like you were wrong about Murdo Edeema?"

"Murdo was the one who was wrong."

"You were all wrong. I'd never be part of your organization."

Miss Dubs laughed and said, "You already are. You think we're the enemy? We're you. Who do you think made that knife in your belt? Who do you think packed your parachute or fueled the airplane you jumped out of?"

"Smuggling? Sanction busting? Murder?"

"Wars don't just happen on their own, Lieutenant." Miss Dubs pointed the gun at Ash. "And I don't remember you complaining about the war. Now put those papers in the folder and give it to me." Ash stuffed the folder and then tossed it across the floor. Miss Dubs picked it up while keeping the gun aimed at the admiral, saying, "As much as I'd love to stay and shatter the rest of your illusions, I have to go."

Miss Dubs tugged Garrett to the front door and issued a warning: "If I see you once I get outside this door, I'll kill him." Without taking her eyes off Ash, she pulled the door open. "I'm quite serious."

Miss Dubs had backed halfway out of the house when a baseball bat suddenly swung down through the doorway and struck her across the base of the neck. She collapsed where she stood, knocked out cold. The admiral darted to the sitting room, trying to calm himself by taking deep breaths.

From behind the door, the batter appeared, so disheveled that it took a few beats for Ash to recognize who it was.

"Wild, you're not dead," Ash said as enthusiastically as his declining physical state would allow.

The big blond SEAL studied the bat and said, "Those neighbor kids really should learn to put their stuff away. Somebody could get hurt with this."

Ash shuffled his wounded body over and weakly hugged his friend. "I thought you'd been fragged in that explosion."

"An old trick I learned back in the Med. Let's just say electrical wires and bilges full of fuel don't mix. How about you? I heard shots."

"I had to wound the steward," Ash said, motioning across the floor. "He was one of them, along with her."

Sirens screamed through the night. Outside police cars and ambulances clogged the street, each skidding stop seemingly an attempt to outdo the previous one. The street was alight. As legions of cops and a handful of paramedics descended on the Garrett residence, Wild looked at Ash and said, "One thing's for sure: When you say you've got a war, you really mean it."

Ash managed a pained smile, and then considered Miss Dubs at his feet with her dress partially hiked up and her skinny white legs contorted at unnatural angles. Next to her was the folder, its contents spilling out. But the world was fading from view. The last image Ash had before passing out from loss of blood was that of the damning collection of papers firmly in his grasp.

EPILOGUE

The parking lot of the military air terminal at Andrews Air Force Base was densely packed with cars along the rows near the entrance. But across the expanse of asphalt was a lone car, a late-model import, backed nearly into the forest that bordered the western edge of the facility. Although the car's gentle rocking motion may have drawn the attention of any passersby, fogged windows would have prevented them from seeing the occupants, which was certainly fine with the two lovers tangled in the backseat.

The rocking stopped as abruptly as it had started. Inside, Ash and Melinda sat up and struggled to put their clothes back on within the confines of the two-door. Before Ash tucked himself away, Melinda took him in her hand and said, "Well, goodbye, little fella. I won't be seeing you for awhile."

"He'll be back," Ash returned. "And he goes by '*big* fella.'"

Melinda looked across the backseat, forcing a smile. Ash saw the corners of her mouth jerk downward as she fought tears, and as he reached over to comfort her, she broke down. "I'll be back," he said.

"This is why I swore I'd never date a guy in the military." She wiped her eyes. "Oh, well, what are you going to do, right?"

"Well, for starters, you're going to email me every day. And then I'm going to call you anytime I can sneak my way to a phone. Before we know it we'll be spending weekends in bed again."

"Don't do anything stupid over there."

Ash raised his right hand and said, "I promise I won't."

Melinda sat up again. "We'd better get you into the terminal."

Ash shot a glance at his watch and frowned. "It's about that time, isn't it?"

Ash parked the car closer to the entrance and grabbed his hanging bag out of the back. Through the automatic doors, they heard the announcement over the public address system requesting that all passengers for Chartway Aviation flight 105 to Bahrain check in at the gate.

"Well, that's me," Ash said, letting his bag fall from his shoulder as he faced her.

They kissed much longer than those concerned with the opinions of strangers would have, and then she took his face in her slim hands and said, "Be careful, dammit."

"Always."

After one more kiss, she walked away, stopping to look back on her way through the sliding doors just to make sure he was still watching her. He waved jovially, hoping to ease her mind. With one final pretty smile, she was gone.

Reaching the gate, Ash found Wild fast asleep, with his legs propped against his own hanging bag. Ash nudged the other SEAL's foot, and Wild bolted upright, mumbling, "What, what?"

"Did you check in yet?" Ash asked.

"Yeah. Damn, why did you wake me up? I was having a great dream about last night."

Ash showed his ID to the petty officer at the counter and put his initials next to his name on the manifest. On his way back to grab a seat next to Wild, he was surprised to run into Vice Admiral Garrett. "What are you doing here, sir?" Ash asked.

"You don't think I'd let you go back to the war without wishing you luck in person, do you?" the admiral said.

Wild came up from behind and extended his hand, saying, "Sir, I just wanted to thank you for your help in getting these orders. I owe you one."

"See if you feel that way in a month or two," Garrett laughed. "Besides, I'm the one who owes you guys."

"Did you go to Miss Dubs' arraignment?" Ash asked.

"You think I would miss that? That woman almost ruined my career . . . my *life*. I still can't believe all that was going on under my nose, but let's just put it this way: I wasn't the first flag officer she fooled; in fact, there were some others she fooled much worse, you know, not just dirty bombs but ICBM-type stuff."

"So she'd been operating like that for a while, huh?" Wild asked.

"Years. Decades. Allegedly, her history of illegal doings goes all the way back to the Cold War. Name an enemy—the Soviets, the Sandinistas, the Serbians—and she probably has her fingerprints on dealings with them. And this aide placement business—well, that's a story in itself. At least twelve of the UGS indictments are against former aides that she brought into the organization."

Wild looked at Ash and said, "You could've been number thirteen."

"Not only did I miss the big salary," Ash returned, "I missed the jail time. So you think UGS is going down hard too, Admiral?"

"They already have," Garrett said. "Along with Le Monde, this French company. It was quite an organization. Miss Dubs was just the tip of the iceberg. There were dozens of folks around the world above her, and most of them have been nailed already. Anyway, UGS folded a few weeks ago. In fact, you want to hear something ironic? The Huntington Group receptionist applied for Miss Dubs' position—Allison was her name, I think. She had a great résumé and was attractive, but that would've been too . . . too . . ."

"Fucking bizarre?" Wild offered.

"Yeah, that basically captures it."

The intercom crackled with another announcement: "Chartway Aviation flight one-zero-five is now ready for boarding. All passengers for Chartway Aviation flight one-zero-five to Bahrain please make your way to the airplane."

"Take this before you go," Garrett said, producing an aiguillette and handing it to Ash. "This was the one you wore. I wanted you to have this for good luck."

Ash considered the braided loop in his hands and said, "Good luck, huh? I'm not sure this brought me any good luck."

"Well, it brought me good luck. Keep it as a reminder that no matter what happens or who you piss off along the way, you've got a three-star on your side." The admiral extended his hand. "The war looks like it's winding down, but I'm sure there'll be a lot of work to do on the backside. Keep doing us proud."

Ash nodded and tucked the aiguillette in the side leg pocket of his desert cammies. "All right, gentlemen," the admiral continued, rubbing his palms together. "I've got to be getting along; although I'm not really sure where I'm supposed to be next." He pulled out a memo pad and flipped through a few pages, musing, "You know, Miss Dubs may have been up to no good, but she sure kept me organized."

Ash hoisted his hanging bag over his shoulder and shook the admiral's hand one more time, saying, "Thanks for taking the time to see us off, sir."

"I still don't have an aide, you know," the admiral returned. "The truth of it is, Ash, you were getting pretty good at the job. And this time I'd be the one who picked you."

Ash shook his head and said, "With all due respect, sir, I think I'd rather have an M-4 rifle than a daybook in my hands."

"Fair enough. But if you ever change your mind, you know my number."

Garrett walked away following still another hand-shake, and the two SEALs queued up in the line out the door. Before they crossed the tarmac, they placed their bags on a pallet that would, in turn, be hauled en masse by a forklift and strapped down in the cargo hold aft of the seats—evidence of the government's no-frills approach to getting personnel into theater. But in spite of the inelegance of the procedure, Ash had yet to have any baggage lost on a government charter flight.

Ash studied the 747 as he walked up the portable stairway into the charter jet, looking for the Chartway logo, but the bright white airliner was unmarked and very clean, as if it had just been washed or maybe even painted. They passed the flight attendants—surprisingly attractive for a charter flight—as they made their way aft along the port aisle. Although there had seemed to be a crowd in the line on the way out to the jet, once the passengers loaded, there were a lot more seats than people aboard to fill them. Ash and Wild laid claim to one of the center aisles, each man spreading himself across three seats.

"I stopped and got some fresh reading material for the trip," Wild announced, rooting through the plastic bag in the seat next to him. "What do you want first: *Maxim* or *Stuff*?"

The voice of one of the flight attendants purred through the intercom: "We'd like to direct your attention to the card that contains some safety information in the seat back in front of you. If there is a sudden loss of cabin pressure, an oxygen mask will descend from above you. Put the mask over your face and mouth, and breathe normally. In the unlikely event of a forced landing in water, your seat cushion can be used as a life preserver until you enter one of the rafts that will deploy automatically. If you are currently in an exit row and feel you are unable to handle the responsibility of opening the door in case of an emergency, please tell one of the flight attendants and she will reseat you. We welcome you aboard UGS Air—*er,* I mean, Chartway Aviation's flight to Bahrain. The employees of Chartway thank you for your service to our nation, and ask that you let us know what we can do to make your flight more comfortable."

Ash and Wild traded concerned looks as Ash asked, "Did I just hear what I thought I heard?"

"I think you did," Wild confirmed.

Ash called over the nearest flight attendant, a statuesque black woman, and said, "Excuse me, ma'am. Did the other attendant just say 'UGS' during that announcement?"

The flight attendant rolled her eyes and said, "We've all been doing that lately. We just changed our name from UGS Airways to Chartway Aviation, and it's obviously taking a little while to sink in."

The pilot called for the attendants to take their positions for takeoff, and the black woman rushed aft to belt herself into one of the fold-down seats.

"What do you want to do?" Wild asked.

"It's a new company, right?" Ash replied. "Besides, do you know of another way to get over there?"

"No."

"Miss Dubs was wrong, wasn't she? *They* are not *us,* right?"

"No, they're not."

Ash turned his attention the opposite way, across the empty row of seats on the left side of the cabin and out one of the windows, watching the buildings and trees go by in the distance as the big airplane taxied into position for takeoff. Just before the four engines roared to full power, he looked back to his friend and said, "Then, let's go fight."

And Wild smiled.

Penguin Group (USA)
is proud to present
GREAT READS—GUARANTEED!

**We are so confident that you will love
this book that we are offering a
100% money-back guarantee!**

If you are not 100% satisfied with
this publication, Penguin Group (USA)
will refund your money!
Simply return the book before
September 1, 2005 for a full refund.

**With a guarantee like this one,
you have nothing to lose!**